OUT OF THE NIGHT

Claire Baird is the perfect wife and mother. Her role in life is to be the exemplary army commander's wife. But Claire's ordered world explodes when a young woman with a devastating revelation arrives on her doorstep to confront her, in full view of Claire's fellow army wives. Claire, who has striven to support her husband's fragile confidence, to keep up the morale of the often anxious army families, to cope with the adolescent mood swings of her fourteen-year-old daughter, Leah, is now going to need all her reserves of strength and compassion. As tongues wag, all that she has so carefully constructed is threatened with destruction: her marriage, the trust of Leah, the good opinion of the wives, and even her own sense of self. Her capacity for love and forgiveness will be tested to the full. But Claire has reserves of strength that astonish everyone, even herself.

OUT OF THE NIGHT

Margaret Graham

CHIVERS PRESS
BATH

First published 1998
by
Hutchinson
This Large Print edition published by
Chivers Press
by arrangement with
Random House UK Ltd
2000

ISBN 0 7540 1372 3

British Library Cataloguing in Publication Data available

Printed and bound in Great Britain by
REDWOOD BOOKS, Trowbridge, Wiltshire

For Sue, and Sylvia

AUTHOR'S NOTE

Since this novel is set in a military context I must make it quite clear that the Severn Regiment and its personnel and experiences are not based on any actual regiment and neither is the situation on the married quarters patch.

Out of the night that covers me,
Black as the Pit from pole to pole,
I thank whatever gods may be
For my unconquerable soul.

In the fell of circumstance,
I have not winced nor cried aloud:
Under the bludgeonings of chance
My head is bloody, but unbowed.

W.E. Henley, *Echoes*

CHAPTER ONE

Anna Weaver knelt back on her heels in front of the television. She checked the clock on the mantelpiece. Half an hour before the evening news. That was fine, and anyway, there was no guarantee either of the Bairds would be featured. She had to be ready though. Her hands trembled as she reached for the videotape.

At the edge of her vision she could see the answer machine blinking. She'd been almost beside the phone when it rang and had heard the strain in her mother's voice. 'Hello Anna, it's me. Come on love, pick up the phone. Anna, talk to me.' She hadn't. She'd just waited. 'Have you decided, Anna? Please be careful. Remember what the counsellor said. Don't thrust this at her. There are ways of doing these things, just remember that. Please phone me.'

She pushed the tape into the machine, easing herself into a sitting position on the floor, her legs tingling. She pressed play, and volume. A camera panned the mountains of Bosnia in all their terrible beauty, before focusing on Lt.-Col. Mark Baird of the Severn Regiment as he negotiated with local militia who were obstructing a United Nations High Commission for Refugees aid convoy destined for Travnik in Central Bosnia.

She pressed pause, drawing closer to the shimmering screen, studying his features, the way the light fell on his thin face, the hazel of his eyes. She pressed play and watched the cold wind tugging at his light brown hair. Against the

1

gesticulating Croats you could see that he was not a tall man, quite slight, but wiry.

Word for word she parroted the correspondent as the camera closed in, and the lorries revved, and Mark Baird and his team stood full square to the jostling, obdurate men. Their breath was cloudy in the cold. The snow on the mountains reflected no sun. Word for word she asked Lt.-Col. Mark Baird his opinion of the progress his men were making as they struggled to fulfil their mandate. Word for word she duetted his frustrated, clipped reply. A reply almost drowned by the revving of the lorries as they began to move, escorted front and rear by Baird's Battalion Group armoured vehicles.

The tape seemed to jerk as the footage changed to Mrs Claire Baird at the Army Wives Coffee Club on the married quarters patch in England. Children were scrambling over the playgroup equipment which was set up at one end of the large room. Mrs Baird smiled at the interviewer, battalion wives stood alongside. Above them all was a banner proclaiming the opening of their Wives Aid for Bosnia campaign. Again Anna paused the tape, capturing the tired face, the frozen smile, the lines beneath Claire Baird's blue eyes, the long navy cord skirt and white blouse. Her mousy hair had obviously seen a few rollers the night before, but really needed a good cut, colour and blow-dry.

Anna stared. The trembling began again. She pressed play, and reactivated Claire Baird whose voice was calm and measured as she said, 'Of course we're anxious but the morale of the wives and families is high, and our commitment to raising funds for Bosnia aid is total. It helps us to feel involved in the lives of our husbands, or sons, or

2

brothers, or fathers. It makes us feel less helpless in this tragic situation.'

Anna didn't join in word for word with this woman. She wanted to listen. She didn't join in, either, when the wives at the Coffee Club blew kisses to their men, or waved. She just watched as Claire Baird put out her hand to the child who ran at her waving a painting. She watched as she lifted the child, took the picture and said, 'Sam, wave to your daddy.' As the interviewer identified Sgt Wilson's four-year-old son, the painting smeared blue on to Claire Baird's blouse. She merely hugged the child, and smiled.

The phone rang again. Anna didn't move. The answer machine clicked in.

There were more pauses, more roads, more Lt.-Col. Mark Baird traversing steep inclines, bulked up with flak jacket, helmet, more gunfire, more distant bombardment of other towns as the Serbs continued their advance. More tension, checkpoints, refugees. On and on it went. She checked the clock. Five minutes. She pressed stop, knowing the precise point at which the compilation of news fragments was complete, and waited.

She sat all through the news, but there were only reports about Sarajevo—the bombardment, the hunger, the outrage. Nothing about him, or the fund raising for Bosnia. No recording was required.

She shut down the television, and stared at the blank screen. It was so quiet. She pushed herself up from the floor. She looked again at the flashing answer machine, but went instead to her desk, picking up a photo, looking at it for a long moment, feeling as though she could hardly breathe. Her hands were trembling again. She put the

3

photograph of the baby into the buff envelope, then the letter she had written to Mrs Baird. She sealed it, placed it neatly on her blotter, and only then did she move to the phone, press her parents' phone number. The receiver was snatched up on the first ring.

'Anna.' Her mother's voice was eager.

'Hi, Mum. I have decided. I'm going to send it to her. Now's the best time when he's away.'

Her mother hesitated then said, 'We're here for you, love, any time, night or day.'

'I know you are. You always have been. You always will be.'

CHAPTER TWO

Claire Baird woke to the muffled thump of the heating flashing up. She turned over, pulling the duvet tight around her, and dozed. It was nine when she woke, by which time bright light was coming through the subdued blue and green 'wishy-washy' curtains, or so they had been labelled by Mark. She lay still for a full minute, remembering, wondering, allowing herself one glimpse of the past. It was the only time she allowed herself or she would not survive.

The minute over, she opened her eyes, stared at the curtains, the dressing table, the chest of drawers, Mark's wardrobe, all the things she used to centre herself again. She hurried into their bathroom, stripping off her pyjamas; there were a few perks to a husband's deployment. She knocked on the wall backing on to Leah's room, calling,

4

'Come on, come on.'

Before showering she put rollers in her hair, hoping the steam would do its stuff and bounce everything up enough to pass muster for another day. There was definitely more grey, she thought, peering into the mirror. Her mother had been grey before she was forty. 'Who wouldn't be, with a daughter like you,' she'd said.

Claire hurried into the shower, washing quickly, drying herself, then on and off the scales. Nothing gained, but nothing lost either and Christmas mince pies would be here before they knew it. It wouldn't do. She dressed suitably for church, then used the bedroom phone to make arrangements to visit Annie Bates, the wife of the wounded Corporal, in the afternoon. Thank God it was only a shrapnel wound—upper arm, Mark had said when he rang with the news last night. Hurrying along the landing she called, 'Hope you're up.'

'All right, all right, I'm coming.' Leah's tone was verging on the savage but it always did until she'd eaten. Claire held to the theory that primal instincts were 'born again' in all fourteen-year-olds and her own daughter was no exception. Mark you, she'd been excessive yesterday after the grounding penalty for being late home after the Youth Club but maybe she'd blown herself out.

In the principally white kitchen, Claire switched on the radio, catching the news as she pushed square bread into the toaster and boiled the kettle. She fished out the low-fat spread for herself and normal for Leah, listening to the disengaged radio voice informing the nation that aid was still reaching Sarajevo in spite of the almost constant bombardment. She grabbed the Marmite and

5

heard a different voice reminding everyone that a Serbian general had openly declared his aim of replacing most of Bosnia's Muslims with Serbs.

As she made the tea Leah dawdled into the kitchen. Claire thrust toast at her, waving her towards the table. 'Take, eat.' She poured tea into mugs. 'I'll be back, just loading the boot with Muriel's tombola prizes.'

She didn't expect an answer, and neither did she receive one. The kitchen door opened into the double garage. At the last meeting she and the Wives Club had packed into cardboard boxes last year's Christmas bath salts, unread books and heaven knows what else the patch had donated. It was these she now heaved into the Volvo, hearing in the background the radio change from Radio 4 to Radio 1. It would appear that Leah was fed and watered, so communication could commence.

She slammed the boot, entered the kitchen, washed her hands and dried them on the environmentally friendly kitchen roll that appeased Leah's current obsession—the planet. Leah chose to speak halfway through another piece of toast. 'The stand-in padre's going to love the rollers.'

'I intend to remove them.'

Claire looked carefully at her daughter's striped blue, green and red leggings, and the long—well, what was it? Some sort of tunic in a startling configuration of style and colour. 'The question is, do you?'

'Do I what?'

'Intend to remove that lot. It's the worst fashion statement I've ever seen.'

Leah gulped her tea, waved the last remaining corner of her toast at her mother. 'There will be

6

others, believe me.'

Claire laughed and sat down opposite her daughter. 'I do, I really do believe you, but at least substitute single tones, please Leah. It is church, and it is lunch at Muriel's afterwards. She might be Dad's godmother and besotted with you, but she is also a general's widow and somewhat conservative.'

Leah drained her mug and rose. Her mother said, 'Take that mug to the sink. Hey, and the plate. You *are* changing?'

Leah seemed to consider. Eventually she nodded, clumping out in her Doc Martens. Claire watched her go, feeling that she was making inroads into the pubescent minefield her daughter had become. It seemed that excessive statements were presented in the expectation of being negotiated down, but down to something that nonetheless broke rules, leaving Leah feeling that she had won.

Claire tidied up. After all, why not leggings? At least Leah was coming, and that's the battle she hadn't expected to win. She changed back to Radio 4.

At 10.15 a.m. they turned left out of the drive, into the majors' quarters. Leah nodded towards Liz Gibbons's drawn curtains. 'Lucky old Liz.'

Claire grinned at Leah. 'Never mind, virtue has its own reward.'

Leah's silent but expressive response was much as she expected. She laughed and Leah joined her, spluttering. 'Liz has conjured up another important surgery meeting to coincide with church I suppose, Mum? Otherwise known as her usual ducking out.'

'Spot on.'

'How can you two be so different when you grew

up together and are practically joined at the hip? Just think, if you were a bit more laid back we could still be . . .

'Save your voice for the hymns.'

Robert Briggs, the Families Officer, was waiting for them outside the garrison church. He smiled at Leah, jerking his head towards the door. 'Tom's gone on ahead.'

'Bit eager, isn't he?' Leah grumbled.

'Not sure I'd put it that way.' Rob flicked a look at Claire, and they grinned at one another. Leah strolled on, catching sight of Tom, Rob's son, in the porch. She quickened her step. Wives and children were converging, smiling acknowledgement at Claire and Rob as they passed. Claire chatted to some, stooping to speak to the children, most of whom were in the playgroup. One asked, 'Will our flowers be there, Mrs Baird?'

'They most certainly will, and just as beautiful as when we arranged them on Friday. Hurry along with Mum, and I'll see you inside.'

She and Rob walked on behind, stopping again just to the left of the entrance. Rob drew out his diary. Claire sighed, 'I knew I should have stayed in bed.'

'Tut, Mrs Baird. Just a few things. Now, I wanted to talk to you about having a re-run of Bonfire Night. Although it was rained off on 5 November, the bonfire's still there, nicely dry now, and the fireworks are cluttering up the place—could even be called a fire hazard.'

Claire was digging into her bag for her own diary. 'If you're that worried about them Rob, bury them in a bunker.' Her tone was dry. 'Anyway, you know I hate the damn things. Do you really think

8

we need to try again?'

He laughed, turning the pages. 'I rather think we should. It'll get the wives over the hump leading to Christmas.'

All the while women approached the church, chatting, smiling across at them, some shyly, some confidently. She greeted them all by name, prompting Rob when memory failed. Eventually she agreed to the belated Bonfire Night as they had both known she would. 'But only if you pick a date and help sort it out,' she insisted. 'I've the mayor's fashion show to compère in return for his attendance in full regalia at the first anniversary of the playgroup, which, my dear Rob, I might remind you I'm still running, plus the Wives Club, the—'

He gripped her arm, then grinned. 'All the previous arrangements are still in place—that just leaves the food. Otherwise all you need to do is swan around with a sparkler in your hand.'

'Oh, *just* the food.' Claire waited.

Rob looked into the middle distance. 'Maybe the Wives Club could do their usual brilliant best.'

'We did our brilliant best a week ago for the original bonfire, remember, and ended up scuttling for cover from the deluge, and eating it in the old theatre while the kids did the conga round the auditorium for about two hours, when not tipping over the seats stacked at the side.' The electronic bell was tolling. They moved to the entrance. It was dark in the church, and as full as it had been when the battalion had been deployed, unaccompanied, to Northern Ireland. Why not? she thought, if you still believed in such a thing as a kindly God.

They walked to the front pews where Leah and Tom, together with Maud, Robert's wife, waited.

9

Claire whispered to Rob, 'The wives have done enough so I'll get a couple of hot dog stalls in. Take it or leave it, Robert Briggs.'

'I'll take it.' He stood back to let her enter the pew first, whispering, 'You going to B Company's tea and stickies this afternoon?'

She shook her head, kneeling on the hassock alongside him. 'Summoned to lunch at Over Setton. Liz is going sort of in my place.'

'Our second-in-command's wife couldn't pull a surgery meeting out of the bag?'

'That was this morning.'

As they resumed their seats he peered past her to Leah in her leggings, and Doc Martens. 'Off to Muriel's, eh? Well!'

'Well indeed,' she said.

As they searched for hymn number 281 Rob told her that he was seeing Lance Corporal Bates's wife at 12.30. She nodded, turning the pages of her hymn-book. 'I'm there at three. At least it means I can legitimately leave Muriel's at a reasonable time. I mean, I do love her dearly, but a little goes a long way.'

All around them, as female voices swooped and teetered in a church which was better suited to the compulsory enthusiasm of Regimental Church Parade, they swapped information on individual 'patch' problems. There was nothing new in the litany of separation, loneliness, debt, ill health, ongoing marital or children problems, but that didn't make it any less miserable for those involved and the thought depressed Claire.

As the hymn soared to a climax, Rob nudged her. 'If you've a minute, add Sergeant McKay's wife to your list. Their lad's been cautioned for

10

shoplifting and she feels the word is tutting at a senior NCO's wife letting the side down—she's on the way to Annie Bates's.'

Claire agreed, staring at the stand-in padre. The veins were standing out on his temples as he strained for the last note of the hymn. He held it while all around voices faded away in dribs and drabs. The organ squeaked. The padre ceased and Claire felt relieved for him. This man must learn to pace himself.

As they sat she scribbled 'Sharon McKay' beneath 'Annie Bates' and wondered how she was going to recover the time sliced from her essay-writing slot. Sadly, time, tide and A levels waited for no one, damn and blast, but at least Leah could see the benefit of working for exams at the proper age.

*　　*　　*

The actual lunch with Muriel was better than expected. Muriel's grandson, Dan, was there complete with earring in one ear, and a ponytail. He too wore Doc Martens. Claire and Muriel walked in the glorious gardens afterwards leaving the two youngsters to 'share a pair of rubber gloves' as Muriel put it, pointing towards the sink.

Now, as she led Claire arm in arm in a slow march past the boxed herb garden, she boomed, 'So glad you could come, m'dear. D'you think Leah liked the spotted dick? Didn't eat much—thought it was her favourite.'

Claire patted Muriel's gloved hand. 'It is, but she's gone past the age where they eat mountains and still need a pit-stop within the hour. I could tell she liked it, though. It was the thought as well, bless you. By the way, sorry about the leggings.'

Muriel barked a laugh and pointed out the holly she had planted to prevent the sheep breaking through from the field beyond. 'Seems to me that these days it's either leggings, or belts that masquerade as skirts. At least with leggings she won't get chilblains on her backside.' Her cairn terrier, H.J., was roaring backwards and forwards and round them. 'Oh, I don't know, it's a changing world, m'dear. All I had to worry about with my lot were constipation, and brushing of teeth, all that sort of thing, but now it's repression, gender merging and Lord knows what. I mean, the boys wear earrings and the girls wear workman's boots. Of course Dan's father's in a lather in case he develops an interest in soft furnishings instead of charging off to Sandhurst.'

Claire roared with laughter. 'It's a phase.'

Muriel grumbled, 'It's one he'd like to thrash out of him. I tell him, be like me—softly, softly.'

Claire slid a look at Muriel as they reached the sundial in the centre of the white garden. Muriel was smiling broadly. Claire grimaced. 'Softly, softly, my foot. OK Muriel, so why are we patrolling the garden? It's always a lead into something else.'

Muriel brought out secateurs from her husky and set about a late-blooming rose. 'They've no business flowering now.' She handed the damp-stained buds to Claire. 'There, take these home with you. They might respond to some TLC.

Claire waited. Muriel rammed the secateurs back into her pocket and took her arm again. They began their slow march back to the house, H.J. still mounting a top-speed reconnaissance. 'Been talking to our local vicar. The village drama group's lapsed, y'see, natural wastage apparently, but a rump of keen and, what's more living, members are left. Don't you think, my dear girl, we could do something more to boost the Bosnia Fund? It's time we brought back the pantomime to the base, only this time made it a joint civilian/military effort.'

Claire tensed. Muriel sensed it. 'No wait, Claire.'

Claire didn't. She said, 'The Bosnia Fund is doing quite well enough, you know, Muriel, and our Drama Club is happily defunct.'

Muriel dragged her to a halt. Above them rooks flew away from the old oak to the left of the barn. 'Claire m'dear, it is what is needed, trust me. For the greater good, not just the Fund.'

Irritated, Claire tried to walk on, but Muriel held her back. H.J. skidded to a halt and legged it back, taking a rest beneath the leafless lilac. 'I don't want to discuss this in front of the children, Claire. I repeat, we need it from the point of view of the battalion, or at least the battalion wives.'

Claire pulled away, crossing her arms, and staring at the elegant ivy-covered stone house which had once been a brewery. She made no effort to hide her feelings and half shouted, 'It's all right, everyone's settling down.'

Muriel shook her head. 'Look my dear, the resentment is still there not as much, but now the men are away it's biting again, and it will continue to do so. For goodness sake, Claire, Mark put up a real black. You know it and I know it. The only one who doesn't seem to is Mark.'

Claire watched as Muriel poked at a worm cast, and felt dragged down by the thought of the efforts

13

she had made to repair the damage Mark had caused when he took over command. For months she had argued quietly but firmly against the increasing number of courses, the escalating open days, the ridiculous number of exercises the men were subjected to, exercises that ran virtually back to back. 'The strains are bad enough for the families at the best of times,' she had explained repeatedly. 'This is all too much.'

He hadn't listened, insisting that he was acting, and would continue to act, on the advice of the Brigadier. He had insisted that these were matters of which she knew nothing. After all, who was it that had been promoted? He had spelt out to her the requirements of his job in today's army, an army that was being downsized as the 'Options for Change' policy got under way.

His voice had been fraught as he yelled, 'We all need to exhibit a positive attitude. One way of doing that is to up the activities, show zeal. Do you want the men to be made redundant? How will that help them? Do you really want the Severn to be amalgamated? Do you really want me to retire with the label, "the guy who lost the regiment"?'

Quietly she had said, 'The claims you are making on the officers and men, not to mention yourself, are too great. It's a form of moral blackmail. It must stop.'

It hadn't stopped, so she had taken upon herself the role of mitigator in the only way she could. She had taken care of the wives to the best of her ability. She had established a playgroup, a close working relationship with the Families Office. She had been available day and night to discuss problems of any sort. She had organized sports

14

days, fun days, every conceivable damn day, and slowly the wives' morale had appeared to steady, and, as a knock-on effect, that of the men.

Muriel was off from the blocks again, her great voice thundering across the garden. 'A panto is jolly, it will bind them together while the men are in danger, and it'll get the patch into good shape for their return. The village is keen and what's more, they have bits and bobs of costumes and props expertise. The village carpenter was on the committee and he's champing at the bit. Look on it as a good exercise in PR, and a way to remind those potential redundees of the *realities* of life outside.'

The kitchen window was steamed up. Claire pictured Leah toiling over a full sink, but perhaps it wasn't toil with Dan beside her. Muriel didn't have a dishwasher: she didn't hold with that sort of flabby nonsense.

She began walking towards the house again across grass sodden from the night-time drizzle. God, she hadn't the time or energy to do a panto. She felt a headache begin. She stopped, turned, looked at Muriel. 'Surely I'm doing enough?'

Muriel was standing where Claire had left her, her arms akimbo, her legs as though planted into the ground she loved. 'Trust me, the patch is still simmering. Oh damn it to hell, I could shake that husband of yours until his teeth rattled. Even his mother's worried.'

Claire shook her head slowly, almost allowing her rising anger to show, but managing somehow to restrict it to irritation. 'And how did Belle know anything about this? Has she developed extra-sensory perception, or have tittle-tattle letters been

15

winging their way to a certain vineyard in Tuscany by any chance? For God's sake, Muriel, you're a meddlesome old—'

'Bag?' queried Muriel, quite unmoved. 'Well, I dare say I am, but she's my oldest friend, and he's my godson, stupid little bollock that he is. He's lost his way, Claire. He's put personal ambition before the battalion, before the men.'

Claire felt the irritation drain into something approaching disbelief and said, 'You don't really believe it's ambition, do you? Because if so, you don't know your godson at all. It's fear of doing a bad job, of being found lacking.'

The two women stared at one another, then Muriel shook her head slightly. 'No, of course I don't, and I'm taking on board everything you say and I agree with you. It's just bloody unfortunate that at a time when he was full of the uncertainties of the newly promoted he was expected to pick up a hot potato. He cocked up, no thanks to that damn brown-noser Brigadier Fransten yapping in his ear.'

Muriel bent to H.J., pulling his ears gently. The cairn was panting, his eyes bright and full of love. 'Nonetheless, he should have said no, like all good girls do. He should have put the welfare of his men and their families before the requirements of the prat who was only out for reflected glory. Those exercises tore the men away from their families unnecessarily; the whole damn situation was counterproductive.'

'Muriel, it's averted amalgamation with another regiment . . .' Her voice trailed away because she was unconvinced.

'In the Severn's case amalgamation was never a

strong possibility, whatever the Brig. said, whatever the Government's downsizing threatened. Mark should have exercised judgement, and seen that. And in spite of it all there is redundancy looming, though perhaps not as much as there would have been, I grant you that.' Muriel's voice was firm, as she tossed some old prunings into the nearby wheelbarrow. Walking towards Claire, her voice dropped. 'Now, however, they're away, in possible danger, and haven't had the time to consolidate their family situation. It's unforgivable.'

The two women stood close together now. Claire murmured, 'It's all such a shame, Muriel, when you think how much he loves the regiment. Not many newly promoted lieutenant-colonels would wait two years for command of their own regiment, rather than go somewhere else. I'm just so sorry it's gone so wrong.' Her voice became more determined. 'But he's rising to Bosnia, that's obvious. It's taking its toll but he's doing a good job.'

Muriel slapped her lightly on the back, nodding her agreement. 'Hey, last night I was remembering when Belle gave him his first pair of long pants. It was at the vineyard. Proud as punch he . . .'

Leah and Dan were shouting in unison from the kitchen, 'Coffee's up.'

Muriel waved. 'On our way.' Arm in arm they proceeded and Muriel's voice could almost have been called gentle had it been a few decibels lower as she said, 'Think about the panto, Claire. Good for the village, good for the patch, good for Bosnia. I'll fund the production and the takings can pay back half of the outlay. There you are, all obstacles removed.' Claire raised an eyebrow but said

17

nothing.

They had reached the terrace. Terracotta pots with winter flowering pansies were a splash of colour against the fading afternoon. Muriel said, 'You know, m'dear, before my old devil took to pushing up daisies I found the Drama Club a great asset to wifely morale. It unearths skills in these little souls that they never knew existed. It creates intimacy across all ranks.' Now her voice really was quiet.

Claire said, 'I'll think about it, that's all.'

*   *   *

That afternoon, while Leah finished her homework, Claire visited Annie Bates, who was no longer upset about her husband's shrapnel wound, but relieved. 'Lightning doesn't strike the same place twice, does it?' she asked Claire. Claire knew that it did, but agreed with her. Over a mug of coffee she told Annie that Mark had phoned the previous evening, telling her the news of Eric's wound, assuring her that he was fine. Annie asked, 'He phoned specially, did he?'

Claire was reassuring, though Mark phoned every Saturday at 2230 hours. He was a great one for routine, especially when stress was escalating. 'Oh, yes, his concern has always been for his men. That's what all the extra work has been about, hard though it was at the time.'

'They still want redundancies though,' Annie said doubtfully.

'But not as many as might have been the case,' Claire insisted. She spent half an hour with Annie. The two small children came and sat with Claire.

Emma on her knee, and Jody close up on the sofa. She told them of the fireworks they would be painting at playgroup next week, and of the bonfire that would be scheduled for the near future.

She spent a similar time with Sharon McKay, agreeing that she too would feel like pulling the head off her child if she pinched batteries for her personal stereo and then did a runner down the high street with the security guard in hot pursuit. 'But there but for the grace of God go many of our kids,' she reassured Sharon.

Their children were both the same age, and knew one another from the Youth Club and Claire was relieved, as she frequently was, that Leah had been eager to join, when some officers' children felt it beneath them. It reinforced her efforts to be as approachable as possible.

She called in on Sally Coates, the RSM's wife on the way home. She and Sally had worked closely together since the early days of Mark's 'reign' and though nothing was ever said, an understanding of the situation and a mutual respect had been established, a respect that had become a friendship.

Sally had just bought a cappuccino machine and tried it out for the first time while Claire was there. They sprinkled sugar on the froth and developed moustaches with the first sip. It was good, but both agreed that without the hot Italian sun and the doe-eyed Italian males it fell short of perfection.

Moustaches removed, they talked business and Sally filled her in on current problems, though she said she had already left most of the information on Claire's answer machine. On the way home Claire called in on her playgroup colleague,

Captain Baines's wife, Clarissa, and dropped off the register for Monday morning, checking at the same time whether she needed to collect more card as well as glue from the cash-and-carry in the morning.

Finally, because Liz's house was in darkness, she checked with Major Sissons's wife, Jean, that the tea and stickies had gone well for B Company. They had, and Jean told her that Liz had gone on to her mother and would be back late. Claire bit back her disappointment, drove the thirty metres to her own house, hearing the familiar crunching of the gravel beneath the wheels as she passed between the two gateposts. She garaged the car, walked into the kitchen, called up to Leah, 'Want a cuppa?'

'No thanks.'

The answer machine was blinking. She listened to the messages, fast-forwarding Sally's for the time being, then noting the phone numbers of wives who had called, and the changes to the Wives Club outing in January that Sara Green of C Company was arranging. Finally the mayor reminded her of their meeting tomorrow.

Using the *Yellow Pages*, Claire noted down hot dog possibilities. At the kitchen table she started mapping out the mayor's fashion parade script, then began work yet again on her history essay, preferring the informality of the kitchen table to the study.

Above her Leah's music began to pound. She called up, 'Do turn it down.'

Nothing happened. She took the stairs two at a time, knocked on the door. 'For goodness sake, I can't hear myself think.'

20

The music subsided slightly. Leah yelled, 'It's the only way I can think, and if I've been grounded for being a measly five minutes late home from Youth Club, the least you can do is allow me this small pleasure.'

'Perhaps from now on you won't be late.' She noticed the chipped paint on the door. It had probably happened when Leah slammed into her room after the penalty was imposed.

'But five minutes, Mum? You over-react, you know. You always do. I heard Liz tell you that the time before.' Her voice was hard and angry.

'Parents worry.'

'You do, you mean. What do you think I'm going to do, have sex on the mess steps?'

'Leah, be quiet, and turn the music down.' Now Claire was shouting as well.

'You make a fool of me, you know. Fuss, fuss.'

'I'm not arguing about it again. Just turn the music down.' Leah did, a fraction.

*   *   *

Downstairs Claire took an aspirin and tried again, pondering the causes of the rise of Fascism in Europe between the wars. At six, she made a snack supper of Welsh rarebit for them both and was ironing Leah's school clothes when the phone rang for the umpteenth time. She left the answer machine to log in until she heard Mark's voice. But it was Sunday. She dashed into the hall and snatched up the receiver. 'It's me. Is everything all right?'

He sounded even more stressed than he had last night. 'Fine. Just didn't get much of a chance to

21

talk to you yesterday.'

'But everything's all right?'

'For God's sake Claire, hardly all right, or don't you watch the news?' She was used to this and waited, picturing him lowering his head, talking as directly as possible into the mouthpiece in case anyone was passing and thought he wasn't hacking it. What she wasn't used to was a phone call on Sunday. Her mind was racing. She said calmly, 'Usual bag of nails then?'

'Bit of a problem in the mess last night, after I rang. Honestly Claire, it makes you wonder why you're out here. There I was, just off the phone to you about Eric Bates and some idiot local press interpreter ambushes me in my own bloody mess and lambasts me for not doing enough. Hell's bloody bells, as if it's not enough to be out there taking flak I have to watch my back when I'm having a beer.'

Claire said softly, 'Oh Mark.'

'Anyway, I don't want to talk about it. All too bloody silly. How are you two?'

Claire lifted her eyes to the ceiling. The music was thumping again. 'Fine, absolutely fine.'

'Good, but while I'm on, what news of Liz? Is she still banging on about taking the partnership at the surgery? She's the bloody end you know, because it's got Ben all wound up. He's talking of taking redundancy rather than have her and the girls stay put when his next posting comes through, though why the hell she can't make do with that once a week woman's clinic she runs I don't know. I need Ben full on, Claire, so have you talked to her yet?'

Claire brushed her hand through her hair,

22

staring into the gilt mirror which hung above the phone, her headache up a notch. In the background she could hear male voices. 'Five minutes, OK?' Mark asked, his voice muffled as he turned from the mouthpiece. 'No hurry,' was the reply.

Claire said, 'Yes, I've talked to her and she's trying to get more time to make the decision. She knows Ben needs to concentrate, she's not a fool.'

'Sometimes I wonder.'

Claire said nothing, just fiddled with the message pad and into the silence Mark said, 'One more thing, then I must cut and run. I had a letter from Muriel. She can be such a big mouth, can't she, and then out of the blue she comes up with a complete gem. She should have managed to run it past you by now, the pantomime, I mean. You'll do it, of course.'

Claire stared into the mirror again, feeling a great anger growing, making her too hot, and her hand shake.

'Claire?'

She swallowed, and when finally she spoke she was as quiet and calm as usual. 'But I have my exams in the summer. I have hardly a spare moment as it—'

He cut in, his voice impatient. 'Oh, Lord, Claire, if you could see the chaos out here, you wouldn't hesitate—the panto would be for the Bosnia Fund, after all. Apart from that, think of the wives. Muriel's quite right, it would lead to a sense of achievement. It's just a question of prioritizing, deciding what can be moved; you can delay your exams until next year, surely? Come on, Claire, you know how much I rely on you, don't let me down.

23

I'll call next week to find out how it's getting on, usual time. Love to Leah.'

With a click he was gone, just like that. Claire pressed the receiver hard against her cheek. It was cool. She could see into the kitchen where her essay notes still lay on the table, where the ironing was half finished. Upstairs in the spare room was her playgroup artwork, tomorrow there would be more, and more phone calls from wives, more . . . She took a deep breath, pressed the phone rest. She wouldn't let them do this to her, she damn well wouldn't. She clattered the receiver on to the rest, then walked to the kitchen table. How could she manage to do a pantomime as well as this. How?

She couldn't. She looked at her schedule, trying to find windows. In the end she gave up, because she could still hear his voice, still sense his tension, and knew that he'd spoken the truth when he'd said he relied on her.

She returned to the phone and reluctantly dialled Muriel's number.

'Hello, hello,' Muriel shouted, as though her voice had to reach Claire without the benefit of the phone line.

Without preamble Claire said, 'You didn't tell me you'd written to Mark.'

There was a pause, with only Muriel's hefty breathing to be heard. At last she spoke, sounding embarrassed: 'Claire, sometimes I appal even myself.'

Claire straightened and thrust aside the wooden paper knife she had been toying with. 'Well, that's a relief,' she said drily, 'and let me warn you that if we're short of the back end of a cow, you know whose door I'll be knocking on.'

24

Muriel's laugh of relief boomed down the line. Claire held the receiver away from her ear. 'Splendid girl, knew you'd do it. I'll send you photos of our village productions, so you can see their range of costumes, bit moth-eaten . . .'

'Good-night, Muriel.' Claire put the phone down. Her hands were trembling as she picked up the paper knife. She looked through into the kitchen: the iron was clicking as its thermostat cut in, her work was still piled on the table. The paper knife, a varnished mallard duck that tapered away to a flattened tail, rested on her palm.

It was this tail that she snapped.

CHAPTER THREE

From the turret of his Warrior tank, Mark could hear the Serb artillery as it pounded the north-west. He had been hearing it since they'd left their Vitez base, but it was all par for the course. Also par for the course was the trickle of refugees, moving east away from the Serbs, but at least it was only a trickle, which meant no more territory had been lost.

He looked down at a small group as they passed, then ahead, adjusting his earpieces, trying to shut out all but the radio nets. But still he saw them, and they could have been the people he bumped into in W.H. Smith, the people who came into any British town on market day, the people who sat on PTA committees, parish councils. It was this recognizability which always shook him, and shook his men, and it was with difficulty that he dragged

25

his thoughts away from a sudden image of Leah and Claire toiling along such a road.

He stared instead at a deserted farmhouse with blank and broken windows and empty corrals where there should have been livestock. High above the farm was a field of winter grass, above that an escarpment where snow glistened. In the valley the sun caught the naked branches of the apple trees. Pigs were rooting. Had they come from the corrals, or did they belong to another farmer who had stayed, more in hope than good judgement? Maybe the farmer had chased his neighbour off? Maybe one was a Croat, the other a Muslim, or a Serb?

He pressed his left earpiece to clarify the information that was coming through from the Vitez Operations Room, and then the right as information came through from some of his reconnaissance troops on the ground. Could a brain be ambidextrous? Well, if it couldn't it had better soon learn. He found the familiar cacophony routine comforting as they headed to the Maglaj area where they had two reported roadblocks. The first was nuisance value, the second was holding up an UNHCR aid convoy.

Mark slapped his gloved hands together in exasperation, and for warmth, seeing the Warrior commander, CSM Franks beside him in the turret doing the same. Dear Lord, did these idiots want their people to be helped or not? He'd bring it up with the local commander in Maglaj when they sat down to a 'reach out and keep the lines of communication open' meeting yet again.

His thoughts were interrupted by a voice in his earpiece giving their expected time of arrival at the roadblock. It was Lance Corporal Jones, his signaller, who was being bounced around in the rear of the Warrior with the interpreter, Captain Jeremy Baines. Mark acknowledged, his skin aching from the cold. Above him the sky was grey and bleak; a few birds flew across his angle of sight. He rubbed his mouth, worried because soon there'd be snow, real unrelenting snow, and somehow he had to keep the aid coming. His stomach knotted in its usual bloody fashion. He spoke into the intercom in an effort to distract himself, dropping his shoulders, relaxing his muscles. 'Never mind, it could be worse. We could be sipping tequila on a sun-drenched beach. Just think of that.' Beside him CSM Franks laughed.

'I'd rather not, thank you, sir,' Lance Corporal Jones replied. 'Don't think I could bear not to be here, having every bone in me body rock'n'rolled.'

It was another three kilometres before the first roadblock was spotted. It was on the part of the route that skirted a Muslim village with its tiled roofs, and balconies set against the backdrop of the mountains. At the windows he could see their flags flapping in the wind; one was snagging on an empty windowbox.

Once there would have been geraniums in the windowbox, he supposed. But that was once upon a time. Is that what they told their children—once upon a time we had flowers not flags, flowers not guns? He sighed as the Warrior slowed, sighed at the sight of the villagers spread across the road. How many times had they done this, how many times would they do it in the future?

The distance between the Warrior platoon and the men was closing. He could see ten men, their

27

coat collars turned up against the cold. Some stamped their feet. He could see their breath clouds; some were the age of the lads who sat smoking and flirting in bus shelters back home, though others were old enough to be their fathers. What had they done, looked out of the windows this morning and thought, hey, nice day to be bloody minded?

He knew this was unfair. He also knew that in their place, at a time like this, he would have done the same if a neighbouring village set up a roadblock as the Croats had done, just a kilometre along the road. Drawing closer he picked out two men who wore balaclavas and combat jackets and cradled ancient rifles as though they were babies. These two were amongst the ones who didn't stamp, and neither did their eyes move from the Warriors. Instead they purposefully positioned themselves in a flanking position either side of the road as the tanks approached. Was that to make sure the group didn't break and run? Just then one of the young boys turned as though to flee but an old man in the centre barked at him and he held firm. Ah, so it was the villagers who were in control after all.

The Warriors were very close now and still the men did not move from their path, heedless of the bulk, and the noise. Damn, he'd feared they wouldn't but sometimes Warrior intimidation worked. Mark let his driver roll forward to within three metres before ordering a halt. He spoke into the intercom: 'Out of the warmth, Jeremy. Time to earn your keep.'

Once debussed the ground felt amazingly steady beneath his feet. Usually there was at least a bit of a tremor in the old pins, but the constant patrolling as he filled in for his 2IC, Ben Gibbons, who was nursing a badly sprained ankle, had broken him in nicely. He didn't ordinarily lead from the front, preferring an overall view from the command centre, but maybe a change would be good.

Behind, the crews were at the ready, the Warriors growling. Near the verge were anti-tank mines, but his men knew all about those. It might be a good idea though to remind them all again at Formal Orders. After all, it wouldn't do to have them taking their necessaries home in a jiffy bag.

The Muslims had stopped stamping and stood immobile as the older man came forward a mere half a pace, flanked by two other villagers. Again Mark assessed the positioning of the others but nothing had changed except that moving in on his left and right were the two men with weapons. They stopped on the periphery of his vision. Switching into Serbo-Croat, Baines established the leader's name: Enver. 'That's all, sir. Enver, no way we're being given any more.'

Slickly Mark and Baines slipped into the routine he had inherited from Ben. Push, smile, negotiate. Push, don't smile. Louder, brasher, harsher, keeping an eye on any riflemen. These were no longer cradling their weapons, but standing at the ready.

Jeremy translated Mark's final request for passage. Enver shook his head as before. The wind was snatching at his coat, and at Mark's flak jacket. The old man's expression was blank, obdurate as he pulled the makings of a cigarette from his pocket. Deliberately he rolled one, licking the paper, cupping a match between gnarled nicotine-stained hands, and inhaled. The limp thin cigarette burned quickly in the wind. He exhaled out to the side, coughing, breaking the stare.

Mark took another pace forward, seeing Jeremy move with him. The old man drew again on the cigarette. God, it was cold. Mark repeated loudly, clearly, with Jeremy interpreting just one word behind, 'You have no right to obstruct a UN patrol. I insist that you remove your men. We are tasked to facilitate humanitarian aid convoys, and you are preventing this.' His voice was louder now. 'We are attempting to save others, including your own people, from starvation.' The two hooded men moved in a pace and he was bloody glad of the Warriors behind him.

The cigarette had burned down. Enver squinted, took a last drag, then dropped the stub to the ground, looking at it, though Mark did not. He never took his eyes away from Enver.

'I repeat. You have no right to impede the UN patrols, Enver.' Mark pressed closer still, his voice quieter, man to man and now Enver lifted his head and stared at him. Eye to eye contact was what it was all about, or so the pundits said. Great, let's just wait until the cigarettes are finished, until the guy is good and ready to face you; it's not as though the UN has anything better to do than hare up and down playing silly buggers all day.

Enver spoke slowly in that nicotine hoarse voice, and Jeremy just as slowly translated, 'We protect our own.' Brief but to the point, Mark thought.

He moved even closer, to within inches from the man who was exactly his height, a man with large pores, leathery weatherbeaten skin, nostril hair, and rheumy eyes which were not in fact blank any

30

more, but full of pride, and of panic. Mark smelt the nicotine and garlic on his breath, the woodsmoke and animal odour on his coat. A cock crowed in the village and a dog barked.

He became even quieter, even more man to man, but increased the tempo, speeding up his delivery. 'We are here on the instructions of the UN Security Council and you are preventing us from doing our duty, from making the distribution of aid possible. You prevent *us* from helping *your* own. Enver, we must go through. We will go through, you know that, but I would prefer that it was with your permission. After all, what would the commander of your forces have to say about this, for Maglaj is our destination.' Threaten, nicely. Next stage, threaten nastily.

Enver stared into Mark's eyes as Baines translated, though sometimes he faltered as he covered Enver's replies. Behind him Mark heard CSM Franks cough, heard the wind, heard chickens clucking at the roadside. Again a dog barked. Enver stepped back, swinging round to Jeremy, his voice still hoarse but now animated, almost desperate, and spittle formed at the corners of his mouth as his hands reinforced his points. Jeremy frowned. The man repeated himself. Jeremy nodded, rubbing his forehead as he searched for a word, saying quickly to Mark, 'Sorry, sir. Strong dialect. Bit of a struggle here, both sides.'

Jeremy spoke to Enver again. When he'd finished Enver looked across to the village, then back to Mark.

It was as though it was just the three of them standing in the cold, on this road. The idling Warriors had melted into the background, the wind

31

seemed quieter. Enver's men did not move, did not intrude.

Come on, for God's sake, Mark wanted to bellow. The wind was making his eyes water, his nose run, and what sort of a pillock would he look dragging out his handkerchief at this point. Damn it, it was so bloody stupid because they'd open the road, these people always did—or had done up to now anyway. His stomach twisted. They had to, because under the damned mandate he had no authority to force his way across. They had to, or his battalion's credibility with the local commanders would take a step back, and that is what his company commanders had spent their time establishing. How else could they keep the aid flowing?

They had to, or it would be the great Lt.-Col. Mark Baird who'd fouled up.

Still Enver stared. Mark blinked, sniffed. A woman called from the village, a child cried. It caused a loss of concentration for Enver, who stared at the village and then at the Warriors. His sudden descent into total despair was shocking to watch. Almost immediately his shoulders bowed and all pride vanished and after a moment Enver turned to his men and waved them to the side of the road.

His relief overlaid with pity, Mark held out his hand. The two men shook. Enver followed his men, and Mark stared after him, before turning away with Baines. 'Every day the same,' Mark said carelessly, but he was disgusted with himself, and felt as though he'd just trampled on the poor bugger.

*   *   *

One kilometre further on they came to the stalled
UNHCR aid convoy just where the road narrowed.
There was no way Mark was going to direct his
driver, Corporal Hancock, to lead the Warriors
alongside since it would take the platoon too near
the verge. Shanks's pony again. Damn. It would
have helped set the right atmosphere to have the
Warriors growling in intimate back-up as before.

They made their way on foot to the head of the
convoy, the sickening smell of diesel from the
idling lorries proving superior to the forces of the
wind. As Mark walked he searched the verges, all
the while acknowledging the disgruntled greetings
of the drivers. Yep, there were the mines and when
the snow was thick they'd be covered, but still
active.

As they approached the lead lorry, which was as
mud splattered as the rest, the convoy foreman
leaned out of the window, gesticulating, forcing
Mark to stop as he yelled down at him, his
exhausted face almost as red as his straggly beard,
his accent broad Geordie. 'I'm sick to bloody death
of this, man. It's enough driving this bloody
truck over these bloody roads, through these
bloody villages without this bloody nonsense. If it
goes on I'll drive over his bloody men and their
bloody guns.'

Mark nodded up at him, grinning. 'I think I get
your drift, just hold on.' Mark had had to shout,
because even with the engine idling the noise was
terrific. Over his shoulder Baines too shouted up to
the driver, 'Breathe deep, think pure thoughts.'

The man stared at Jeremy as though he was

33

witnessing the coming of the Magi, then shook his head, lifting his hands in a gesture of surrender. 'All this way and what do I find at the end of the tunnel. Not a light, but a bloody comedian.'

Mark shouted, his grin broader, 'Your contact with Captain Baines is brief, whilst sadly mine is not.'

They proceeded to the checkpoint which was manned by Croats in combat gear. Two carried Kalashnikovs held at the ready. A press Land Rover was drawn up immediately in front of the checkpoint. Oh wonderful, the usual audience. Beyond them was a village and this one flew Croat flags. Behind the village the pine trees came almost to the houses. The air seemed thinner, colder. Mark guessed that the road they had just driven along must have been a tighter gradient than he'd realized.

Mark spotted Charlie Bennet, a grizzled tabloid journalist, the ponytailed Arthur Pierce, and another journalist he knew less well called Anthony someone or other. They were bunched close to three Croats, one of whom was presumably the local leader, and it was he who noticed Mark and stiffened. Arthur half turned, waved. It was then Mark saw Gordana Sevo, the young Muslim press interpreter. She was offering cigarettes to the Croats, smiling as one of them spoke, translating for Arthur, who swung back to the group. Mark's heart sank. He'd hoped his first meeting with Miss Sevo in the mess last night would be his last.

'A neurotic off-the-wall interpreter. That's all we bloody need,' Mark murmured, striding forward, catching the edge of a pothole, almost tripping. 'Damn and blast.'

34

Baines said quietly and urgently, sticking close to Mark, 'Actually, she is, sir. All we need I mean. That's what I was trying to explain before she got a little overexcited.'

'So, that's what you call it, is it?' Mark snapped. Jeremy stuck at his side, talking quickly. 'Think back to the roadblock, sir, I was floundering with the dialect, and to have known something about the village would have broken the ice. We're very stretched, sir, and Miss Sevo's only very temporary with the press and these local interpreters are worth their weight in—'

'Quite finished, Jeremy?' They were skirting the Land Rover, and almost at the checkpoint. Jeremy said, 'I think so, sir.'

'Let's get on with this bloody war, then.' His voice was low enough for only Jeremy to hear.

'Er, bloody peace is the word you're looking for, sir.'

'Don't push it, Captain Baines.' His voice was crisp.

'No, sir.'

As they reached the group Arthur flashed a look at him. It urged caution. The journalists stepped to one side, but Gordana stayed put, returning the cigarette packet to the pocket of her anorak, her gloves making her clumsy. Mark watched as she pulled the gloves off with her teeth, then stuffed them into her pocket too. On her back she carried a small rucksack. Her black hair was tied back but a strand was loose as it had been when she had gone for his jugular and accused him of clutching the mandate to him like a security blanket, and of being grateful that it forbade direct action, allowing him and his men to stand by looking pretty as her

35

people were driven from their homes, or killed.

Hanging on to his temper somehow, he watched as she shook Jeremy's hand, but as she turned to him he dug his hands deep into his pockets and stared beyond her to the Croats. She shrugged and turned back to the Croat leader, picking up where she'd left off, or so Mark presumed, turning into Jeremy's translation of the conversation as the trucks idled and the wind rose.

It became clear then that Miss Sevo was giving him a testimonial that most colonels would die for. Mark was confused, but not for long, for almost immediately he was thrust into the roadblock routine with Baines and Gordana Sevo working in tandem. During a pause Gordana brought out her cigarettes again, chatting casually to the Croats as she offered them round. In no time at all her fingers were red with cold. The cigarettes were taken and lit from the stubs of those she had offered earlier.

Some progress was made, but not enough, and now Mark grew impatient, stamping his feet to try to regain some feeling, almost shouting as he said, 'Within two hours I'll be speaking to your local commander.' As Baines interpreted, Gordana Sevo fed him every name of the local commander's team in Maglaj. Baines presented them without pause, then stalled. Gordana took up the pace, laughing a little, reaching out to attract the local leader's specific attention, talking, then holding her sides and panting. The local leader roared with laughter. All the other Croats were smiling now.

Mark snapped a look at Baines, who whispered, 'It's a bit of a bloody gift, sir. She's told them that her father taught one of the local leaders in Maglaj

36

and she's let this lot know that this particular article was placed last in the three-legged race on sports day. She seems to be getting them on side, or let's hope she is; they're an obdurate lot.'

At that moment there was a torrent of Serbo-Croat from the leader and Jeremy was all attention, but it was obvious to Mark he was floundering. He watched as Jeremy muttered to Miss Sevo, who turned to Mark. 'He says, you tell him from me that old stinker's days of running are over unless he loses that beer gut. Or words to that effect, Colonel Baird. I would not distress you with the verbatim translation.'

Away to the left a dog was barking furiously, but then there was the sound of an old man shouting, and a yelp, then silence. For two pins Mark could have given Jeremy a good poke for letting this girl step into the breach; first a bollocking from her, then a eulogy, and what was this? Her saving the bloody day? Or was it? Why didn't everyone just get on with it? He snapped: 'So where does this leave us, Miss Sevo? Is this just a *tête-à-tête*, or can we go through? Forgive me if I'm not a mindreader.'

Next to him Jeremy looked at the ground. Arthur and Charlie tutted and stared at the sky. Gordana turned from Mark to the Croat leader. She spoke to him again, nodding and smiling at his reply. She turned to Jeremy, the smile gone. 'You heard? Then please inform your Colonel, slowly and in words that even he can understand, that he may proceed, but to remember to speak to their sports day star. Tell him it should help his meeting in Maglaj considerably.'

She looked away, up at the sky, groping for her

gloves and putting them on. Jeremy looked at Mark, knowing he had no need to relay a message which his Colonel had heard quite clearly.

Mark nodded uncomfortably, avoiding Jeremy's eyes, stepping forward to shake hands with all three Croats, who gestured to the lorries. Stepping back he saw that Arthur had grabbed hold of Gordana and was shouting at her above the revving. What now? Mark thought as he stepped out of the path of the convoy foreman who was creeping his lorry forward, the great wheels churning the mud on the road. Light snow had begun. Gordana called to the Croat, who nodded. Jeremy said, 'She's asking if the journalists can take photos and they've agreed.'

Arthur called, 'Best side please, Mark.'

Mark ignored him as the lorries churned past. Behind them would be the Warriors. He could walk to them, but why bother. 'Let the mountain come to Mohammed!' he shouted above the noise to Baines, then stopped, closing his eyes. Was he mad? Miss Sevo was Muslim. He turned round anxiously, braced for another diatribe, but Jeremy and Miss Sevo were talking intently some distance away, Jeremy taking notes as Gordana read to him from her notebook until she darted a look across at Mark, speaking urgently to Jeremy. He nodded.

She tucked her notebook back into her backpack which she slung over her shoulder and together they walked towards him. Mark looked away. Damn that bloody Baines. He braced himself as she reached him, though Jeremy had stopped a yard or two away. She shouted above the roaring lorries, 'Colonel Baird?'

'Miss Sevo?' His voice was cool and almost drowned by a lorry slipping its gears alongside them.

She seemed to be groping for words. She shot a glance back at Jeremy but he was coughing in the rising exhaust level. She turned back to Mark, and his shoulders were almost in spasm as he waited. Still she said nothing. As the lorry finally sorted itself out and picked up speed Mark was the one to speak, and he reluctantly said what he knew he should have said far sooner. 'I must thank you for your assistance today, Miss Sevo.'

Beyond them Jeremy was studiously leafing through his notes. Gordana smiled briefly, took a deep breath and raised her voice above the noise. 'Perhaps we may treat it as my attempt at an apology, Colonel Baird, for my bad manners, for my attack on you which you did not deserve. I was tired, too many wines, too much idiocy. Tired after my months in . . . Well, just tired.'

He stared, surprised.

She kicked at the ground and dug her hands into her pockets, finally looking him in the eye. 'Yes, I am very sorry.'

He was disconcerted, wrong-footed. After a moment he said, 'Then I repeat that I am grateful for today.' This time the tone was better, and it was partly because at this moment Miss Sevo looked pale and tired and remarkably defenceless.

She started to turn away, then swung back, words tumbling from her, her face reddening. 'Colonel Baird, Jeremy tells me that you are in need of another interpreter. Now that you have seen my capabilities . . . You see, my time with the journalists is brief, temporary. Tomorrow it is at an end . . .' She stopped as Mark stared from her to Jeremy, shaking his head in disbelief. What a

39

bloody nerve, just wait until he got Jeremy to himself. Miss Sevo said, her face tense, 'Colonel Baird?'

Struggling to keep the indignation from his voice, he said, 'Thank you for your interest, Miss Sevo, we'll bear you in mind.' The lorries were still grinding past, diesel fumes were heavy on the air, mud was spraying. He began to walk away, but she came after him, pulling at his arm, her voice high pitched. 'Thank you, thank you so much, Colonel Baird. It is such a—' she searched for a word—'comfort to be borne in mind.' With that she stalked back to the journalists, passing Jeremy who appeared to have noticed nothing as he studied his notebook. Nonetheless, he hurried to Mark before Mark could shout for him to do so, listening to the bollocking he received, then saying, 'Sir, she needs a job, just as much as we need her.'

Mark glared and turned to wait for the convoy to roll through. 'Enough, Jeremy. She's too volatile, too unreliable. You can see that for yourself.'

Jeremy pressed his point, pleading for five minutes of his Colonel's time, which for some crazy reason Mark found himself allowing: he listened as Jeremy pointed out that Gordana Sevo had been in Australia when the whole mess had begun, that on her return she checked that her parents were all right in their perfect little village in the north-west, and then found work in Sarajevo. 'She was there when the bombardment began and stayed because, well, a matter of honour really.'

Mark closed his eyes. 'I don't really feel I need the girl's life history, Jeremy.'

'Bear with me, sir. Her parents' village fell to the Serbs, and Bosnian Serbs. Her mother and the

40

village were sent in sealed cattle trucks to Zagreb before Croatia closed its borders. Her father was led from the village by the militia because he was one of the . . .' Jeremy hesitated, then shrugged, 'one of the Parish Council, if you want to think of it in our terms. She doesn't know whether he's in one of their concentration camps, or buried in a deep pit he was forced to dig.'

Mark stared after Gordana who had reached the press Land Rover. She opened the door but didn't climb in, just stood there, her head down. God almighty. He turned away, seeing the village in the gaps between the lorries, thinking of Enver, and all the others he met every day, and all the sights he'd seen, and his stomach knotted again. He didn't need to know any of this; it was bad enough trying to stay detached as it was, for heaven's sake. After all, it was a civil war, no matter that Miss Sevo had called it an invasion by the Serbs in the mess the other night, with the Croats not far behind. In his book it was civil war and neither he, nor any of his men, could afford to recognize it as anything else, and anyway, she wasn't his responsibility. If she wanted to help so much, why didn't she just settle down, start behaving like a reasonable human being instead of popping up from nowhere and going ape the first time she set eyes on him? He said as much to Jeremy, who shrugged as the last of the lorries rumbled past and their Warriors approached. 'She was being wound up in the mess by a freelancer.'

'And just now?' Mark's voice was cold.

'She lost it. It's just so important to her.'

'She should go to her mother in Zagreb, or back to Australia—get away.'

41

The Warrior was almost here, thank God, and so Jeremy would have to wrap it up, Mark thought, slapping his hands together. Jeremy said, 'She's just managed to get out of Sarajevo, but with the usual gift—a shrapnel scar on her arm. Now she wants to be of practical use while she waits.'

They walked the few yards to the Warrior which was rattling and throbbing like Mark's head. Shrapnel? Dear God. He hesitated. The road was muddied from the lorries. Diesel still hung in the air. He realized that the wind had dropped and stared across at the mountains. They looked beautiful, but they could hide artillery, they could hide militia, that was his problem, not a young girl with a shrapnel scar. 'Waits?' he queried.

'For news of her father. Isn't that what you or I would do? She's collecting . . .'

'Leave it now, Jeremy. Just leave it.'

CHAPTER FOUR

Anna Weaver checked the clock in her hairdressing salon. It was 8.30, but her first clients had already arrived. This 8.30 start was something she'd suggested to her mother, Lynne Weaver, soon after she'd become a fully qualified stylist. They'd implemented it seven years ago, on Anna's eighteenth birthday, 10 April. Her mother had smiled. 'We'll take it in turns to open up. After all, it's about time we became full partners.'

It had proved a popular move, especially for those ladies who were going to London on cheap day returns with travel limited to the later trains. It gave them a chance to have a quick 'going over' before socking it to Oxford Street. 'Well, I wouldn't put it quite like that,' her mother had chided while her father had raised his eyebrows over the *Daily Mail* he took hours to read at breakfast after he had been made redundant.

There was a gentle murmur of gossip in the peach-themed carefully lit salon. Before her parents had moved to Cornwall her father had put in a false ceiling and recessed the lights. 'Marry a plumber or an electrician,' her mother had once instructed. 'If nothing else, they're handy to have around.' Then she had laughed, that great pealing laugh. But somehow marriage seemed too far away, impossible until she had . . .

Again she looked at the clock. 8.40 a.m. She caught her head stylist's glance and nodded, mouthing, 'Yes Cheryl, she should get it this morning.'

All three stylists were in. Monday was often busy, especially once Christmas began appearing on the horizon. Jody the apprentice was washing Mrs Philips's hair and was all elbows and effort. Anna walked across and whispered, 'Gently, leave a little hair for me to blow-dry, Jody. Bald is not in fashion.'

Jody flushed, stopped, said, 'Sorry.'

Anna touched her arm. 'Don't worry, you're here to learn. Just imagine it's your own head you're working on and you'll get it right.'

Cheryl's client, Mrs Smithers, was just leaving. She'd come for a quick comb-through and was heading for a job interview. 'Good luck,' Anna called. 'You look great.' Cheryl had always been good; even when they'd been at college she'd had a

43

sort of flair.

Mrs Smithers turned in the doorway and waved. 'Thanks, Anna, dear. Give my love to your mother.'

Cheryl hung up the flowered gown, then checked the appointment book. As she did so, the phone rang. Anna tensed, watching and listening, but it was only a request for a cut and blow-dry. Cheryl replaced the receiver, and wrote it in the book, by which time Mrs Philips was finished at the basin and would soon be installed in front of the mirrors ready for Anna.

Cheryl saw this, and beckoned Anna over to the appointment book. 'Just a minute, Anna, bit of a muddle here, I think.'

Cheryl's hair was deep auburn today. It had been strawberry blonde on Friday, but then she was naturally ash blonde and could take all sorts of colours. Anna caught sight of her own mousy hair. OK, highlights helped but, oh, to be blonde . . . oh, to be so many people . . .

She stood with Cheryl, following the line of her finger in the book. It was Saturday's page. 'Forget the book,' Cheryl murmured. 'You've sent the photo recorded delivery, I hope, so she has to sign for it, actually have it pressed into her hands? So she can't deny having received it?'

Anna snatched a look around the salon. Everyone was busy. 'Yes.'

'You gave her both phone numbers—the flat and the salon?'

Anna nodded. Cheryl said, 'So now we wait.'

Again Anna nodded. 'Yes, now we wait.'

CHAPTER FIVE

Over breakfast, which she ate standing at the breakfast bar, Claire checked her schedule, but there was hardly any slack. The clock chimed 8.45. She shouted without looking up, 'Leah, get down here. I won't tell you again.'

A bedroom door slammed and she heard her daughter's slow tread on the stairs, the thump as she dropped her weekend bag in the hall, the dragging of her feet on the tiles. 'Pick up your feet,' Claire called.

Leah said from the kitchen doorway, looking neat and normal in her navy blue uniform, 'I'm not a morning person.'

Claire smiled at her. 'There's toast here or cereal on the table.'

Leah read from the schedule as she reached across the breakfast bar for the toast. 'Return Leah to school 9 a.m.' Claire tapped the pot of Marmite with her pen. 'Come on, we haven't a lot of time.'

Leah spread margarine, shaking her head at the Marmite, took her toast to the table and slumped into a chair, peeling the crust off the toast. 'What would happen if someone deleted the lot? Would your life grind to a halt? Would it be as though you were a puppet and someone had cut your strings?'

Claire watched her daughter put aside the toast, uneaten, and instead pour cornflakes and milk into a bowl. 'I'm delighted that you aspire to imagery in spite of not being a morning person, but cut the melodrama. And don't even think of reaching for a rubber because, schedule or not, I wouldn't forget

45

to return you.'

Claire checked through the visits she had to make on the patch and found that the only half-hour she could create to find a pantomime script in the library was on her way back from returning Leah. She threw down the pencil. Leah was still fiddling with her spoon, not eating much; her discarded toast was in a heap on her plate.

'Come on, you need something in your stomach. You asked for cornflakes so I bought cornflakes.'

Leah stared at her. 'What with Dad away all the time, and you rushing around doing his bidding it's no wonder you bunged me into boarding school.'

Claire hung the schedule back on the hook, smoothed down her skirt, took a deep breath and only then did she turn. 'You asked to go, if you remember. I was the one who protested, so nothing would make me happier if you wanted to do 'day' again—I'd speak to the headmistress immediately. But if we're posted again, and it's in the middle of your GCSEs, we'd be in trouble—just as you said. It's up to you but you wanted to be with your friends.'

Leah sagged, staring out at the garden which was mainly down to bushes. 'It's not up to me, it's up to the pathetic army.' Claire followed her gaze. When they retired to a home of their own she would have the chance to see the beds they planted bloom. Claire said, 'Well, at least Dad has a job. Thousands are out of work.'

'That's a cop-out, Mum.'

Claire smiled gently at her daughter. 'I'm just not up to philosophical discussions on a Monday morning, especially when I'm not going to see you for a few weeks. I'll miss you, darling.'

46

Leah studied her cornflakes. 'Do you ever think that life's like these—soggy.'

Claire laughed aloud. '*Soggy* I could deal with.' She went to her daughter's side, stroked her brown hair. Her hand was trembling because she was tired, so damned tired. Leah hugged her. 'I'll miss you too, Mum.'

*   *   *

They left the house by nine, dropping the newspapers off at the recycling skip at the rear of the NAAFI. The recycling campaign had been led by the Wives Club last year and could be deemed a success, and in such a way her life was measured, Claire smiled wryly. In campaigns completed. Not so very different from the battalion.

Leah arrived at school on time, darting out of the car in front of the mellow stone building before Claire could attempt to kiss her. In town, Claire managed to park in the short-stay, and ran to the library, coming out into drizzle with a few scripts of *Cinderella* and one of *Peter Pan*, though how the hell they'd manage Peter flying through the air she couldn't imagine. How the hell would she manage any of it, she wondered as she backed from the car park. Her expertise only extended to the playgroup nativity that she'd been up half the night planning. She was still dithering about who should play Joseph. Was little Sam, Sergeant Wilson's son, confident enough? He was such a shy soul with a voice that was little more than a whisper, quite unlike his father who could silence the whole parade ground with just an indrawn breath. But perhaps living with Sgt. Wilson made one whisper?

47

Before driving to the house she staggered into the playgroup at the Coffee Shop with a big box full of paints, Play-Doh, glue and card. Perched on the top was the nativity script and cast list. Clarissa Baines hurried to take one end while Private Evans's wife, Josie, led the children in 'Ring a Ring a Roses'.

They shoved the box into the large cupboard the playgroup had taken as their own. Next to it was the cupboard for the Mother and Toddler Group, another of Claire's innovations. They were both panting as they straightened and flexed their shoulders. Claire grinned. 'Remember I'm on Mother and Toddler duty this afternoon, so if there's anything urgent to report about this morning, leave me a note here. I'll see you at the Wives Club committee meeting this evening. Have I got a surprise for you all!'

Clarissa sighed, hands on her hips. 'I hate surprises. The last one was the Guy Fawkes food, and look what happened to that.'

Claire shook her head. 'You ain't seen nothing yet.'

*   *   *

Back at the house the first thing Claire noticed was the insistent blinking of the answer machine, and the mail put neatly on the hall table. She called to her cleaner, 'Hello, Mrs Todd.' She didn't bother to take off her long black mac, but pressed the play button, pencil in hand.

The first call was from Rob, asking her to meet him at Private Wilt's house at midday. He reeled off the address and gave a short summary of the

48

problem. She jotted it down. Debts. Threatened walkout by wife. He ended, 'Sorry, know it's hectic but Sally is out for the day, so I knew you'd want to be there. Oh, by the way, the pregnant kid at Mons Close—can you nip in there too sometime? Bit of a follow-up needed, I'm told. I've heard about the panto. God help us.'

Us? she ground out silently.

She took down the next, which was from Maureen, Corporal Hill's wife, at the HIVE, Help Information Volunteer Exchange, the information and advice centre run by some of the wives next to the Coffee Shop. 'Claire, you know you said you'd stand in if necessary? Well, we're stuck on Thursday. I know it's college but just this once?'

At last the messages were finished and Mrs Todd called through the door, 'Some photos came, or somesuch. One of those *"Do Not Bend"* jobs. I put it with the rest of the mail.' Claire ignored the pile but checked her hair. It had collapsed in the damp.

'See you, Mrs Todd,' she called as she rushed out again, revving the Volvo, spinning the wheels on the gravel, killing her speed as she cruised on to the road. What was the Wilt girl's name? Anne, Audrey? Damn, she couldn't remember.

She drove slowly over the sleeping policemen, leaving Volvoland—or the officers' quarters—with its fences, hedges and garages, and entering 'the rest'. She drove down street after endless street of faceless glum houses that decreased in size along with rank. She tried to put a face to Mrs Wilt. Had she been at the abortive November 5th? Or the summer activities day? The husband was in Ben Gibbons's company according to Rob, so perhaps

49

she could persuade Liz to drop in later.

As she turned left she gave up on the name, and was angry with herself, but not just about that. The Neighbourhood Network she'd set up should have picked this up. They'd have to be more vigilant, but there was such a fine line between interference and awareness, and the network representatives had their own strains too.

Rob was parked outside the Wilts' house and it looked as though he'd just arrived, because his windscreen wipers were still working. As she looked they stopped and he met her at the head of the path. There was a yellow Tonka truck out in the rain. 'Anne or Audrey?' she queried as they reached the door. He put her straight, adding that Wilt had been trickle posted. Again she was angry with herself because someone posted individually rather than with the battalion was invariably isolated and lonely. She insisted as she knocked, 'Make sure you let me know these things.'

They heard footsteps and the door opened. 'Audrey, how are you?' Claire said. The girl burst into tears and just stood there, her hair lank, her face pale. While Rob stared aghast Claire stepped past him, putting her arm round the girl and leading her into the lounge-diner. There was no chance of her not knowing her way, as army quarters could not be called creatively unique. The furniture was the usual ghastly army issue: practical, not beautiful, with the sofa covered in stretch nylon. She sat down, patting the seat beside her. 'Come on, tell me all about it.' There was a smell of tinned soup heating.

The girl wore trainers, navy tracksuit bottoms, and a loose sweatshirt. Claire envied her the comfort. Her own shoes rubbed at the heels, her woollen skirt prickled. She should throw the damn thing out but it didn't crease and kept her looking reasonably as a colonel's wife should.

Rob was in the room now, sitting by the electric fire. One bar was on. A baby of about a year was asleep in the pushchair and a television flickered soundlessly in the corner. Together they listened as Audrey said, 'I'm going. I've had enough, I've just had enough, that's why I rang your office this morning.' She nodded at Rob. 'I thought I should tell someone, couldn't just leave the place, could I? Got to do Marchout.'

'I'm glad you rang,' Rob said. 'We don't want you to go unless there really is no other option. We'd miss you but not as much as your husband would. It's probably the thought of you that's keeping him going.'

Audrey hugged herself. 'I don't care what he thinks. All this is his fault. He's the one who wanted the car and I didn't know things were so bad until he'd gone. And on top of that, this morning I gets this letter from him saying he's lost his binoculars and he hasn't been keeping up with his kit insurance. We've got to pay £150 and I can't stand it.'

Claire and Rob explained that the HIVE could help with financial advice, that the Families Office was available for support, and there was Claire, or Bridget, the network representative round the corner, or Sally, the RSM's wife. That perhaps she shouldn't leave yet, she should have another try at making friends who would share her worries. That civvies often didn't understand the worry of wives with deployed husbands.

51

'But you see,' Audrey said, her tears finished, her face pale. 'How can I tell anyone how I feel? They all want their men home and I don't think I do, not any more. I hardly saw him before he went and now he's gone for six months and I can't even remember what he looks like. I just feel I want to kill him for getting me into this. I want to take my Julie and go home to me mum.'

The curtains looked as though they were made from brown sacking and the carpet was heather-pink. Along one side was a huge rosewood cabinet which made Claire sigh. When would these kids stop going mad on the German postings, buying up everything and finding no room for them when they returned? But why hadn't she somehow made Mark give all these kids a chance?

Rob, making 'drinking tea' signals, escaped to the kitchen. She called after him, 'Turn off the soup, please, Rob.' The baby stirred, settled, Audrey became calmer and Claire suggested that she come along this afternoon to the Mother and Toddler Group with Bridget Murphy who lived at number 14. The girl seemed to shrink. When Rob brought the tea she took a mug, clasping it as though it was a life raft, but didn't drink. Her wrists were thin, her fingers too, and her wedding ring seemed too large. Claire hugged her, saying gently, 'Don't worry, I'll contact Bridget. She'll phone you, then you can walk in together. I'll be there.'

The girl pulled at her sweatshirt. 'You see, she can't phone. It's cut off.'

Unsurprised Claire said, 'I'm in the HIVE on Thursday. Come in, and we'll chat to the financial adviser and sort out how to pay these off. Nobody's going to bite your head off, they just want to know how much, and how regularly you can pay, then if necessary we can deduct what's necessary from your husband's pay.' Rob nodded.

'I don't know. I told me mum I'd come home, but I don't think her boyfriend really wants us.'

'Well, we do.' Now Claire used her secret weapon. 'Oh, and just think back to the Marchout, all the work, then those fingers searching for dirt along the top of the wardrobes, in the oven. Why not give us another try?'

The thought of the Marchout usually did the trick, at this stage anyway. Today was no exception, but as they left Audrey said, 'I didn't know it would be like this. I want a husband who's here some of the time.'

*   *   *

Rob saw Claire to her car and the drizzle seemed lighter. She unlocked her door and threw her handbag on to the passenger seat while Rob held the door for her. As she turned to thank him he said, fiddling with the catch and looking anywhere but at her, 'I've been wanting to talk to you, Claire. The percentage of marriage break-ups has increased this last year. Yes, we can put some of it down to the inevitable strain of an army being asked to do more with less, but at the same time we can't have the same pressures put on the families when the battalion returns. The pressures Mark—'

Claire put up her hand, her voice crisp. 'Don't let's spoil a good friendship, Rob.' She settled herself behind the wheel while Rob shut the door wordlessly before returning to his car. She lowered the window, calling to him as he opened his car door, 'It won't happen, trust me. And make sure you're available for the first panto reading. You men will never have been so popular. You're just right for one of the Ugly Sisters.'

Rob grinned, winked, and half saluted.

*   *   *

That afternoon Claire took tea with the mayor in his parlour to discuss her script for the fashion show, and also found herself discussing the stall the mayoress felt the Lt.-Col.'s wife would like to run at the mayor's Christmas bazaar. Somehow, in a discussion that took for ever and too many scones, it was decided she had agreed. Then there was the obligatory chat about Bosnia and the hopelessness of the situation, and a quick update on the first anniversary 'do' of the playgroup which was planned for the coming Saturday, and which Sidney Harris, the mayor, had agreed to attend in full regalia.

Claire always found this room oppressive with its dark panelling overlarded with plaques on which the names of previous mayors were listed in gold. As she gathered up her handbag and briefcase, it occurred to her for the first time that it was because it reminded her of the mess.

It was dark as she walked to her car and past 6.30 p.m. when she arrived home. She threw soup into a pan and decided such meals were the badge of any service wife, regardless of rank. She toasted two crumpets, gulped them down, checking the clock as she did so, because the Wives Club Committee was due at eight.

After noting the calls on the answer machine

and phoning Leah she galloped upstairs, showered, threw on jeans and a sweater. Her hair was really past resuscitation, but she put in a few rollers and dried it sitting on the bed, trying to breathe slowly, trying to relax for just a moment. As she did so, she heard the doorbell. It was only 7.30. Damn, damn.

She tore her rollers out. Her hair was still damp and she looked absurd. Barefoot she hurried downstairs, hearing Liz shouting through the letterbox: 'Let me in, let me in. Enemy at the gate!'

The tiles were cold as Claire yanked back the curtain, calling, 'What on earth are you on about now?'

Liz Gibbons almost fell into the hall the moment the door was open, but Claire hardly noticed because she had already started back up the stairs again, saying firmly, 'You're a darned nuisance, and now I've got to put my rollers back in.'

She plonked herself on the bed and began again, hearing Liz shouting as she came along the landing, unable to decipher a word until she hurried in, pointing at the rollers. 'No need for those. What I've got to tell you will make your hair curl on its own.'

Claire ignored her. Again she checked her watch. As she clicked the hairdryer on Liz knelt at her feet, shaking her knees. Her face reflected the fact that she'd heard shocking but beautifully repeatable gossip. 'She's back, here, on the patch. The 'Orrible Oracle's back.'

Claire clicked off the hairdryer, her heart sinking. She snapped, 'Liz, cut it out, that's not funny.'

Liz shook her. 'Don't I know it. Just heard it from the horse's mouth. Well, Jean Sissons's anyway.'

'Mollie Perkins is back? I don't want to believe it.' It seemed astonishingly quiet in the room, and Claire felt a wave of incredible tiredness. She cupped the mouth of the hairdryer, pressing her hand hard against its guard which was almost too hot.

Liz still knelt, her dark hair held back in two clips. She wore a black polo neck and black jeans. Claire removed her hand from the dryer, examining its redness, managing a laugh. 'So you've dressed appropriately?'

'Spot on. No room for flash on a night like this.'

As Liz sat back cross-legged on the floor she reactivated the hairdryer, shouting above it, 'Where's she staying?'

Liz jerked her head towards the window. 'With Jean. So within earshot and eyeshot.'

'Damn.'

'Exactly. But who else would have her?'

Claire dragged out the rollers. 'We shouldn't be saying this, it's not on. After all, the fact that she's come back must mean something, she's obviously decided she misses us.' Yes, that was it. This time she'd be easier. This time there'd be fewer ruffled feathers to smooth, less nonsense to sort out in her wake.

Liz was winding the flex round the hairdryer and her face was seriously noncommittal as she enunciated, 'Apparently she didn't find the villagers supportive enough. She felt that only the patch would be appreciative of the stress she was going through.'

Claire was on her feet, busying herself by drawing the curtains. She pulled at a loose thread,

56

snapping it, and wound it round her finger as she headed for the door. 'Well, that sounds hopeful, as though she's seen the other side of the coin. We'll cope, we always do. Come on.'

Liz was right behind her as they entered the kitchen. 'It sounded to me pretty much as though she still thinks she is the only one going through any sort of difficulty. You'll have to keep the lid on her, Claire, right from the start. Incidentally how's Nigel Perkins coping in Bosnia? He's such a pillock he must be a dead weight for Mark.' Claire said nothing and Liz laughed as she lolled against the breakfast bar. 'Yes, OK, you know, but you're not saying. Fair enough but it must have been all his Christmases rolled into one when Mollie stalked off like that. Poor sod, how could she expect him to be made up into Lieutenant-Colonel?'

While Claire put biscuits on to two plates she wished, not for the first time, that she could operate a ranking system like Mark, at least for someone like the 'Orrible Oracle, as she and Liz had christened bloody Mollie. Then she could just tell her to shut up and butt out if she even began to look as though she was causing trouble with that damn tongue of hers. Liz put cups and saucers on to trays. 'Instant or cafetière?' she asked.

'Instant.' Claire eased the thread from her finger and dropped it into the flip-top bin. It smelt of bleach. Good old Mrs Todd.

Liz put the coffee near the tray. 'Why is it that everyone takes an instant dislike to Mollie?'

Claire murmured, as she filled the kettle, 'Because it saves time.'

Liz shrieked with laughter, then sobered. 'The trouble is, people don't change. Her "easier" is

57

everyone else's bitter and twisted. She's a boil that needs lancing.'

Claire checked the clock—8 p.m. 'Spare us the clinical details.' Then a thought struck her. 'God, that means she's coming tonight, just when I have . . .' She stopped, remembering that Liz had yet to learn of the panto. She grabbed the coffee, spooning it into the cups.

'I gather so from Jean. She was going to let you know but I said I'd be seeing you.'

Claire gestured at their clothes. 'Did you tell her we'd gone casual?'

'I was too shell-shocked, but her casual would be one string of pearls less. Jean'll brief her, so don't fret.'

They each carried a plate of biscuits into the sitting room, then closed the curtains and brought through a couple of dining-room chairs to make up the numbers. As Claire positioned the chairs, counting round, she saw Liz looking at the scripts on the coffee table and swallowed. Liz leafed through them before letting them drop to the table and said nothing for a moment, then she turned to her, her hands on her hips, her face a mask of fury. Don't do this Liz, not now, Claire thought. I don't need it, not now. Not *now*, understand. She started to walk towards the kitchen but Liz sprang after her, grabbing her arm, spinning her round.

'Are you mad, Claire Baird, or just utterly spineless? I'd heard a rumour that Muriel had a bee in her bonnet but I knew you'd refuse because you haven't time. We've talked about the importance of your exams, about this being your year now that you've got Mark through the worst of *his* pig's-ear, about nothing getting in the way . . .'

58

Claire pulled away from her. Leaning on the back of the armchair she stared at the mantelpiece, not at her friend. The chrysanthemums in the vase were past their best, the water probably smelt. Bad old Mrs Todd. Liz came closer. 'Don't close up on me, Claire. Why the hell have you agreed to this?'

Claire smiled and shrugged, but there was no answering smile from Liz. Claire explained, 'Muriel wrote to Mark. They both decided it was a good idea—and it is, you know.'

Liz sliced her words to a halt. 'Damn that. Your exams are a good idea, good health is a brilliant idea. I mean when do you intend sleeping?'

Claire gripped the back of the armchair. She had replaced the covers last year so that the beige background behind the dark brown flowers would pick up the flat beige of the curtains. It had been a mistake because it showed the dirt too much. She said. 'It's taken care of. I'm dropping English. I arranged it today so there's nothing you can do about it. It'll give me a window in my schedule. I really don't mind.'

Liz grabbed her arm. 'Look at me and say that again.'

Claire looked up. 'I really don't mind.' It sounded as though she meant it.

Liz put her hands to her head, and it seemed for a moment as though she was going to tear her hair out. 'Why do you do it? Why do you always give in? You never used to be like this when we were kids. Look, just tell them to take a running jump, for God's sake. They have no right to put this on your plate, you've done enough. Just say no, damnit.'

Claire could hear voices coming up the drive and said quickly, 'I can take English in the autumn, or

59

next year. It's called compromise, Liz, so get off my bloody back. I'm still taking history, and there's no rush.' She started towards the door, but Liz grabbed her arm again. 'Just you wait a minute, Claire Baird.' Her face was close. 'It's not compromise, it's lying down with your legs in the air. Why do you make such a martyr of yourself— just tell me that? If there has to be a pantomime, get someone else to do it.'

The doorbell rang. Claire pushed her friend aside. 'It doesn't work like that, and you know it, so stop hassling me, and try helping.' Liz gestured to the room.

'I'm here early, what's that if it's not helping? What else do you want me to do, plump the cushions?'

'Well, that's a start. Look, just keep your voice down. We have to accept that Muriel and Mark are right, it would be good, could even be fun, and I need to be seen to be at the helm. But don't worry, it will be a team effort.' Liz shook a cushion at her, before positioning it perfectly on the settee, standing back, mockingly admiring her work, calling softly as Claire opened the door into the hall, 'You're your own worst enemy. Just plonk it on to someone else, the whole damn thing.'

Claire paused, her hand on the door. The bell rang again. She said, grinning, trying to lighten the atmosphere. 'You're offering, are you?'

Liz flushed as she picked up another cushion. 'That was below the belt. I would, but I've a job to do.'

Claire could hear the women chattering on the porch. One laughed. It was high pitched, so Clarissa had arrived. Claire's face was quizzical as

60

she said, 'One day a week?'

'Well, of course I'll do something, but nothing regular. I'm not reliable enough—what if my hours are increased? Anyway, it's no good going on, because you know I won't give in to bloody pressure like you, so get the door, Claire Baird, or they'll start hammering it down.'

Claire raised her eyebrows. Liz said uncomfortably, 'Well, with a bit of luck the committee will veto it and no one will have to do anything.'

*   *   *

By nine o'clock the committee had finished with Wives Club business, and sat drinking tea or coffee. All were dressed in tracksuits, jeans or similar, except for Mollie, who wore a matching Jaeger skirt and top and one string of pearls—her casual rig. Nonetheless, Mollie had volunteered to organize the Wives Club meeting for March, which was a first, and therefore encouraging. The fact that she was intent on a swimming evening at the local leisure centre was unfortunate, but couldn't be helped.

Briefly, Claire shared with the company commanders' wives the most recent problems that had arisen amongst the men's families, including Mollie in this as the wife of the officer commanding B Company. Mollie made great play of writing the details down in a small leatherbound notepad, saying as she did so, 'Nothing changes, all so tedious. Debt, marital discord, not coping on their own. Surely they know what they're getting into?'

61

Liz said, 'Well, you were quick enough to do a runner when the going—'

Claire cut in swiftly, 'Maybe Emily, our Army Wives Federation representative would give us an update on her side of things.'

Claire caught Liz's eye, and her apology, and smiled, knowing that Liz had only said what everyone else thought. Claire heard nothing of Emily's federation news as she ran through her introduction to the pantomime project again and again. When the update was finished she took a deep breath and, careful not to look at Liz, said, 'I think now's about as good a time as any to bring on the good news.'

The women turned to her, their faces curious. Liz chimed in, 'Oh no it isn't.' Her voice was robust, full of laughter, but beneath it Claire could hear the anger.

Claire grinned and pointed to the script on the table, her rehearsal blown sky high but this way was better.

Liz, her hands open to the heavens, asked: 'Any guesses?'

Sally, the RSM's wife, groaned. 'I'd heard the rumours.' She was shaking her head in disbelief, and exchanged glances with Liz. Sally's hair was freshly permed and it made her look different, too tidy and mumsy. Claire chanted, 'That's no rumour, that's the truth.'

Lt. Netherton's wife, of B Company, asked, 'This poor taste routine isn't leading where I think it is, surely?' Claire explained about the panto, half hoping for a great handsdown, but it didn't happen. Instead the women were nodding and passing the scripts around. The only two not fighting for one were Sally and Liz, who just stared into their cups.

After five minutes Claire called them to order. 'It's a yes, I gather?'

Jo Franks, the wife of Mark's CSM, raised her hand. She looked as though she should have been a farmer's wife with her round face, her healthy complexion, her bobbed hair and practical hands. 'If we go ahead I think we should write our own script, based on a traditional story, of course. We could tailor it to our situation, get a bit topical, bring in the regimental characters, and something about the village, then video the show and send it out to the men.'

More suggestions followed thick and fast until Liz, her face set, rapped on the coffee table. 'Claire can't and mustn't do this single handed, it's too much, and let's face it, the old bag's only ever done a nativity before now. We're talking polystyrene boobs here, girls, and men in drag, and one of those might have to be the village vicar. We need a team on this.'

Everyone was laughing except for Mollie and Jean, whose disapproval was evident in their rolling Les Dawson shoulders and sucked teeth. Claire wanted to hug Liz to within an inch of her life.

Liz said, 'So we need a hands-on producer to help Claire, a steering committee, and yes, let's write our own script. Volunteers?'

Jo Franks said to Claire, 'I could definitely write it, and I've experience of producing.' Next to Liz, Mollie turned to Jean, whispering loudly, 'But she's only a sergeant's wife. It wouldn't do for her to be the producer—in charge of us all.'

Liz gaped. Jo coloured and Claire wished yet again that bloody Molly had stayed in deepest

Devon. Sally leaned forward but Claire was already on her feet, hurrying to the sofa. She crouched before Mollie, saying quietly, 'It would "do" very well. Apart from Jo's other attributes she has an English and Drama degree and I would remind you that while the men are away we must all pull together. I know I have your commitment to that premise. In fact, I insist upon it.' Her voice, though level, held all the disappointment of her day, all her anger at the situation, all her irritation at this stupid woman, and it caused Mollie to flush, and to stutter, but Claire didn't want to hear any more from her. She held up her hand, resumed her seat, and raised her voice, 'Now, is everyone happy with Jo writing the script?'

Everyone was, and they began firing suggestions as Jo took notes almost as though she had never heard of Mollie. Claire glanced at Liz, saw her support and was able to smile as she turned to Jo, giving her the vicar's phone number so she could glean how many villagers would be interested.

Sally said she'd put feelers out round the patch. Maureen would get someone at the HIVE to run up some posters. Soon the machine was in motion and even a phone snow-line had been set up by the time the meeting drew to a close. At Jo's suggestion the next meeting was arranged for Thursday to approve the script.

'Only three days?' queried Jean tentatively.

'Are you sure that's not rushing you?' Claire asked.

Jo shrugged. 'No, I'm supplying teaching and I've nothing this week so it's fine. Besides, if you're happy with *Cinderella* I've a skeleton that I can fiddle about with. The sooner we know the minimum cast we can get away with, the sooner we can hold readings. Provided of course there *are* some out there who don't mind making idiots of themselves.' She had relaxed and suggested that she and Claire have a quick meeting within the next week to pull together a steering committee which must include stage manager, costumer, etc.

Claire nodded. 'We'll sort that out on Thursday?' As Jo agreed, Captain Clooney's wife, Chris, gestured that she must go. It was ten o'clock. The babysitter had school tomorrow.

They drifted off in ones and twos, Mollie and Jean leading the way, Mollie all bristles and wounded pride even in the face of Claire's conciliatory overtures. Jo and Sally left together but not before Claire had taken Jo to one side and made sure she knew that she was a godsend.

Soon there was only Liz left in the sitting room clearing the cups on to the tray. Claire met her in the kitchen and together they stacked the dishwasher as Liz grumbled, 'I'm bushed. I could have done without the advent of Mollie.'

'Busy day?' Claire sympathized, her own head aching.

Liz tipped the remains of the coffee into the sink. 'Difficult, more like. We talked about the partnership.'

Claire braced herself but Liz continued, 'You're right, you always damn well are. I talked about moving the deadline and it was no problem for them. They've absolutely promised they'll wait three months before they approach anyone else, so you can all relax. I'm not going to pressurize Ben but I still want it, Claire, I've had enough of being an appendage. I want a career, and that means not

65

moving again, and if it means Ben getting out, well . . .' She drew breath. 'Anyway he'll be back on leave in January and we'll decide then, calmly and rationally.'

Claire stopped pouring powder into the dishwasher. 'Calmly and rationally, eh?'

Liz laughed aloud. 'Well, if some fairy godmother can turn a pumpkin into a coach. miracles can obviously happen.' She headed for the hall, then came back. 'Come to think of it, how do we turn a pumpkin into a coach?'

Claire said, 'Get out of here.' She followed Liz into the hall. 'Jo, bless her, is bound to know all about transformation scenes. I could have killed Mollie, but perhaps I should have handled it better, seen the remark coming and diverted it.'

Liz was shrugging into her mac. 'I told you that woman is a boil that needs . . .'

Claire put her hands up in surrender. Liz took no notice and ploughed on. 'But you didn't quite lance her, just put a poultice on the situation, quietly and efficiently, and I know it's not the right thing for a CO's wife to do, but just once I'd like you to smack someone in the mouth. And just for once I'd like you to realize that someone else's bad behaviour is not caused by some failure on your part.' Liz stopped and reached out, picking up a manila envelope from the phone table. 'Ah, photos. Maybe there's a pumpkin costume in amongst the village props?'

She handed it to Claire. Together they walked to the door. Liz shook her head. 'Though why on earth Muriel sent it recorded delivery I can't imagine. They're hardly the crown jewels.'

Claire looked. The postmark wasn't local and

the handwriting wasn't Muriel's. She said, 'Perhaps it's come from someone who was once at the Drama Club and has now moved on. Muriel is the end though, she must have set it up even before she asked me, because it was posted on Saturday, for God's sake. Tell me, why aren't I surprised?' Her tone was ironic. As Liz opened the door she prised open the envelope.

'Well, is there a pumpkin amongst them?' Liz asked, about to step outside.

Claire read the letter paper-clipped to the photo. The writing was clear and bold. She stared beneath at the perfect, beautiful baby lying in her bonnet and matinée jacket in her carrycot. She stared and didn't hear Liz ask, 'What the hell's the matter?'

The cold night air was seeping in through the open door, past Liz, coming to her, and with it came darkness, such a darkness, swirling, sweeping, roaring. It swamped her. She pushed the photo back in its envelope. She tugged at her collar, trying to breathe and in a moment Liz was by her side, her arm round her. 'For God's sake, what is it?'

Liz's arm was warm, strong. Her voice sent the darkness back into the sky, back out there, but she was still so cold. God, she was cold. So cold. She stared at the curtain, the one she had made, the rail she had put up, seeing the flex of the drill trailing, hearing Mark worrying about the Marchout.

She drew a sudden breath, pulled away from Liz, from the safety of her arm. She said, going to the door, gripping it, needing its support, 'I'm tired. Just tired. Terrible headache. No pumpkins, Liz. Not even a magic wand. Nothing of any use. I must

67

go to bed.'

Her voice was thin. It came from somewhere else, not in her, but that was wrong. Of course it came from her. She shook her head, looking at Liz. At the glorious hair, the full figure, at the woman she knew best in the world. She wanted to say, Don't go. Don't leave me with this. She said instead, smiling, 'Hey, must fit a rest into my schedule.'

Liz tightened the belt of her ankle-length mac, an answering smile on her lips, a smile that didn't even begin to reach her eyes. 'Why not, there's a first time for everything. Claire, you shouldn't be getting headaches that spark up like this. It's too much, I keep telling you the whole bloody set-up is too much. You make sure you use that steering committee, you understand?'

Claire pointed towards the drive, as though directing traffic, a grin slapped on her face. 'Stop dithering.'

Liz tugged once more at her belt, turned up her collar.

Outside it was misty and there was a smell of bonfire on the air. She hesitated, half turned. 'Claire,' Liz touched her friend's cheek. 'You need a break.'

'Liz, please.'

Liz half shook her head, then walked away, head down. To Claire the gravel seemed noisier than usual.

Claire closed the door carefully, then leaned against it, sliding down to the floor. She removed the photograph, and the note, and both were too heavy for her to hold, their weight too great. The ache in her arms made her gasp, and the gasp became something that was not a howl, not a moan, it was a rasping snatching sound that tore at her throat and went on and on until it was all that existed in her world.

CHAPTER SIX

The Operations Room of the Vitez base hummed with the murmur of voices as it always did and Mark relaxed for a moment into the familiarity of the place. He glanced up at the reinforced ceiling, then tracked across to Ben who was pouring over a map with the Watchkeeper.

He shook his head. Ben saw and hurried to his side. 'You all set? OK?'

Mark swore gently.

Ben laughed softly, 'Not a happy bunny this morning, are we, Colonel?'

'Sod off, Ben, don't get cocky just because your ankle's keeping you out of the line of fire.'

Ben continued to laugh while the radio nets crackled and phones rang. Lt. Andrews walked by with a plastic cup filled almost to the brim with coffee. 'Kind of you,' Mark said, taking it off him. Lt. Andrews sighed, and returned to the coffee machine to start again.

'Capitulation is thirsty work, I should imagine?' Ben was staring into the distance, but he couldn't suppress the laughter and it broke out again.

Mark stolidly drained the cup, straightening his shoulders as he tossed it into the bin. 'Hardly capitulation—I prefer to look on it as tactical necessity but I just hope Baines remembered to

69

mention to Miss Sevo that today is a try-out. If I find, however, that Baines has no real need to be in Turbe with that particular liaison team I will personally convert his guts into garters in the slowest, most painful way known to man. It's just a shame that it's such a long bloody day.' He patted his combat jacket, turned to Ben and grinned. 'If I don't return I shall expect the highest posthumous decoration for gallantry above and beyond the call of duty. No need to try and recover the body, there won't be one. She's bound to have a taste for raw meat.'

Ben watched him stalk away and called, 'Never say die.'

He heard Mark's reply loud and clear. 'Don't be so bloody ridiculous, what's this, if it isn't walking into the valley of the shadow of death.'

The rest of the Ops Room heard him too, and laughter grew. It underlined how much the men were putting the start of Mark's command behind them and getting on side, stupid prat that he was. Mind you, there was still room for improvement but you couldn't have everything. Ben shook his head, irritated and relieved.

*   *   *

Mark and Gordana Sevo sat in the back of his Land Rover. Neither spoke, and he was thankful to be left in peace as he tried to schedule the battalion tasks that loomed, and wrote memos to himself in his notebook, agonizing over the fact that there were not enough hours in the day.

As they crossed a ravine using an old but hopefully sturdy bridge, Lance Corporal Simms bullied the windscreen, clearing the mist and Mark wished he could clear his own mind as efficiently. He was trying to remember which Muslim commander had just lost his family: was it the one he was meeting today? Damn and blast, it was no good. Jeremy would have to come back on board and they'd get someone else to hold the Liaison Officer's hand in the Turbe area. He needed briefing on the personalities, he needed someone who knew instinctively what was required. He did not need this chit of a girl.

He wiped the window. In the distance was the sound of fighting, and over to the east smoke was drifting into the sky. One neighbour turning on another? He'd hear soon enough over the radio. They thumped down and then out of a pothole. Lance Corporal Simms cursed quietly under his breath and Gordana Sevo made a grab for her small backpack as it slid off her knee. Mark turned, checking that the other three Land Rovers were still with them.

Beside him Gordana unbuckled the strap of her backpack and took from the front pocket a red notebook. Removing a folded typewritten sheet from inside the cover, she offered it to him. 'Colonel Baird, here is background to those we meet in Tuzla today. It helps if you know where these men are coming from.'

He turned to her, surprised and relieved, but almost disappointed because it had removed his cause for complaint. Reluctantly he said, 'Thank you, Miss Sevo.'

He scanned the page. There it was, neat, concise, everything that he needed. One was a former Yugoslavian Army officer, another a

71

teacher. Details of children, members of family cleansed, missing.

He said, handing it back. 'Useful. I'm grateful.' The words were right, the tone was not. She waved it towards him. 'Please, that is for you. I have mine. It is not just my information, you understand. It includes that which Jeremy and your liaison officers and permanent interpreters collect for your Intelligence Cell.'

Mark bowed his head, and said, his voice heavy with irony, 'Yes, I do understand the system, since I am the one who inherited it, and improved upon it.'

She coloured, and he knew he'd been a bastard but then, why did she have to go out of her way to be so clever?

He took the paper from her and she busied herself pushing her notebook deep into the front pocket of her backpack. It was bleached, scuffed and stained, and much like the one Leah had for her sports kit. In spite of himself he softened. 'Your filing system?'

Staring ahead at the wooded valleys and the mountain ranges she said, 'Yes, my filing system.' Mark studied the typed notes again, trying to keep the thread of the facts, and was close to memorizing them when she spoke again.

'Colonel Baird, if I might suggest . . .' She stopped. Mark stared at her absently, trying to hang on to the names, feeling them slide away. Damn.

Gordana cleared her throat nervously but her voice was firm when she said, 'Face is important here, in Bosnia. Perhaps you are aware that in the eyes of neighbouring states we Bosnians are like

72

the Irish: the butt of jokes. However, just as the Irish, we have our sense of honour.' Though her voice was strong her fingers were nervously working the strap of the backpack.

The Land Rover juddered and jolted and Mark wished to hell that she'd get to the point. Jeremy knew when to speak and when not; this just wasn't going to work. She continued, 'It is important, I think, to distribute yourself evenly amongst both Croat and Muslim leaders. If not, UN favouritism is perceived, honour and face is jeopardized. Positions are taken. You will find that suddenly roadblocks are not discouraged. Today you visit a Muslim commander, with only a brief stop in Vares to talk to the Croats. It is a mistake. To their leader it could seem almost patronizing, a favour to a child.'

Mark stared blankly down at his notes, scarcely able to believe what he'd heard. Was the girl stark staring mad to think he didn't know this? She began again. 'Colonel Baird, I hope you understand that I do not criticize, in fact I applaud your goodwill. I just feel that it is a point worth making.'

He turned to her, his outrage manageable, just. 'I can't imagine how I've managed to cope for so long without your input, Miss Gordana. I'm sure that single-handedly you will pull the UN force into something to be proud of, and in the meantime I presume you have a stopwatch. I presume you will time each meeting to the second and log it in your files. Just so that we are absolutely fair. I was at Vares last week.'

Her hands became instantly motionless. Lance-Corporal Simms's eyes were on him fleetingly but it

73

was long enough for Mark to interpret his expression. It was not warm.

Mark cursed inwardly. Just wait until he saw Baines. 'Checkpoint, sir.' Simms's voice was carefully neutral.

*   *   *

At the checkpoint Miss Sevo plied the Muslims with cigarettes, chatting to them, then translating Mark's request. It seemed that in record time the Land Rovers were heading in the direction of the old ski resort of Vares and Mark acknowledged to himself that she was good, but even so, she just caught him on the raw, and then he went over the top and... As they ran alongside a few pines clinging to the edge he said stiffly, sitting right up against the door, whilst she sat against the other, intent on her notes. 'Miss Sevo, I must apologize, but...'

She interrupted, glaring round at him. 'No, *you* must do nothing. We are all in *your* hands. We have no power, no redress.' She returned to her notebook. There was only the sound of the Land Rover; the rumble of the tyres on the uneven road surface, the change of tempo as Simms changed down to negotiate a hairpin bend. The valley dropped away but the vivid autumnal orchards were still visible in the thin sun. Exasperated, Mark rephrased his apology. 'Miss Sevo, I would like to apologize.'

Gordana held her notebook loosely. A strand of hair had escaped from her clips and it touched her cheek, swinging in time to the Land Rover's motion. Mark waited, absorbed in this small

74

movement until Miss Sevo secured it. He dropped his gaze. Her notebook lay on her lap.

He looked at her again, and she was smiling. There were laughter lines at the corners of her eyes, burned deep as though the sun of Australia had caught a careless joyous moment and decided to preserve its memory for ever.

She said, 'You are kind. As always I am too knowing, but more than that, I respond too harshly. It is something that has crept up on me. I don't think it is a true emotion, but something that comes from nowhere, or perhaps from tiredness and stress, and makes my words sharp and cruel. Then I wish that I could take them back. I wish that I could climb above this irritation.' Slowly he nodded at her as her smile faded and an earnest line formed between her eyes. In his mind he re-ran her words, startled, because this young woman had just described himself.

After a moment he slowly shrugged. 'Perhaps you would give me a general brief. That village, for instance.' He pointed to a crow's nest village.

Until they reached Vares she talked him through the makeup of the villages she knew from experience and those she had learnt about. She listed in her book those she knew nothing of. 'I will fill in these gaps. It is only when you need details about your own land that you realize how little you know it.'

In spite of himself Mark agreed with her again, and found himself listening intently as she told him of the farmer down to their left who lived in the idyllic farmhouse by the river, but who had no diesel for his tractor. 'In the spring there will be no ploughing, instead they will dig what they can by
75

spade.'

He looked when she pointed to houses high in the mountains. 'Skiing chalets once, in the days before . . .' Her voice petered out, and then she asked briskly, 'Do you find the information that your Scimitar squadrons provide helpful?'

He nodded, keen to follow her lead away from emotional areas. 'Yes. Bloody boring though it is for them no doubt.' She grinned, saying, 'They just park, duck, and observe front-line positions. At least the rest of us talk, and make contact with living breathing beings.'

He was relaxing. Remembering the nicotine and garlic breath of the old man at the roadblock he laughed. 'A bit too much direct contact sometimes.'

*　　　*　　　*

They spent thirty-nine minutes at the Croat HQ and as they approached Tuzla he whispered, 'Stopwatch at the ready, Miss Sevo.'

She looked at him uncertainly. 'Colonel Baird, we have no need to be exact, it was the principle I was discussing.'

He heard himself laughing again. 'I quite understand that, of course.' He realized that he was feeling quite relaxed and was astonished. They picked up Captain Sandy McGregor, Liaison Officer for the area, from C Company's base at Kladanj and sped along 'bomb alley' to Tuzla. Captain McGregor briefed them all the way, but told Mark no more than Miss Sevo had done already. Mark caught her glance, and they both nodded.

Entering Tuzla, which was all grey concrete and

worn apartment blocks, Mark found himself telling Miss Sevo of Vienna, and the equally grim apartment blocks which had been shoved up long ago to house the returning bureaucrats after they no longer had an empire to administer. He told her too of the wine tasting he and Claire had endured at 8 a.m. when all they had wanted was to grab a bottle of reasonable plonk from the wine shop and make it to the airport on time. Her laugh was full of fun, full of something that had gone from this country. She said, 'Pissed before breakfast. I thought that was the prerogative of students.'

Surprised, he grinned. 'Ah yes, you have obviously travelled in Australia.'

She smiled. 'My father also prepared me well. He was a realistic man.' The smile faded and didn't reappear until they reached the Muslim headquarters.

An hour later he could still taste the slivovitz and the coffee, and smell the crude tobacco on his uniform as he entered the hotel in the centre of Tuzla where they were having lunch. As he pulled out Miss Sevo's chair he could still picture the Serb positions flagged on the Muslim maps in their HQ. Maps which had been spread out on tables and held down at the corners by overflowing ashtrays. Phone lines had sprouted from unlikely places and were looped along the ceiling; they rang endlessly as Miss Sevo and Sandy McGregor translated the proceedings, lifting their voices over the rattle of gunfire and thump of mortars, just as the Muslim commander was doing, ignoring the steady trickle of plaster from the cracked ceiling.

Lunch was pizza and beer. Both were cold, and Mark picked at his as he listened to Sandy's assessment of the situation while Miss Sevo wrote carefully and continuously in her notebook, picking at the dry bread which accompanied the meal until she surreptitiously reached into her backpack and brought out a green notebook. As Mark watched she wrote rapidly, crosschecking against the other, and now she had Mark's full attention. Why did she need two? Who else was she feeding this information to? Probably just a precaution in case she lost one? With his brain clicking over, Mark sat back, puzzling, but then he saw her lay aside her pencil, take out a paper bag, and slip her pizza into the backpack. Embarrassed and unseen, Mark swung back to Sandy.

Captain McGregor was saying, 'Don't you agree, sir?'

Mark nodded, his appetite gone. Agree? To what? He said, 'Run that past me again, Sandy, I was miles away for a moment.'

Captain McGregor did so.

*   *   *

They left Captain McGregor to be picked up by one of his men at 1600 hours, but only after Mark had visited the President for Refugees. He was bone tired by the time they left Tuzla, this town born out of Tito's more paranoid moments, a town which reminded Mark of a wartime film set and no longer of Vienna, which seemed centuries away from where he was now.

They roared south on the main Sarajevo road, then diverted into the mountains to avoid the Serb front lines. The track was narrow and dangerous and he ordered convoy lights because the track was in full view of the Serb artillery on the hills overlooking Sarajevo.

He said to Miss Sevo, 'I'm sorry, there is a risk, but I need to re-familiarize myself with this road in case we have to use it.'

'I know of the risk,' she replied.

Mark scratched the back of his hand, sounding awkward as he said, 'I assume you realize that it is to your advantage not to be taken on because there would be this sort of danger every time you travel with us. There would be danger even if you didn't travel, for there are some who will feel that those who we employ are the enemy as much as they think we are. Penalties could be extracted.'

She nodded, the edge back in her voice. 'You mean a sniper could blow my head to pieces. Yes, of course I know that, Colonel Baird, but all in my country are in danger. Do you think I am an imbecile? Do you think . . .' She fell silent.

For God's sake, he had only been trying to explain the job because he had half convinced himself that she could have it, but no, he had been right all along, she was just too much damn trouble. In silence they proceeded through the danger zone and through the next two checkpoints, but were stalled immediately after that by a small landslide which was clearly visible in the moonlight. A group of Croats from the third checkpoint were clearing it, and Mark's platoon joined them while Mark paced nearby, watching for a moment as the clink of spade on rock almost drowned out the deeper sounds of the Serb bombardment of Sarajevo, a good ten kilometres away.

After a few minutes the chill in the air was too keen and he started towards his Land Rover, then

79

thought better of it as he saw Miss Sevo still sitting in the back seat. He resumed his pacing, staring across at the flashes and explosions bursting in and above Sarajevo, finally walking back to the cluster of pines at the rear of the Land Rovers, taking care to look only ahead. In the shelter of the trees it seemed warmer, but he could still hear the artillery quite clearly.

What must it be like to be the UN presence there? Bloody hell, he thought he was stressed; that must be a nightmare. How would you keep the lid on the impotence, the humiliation of having to witness and endure to that extent without response? He heard the click of a door, a slam, and saw movement by the Land Rover. Miss Sevo was coming towards him. He waited, a lamb to the slaughter, but what else could he damn well do— scarper? He jammed his hands in his pockets and stared again towards Sarajevo.

'Under different circumstances that would be a striking sight,' he said as she reached him, and wondered if that statement sounded as crass to her as it did to him. Well, if she was true to form he'd soon find out. He bunched his hands.

Miss Sevo crossed her arms and half turned. 'It is history being made. It is man's inhumanity to man. What is it your Douglas Hurd said? I can't remember his exact words, but to the effect that it is only because of the media that public opinion has forced action on Bosnia, that there is nothing new in all of this. I often wonder if he meant that therefore, nothing should be done, so dry your eyes, stiffen your upper lip, and stop fussing over an insignificant event? What do you think, Colonel Baird?'

The look she gave him was not aggressive, and to his surprise he realized that it really had been a question. He thought, then answered slowly, 'As a soldier I would like to do more, but as a politician I would see the murky waters. So you can see, Miss Sevo, I don't know what to think. I simply follow . . .'

'The mandate,' she finished for him. The edge was back. He wanted to move away from her and all that she was about to lay at his door, but for God's sake, she'd only follow.

Around him the wind almost bent the trees, and snow fell through the branches. He looked up, picturing the summer here, with the air so pure and laden with the scent of pines. And the views? Well, they'd be spectacular. He stopped himself. Once they would have been spectacular. Behind him the men laboured and cursed softly, boulders crunched, spades clinked, and over it all was the gunfire, and now, her voice.

'Over there, in Sarajevo, are my friends. They do not sleep on their pillows, instead they place them at the windows, along with their wardrobes for protection. In their homes there are no longer roses, these are outside now, they are the thousands of mortar impact points, our "Sarajevan roses"—blood red. When my friends walk, or scuttle, or run through the streets it is on the glass of windows that did not endure. When they are shot, it is the crunch of glass beneath their bodies that is the last sound they hear, not bullet, or shrapnel. Yes, it is the crunch of glass.'

He wondered if that was what she had heard when she had been hit by shrapnel, but he said nothing, because the one thing he was learning was

81

that whatever he said it wouldn't be right.

She sniffed her anorak. 'Today we smell of tobacco smoke. Down there their clothes will smell of soot and smoke, and dust. Dust smells, you know, Colonel Baird.'

Mark turned to check on the landslide. Come on, for God's sake. He saw that it was cleared. He heard Lance Corporal Simms muttering as he returned, 'Bloody load of spastics, they are. If it'd been left to us we'd have had it cleared in no time.'

*　　*　　*

They reached their base on the outskirts of Vitez at nearly 2030 hours and drew to a halt outside the building which housed Miss Sevo's flat. It was almost next to the press house, and not far from the one he, as CO, had taken as his own. All were just outside the entrance to the base.

She stood on the pavement, looking at him. He knew what it was she wanted to ask, but he couldn't take her on, she was good but like a bomb that kept threatening to explode, though he wasn't going to be fool enough to tell her the verdict himself. It was enough that he'd prepared the ground. He'd leave it to her white knight, Baines. He said, 'Good-night, Miss Sevo. Thank you for your services. Someone will be in touch.'

It was as though a shutter came down over her face, but she nodded as she closed the car door and walked into her house. Not for the first time today Lance Corporal Simms caught his eye in the rearview mirror, but the expression was guarded. Bloody good thing too, Mark thought, because he didn't want judgement, not about something as trivial as this. Not about anything, in fact. He'd had enough of that to last a lifetime over the last year.

Lance Corporal Simms drove through the gate and the sentry saluted. Simms dropped Mark at the door. Reaching his office, Mark threw his flak jacket on the chair in the corner. He had radioed through to Ben in the Ops Room on a regular basis whilst on patrol, and in a moment he'd report down the line to the Brigadier but that could wait for a moment.

There was a knock on the door. It was Ben, who stuck his head round, grinning. 'Still with us then, unscathed, untouched by man-eating interpreter. Meet you in the mess. Drinks are on me.'

Mark dropped into his chair. 'Push off.' He was grinning but as Ben disappeared down the corridor he sank his head into his hands, rubbing his eyes. He could see her putting the pizza in the bag. He could hear her facilitating his task with the local commanders, with the Croats at the checkpoints, the landslide. Yes, she was good, but bloody hell . . .

He threw himself back in the chair, looking at the photograph of Claire on his desk. No way. No, he wasn't having her. Good God, he didn't need any more women on his case. They never knew when to keep their mouths shut and if they weren't giving unasked-for advice they were looking hurt. He thought of Claire. OK, he might sometimes have been a bit short, but bloody hell. He dragged his fingers through his hair, catching sight of the pile of papers on his desk which had grown since this morning and wearily reached out and took a form from the top. At least this he understood.

CHAPTER SEVEN

On Thursday Anna Weaver waited for the traffic lights to turn green, snatching a quick look at directions she'd written out and Sellotaped to the dashboard. Her hands felt as though they were locked on to the steering wheel. She forced herself to relax her grip but the tension remained; tension that had dug deeper with every second that had passed since receiving the returned photograph. It hadn't even been sent recorded delivery.

How could Claire Baird be so careless with something she must have known meant so much? What if it had gone astray, lost for ever? How could she scrawl on that posh paper *I'm so sorry, but you are mistaken. However, please accept my best wishes for your future.*

The car behind hooted. The lights were green. She accelerated, heading out of town towards the main road. Well, Claire Baird, it's not finished yet. I refuse to let this be the end. Her eyes flickered again to the route. She reckoned it would take an hour and a half, that was all.

*   *   *

Liz rapped on Claire's kitchen door, and came straight in. 'Am I the first?' She pulled the multicoloured silk scarf from her head and stuffed it in her pocket. 'Darn drizzle.'

Claire raised an eyebrow. 'My word, you're keen. I take it this means you want to be first on to the *Cinderella* steering committee?'

84

'No, my dear Mrs Baird, it doesn't mean that, but a good try. What it means is that my caring compassionate side is asserting itself—I'm checking up on you, though I wanted to come earlier.' Liz lolled against the breakfast bar where freshly baked bread cooled on wire trays.

'How is your mother now—better for your ministering?' Claire was rummaging for the corkscrew in the drawer.

'Just a spot of flu, and yes, she's fine.' Liz spotted the wine glasses on the tray. 'Oh, I see it's bribery and corruption time. Get the girls blitzed and they'll be anyone's, even Cinderella's.'

Claire's headache threatened to split her skull but somehow she smiled and murmured, 'That's the general idea.'

Liz tapped the base of the bread. There was just the right hollow sound. She picked off a piece of crust, her eyes fixed firmly on Claire, her expression one of concern, tinged with confusion. Claire wouldn't acknowledge either. Instead she reached into the pantry, collected several packets of crisps and tossed them across to Liz. 'Stop cluttering up the place and do something useful. Dig out the earthenware bowls and remember that tonight we are in the presence of righteousness— the vicar from Over Setton will be amongst us—so appropriate behaviour, please.'

Liz's voice was muffled as she rooted, head down and bum up, for the bowls in the dresser. 'The vicar?'

'Absolutely. He's Muriel's emissary and will be accompanied by the warden, who was the doyen of the village drama group before it became defunct. Apparently he's panting for a part.'

Liz laid six bowls on the table, blowing her hair out of her eyes. 'Two men in our lair but they're of the cloth; that just about sums up my day.' She tore open the crisp packets and shook the contents into the bowls. 'Still, if they come in their long black frocks they're already halfway to becoming the Ugly Sisters.'

'*Appropriate* behaviour, Liz,' warned Claire, finding a laugh from somewhere. 'Especially, my dear girl, where Mollie's concerned.'

Liz disposed of the crisp packets in the bin, dusted off her hands and returned to the table. As she sat down she pointed to the loaves. 'Enough of the meeting, what's with the bread? You only pound hell out of poor defenceless dough when there's a crisis.' She became serious. 'What's happening, Claire?'

'I needed bread, that's all.'

Liz picked out a couple of crisps. 'No, that's not all.'

Claire reached for the ashtrays. 'Are you smoking or not?'

'Stop changing the subject. You don't look right. You look, oh, I don't know—distracted. What was the photo of? And yes, I am smoking—you're driving me to it.'

Claire concentrated on opening a bottle of white wine, glad that the reluctant cork was demanding all her attention. She strained, and with one final wrench it was out. The second was easier and she put both in coolers. Now her voice would be steady. Now she had found the laugh again. 'Good heavens, I'd forgotten about the envelope. No, that was nothing—just someone's marketing ploy.'

It was something she'd worked out during that

long Monday night, a night in which the pain, and the longing, and the loss had returned in even greater force than she had ever thought possible. It still remained.

She tossed the corks into the bin, jerking her head towards the sitting room, grabbing the coolers and Chablis. 'Bring the crisps, there's a good 'un.' In the sitting room she found room for the bottles on the side table. She placed them in the centre. Yes, the dead centre. She touched both. Still cold. As cold as she'd been when the photograph arrived. As cold as . . . She let her hands drop to her sides.

Her arms ached, because they were empty, they held nothing. She turned, a bright smile on her face.

Liz was standing, holding the tray of crisps, her eyes searching.

'OK, OK, Doctor, I give in. It's the pantomime. You were right, it is a bit too much, and Mollie's return hasn't helped and so it's all just suddenly got to me.' She felt her voice begin to shake and stopped abruptly. Liz hurried to her, but Claire stopped her with a gesture. 'No, don't sympathize, or you'll set me off. Just put the darn crisps round and help me get through the evening.' Her voice was quite steady again, her smile working well.

She fetched the glasses from the kitchen and on her return found Liz flicking through the script that Jo had brought round in the afternoon. Claire asked, 'You've seen a copy?'

Liz dropped the script on to the table; she was picking at the crisps, fumbling for one that folded over on itself—her absolute favourite. She found two and smiled at Claire, waving them triumphantly. 'Indeed I have read it, and there's a witch—the 'Orrible Oracle . . .' She waited. Claire grimaced and said, 'It must be a coincidence? Only you and I call Mollie that.'

Liz shook her head. 'Or sleight of hand revenge, and why the hell not. Let it go. Apart from anything else it'll be the best therapy for you to have a bit of a hiss and a boo at the stage version. It'll render the real one less of a pain.'

Claire laughed. 'That's your prescription, is it?'

'Absolutely.'

God, Claire thought, if only life were that simple. Again she felt herself begin to shake but at that point the doorbell rang and Liz whooped and dived for the wine. 'Great, now we can get cracking.' But her eyes were still concerned.

* * *

By nine o'clock the script had been accepted and Sally distributed the proof poster the HIVE had already run off. 'All we need is to add an audition date.'

Claire said. 'We'll come to that later but let's see who's going to distribute them once we've sorted out the details. I'll put some in the Coffee Shop, the NAAFI, and the Federation Register of Employment office.' Liz offered to put one in the doctor's surgery. Clarissa, Emily and Maureen came up with some useful suggestions too.

Claire asked Jo, 'How soon do we know if it's viable? Do people flood in the day the posters go up, or is it a trickle situation? What I'm really trying to ask is when do we start panicking and scrub the whole thing.' She tapped her pen on her notepad.

Liz called, 'You call that a panic—it'd be a celebration in my book.' Instantly there were boos and hisses. Maureen and Emily shook ferocious fists. Mollie said, 'That attitude is unhelpful, Liz. Don't you agree, Vicar?'

The vicar who had contented himself with a dog collar rather than a full black 'frock', winked at Claire as he turned to Mollie. 'I feel Liz isn't quite serious, Mollie.'

Claire kneaded the back of her neck and caught Liz's eye, shaking her head slightly. Don't say it, Liz, don't say, 'I shouldn't bet on it.' Liz nodded to Claire, her smile warm. Claire continued to knead her neck, knowing she could read her friend like a book, knowing that Liz thought it reciprocal. But it wasn't. For there were chapters that must stay locked. *They must stay locked.*

Liz asked Jo, who sat next to her on the sofa, 'What if we don't get enough to fill the cast list?'

Jo, taking a light from Liz, sucked greedily at the smoke as she sat back. Tonight her short nails were varnished a soft pink. She grinned at Liz. 'I refuse to consider such flabby talk.'

Mollie drew in her breath, Liz and the others laughed, even Jean. Jo continued as she sat back, exhaling. 'However, if it should happen, some of the cast can take on an additional role. The problem comes when they're changing costume and a zip gets stuck. I mean, look here.' She leafed through the script and found the transformation scene at the end of Act I when the pumpkin becomes a coach. 'We've mice who transform into coachmen. So we'll slot in new coachmen, and scoot the mice into the dressing room, quick-change them for the ball. It should be fine but there's always one who manages to get half strangled by her costume in the rush.'

Again Claire fixed Liz with a glance but this time there was no stopping her. 'We'll just have to put all those we hate into the most intricate costumes.'

Over the laughter Mollie could be heard. 'Only you would think of that, Liz. Do forgive us Reverend Masters.'

Claire butted in. 'The men will be a problem ...'

Clarissa Baines called out, stretching forward to take a crisp, 'And it were ever thus.'

Jo scribbled in her notepad. 'Thanks for that, Mrs Baines. It'll make a line for one of the Uglies.'

After reminding Jo that they were all on first-name terms Claire said loudly, 'However, the $64,000 question is—are you going to be our guiding light—our producer—in all this? We still haven't had that assurance from you.'

Jo shifted uncomfortably, her glance taking in Mollie then returning to Claire. She fiddled with her white polo neck. 'The problem is, that if we're talking about attracting participants the organizer has to be you. You walk on water as far as the patch is concerned so if it's your baby they'll be queuing up.'

Claire hung on those last words and it was as though the room had darkened, as though cold seeped from every corner. 'Claire?' Jo queried, her face concerned.

Claire shook her head and found she was in the midst of chatter, of light, of warmth again. She protested quietly. 'But I don't know enough.'

'No, she doesn't and I won't have her overloaded.' Liz tapped her ash into the 'Greetings from Margate' dish that Leah had brought back when she was six.

Mollie said, 'Being overloaded is part and parcel of being a CO's wife.'

Sal teased, 'Left to Claire we'd be drowned in schedules and stuck in nativity mode. We already know that's the limit of her experience.'

Claire smiled, brushing back her hair. 'Well, thanks a bunch.'

The Reverend Masters winked at her again and beside him the warden, Tom Smith, guffawed. Jo stubbed out her cigarette. 'My proposal is that I come in as co-producer/director with Claire. That way she's still the figurehead and we share the load—a problem halved?' She looked around the room. Everyone was nodding, even Mollie, though it was the merest of movements. Jo continued swiftly, 'So, we set up a steering committee, including the company commanders' wives, that way there's a point of contact for the reluctants of the patch, a sort of loyalty bond.' Liz looked as though she'd sucked a lemon, but slowly agreed, as did the others.

Jo grinned and carried on. 'We'll send round forms to all those who are interested, get them to put down their strengths and weaknesses because it's not only actors, but the backroom personnel we need as well.'

Mollie crossed her legs, smoothed her pleated skirt, and cut across the chatter which had broken out. 'In my village I was involved with the WI drama, so I consider myself experienced.'

Claire sagged in her chair, Liz looked as though she was going to vomit, but not Jo. She said, 'In a moment I'll ask you to write the details down for me. It would be such a help. I know that those who offer first are going to be the backbone of the thing. Claire and I can put them in the roles that we feel will benefit the production most.'

Claire met Sal's gaze. Just what role would Jo find for Mollie? Something that diverted her from the main drag, she felt sure, and what a brilliant RSM's wife this girl would make one day. She just hoped CSM Franks appreciated her, but he was a bright fellow, and nice with it, so he probably did. Long may it stay that way. Again she felt the darkness.

'Claire.' Jo was trying to get her attention. 'Claire,' she repeated. 'I suggest a steering committee meeting tomorrow evening so we can get under way. We'll need to fix audition and rehearsal dates, personnel for scene painting, props and so on. People will come along to the auditions who haven't approached us earlier, so we must have a good supply of forms. We'll need a wardrobe committee and so on and the two of us need to produce a critical path.'

The next fifteen minutes was spent firming up the steering committee, which comprised the Reverend Masters and Tom Smith. The company commanders' wives, Sally Coates and Clarissa Baines, also volunteered.

As they finished Jo reached into her briefcase and brought out a sheaf of forms. 'I just happen to have upon my person . . .'

Liz grumbled, 'Let me guess—forms?'

Jo handed them out. 'Exactly, Liz. Can you all fill in your details, then we're off to a flying start. Vicar, while I think of it, can you chat up the village Youth Club? We could do with some dancers between scenes, as well as some in speaking parts.

I've had a word with Barbara at the garrison Youth Club. She's getting our lot on side. The chicken we're having as Cinderella's kitchen friend is a bit of a problem; we'll need a man in tights for that and it's the legs we'll be auditioning.'

The vicar in his turn handed her a list of the scenery they had beneath the stage in the village hall.

Mollie said to Claire, 'Didn't you say Muriel Haynes was sending round photos of the costumes? I should see them, as I've put wardrobes as my strength.'

Claire stared at the form she was filling in, the words suddenly dancing and blurring. Her hand had begun to shake. Laying down her pen she took a deep breath and miraculously her voice was quite steady as she said, 'They haven't arrived yet, but I'll bear that in mind.' She touched her mouth. She smelt the bread, felt the ache in her wrists from the pounding, the ache in her head. Why didn't everybody go—just go.

*   *   *

Anna parked her car beneath the street light at the head of Mons Road. She released her seat belt and leaned across, lowering the passenger window, calling to the two women who were walking along beneath umbrellas, 'I'm looking for Ypres Place, Mrs Baird's house.'

One of the women stooped, looked into the car, a query in her eyes. Anna gestured to the envelope. 'I'm delivering some photographs.'

'Oh right. You go on this road, OK. Turn right at the phone box, go on to the next left. Keep going.

93

It'll be facing you, right?'

Anna repeated the directions. Her windscreen wipers were squeaking. The drizzle had stopped. Mechanically she switched them off. 'Yeah, that's right,' the woman confirmed, smiling slightly before rejoining her friend and walking on.

Anna wound up the window, clicked in her seat belt and drove on, turning right at the phone box, then next left. There was a large house facing her. Her breathing was too fast. She stopped a few yards from the open gates. A curved gravel drive led to the house. The porch light was on. The room to the right of the door was occupied, judging from the light showing through the gap in the curtains.

She turned off the lights, then the engine. She felt sick. She hadn't the strength to take the key from the ignition, undo her seat belt. All she could do was sit, trying to get her breath. Her legs were shaking, the window was misting.

She stared at Claire Baird's house, at the room where she must be sitting. She checked her watch. Ten o'clock. There were no cars in the drive. Claire Baird was alone. She would approach, she would knock, the door would open . . . Anna dropped her head into her hands. Then what? Then what? All these years and then what?

She dug her fingers into her scalp, counted to three, opened the door, snatched up the envelope and hurried towards the house. Sodden leaves muffled some of her footsteps, but not all, by no means all. She slowed, walked on her toes, the gravel crunched. She breathed through her mouth. There was no drizzle, just dampness in the air, a dampness that chilled. She was trembling as she drew closer. The porch light reached as far as the

94

laurel bush, where she stopped for a moment.

It was then she heard a burst of laughter from the room, and voices. She stopped, unsure. The front door opened and she heard several voices, not just one. Not just Claire Baird's.

She turned to flee but she would be seen, and heard. Instead she ducked behind the bush, brushing against the wet leaves, her heels sinking into the softened lawn. She gasped for breath as though she'd been running and put her hand to her mouth. Gradually her breathing slowed.

Through the gaps she saw light shaft from the door, but it reached no further than the porch light. Safe in her darkness she heard a woman say, 'Sorry to rush, Claire. Mandy needs me sitting on her if she's ever going to finish her course work.'

Claire Baird, dressed in jeans and a polo neck beneath a shirt, touched Mandy's mother's arm. 'The others are on their way, Sally. You're OK for tomorrow's meeting, and there's the playgroup celebration on Saturday. To be shot at dawn is the penalty for a no-show.'

Sal laughed. A vicar and another man came then, stepping down the drive with Sal. The vicar was saying, 'We left our car in Liz's drive, don't know why but I thought your drive would be chock-a-block.' The gravel drowned Anna's breathing, but not the image of Claire as she waved to the vicar, not her voice as she said 'Thanks for coming.' She seemed smaller than she had done on the television and even more tired. Her voice was the same, and her gestures.

Anna eased her weight from one foot to the other. Her feet were damp, her toes numb, but she barely noticed. Her eyes were fixed on Claire. It would be soon, very soon, and suddenly the trembling ceased, her breathing was deep. It was as though nothing more could be done than had been done. The waiting was almost over. More women came out and walked along the drive, their voices muted, most discussing the weather and already longing for the spring.

$$* \qquad * \qquad *$$

Jo and Liz said to Claire, as she held the door, 'Are you sure we can't help clear?'

'Quite. It's Mrs Todd's morning tomorrow, and she'll sort it out.'

Jo stepped on to the porch. 'Good, it's stopped drizzling.' She turned. 'I think I'll just catch up with the others. I want to pin Mollie down to wardrobe. It's a section where she can work alone on her own little machine.' Her face was impassive but Liz roared with laughter and waved as Jo walked briskly away. Liz slipped her arm into Claire's and together they stepped down on to the gravel, walked a few paces then stopped. Claire murmured, 'That young lady is going to be a gem.'

Liz tugged her arm. 'Please let me help clear up.'

Claire shook her head. 'Go on, we all need an early night.' Liz walked on. For a moment Claire watched her, then raised her hand, wanting to call her back. She clamped her lips shut. No. She must not. Instead she rubbed her forehead and as she did so there was the sound of a breaking twig. It came from the laurel. Claire turned to look, to listen. She waited but there was nothing more. She shrugged, but there it was again. 'Who is it?' she whispered, staring into the darkness.

There was movement now, and a rustling. 'Who's there?'

She stared at the girl who moved out from the darkness of the bush. The light was dim but there was enough to see the eyes, those eyes. Those dark eyes. Claire backed.

The girl spoke. Her voice was high pitched, her words rushed. 'I'm sorry, I was waiting for everyone to go. I just wanted to talk to you. That's all. Just to talk to you.' It wasn't a voice Claire recognized, but the eyes, oh God, she recognized those. Claire put up her hand; her legs were like water but the girl came on. The light was on her now, and the eyes faded, somehow they just faded. Claire whispered 'Who are you?' But she already knew, of course she already knew.

Liz called, 'Claire, are you all right?' Claire heard her, and held up her hand, but this time to send her away. Oh yes, she must go away. The girl, her eyes holding Claire's, held out the brown envelope which had contained the photograph. 'I had to see you.'

Claire's arms ached as she ignored the envelope, her voice shook as she said, 'Please, you must go. For your own sake you must go. Trust me.' The girl just stood there, her short hair moving gently in the slight breeze, her face pinched from the cold, a face Claire knew she would remember for the rest of her life, even as she insisted, 'My dear, you really are mistaken.'

Anna said, 'No I'm not. Look at this again and tell me I'm not.'

Out of the corner of her eye Claire could see Liz standing stock still. Much further away, from the head of the drive, Claire could hear the murmur of

97

concern from the others, and it was growing. Soon they too would be here.

The girl came closer, the gravel crunched. All around was the dripping of water from the leaves, all around was the blackness, the cold. The girl still held out the envelope. Within reach of Claire she stopped and repeated, 'Look at this and tell me I'm mistaken.'

Mollie's voice was strident and carried clearly from the road. 'Is there a problem?'

Liz stepped forward, asking urgently, 'Claire?'

Again Claire flagged her to a halt as she whispered to the girl who was so close, so very close, and whose light perfume she could smell. It was like apple, like the sun, like . . . She whispered to the girl who was so close that she was almost within touching distance, 'Please go away.'

Instead Anna took the photograph from the envelope and held it up. It was illuminated by the porch light. 'How can you pretend it isn't me? How can you?'

Her voice rode in on a tide of greater darkness, a deeper cold which was drowning Claire. The girl shook the photograph, and light seemed to skid across its surface. Abruptly Claire stepped back, bursting through the darkness, gulping at the air, shouting, 'Because you're wrong. You're wrong. It never happened.' She took another step backwards, another. Anna followed, pace for pace. Claire hit out at the photo. It fell. 'Liz, help me, get her away. It's not me, she's mistaken,' she cried. Liz darted forward. Mollie called again: 'Shall I get help?'

Liz shouted, 'Leave it, Mollie. Everything's fine. Bit of a misunderstanding.' She rescued the photograph from the ground. Leaves clung to it.

Anna snatched it from her, pale with shock and outrage. She picked off the wet leaves heedless of Liz who had taken her arm, saying, 'Come on now, there's obviously been some mistake. Let's find somewhere warm to talk it through.'

Anna heard the voice, but the sense eluded her as she frantically examined the photo and saw how the leaves had smudged the baby's face. Liz repeated herself, and now Anna pulled from her in a frenzy of hurt and rage, shouting at Claire, 'How could you? It's the only one there is. How could you?'

Claire just stood, rocking on her heels, seeing Anna's heaving shoulders, seeing her anger and pain, seeing Liz take her arm again, seeing Anna hit her away, hearing her screaming, 'OK, I'm going, but sod the lot of you. Sod you all.'

Claire watched as Anna ran down the drive, her coat flapping, watched as Anna stopped by a rose tree. She wanted to move, follow. But she must not. That had been decided long ago. So she stayed, rocking on her heels as the girl turned and almost fell. Claire's hand came up. Anna steadied, stared but it was too dark for Claire to see her face, too dark, too cold. At last Anna Weaver called, 'Who wants you for a mother anyway? My mum said you were a nice woman, someone who'd really wanted to keep me. How could she say something so nice about someone like you?'

There was no more pain in Claire as the girl ran on. There couldn't be. How do you increase what is already total?

Anna Weaver ran on into the light from the street lamp and Claire watched her skirting the other wives, groping in her pocket.

Anna found her keys as she reached the car. She fumbled for the lock, the breath heaving in her chest. The key went in, turned. She wrenched open the door and collapsed into the seat.

Orders were being given by her mind. Ignition. Gears, accelerate. The wheels spun, but then held. Drive. Drive.

*   *   *

Claire clung to the porch upright, her legs gone, her arms aching, listening to the screech of the tyres, the roaring engine that faded, faded into nothing. No one moved until Liz lifted her hands and dropped them again to her sides. Now the others hurried up the drive. Claire dug her nails into the post. 'Get rid of them. Please get rid of them all.' Her voice was harsh.

She watched Liz gather the women up and usher them away from her. Yes, that's right, get everyone away. She released her grip on the post. She staggered, recovered, somehow reached the doorway. Almost there, almost safe. She shut the door behind her and leaned against it. Her whole body trembled. She was cold, icy cold. It was dark, so dark, even though the light was on.

Liz pounded on the door. 'OK, they've gone. Now will you please tell me what the hell is going on?'

Claire's lips were almost too stiff to move. She struggled, then managed to say, 'Go to bed, Liz. Just go to bed.'

There was silence for a moment, but only a moment. 'Claire, I don't understand.'

Claire forced words from her mouth, words that somehow had no connection with her mind, a mind which was elsewhere, which was going where she didn't want it to, a mind running wild. 'The girl made a mistake. She sent the envelope to me thinking I was her mother and of course I returned it but it bothered me a bit, that's all. The whole sad thing bothered me and I didn't want it to upset you as well. Now, go to bed, Liz.'

Liz shouted, 'Claire, come on. This girl springs out of nowhere and now you lock yourself in. If she's a nutter we should tell someone.'

'She's obviously troubled, but it's over. No need to tell anyone. Go to bed.'

The door was hard. Claire gripped the curtain and held it to her face. It was warm. At last there was something warm. She drew the curtain round her.

Liz's voice was quiet but urgent as she said, 'Just let me in, let's just calm one another down. Please, the rain's started again. Come on, you idiot, let me in, lead me to the gin and we'll talk it through.'

It was so good here, hidden in the curtain. So quiet, so warm. 'Please, go to bed,' she repeated.

Liz banged on the door. 'I can't leave you like this.' She waited. Claire did nothing, said nothing and at last she heard movement on the other side of the door and Liz's voice. 'OK, you win. Just hope the poor kid's OK, she roared off at a hell of a lick.'

Claire said nothing.

Liz walked slowly down the drive. It wasn't raining but she'd felt a complete pillock shouting through the door with Mollie watching. The least

Claire could have done was to let her in after something like this, but the old girl had been damn right about it being a sad scene and right now she could do with a gin, not with having to calm this lot down. She realized she was shaking.

They were in a group outside Jean's. Mollie beckoned her over, pulling the collar of her coat higher. 'What's happening?'

Jo and Maureen rounded on Mollie. 'It's really none of our business.'

Liz flashed them a quick smile. 'It's fine. Just a rather sad young woman with a bee in her bonnet. A case of mistaken identity, apparently. Well, obviously. And Claire's had just about enough for one day, that's all. She's pulled up the drawbridge.'

Mollie smirked. 'Yes, I saw you shouting through the door. I wondered if I should come and see if I could help her. But it's odd, you know. For a case of mistaken identity I must say she looked remarkably like Claire as she got into her car. And Leah, come to think of it.'

Liz, whose feet were becoming numb, wanted to break away, get to her house, pour herself a drink, or throttle Mollie. How could the bloody woman say something like that when it had been too dark to see properly? She turned back to look at Claire's house and saw the street lamp. She hesitated, wondering, her heart sinking, but then she brushed the idea aside. What rubbish, of course she would have known about a child, and anyway, Claire had never lied about anything.

Mollie was looking at her, her face eager and malicious. Liz shook her head. 'You just can't stop yourself, can you? That woman in there is worn out, then she has this scene on her doorstop and you can't resist sticking your oar in and making something of someone else's tragedy. Think of the poor kid roaring off into the night. Think of your CO's wife having it all on her doorstep when she's up to her eyes. Good God almighty, we certainly know you're back on patch, don't we?'

Mollie, apoplectic with rage and affront, turned to Jean, who leaned forward and touched Liz's arm. 'But there was a considerable likeness.'

Jo spoke now, her hands deep in her duffel-coat pockets. 'The thing is, Jean, there are types of looks, and it was probably just that we saw they had similar shaped faces. I mean, her eyes were nothing like Claire's.'

Liz brought out her cigarettes, offered them round. Only Jo accepted. Liz inhaled, needing a moment. Then she shrugged.

'Come on, the old bag needs our support, girls, not a lot of nitter-nattering. Let's get to bed.'

Mollie drew herself up, her voice rigid with dislike. 'I'd not call it nitter-nattering. After all, if that girl had proved to be her daughter it could have done as much damage to the patch as her husband's shenanigans. Imagine turning away your own child, just like that, in front of other people. Imagine setting that sort of example, when you've set yourself up as a saint. It would have caused divisions, people would have taken sides. It would—'

Clarissa Baines swung round. 'Just for once will you shut up. Claire did not set herself up as a saint, she just does her job better than anyone else I've ever known, and quite frankly more of the senior wives could follow her example. There's one I can think of in particular.'

103

Jo and Maureen were nodding but now Liz stepped in. 'Come on, let's stop this, it's all totally absurd. Claire is not the mother of that young girl so the situation has not arisen and will not arise. Look, she needs a good night's sleep, and so do the rest of us from the sound of this, so let's get to it, doctor's orders.' Liz stood firm until the unsettled group dispersed, but not before Clarissa and Liz had apologized to Mollie, and Mollie had reluctantly murmured an apology in return.

Once inside her own house Liz phoned Claire. The answer machine logged in. Liz said, 'Pick up the phone, Claire. Just pick up the phone, I need to talk to you, to know you're all right.' She waited. Finally she heard Claire say, 'You woke me. I'm fine, just knackered, you silly old tart, now go to bed.'

Reassured, it never occurred to Liz to wonder how Claire could hear her message in the bedroom when the answer machine was in the hall.

*   *   *

Claire returned to her nest behind the curtain, curling up on the floor, feeling the terrible ache in her arms. An ache which had begun twenty-five years ago in the unmarried mothers' home when she had held Anna for the last time. Then her daughter had smelt of breast milk, not of perfume. Pulling the curtain closer Claire whispered, 'I wanted to do the best that I could for you, in the six weeks I had. They said not to feed you, but I did.'

Anna's skin had been as soft as down, her fingers had curled around Claire's forefinger. 'My finger. You held it as though you would never let me go.'

104

Matron had come from behind her desk and prised Anna from her arms. 'She took you. Your fingers gripped so hard but it wasn't any good. Nothing was any good.'

Matron had lain Anna in the carrycot. 'You were dressed in the clothes I had knitted. I can't knit, but I did those, the ones in the photograph. Somehow I did those.

'Matron sent me to walk in the grounds with Teresa, the assistant matron, saying, "When you come back it will all be over and it will be time to start your life, again." That's what she said, and in a way I did.'

Claire curled tighter still, moaning a little because the ache was so intense. 'They came and took you when I was walking beneath the magnolia tree. It was a late spring and still it was in bloom in May. The petals were heavy and white. I can't bear to be near magnolia trees now, because that was when they gave you to two more suitable people. Matron was kind. She promised you would never be able to find me. We both agreed it would be better for you.'

She buried her face in the curtain. 'You shouldn't have come, Anna, you shouldn't have come. You shouldn't have made me send you away again.'

Claire shut her eyes against her life, shut her eyes against the past, but none of her silent tears could change anything and along with the awful tearing pain of the separation came the sound of the surf, the wind in the marram grass, the gulls crying, a girl crying, the girl had been her. A girl that had cried her fear out loud, into the dark eyes of Anna's father.

105

CHAPTER EIGHT

Mark's office was cold but he barely noticed as he mentally clicked down his list, ticking off completed tasks. In the long ago days before promotion this would have brought relief but now it seemed that as fast as he ticked, he had others to add, not to mention those that were lurking, ready to surprise. There was a knock on the door. He dragged his hand through his hair, sat back and called. 'Come.'

It was Ben. Mark shot the same question he'd asked half an hour ago. 'Jeremy called?'

Ben shook his head, limping across the bare floorboards to the desk. 'Not yet, Colonel.'

Mark glared out of his window taking note that the mist hadn't shifted, then nodded to the chair. 'Sit down, Ben, and take the weight off that ankle or I'll have Liz on my case and there are better deaths.'

Ben smiled briefly. Mark rested his arms on his desk. 'Wish Jeremy would call in, it's important we have this Maglaj meeting.'

Ben sat in the chair opposite, looking across at the grey filing cabinets and the smaller desk on the far wall. 'He knows that. We'll hear at any moment.' His voice sounded tired and strained, and come to think of it, he looked it too. Mark asked, 'Your ankle really giving you gip?'

Ben shook his head. 'I'm fine. Look—the reinforcing update is under way so we'll be tickety boo again any minute now. The Ops Room and hospital are having a couple more beams, and in

106

general there are a few more planks to protect windows and doors.'

Mark ticked off another task.

Ben continued. 'However, Jeremy's meeting will stymie your Gornji Vakuf session with Nigel Perkins this morning.'

Mark shook his head. 'I'll get down there tomorrow come what may but it would have been good to get a personal debrief before the Minister descends.' He chewed his lip. He still couldn't decide just how weak a link Nigel was proving. Some weeks he seemed on top, others . . . Anyway, it was something he needed to keep tabs on with the flare-ups getting bigger and bloody better. But he also needed the Maglaj Croat Muslim meeting to come off in order to try and damp down the explosive chaos, especially along the aid routes, not to mention make an assessment of things around there.

He grunted. 'Ever felt like a piece of elastic being pulled at either end?'

'It sounds as though it *should* be nice but probably isn't.' Ben heaved himself to his feet. 'Time to spread a little happiness in the Ops Room.'

Mark half smiled. 'How do you intend to do that?'

'Why, just by being there, Colonel.' His voice was full of self-mockery and his rear view as he made for the door was as cocky as a dicky ankle would allow.

Mark laughed as Ben closed the door behind him, then looked out of the window at the hill where he had spotted Serb ski patrols through his binoculars earlier. He shifted in his chair and dragged his paperwork towards him, working steadily until there was a further knock on the door. He looked up as Ben thrust his head round the door, waving a piece of paper. 'Got it.'

Mark was instantly alert, 'Jeremy?'

'Yep.' Ben came across and put the note down in front of him. 'Maglaj is on.'

Mark sprang to his feet. 'About bloody time.' He scooped up his beret and strode to the door but Ben held up his hand. 'Hang on, bit of bad news. Well, more in the realm of irritating. Personal, you know.'

Mark stopped. 'Oh shit, what?'

Ben drummed his thighs, which was always a sign of tension. 'Our friend and conscience, and he who would be better employed knitting—'

'Get to the point, Ben,' Mark snapped, unnerved by the drumming, his mind already racing around the possibilities because Ben's smile wasn't reaching his eyes and it hadn't all morning, Mark now realized. God, he hoped his 2IC wasn't getting moody, letting things get to him. Damn Liz, I bet she's been on his back again. He waited.

Ben said, pointing to the phone, 'I rang Nigel to wipe out today. He wants a word.'

Mark's mind stopped and focused. Nigel? For God's sake, what now? 'Come on, Ben, get a grip, you're dripping about as though there are sprouts on the menu. You deal with him.'

Ben gestured to the phone again. 'He wanted a word with you, a personal word. It's been put through.' He limped to the door. 'I'll be in the Ops Room.'

Mark strode across to the phone and snatched it up. 'Nigel?' His voice was abrupt.

108

'Morning, Colonel.' Nigel Perkins's voice was tinny. He paused. Come on, man, for Christ's sake Mark wanted to say. Instead he asked. 'Got a problem, Nigel?'

Nigel Perkins blurted, 'No, it's not me. You see, I was in Split last evening. I rang Mollie. Look, Colonel, this is difficult but Mollie thought you should know . . .'

Mark interrupted. 'Your wife thought I should know? What the hell is all this about?' His disbelief at Nigel's trivia made his hand tighten so much on the receiver that it hurt.

Nigel laughed nervously, his voice suddenly uncertain. 'Well, yes. Apparently there was some sort of a scene after the pantomime meeting. Claire was upset. You see . . . Mollie thought . . . Well . . .'

Mark's disbelief had become total exasperation. If it wasn't enough having the women around him having wobbles, now it was one of his company commanders and that just about put the tin lid on it. He burst through Nigel's stammering. 'For God's sake Perkins, has it escaped your attention that we are not on a battalion picnic? Do you really have nothing better to do than pass on "patch" quarrels? Claire is there to sort all that out, which she does in an exemplary fashion, so refer your wife back to her, and be quick about it. You've better things to be concerning yourself with.'

'But you don't understand. It involves Claire, this scene was about Claire . . .'

'Just do your bloody job, and let me get on with mine and that's an order, is that clear? For God's sake man, you've the Minister descending tomorrow. Prioritize, Nigel. Leave the home life behind. If you haven't learnt that by now, there's

109

no hope.' He didn't wait to hear Perkins's reply, but slammed down the receiver, shaking his head, cursing slowly, loudly and with venom. He snapped, 'Ben.'

There was no answer. He turned. The office was empty, the door closed. Of course it was, he'd gone to the Ops Room, and a good thing too, putting through that bloody old woman. He stared at the phone, took in three deep breaths, then phoned Claire. There was only her answer-machine voice, disembodied and unrewarding when he wanted to shake the lot of them.

He could barely wait until 'after the tone' and blurted as it was finishing, 'Claire, what the hell's going on. I'm up to my neck in shit and I have that idiot Perkins flapping about on the line, spinning some tale involving you and Mollie. This is crazy and I can't have the concerns of the patch intruding on my men. Look, if you're not coping perhaps you should think of that HRT stuff. Why not talk to Liz about it? I'll phone tonight.'

Ben was in the Ops Room, hearing the clatter all around, but not listening, because he had talked to Liz last night, or rather she had talked to him, spilling out details of the scene, saying the last thing Claire needed was a stranger launching herself on her like that, because it had to be a stranger. She'd waited, then flowed on: 'If it had been anyone else I would have thought it was her child, but it can't be, I'd have known, Claire would have told me long ago, and anyway she wouldn't have turned her child away.' Ben had said nothing, he'd just shifted uncomfortably, hearing her doubt.

All night he had tried to sleep in his room in the senior officers' house, twisting and turning and

110

trying to put his wife's words to one side, but even here in the daylight, amongst the murmuring and activity of the Ops Room they followed him. It wasn't just her voice that ran and ran inside his head, however, it was also that of Mark on the eve of his wedding to Claire when he had explained to Ben that she had had a child.

Mark had told him up at the bar, well away from the stag night hiatus. He had been rolling the gin glass between his hands as he rambled on about the thought of Claire with another man, the thought that his child wouldn't be the first she had carried. 'That it's all happened, but with someone else,' he'd railed. 'She says that it was all a mistake, that it was just one time, that it meant nothing, but I could kill the pair of them. I mean, you don't expect it of our sort of girl, do you?'

Ben remembered Mark's face, how his eyes had filled with tears and his voice had shaken as he'd continued, almost too quietly to be heard, 'I'm so jealous that, yes, I could kill him for getting close enough to create a child with her. I could kill her for it too.' He had dropped the glass on the bar. It had shattered and he'd cut his hand as he tried to gather up the pieces. Ben had bound it with his handkerchief and while he knotted it, Mark had whispered, 'I tried to walk away from her, but I love her. God almighty, I love her.'

Ben had said, 'It's all behind you now. There's just the two of you, riding off into the sunset.' They had laughed at that, because Claire had an allergic reaction—hives—the minute she approached a horse. They had laughed and the others had called them back to the party. On the way Mark had said, 'You're right, it is behind us. That's exactly what

111

I've told her. I've put an embargo on the subject, told her I don't want to hear another word about it, ever.' He and Ben had only spoken of it once since. It was when they were wetting Leah's head in Cairo, far away from their wives. Mark had said, 'I made the right decision to marry her. It's worked. After all, these things happen. Hell, look at the pair of us—there but for the grace of God go a few of us, eh? It's OK Ben, it's really OK, life's bloody good and I was a stuck-up prat.'

Ben stood resting on his crutch in the middle of the Ops Room, wondering what Perkins had said, wondering if he should have blocked the call, but Mark would meet him at Gorniji Vakuf anyway. He reached Lt. Andrews's desk, stopped. Lt. Andrews looked up. 'Sir?'

Ben looked at him uncomprehendingly. Lt. Andrews repeated 'Sir?'

Ben blinked and said, 'Carry on, Lieutenant.' He walked on to the Intelligence Cell. Listening to their reports, he was wondering as he had done so many times before whether he should have told Liz, though if Claire had wanted her to know she'd have mentioned it herself, he reasoned. But why keep it from her best friend? That was what he'd never been able to understand because the girls had always been so close.

The Intelligence Officer finished the briefing, one that Ben scarcely heard. 'Carry on, Charles,' Ben said, looking towards the door. What had bloody Nigel said?

He waited for Mark, drumming his fingers. God, it had to be the child. How would Mark cope? It was Claire who was always so strong, who was Mark's rock, not that he seemed to realize the fact,

112

or was it just that he couldn't admit it? Anyway, that wasn't the point. The point was why had she . . . ? He shook his head. Well, she *had* sent her away, and that's all there was to it. Poor old Claire but what a bloody mess.

He straightened as Mark hurried towards him. 'Everything all right, Colonel?' Ben asked.

'That man needs a lobotomy, or a divorce. That damn wife of his is reporting some sort of a quarrel, that's all—usual bloody female nonsense, no doubt. Thank God we don't have hormones. I've left a message telling Claire I'll call her later, but I don't mind telling you I'm brassed off with all three of them, and I include Nigel Perkins in that.'

Ben nodded, uncertain whether to speak of his conversation with Liz, but then Mark was off, only to be stopped by the Intelligence Officer. Grimacing, Mark called to Ben over the Intelligence Officer's shoulder: 'You can get the beer good and cold for me tonight. Apparently the flu seems to be striking all interpreters so a wonderful morning is made complete by the news that Gordana Sevo is stepping in. She just happens to be on the spot in Maglaj, and so our Liaison Officer, the inspired Captain Roger Hanning, snapped her up. Hoo bloody ray. I presume the day will go on bringing me great riches.'

*   *   *

Maglaj, a key target for aid delivery, had once been rather lovely and was linked to its newer counterpart by a bridge that spanned the River Bosna. But that was before it had become a front-line target for the Serbs, who bombarded it almost

113

continuously. Mark briefed himself from the intelligence reports that Ben had given him, and he couldn't help wondering just how much information Gordana Sevo had contributed. Quite a bit, from the Intelligence Officer's comments. He stared out. More mountains, more snow clouds, more ravines, more terrible beauty. Turning round, he checked that the other three Land Rovers were in tight formation. They were, and tucked uninvited in the rear was Charlie Bennet's.

Four kilometres this side of Maglaj, and three hours later they drew to a halt at a roadblock, where Gordana Sevo waited, in the same anorak, cords and boots as before. She was chatting to Captain Hanning, who was smoking one of her Marlboro cigarettes from the look of it, and both were shifting their weight from foot to foot in an effort to keep warm. Why hadn't the silly prats waited in the Land Rover?

Almost wordlessly Gordana greeted Mark, but it was the Liaison Officer she accompanied as he slotted in at the head of the convoy. Mark breathed a sigh of relief.

They took a winding track rather than trying to 'run' the main road and approached Maglaj via avenues of damaged houses with blasted roofs and glassless windows. They skirted the scythed power and telegraph poles and burnt-out vehicles, but were unable to avoid the unceasing sound of shellfire. As they steered around a pile of rubble Mark felt a thud, dust flew into the air to his left, and within a few seconds flames soared. Instinctively he ducked, but a fat lot of good that'd do. Again and again there was a thud, and another building was demolished. His frustration consumed

114

him. Yes, they patrolled in Warriors but what the hell good did it do? It was a gesture, that was all. A gesture of what, he wasn't sure. Intent perhaps, but intent only that aid would continue to be delivered no matter what. He flashed a glance at Hanning's Land Rover just ahead. Was all this stoking Miss Sevo? Well, who could blame her. He braced himself as they drew up outside the local force HQ and Hanning and Miss Sevo, by now wearing flak jackets just as he was, ran back to his vehicle, ducking and weaving. Leaping in, panting, they briefed him, hunching their shoulders every time a mortar landed. Miss Sevo was so calm and professional that it was almost an anti-climax.

'Let's go, then,' he instructed, opening the door, only to be ambushed by Charlie, flak-jacketed and with notepad in hand, the others of the press close behind. 'How're you doing, cock?' Charlie flicked a lazy salute at Mark. As Gordana followed Mark on to the pavement Charlie kissed her hand. 'Missed you, darlin'. 'Twas only a few short kilometres but 'twas more than my heart could bear.' Another mortar landed three streets away and they all hurried to the entrance where Roger Hanning grinned and Gordana shook her head. 'You are all hot air, my darling Charlie. You say this, but you leave me dangling.'

Mark stared at Charlie. Good God, he hadn't known there was something between these two, but then Roger mouthed, 'Hangover from the work she did for them, sir. They think she's brilliant, but they've no job to give her.'

Mark shifted uncomfortably. Not another one on the case, for pity's sake, why didn't they give it a rest? He muttered as Hanning took up position
115

next to him, 'You've obviously seen Jeremy recently.' Hanning had the grace to blush.

Charlie now said, turning his attention away from Gordana, 'They're in a bit of trouble if it snows, which it will.' He pointed with his pen at the huge holes in the roofs of those houses either side and opposite where they now stood. 'And still the Serbs come bearing gifts.' He cupped his hand to his ear.

Added to the pounding of the artillery was the odd burst of machine-gun fire.

Mark glared at Charlie, no longer relaxed, itching to slap his hand down, fearing that the idiot would upset Miss Sevo's calm. He snapped, 'You know damn well we're doing what we can.' Suddenly he coughed as the dust from the destruction caught in his throat, then drew a deep breath. Gordana was quite right, it did smell.

Charlie licked his finger and held it up as though testing wind direction. 'Seems to me, someone's getting the wind up, getting sort of unnecessary.'

It was Gordana's turn to snap. 'You talk too much, Charlie. Colonel Baird has much on his mind. On his shoulders rests all of this.' She waved towards the aid lorries which were rumbling towards the centre.

Mark snatched a suspicious look at Roger, but his expression was one of surprise. Mark then glanced towards Miss Sevo to check for sarcasm. There was none. He said, 'Let's get on with it, shall we?'

Captain Burnes led them into the meeting, leaving Charlie to stamp his feet at the entrance. Mark almost, but not quite, felt sorry for him, because in these deserted streets Charlie would

116

find no one to chat to while his press friends took off to photograph the bridge. Not too closely Mark hoped, because it was a sniper's paradise. Charlie had called after them: 'Been there, done that. I'll wait around here, my old cider apples.'

The meeting was cellar based, sand-bagged, smoky, caffeine laden, and slivovitz heavy. The local forces were tired, unshaven, their combat uniforms creased, slept in. Mark sat opposite both, the chair rickety, listening closely to Roger and Gordana's interpretation of the discussions, putting forward his intentions, gleaning information, listening to both parties with the same attention, acutely aware of their need to save face. Yes, it got heated but Miss Sevo was there, reminding him of backgrounds, returning smiles and eventually helping Roger to wind it up for him.

As he shook hands one of the telephones rang. Climbing the steps of the cellar he murmured, 'I never cease to be amazed that in the midst of all this, the phones work.'

'Some of the time,' Gordana said quietly, smiling.

He nodded. He just wished that today, and yesterday, there had been no phones operating between Bosnia and England.

On the street it was still cold and Charlie was still there. He pushed himself away from the wall when he saw them. As he began asking questions, which Mark answered, or not, depending on their content, Gordana brushed plaster dust from Charlie's anorak until small arms fire erupted, a bit too close for comfort. As they broke and ran for their vehicles which had been keeping on the move to present less of a target Charlie puffed, 'Where to

117

now, cock?'

'Well, it's a bit of a leg but *we're* off to Travnik, though I don't know where you're going.' Mark was pulling on his gloves.

Charlie and the rest of the press pack stayed with Roger while Gordana and Mark travelled on to Travnik where they would meet up with the Liaison Officer, and a representative of the Exchange Commission who had agreed yet again to facilitate another cross-the-lines meeting with the Serbs, Mark explained to Miss Sevo.

'Chetniks,' Gordana said as they drove along the track under the eyes of the Serb guns. 'Only civilians are Serbs.'

Disappointed, Mark stared into the mist that was descending. He said crisply, 'That term is unprofessional, Miss Sevo, a cause for concern.'

He met his driver's eyes in the mirror. They were carefully expressionless and as he looked at the road ahead he became aware that Miss Sevo was watching him, her fingers working the strap of her backpack. She said, 'But I was not being partisan, I was commenting, Colonel Baird. I was not aware if you were familiar with the term and my only intent is to help you in your task, now I understand the issues and your commitment. I fear that once I thought you heedless of our plight and now, having worked alongside you, I think that you are not. I cannot apologize enough if you feel I was in any way taking sides.'

Mark swung round, checking for hidden meanings, for cold angry eyes, but as the Land Rover rattled and banged over the ruts and potholes he could see none of this; what he could hear was the pounding of the Serb artillery, and he

118

thought of the dust there must be in Sarajevo, and remembered the shrapnel gouges on the wall. Red-hot metal shards did a lot of damage.

Damn it. Again he checked her face. It was serious, anxious. He looked away, staring ahead. Damn it, why the hell did Jeremy have to be on a roving task? Because the great Colonel Baird had ordered it, that was why.

He shifted himself on the seat, hearing her words again. Anyway, what was the alternative with Jeremy away, it was common sense. They travelled for several kilometres, and he said nothing until he could stand her thin fingers working the strap no longer. Quietly, reluctantly, calling himself all sorts of a fool he said, 'I'll see how the rest of the day goes, and if it's successful I'll speak to Jeremy and my 2IC and we'll try and sort something out.'

He snatched a look at her, and her smile was the one she had used in Australia, the one that had been preserved by that harsh, hot sun.

Settling back he was comforted by the fact that he had left himself a way out, his mind already moving on to the Exchange Commission.

CHAPTER NINE

Anna Weaver had a headache. She gulped down two Panadol with a cup of tea, standing at the sink in her flat the morning after her journey to Claire. She looked out over the little garden planted by her mother with cottage garden plants. It was designed for fragrance but Anna knew she didn't give it enough attention.

119

Mabs, her cat, was hunched on the top of the wall separating her garden from the ironmonger's yard next door—one of the few ironmongers left in this crazy world. She poured the remains of her tea down the sink. Damn shitty crazy world.

The phone rang. She checked her watch. It was 8.14. It would be her mother, her real mother, the one that loved her. Her only mother. She leaned hard against the sink, then swung round and almost ran to the phone in the sitting area, snatching it up before the answer machine locked in.

Her mother didn't wait for Anna to speak but said calmly, though her voice was too high pitched and gave her away, 'Anna love, did you go?'

Anna nodded silently, gripping the receiver with both hands. 'Anna? Anna?' There was no pretence at calm now.

Anna dropped her shoulders. 'Yes, I went.' Her voice was that of an automaton.

'And ... ?' her mother queried uncertainly. 'Anna love, what happened?'

Anna told her now, her voice never varying in pitch or tone until almost the end. Until she told of the photo knocked to the ground, of the leaves on it, the damp. It was then that her voice shook.

Her mother was quiet for a moment before asking, 'What did you do then?'

I ran off. I swore at her. I said who'd want her for a mother anyway.' Her grip on the receiver was even tighter, her headache was worse. She could hardly speak, but she had to go on. 'Her friends were standing at the end of the drive, gawking. I ran to the car. I drove away. She didn't come after me.'

'I'm coming to you,' her mother insisted. 'We'll

120

both come.'

Anna swallowed, struggling against tears. She shook her head, pressed her left hand against her eyes, breathed deeply. 'No, I've clients, I've the shop. Oh Mum.' From the kitchen came the slap of the cat flap and the sound of crunching as Mabs found her dried food. The doorbell of the salon pealed, closely followed by Cheryl's yell through the letterbox. 'Rise and shine.'

Anna said. 'I've got to go, Cheryl's here.'

Briskly her mother brushed that aside. 'Cheryl has a key. She'll let herself in as you well know.' There was hesitation, then in the same brisk tone her mother said, 'Now you listen here, my girl, what you did was wrong. You shouldn't have gone at it like that. Jumping out of a bush, whatever next? I mean, what did the counsellor say?'

Anna sat down, cross-legged on the floor. Mabs came to her, winding herself around her ankles. She repeated, 'I had to approach her carefully, give her time.'

'And did you?'

'No.' Anna's voice was a whisper. 'It all went wrong, you know, Mum. I never thought she'd send me away.'

Her mother's voice was more robust now as she got into her stride. 'Well, we know about you and the thought process, don't we? It's all got to be a big splash and "look at me" and then it all just peters out. Goodness me, we've talked this through for months—I mean we don't even know if her husband is aware that you exist and in you wade, leaving the poor soul with a great mess to clear up.'

Anna shouted now, pushing the cat to one side, 'I don't care about the mess. I want to talk to my

121

mother! I want to know her, just like you wanted to know yours.'

Lynne Weaver took time to answer. 'Then you must phone her, or write to her. You must apologize. You must try again. Do you understand me, you must try again and for once in your life you must see something through, but properly, kindly.'

*   *   *

Lynne Weaver didn't move from the phone when she had finished speaking to her daughter. Instead she remained sitting next to the reproduction table in the bay window of her coastal home. A home which had once been a small working farmhouse and whose land they leased to the farmer in the next valley, whose barns Harry had converted to holiday lets.

The sea was wild this morning, the surf beating against the rocks of the Cornish cove at the base of the cliff to the left of the farmhouse. There were very few gulls, which meant Harry could have a break from cursing and swearing at them as they sat on the roof upbraiding him while he fiddled about keeping the holiday lets up to scratch.

She looked along the coastal path, searching for Harry. He should be back soon with the paper but she wanted him now; not that he could do anything of course, except share it. But that was everything. Yes, he'd share the fear, and the jealousy, perhaps even the relief, this awful relief, in spite of her strong words at her daughter's rejection by her real mother.

She brought out a tissue from her sleeve, dabbed her nose. All these years she'd known the day

122

would come, just as it had with her own adopted mother. Had her adoptive mother suffered as she now was suffering? If so, she hadn't shown it, ever. She had been generous. She had welcomed Sylvie Wilson as a second mother for Lynne, and an extra maternal grandmother for Anna.

But inside there must have been all that Lynne was feeling now. 'You never know until it happens to you, though, do you,' Lynne murmured, wishing her mother were alive to thank.

Through the salt-blurred window she saw Harry, his paper stuck in the small rucksack he carried over one shoulder, puffing as he plodded along the track. But it kept him fit, and that was the main thing. She hadn't moved all this way to be a widow twiddling her thumbs, waiting for bedtime.

She rapped on the window, beckoning him inside. He half saluted, then paused, panting, his hands on his hips as he gazed at the view. Just the sight of him doing that calmed her. He always calmed her and had never given in to the breast-beating that overcame some men when they discovered they were sterile. No one could help getting mumps, after all, she'd told him, and her own sick disappointment had evaporated long ago. After all, they'd had Anna.

He walked to the back door, out of her line of vision. He'd be kicking off his walking boots, opening the door, dumping the boots on yesterday's paper which she always placed by the freezer. She heard the kitchen door shut as he came into the hall. She heard his 'Hello, what news?' In his voice was the same fear, the same jealousy.

When he had settled beside her and listened

123

there was the same relief at Anna's failure, but it was momentary. Taking her hand in his cold ones he said, 'Poor little girl. She needs a good relationship with her biological mother, you know.' He sat back, looking at her, not the view. 'You *do* know that, just as you had with yours. We must allow her her history, her place, just as your mother allowed you yours. We're lucky we won't be discarded because she's had something to imitate and knows how it can work. You must trust her. We must trust her. There's nothing else we can do.'

Lynne kissed his hands, sitting back and rubbing them between her own. 'You're right.' But still there was fear, because the Bairds were so much more than they were, and comparison was inevitable. Would Anna regret what she had missed? Would she resent . . . ? Lynne stopped herself.

Harry said, 'Anyway, the problem will really get going if Mrs Baird's rejection is maintained. What do we do then?'

CHAPTER TEN

Claire turned the shower full on and tried unsuccessfully to drown out the long, long night. Stepping on to the bath mat she pummelled herself dry but still there was the sound of her daughter's voice. She dressed. Everything was different and would always be so because she had sent her child away, again.

She ignored the phone which rang as she brushed her hair. What could she say to whoever it

124

was? Laying her brush on the dressing table she sat quite still, knowing she must move, knowing that she had playgroup at ten, knowing that the world was out there, waiting. That the hours had to be filled, people had to be faced and that night would eventually fall and morning come again and so it would go on, and on.

She picked up the brush, pulling stray hairs from between the bristles, hairs which she balled and dropped in the wastepaper basket. The phone rang for a second time. Again she ignored it, pressing the bristles with her thumb, moving them this way and that, wishing she was as flexible and without feeling.

She let the brush fall to the carpet and walked past the bed in which she had not slept, along the landing, and down the stairs, pausing near the front door, touching the curtain that had been around her all night. She pressed her face into its warmth, wanting to curl up and never leave its dark comfort.

Instead she walked away, to the phone which was blinking insistently. She had today to live through, and then another day. Her arm felt as though it was made of lead as she pressed play, listening to the whirr, the click, and then Mark's voice.

'Claire, what the hell's going on. I'm up to my neck in shit and I have that idiot Perkins flapping about on the line, spinning some tale involving you and Mollie . . .'

Claire pressed her hand to her mouth, harder, harder. Oh God. Oh dear God, what had she done? But by now the next message was playing. Claire froze and listened and now her hand could not have pressed any harder without drawing blood

125

as she heard Anna say 'I'm just ringing to say sorry. I'm so sorry. I shouldn't have pushed it like I did. I shouldn't have come, shouldn't have hidden and then walked out, but I panicked. I heard them coming and didn't want to do it in front of them all, but I didn't wait long enough. It's all my fault. Mum says I'm impatient—always have been. But I really did want to know you, I still do . . .' Anna's voice broke, then she began again. 'She said you were nice. She said you sent a letter when I was a year old. Please, this proves I'm yours doesn't it?' Her voice changed and became angry. 'Or am I just inconvenient, is that why you sent me packing? Were you scared I'd mess up your life, again?' Then another pause, another apology. 'I'm sorry, just sorry. Here's my phone number, in case you ever want to see me.' She gave the number and then hung up.

*　　　*　　　*

Claire was at Leah's school by 10.30. She parked in the space reserved for visitors next to the laundry block. The headmistress had said she would arrange for Leah to meet Claire in the ante-room at 10.30, just prior to mid-morning break.

Claire bullied the windows as they misted up, then opened the window. From the games field came the sounds of girls shouting, whistles blowing.

It was the gym mistress at her own high school who had taken her to the headmistress. The headmistress had phoned her mother, calling her to withdraw her daughter from school immediately. Her mother had come, red faced, almost panting, not understanding the summons, only sure that her

126

Claire knew better than to upset a headmistress who was as worthy of respect as God, or the Virgin Mary at the very least.

The headmistress had told her very quickly why, gesturing to Claire's swelling belly which had been noticed by the gym mistress in the locker rooms. And so it had begun, the reality and the shame that had never ended. Claire wound up the window, shutting out the sounds of girlhood.

She and her mother had travelled home on the usual Greenline bus, but, no, it wasn't usual. At eleven o'clock it was filled with women with shopping baskets. It was not the four o'clock filled with schoolgirls ripping berets from one another's heads, and guzzling honeycomb, or whatever was the craze of the moment.

This time she had sat next to her mother, who huddled as far from her on the seat as possible, looking strangely diminished in her coat which was buttoned wrongly. Her breath had clouded the window as her own clouded the glass now. All Claire wanted to be was one of those other women: normally shopping, normally buying food for their families, normally going home for a cup of tea.

When she and her mother returned home there was no cup of tea, there was rage, a spit-drenching high-pitched rage which Claire endured and accepted and knew she deserved.

There was their instant removal to a holiday let in Lyme Regis—at favourable rates since they would take it throughout the winter, until six weeks before the due birthdate on 10 April. The date was approximate because Claire would not say when it actually happened, would not say with whom it had happened, though she had told her mother how. At

127

the thought she closed her eyes.

At the headmistress's instruction a diagnosis of TB was presented to the school as a cover, and willingly circulated. There was a letter to Liz confirming TB. It was stuffed through her letterbox in the next street by Claire's father. There was the doctor at Lyme who stood above her, prodding, then exploring the place where he, the unnamed father, had been.

The doctor had spoken to her through the nurse, as though he risked contamination if he opened a channel of communication. He did not look once at her face. But her mother, stony faced, understood. Oh yes, she understood and sympathized with him, not her daughter. And Claire understood, and sympathized with them, for by then she disgusted herself.

She understood why her mother barely spoke to her throughout the long days, and why she allowed Claire to walk outside only in the evenings, when her face would be as indistinct as her shape. For five months she had not existed as a person, only an automaton with no rights to an opinion, or a decision. There had been no reality, only letters forwarded by her father from Liz, and hers to Liz talking of the sanatorium patients and little about the treatment.

With every letter forwarded her father wrote kind and caring words and she wished he was with her. But he had to work, in that Woking office, clerk to the solicitor who would shortly be joined by his son.

Claire drew in her breath sharply as someone rapped on the car window. She scrambled to open it. The air was sharp as she did so, the noise from

128

the playing fields loud, the smell of Monday morning laundry strong. A lorry driver grinned at her. 'Move your car, can you, missus? I need to get this stuff picked up.' He nodded towards a pile of breeze blocks.

She wiped the inside of the windscreen with her coat sleeve, backed a few yards, then swung round and parked where it said 'Staff only'.

*   *   *

Leah wasn't in the ante-room, and while the sixth-former who was on reception duty and who had forgotten to pass on the message hurried to inform her, Claire cruised the glass bookshelves in the small room. She moved to the Victorian tiled fireplace which looked as though it had seen nothing as dirty as coal for a good long time. Her coat brushed the faded grasses drooping in an earthenware jug on the hearth. She reached the window and stared across at the hockey field. Hockey sticks were different these days. So much was different. So very much, so how could Leah understand? Her breathing was too shallow, too quick.

She recognized Leah's footsteps and turned, leaning back against the sill, her arms crossed, her fingers digging in, trying unsuccessfully to smile. She had to tell her daughter that she had a sister, and how did she do that?

Leah entered in her uniform, her hair neat in a single plait, her face set. She stopped and didn't look at her mother but at the carpet which stretched between them and for one moment Claire thought that Mollie's girls, also pupils at the

129

school, had completed their mother's task, and spread their gossip on the waters. She stepped forward, her hand outstretched, only to be stopped by Leah's words.

'He's dead then? He shouldn't have been there, the idiot, the stupid idiot.' Leah lifted her head and gazed into her mother's eyes, her face now drawn in dazed grief. Horrified, she rushed forward. 'No, oh no, that's not it at all.'

For a moment Leah remained rigid, then sagged, her face pressed into her mother's shoulder, crying. Claire soothed, 'I'm so sorry, Leah. I should have thought. Oh God, I'm so sorry.'

Leah was still a moment more, then she thrust herself out of her mother's arms, her cheeks wet, her eyes reddened, shaking her head. 'How could you do that to me? What else did you expect me to think? Why are you here then? You always told me you'd come if it . . . For God's sake, Mum, just make me feel a fool, why don't you. I mean I rushed out of the classroom as though . . .' She turned away from her mother, hunching her shoulders, picking at the lock of the nearest bookcase.

Claire stared. As she had driven over she'd prepared what she was to say so carefully and now none of it would come.

'It's Grandma Belle, then?'

Claire dug her hands into her coat pockets, took a deep breath. 'It's not Belle or your father. It's me.' Leah turned, uncertain, her attitude defensive. Claire spoke quickly now because she had done all this so badly and it was unforgivable. 'Yesterday evening a young woman of twenty-five came to the house, claiming to be my daughter. I sent her away.

130

But what she said was true. She is my daughter, your sister.'

Claire watched as Leah stared at her, registering nothing for a moment, but then as the meaning of her words sank in Claire saw shock and disbelief sweeping across her daughter's face. She watched Leah's hands lift then fall. She watched as she looked away, then back at her mother, shaking her head slowly, trying to speak, giving up, trying again, her voice high, her words hurried and disorganized. 'My sister. Your daughter. When...? Your daughter? Why didn't you tell me?' Her voice was rising, but with what?

Claire stepped forward. Leah shook her head, her hand reaching out to stop her. Claire did stop. 'I haven't told anyone, except your father. He knew before I married him.'

Leah walked to the window and stared out at the hockey players. An electronic bell sounded, there were voices in the corridor. 'So, she's not Dad's. Well whose is she then? She came to the house? Why did she come? What the hell's going on? And if Dad knew, why didn't I? I mean, why didn't I know—I've no rights in this family, is that it? How could you keep this from me?' She swung back to Claire. 'God, you bloody hypocrite, all this time you've had a kid, and you sit there like virtue personified giving me a hard time for getting in late. What is it, Mum, d'you think I'm getting up to the same things you did? I mean, why wasn't I told?' She was red, her voice was high.

Claire strode to her, her voice low and urgent. 'Never mind, about being told, just listen to me. I made such a stupid mistake. It was a party...'

Leah cut her off. 'I don't want to hear about it.

131

It's disgusting. I don't want to think of you doing . . . doing . . . that.'

Claire grasped her daughter's hands. Leah tried to pull away, but Claire hung on. 'It was a mistake, you must understand that. And you must never feel that I don't trust you, it's the others I don't trust. You only have to read the newspapers to see what can happen to girls walking alone.'

'Oh, p-l-e-a-s-e, spare me that. But don't for one minute think I'm doing what you were at my age.'

Claire shouted in the face of her daughter's rage, 'I was seventeen and I can't apologize more than I'm doing.' Leah glared at her. Claire lowered her voice. 'I'm just worried when you're late home. Parents do that, they *do* worry you know, but let's leave that for now. I want you to understand what's happened. I want to explain how badly I've handled all of this.'

Leah half laughed. 'I think we've already discussed that, haven't we. Break's almost over. I'd better get going.'

Claire kept her grip on her daughter's hands. 'No we haven't discussed it, not all of it. You see, I was so shocked last night, I sent her away. I told her she was mistaken. I know it was unforgivable but I did it, and I did it in front of some of the wives.'

Leah's face reflected her struggle to understand, and when she did her look of contempt mirrored all that Claire felt for herself. Leah stared at her mother's hands. 'Let me go, please.' Her voice was cold. Claire did so, and her hands felt empty, her arms ached.

'You knew she was yours and you did that?'

Claire stared beyond Leah to the laundry. On

132

the hockey field the marker flags were flapping. She was too tired. Just too tired for any more. Her voice was a monotone as she said, her eyes fixed on the tumbling grey clouds. 'I panicked. I had no warning, she came out from behind the laurel. I had no idea she was there, that she had traced me. It was shock, just such a shock. Please try to understand.'

'Oh, you want me to understand now. Now, when you have been forced to tell me, when the whole thing has blown up and is about to ruin my life. I just can't believe that you did that in front of the wives. For God's sake, Mother, it'll be all over the patch, all over the school, and how do you think that will make me feel? How could you do this?'

The wind seemed to be freshening, and the clouds were breaking up, changing shape. Claire dragged herself back to her daughter. Her voice was still a monotone, but her eyes were locked on Leah's with a desperate intensity as she asked, 'Do you remember the window you broke when you were thirteen? Do you remember that I saw you do it, and you still denied it? Why? How could you do that?'

She saw the anger slowly being replaced by something else, something which, after a moment, became an acknowledgement. Leah walked to the bookcase again. At last she murmured, 'OK, OK. It was panic. It was fear too. I thought I'd be grounded, that Dad would go ape.' She shrugged, turned, and the acknowledgement was joined by exasperation. 'Was it your image? You were scared of what people would think of their CO's wife. Have you just got to be so perfect?' The contempt was back in her voice.

Leah began to walk to the door. Claire called, 'You will stay here until I am finished, do you understand?'

Leah stopped, turned, then shouted, 'I don't understand anything. All this, and what do I tell my friends? They'll hear that you got pregnant, that you fouled up last night.' She was crying. 'Why didn't you just have an abortion like everyone else?'

Claire came to her, and Leah eventually let herself be held, let her hair be stroked, let Claire tell of her ignorance and inexperience which meant she did not, would not, recognize that she was pregnant until forced to by the headmistress; by then she was well over three months. Of the misery and the loss after Anna's birth. Of the joy and pain when Leah had been born. The joy because she could keep this child, the pain because of the deceit, of having to pretend to her neighbours, to Liz, that Leah was her first, that it was all strange to her, remembering Anna all the time. She told her how she could scarcely believe that this child was hers to keep until six weeks had been and gone, and Leah still remained in her arms.

Leah asked, her voice muffled, 'Why didn't you try to find her?'

Claire patted her daughter's back. 'Mothers couldn't do that. Only the child could trace, and that's right. It wouldn't have been fair on Anna.'

'Why?'

'Because she had her family.' The statement dragged at her as the thought always had.

The questions came in a stream now, as they stood together, closer than they'd been for months. Leah asked if Claire had wanted to give Anna

134

away.

'No.'

'Then why did you?'

'Times were different, society would have made it hard for her, hard for me. I was only seventeen and your grandmother . . .'

'What about the father?'

Claire shook her head, closing her eyes. 'He had left the area, gone to Australia.'

'Who was he?'

'Just someone I once knew.' The sound of the sea was breaking through.

'Did you love him?'

'No.' It was almost a whisper,

'Then why did you do it with him?'

Claire tightened her grip on Leah. 'Because, as I've said, I was at a party and I made a stupid mistake. I was very, very foolish.'

Leah rubbed her face against Claire's shoulder, then stepped back, groping for a handkerchief. Claire pulled a tissue from her pocket and tried to wipe her daughter's face. Leah snatched it from her. 'You'll be licking it just like you used to in a minute. I am fourteen.'

Claire half smiled. How quickly things returned to normal. Then the smile drained away. Of course they didn't.

Leah blew her nose, then handed the tissue back. Claire pulled a face, waving her daughter away. 'No way. You deal with it.'

Leah grinned briefly, her eyes still red and her cheeks blotchy. 'Are you going to tell Dad she's come back?'

'Well, I rather feel Mollie's got herself to a phone and locked into her darned husband.'

135

Leah nodded. 'I heard from Mollie's eldest, Monica, that she was coming back to the patch. She's the one with the teeth. We call her Jaws.'

Claire murmured. 'Of course, you would.'

Leah was almost talking to herself. 'That woman's like quicksilver when there's a piece of scandal.'

The word sat between them. Then a bell sounded. Leah said, 'Break's over.'

Claire saw that the players were still on the field. 'Don't they stop for break?' she asked.

'It's the first team, they're fanatics.' The words were all present and correct and in order, but they bounced across the top of an abyss. Leah checked her watch. 'Dad'll be mad you've cocked up.'

Claire's grin was rueful. 'I dare say.'

'You'll be grounded next.' Leah was checking her watch again, shifting from foot to foot, looking anywhere but at Claire. Claire smiled wryly. 'I'd rather like that—I could put my feet up and write my essay. I only got a C last time.' She felt her throat thickening, her eyes filling, and it was because Leah had reached out and was rubbing her arm, saying, 'I always say, don't let the buggers get you down.'

All Claire could do was nod.

Leah said. 'I've got to go.'

Claire whispered, 'I'm so sorry, Leah.'

Leah shrugged, transferring her weight from foot to foot. 'It doesn't matter. It happens all over the place these days.'

'But not to your mother.'

Leah tried to grin. 'Well, not now you mention it.' She was edging towards the door. Claire said, 'I rang Anna before I left. I apologized. I asked her

136

to come whenever it was convenient for her. She'll be here on Sunday. Shall I come and fetch you?'

Leah hesitated, shaking her head slightly, then changing her mind. 'Yes, if you like.'

She headed for the door, then asked, 'I'm the first you've told?'

'Yes, that was most important to me.'

Leah smiled and left.

*   *   *

Claire returned to the patch, ignoring playgroup because Clarissa had stood in for her with no questions asked. Crawling over the sleeping policemen she headed for Volvoland. Leaves were dropping from the trees to lie sodden in the road. There would be plenty to rake up from the lawn at the weekend. She'd burn them when it was dry, something she would not do when she owned her own house: then she'd store the leaves until they became mulch for her flowerbeds.

She fixed her mind on this, not on the houses she passed or the wives who were dragging children along, heads down cagouled to the hilt, and not on Leah whose world had been changed for ever, who would have to contend with the gossip that was probably already winging its way to her, and to her father.

She turned right, the clicking of the indicator out of sync with the swish of the wiper blades. Yes, she'd heap the leaves in a bin that she'd make with chicken wire. She stopped at a junction, and indicated left. What had Anna thought as she drove here last night? Had she stopped and asked the way? If so, who did she ask? A car behind hooted. Claire gestured an apology and turned left. The driver of the car behind, Mavis Hoye from Ben's company, tooted a greeting and waved. Mavis had always said that Claire made her feel everything was under control, made her feel safe. Oh God, what had she done to everyone?

She slowed as she reached Liz's house, but no, she had a mess to clear up, a situation to rectify, a report to present to Mark. Oh God.

She drew up instead outside Jean's. The light was on in the sitting room. Well, it would be on a murky day like this.

*   *   *

Liz stood back from the window, watching Claire approach Jean's front door. She inhaled harshly, taking the nicotine deep, holding it, staring at the woman she had thought was closer to her than her own mother. Now she knew better.

Whilst she, Liz Gibbons, had for almost a lifetime bared her soul, shared every problem, every joy, she, the virtuous Saint Claire, had treated their friendship as though it were a one-way traffic.

She exhaled, lifting her chin, watching the smoke rise. Now, at last, this morning, Ben had told her. A bit bloody late, eh Claire? Just a bit bloody late. I'd have felt a fool anyway, but I feel even more of a pillock now, after riding up on my charger and seeing off the girls on your behalf. You see, I knew what I'd seen but I believed your every bloody word. So, what price friendship? A friendship that's been shown up in front of the others—I mean in front of Mollie Perkins, for God's sake, and there

138

you are, trotting off to repair the damage to her, and bugger Liz Gibbons.

The door was opening. Mollie was there. Claire disappeared inside. Liz stubbed out her cigarette, grabbed her coat and car keys, backed too quickly from the drive and roared off. Yes, go to Mollie, don't even think of how you should speak to me, because it's too bloody late. It's twenty-five years too late. She rubbed her eyes. No. No tears. No bloody tears, Claire wasn't worth it, neither was their friendship. But the bloody stupid tears kept on coming.

*   *   *

Claire left Jean's house twenty minutes later, desperate for fresh air, desperate to be away from Mollie's orgasmic pleasure at her confession and apology, sickened by the grovelling she had to do to placate this woman whose bitterness at her husband's lack of promotion was as tangible as the heavy perfume she wore.

As she walked up the drive towards her car Claire gritted her teeth, stopping at the sound of Mollie's voice, and turning. Mollie stood on the porch, fingering her bloody pearls. 'Claire, dear, I take it Liz didn't know about Anna? She disagreed most forcefully when I thought I'd spotted a likeness. I'll inform her of the facts, shall I, on her return—as my own gesture of goodwill at our new understanding? You did say I was the first of the wives to know, didn't you?'

Mollie looked up and down the road. Claire felt like saying, 'Just shout a little louder and they'll hear you at HQ,' you appalling bitch, but of course she didn't. Instead she smiled and said calmly, 'There's no need, thank you Mollie, I'll tell our steering committee at the meeting tonight, and we'll go on from there.'

Disappointment crossed Mollie's face to be chased away by confusion. She said, hitching up her bosom, 'The meeting, you'll still hold it?'

Claire had walked on. Now she opened the car door and threw her bag on the passenger seat, feeling exhausted. She shouted down the drive. 'Of course. Life goes on, Mollie, just like before.' She slammed the door, started the car, checked her mirror, seeking Liz's car in the drive, needing her, needing to talk to her more than she needed anything else right now. It had gone.

She drew away from the kerb and within thirty seconds was crunching down her own drive.

But life wouldn't be just as before. Nothing would ever be just as before. She parked the car outside the garage, slammed into the house, put on Radio 2, poured a pint glass of water and slumped at the kitchen table. Damn the woman. She felt unclean from the simpering she had done as Mollie perched on the edge of Jean's Parker Knoll chair as though ready and steady for the starter's gun, which of course she was in a way.

Somehow she had kept calm as Mollie branded Anna's visit an unseemly incident. Somehow she had borne it when the woman had nearly fainted with outraged delight at the declaration of the truth, calling the birth of an illegitimate child reprehensible and quite unsuitable behaviour for a senior officer's wife. When Claire had pointed out that at the time of the birth she was seventeen with no inkling that she would become a senior officer's wife, Mollie had been scandalized. 'This is not a moment for levity,' she had yelped.

Claire pushed away the water. It slopped. She pushed back her chair. It grated on the tiles. She climbed the stairs.

She stripped off her clothes in the bedroom, leaving them where they lay, and almost ran to the shower. She let the water blast her, but still Mollie was there, her shoulders back as she surfed the wave of righteousness, proclaiming that Mark should have declined promotion under the circumstances.

At this attack on Mark Claire had at last thrown off the mantle of sackcloth and ashes and shouted, 'I can't help the fact that Nigel has not yet been promoted, and for your information Mark discussed the situation with a senior officer before we married. Perhaps that officer was an extraordinarily enlightened individual, but he felt the situation was tenable. It is only the shock, and my subsequent stupidity the other night, that has created difficulties.'

As the water beat down on her she felt a savage triumph at Mollie's retreat in the face of 'senior officer' and now she lifted her head, opened her mouth, losing herself in the heat, the wet, the sound of the water which at length shut out even that satisfaction, just as it shut out everything else. She stood for minutes like this, not allowing herself to think, to feel. Only allowing herself to be.

Eventually she turned off the water and stood, her eyes still closed, feeling her wet hair dripping down her back and her breasts, hearing the sounds of the house creep in and find her. She sighed, opened the shower door, and wrapped herself in the soft white towel. The mirror was misted. She stared into it and saw nothing, therefore she did not exist. She rubbed her hair with a corner of the towel. Water flicked on to the carpeted floor, the bath mat, the basin. Her skin was heat-pink. Mollie's had been pink when she had finally offered her support, on the unspoken understanding that Mark would be aware of who did support, and who did not.

Claire dropped the towel and walked into the bedroom, finding fresh clothes, dressing, then sitting on the bed as she dried her hair, remembering Liz clutching her knees, announcing the imminent arrival of the 'Orrible Oracle, seeing her crazy earrings, her dancing eyes.

*   *   *

From the landing window, where she'd been on watch, Claire spotted Liz turning into her drive. She ran downstairs, waited for a moment, and then rang her number.

Liz said in reply to her greeting, 'Yes, I'm fine, and yes, I had to go out.' Her voice was cool, detached.

Claire asked, 'May I come round?' Had Mollie spoken to her? Did she know? Damn, damn.

Liz said, 'I'm off to a meeting at the surgery.'

Claire knew there was no meeting and the growing chill that she felt was not from the tiled hall but foreboding. She rushed to the point, pressing one finger down on the pile of letters that had arrived today, most of them bills. 'Liz, I lied to you. That girl is Anna Weaver, she is the daughter I had twenty-five years ago.' She stopped and waited,

142

still pressing with that finger, still managing to remain in control, but only just. Liz said nothing. 'Liz? Liz? Please can I come and see you?'

Liz's voice was low, and wounded, and angry. 'No, you may not come and see me. I believed you last night even though I could see the evidence there, before my eyes. She *looks* like you, Claire. Like you and Leah, but I didn't allow myself to believe anything untoward because you told me it was otherwise. How could you lie to me? Not just then, but for all these years?'

Claire said, 'I haven't really lied all these years, just said nothing. I did lie last night, and I'm sorry.' In the kitchen the radio was still playing and she could hear Whitney Houston, warm and mellow.

'Isn't deception the same as lying, Claire? What else would you call the letters from the "TB sanatorium"? I've trusted you with every part of my life. I've exposed myself to you—but you? No, you've shared nothing if you didn't share that.'

Claire murmured, 'Discretion is different to deceit.'

Liz yelled at her, 'Claire, don't you dare box clever with me. You lied to me, and worse still, you denied your own child. It was for Mark, wasn't it, for his image, and for yours? I really don't know or like you any more, Claire and what's more, I really don't want to.'

Claire was crying now. On top of everything else she couldn't bear this. 'Liz, Liz. It was the shock. You've got to believe me. It was the shock.'

Liz laughed, and it was a harsh humourless sound that made Claire flinch. She dragged her hand across her eyes but the tears kept falling, her sobs were loud in this empty house. Liz said, 'It wasn't shock though, you're even lying about that. You knew she'd found you because she sent the photo. Surely you haven't forgotten I saw you with it? What was it you called it—some promotion or other. You're clever, Claire, I'll give you that.' Her voice lashed Claire and she half leaned against the table, needing its support, her hair hanging over her face, some strands sticking to the tears that were smudged all over her cheeks. 'You're a cruel, manipulative woman, Claire and you've betrayed me. You've all betrayed me because Ben's rung. He knew. Mark told him years ago. I was the only one who didn't know. You even told Mollie first.'

Claire wailed, 'I didn't know Ben knew, and I had to tell Mollie. I had to get that out of the way —it was duty. It was for the patch, for Mark, to try and make good somehow because she rang Nigel and he tried to tell Mark. Then I wanted to talk to you, have the time to explain properly.'

'And you still haven't explained just how you came to deny your child, have you, Claire?' The contempt in Liz's voice echoed that in Leah's.

Claire had to hold the receiver with two hands now. She whispered, 'They promised she would never be able to find me.'

Liz exploded, 'Come off it, Claire, kids have been able to find their parents since 1975. You know that, every bloody woman who's had a bastard must know that.'

Claire dropped her hands and stared at the receiver they still held, hearing that word, the tone of voice, the disgust in Liz's voice. It was such a familiar disgust, one that had started more than twenty-five years ago and gone on and on.

Her hands were shaking. All she could hear was

Liz's voice, telephone tinny. Everywhere else seemed silent; even Whitney had come to the end of her song. She really did not want to hear, or think, or feel, or remember but she knew she had to bring the receiver back, hold it against her ear, talk into the mouthpiece. 'Please understand it was the shock. Just the shock.' She realized with surprise that she was still crying though not with those racking sobs, just a hopeless endless silent weeping.

Liz said, 'Don't keep saying that. I *know* about the photo.'

'Please, Liz, don't tell anyone about that. Please. I didn't think she'd come. I really didn't think she'd come. She has her own family and I thought finding me would just confuse all that. I was doing it for her sake, Liz. I promise you I was doing it for her and the shock was terrible when she came.'

Liz paused, then said, 'Even if I don't tell anyone, perhaps your daughter will, if indeed you ever grant her an audience.'

'She's coming on Sunday, I phoned her first thing. I'm so sorry. So sorry about the whole thing; to you all, but mostly to her. Tonight at the meeting I'll tell the others, but please come. I can't cope on my own. Please Liz, I'm so sorry. I need you. I need you.'

Liz breathed out loudly. 'What are you, Claire, a machine, a totally heartless damned machine? I can't believe you're thinking of meetings at a time like this. Bloody hell, and I thought it was Mark who had become the ambitious one.'

Claire shrieked at her now, 'Don't you understand? Of course I just want to crawl into a hole and die, but I can't, I have to go on as though

145

I don't fill myself with disgust, as though I don't want to turn the clock back, do it all differently. All of it, differently. Ever since it happened I've just had to go on.' The sobs were louder, much louder. The phone went dead. 'Liz,' she gasped. 'Liz.' But her friend had hung up.

*   *   *

At the steering committee meeting held in Claire's house as usual the atmosphere was strained and the conversation stilted, though the vicar had patted her arm, and whispered 'Courage, *mon enfant*,' when he entered. He thought it would help, but it only made Claire realize that the bush telegraph was working as efficiently as always.

Mollie was subdued, but loudly insisted on keeping a place next to her and Jean on the sofa, saying self-importantly to Sally, and including Jo and Clarissa in the confidence, 'There are some who know their duty, and are wholehearted in their support, no matter what.'

Claire wanted to slap her, because she knew that Mollie meant Liz, who had not come early to help Claire set up, as she usually did. Neither had she arrived by 8.30, when Claire finally opened the meeting, taking time as she stood by the mantelpiece to explain that Anna Weaver was indeed her daughter.

It was clearly no surprise, and as her eyes focused on Mollie at least the woman had the grace to flush. Sally nodded sympathetically as Claire explained her shock at the appearance of her daughter, and her reaction to it. 'A reaction witnessed by you all.' Claire's voice was hoarse

146

from her earlier tears.

Jean spoke up in the pause that followed. 'It does seem cruel to do that to you—an extraordinarily selfish approach. She obviously didn't think it through.'

Claire fiddled with the half-empty coffee mug she held, and the strength of her defensive loyalty for her first child took her by surprise. She kept her voice cool as she explained, 'No, on the contrary, she had given it a great deal of thought and sent a letter which I hadn't opened. It was overlooked, amongst bills.' Which was another lie: she just wished she had thought of it this afternoon with Mollie. 'She hid behind the bush because she heard you coming out and didn't want to embarrass me.'

Clarissa Baines spoke up, her voice firm. 'I won't pretend there's not a lot of gossip. It appears we have amongst us the equivalent of the guy with the loaves and the fishes who insisted on distributing his wares to all and sundry.'

Most eyes swung to Mollie and Jean. Mollie smiled conspiratorially at Claire, confident in her role as essential senior wife. She said, 'I thought it my duty to help Claire by making sure that the truth was known. It saves her the task.'

Sally, the RSM's wife, said without any inflection whatsoever, 'With you as a friend, Mollie, who needs—'

Claire cut across: 'Thank you Mollie, but I thought we decided that we would sort things out this evening. I know you were trying to help but perhaps you would allow me to orchestrate how we handle this from now on.' Her tone was conciliatory. She signalled a warning to Sally, Jo and Clarissa, and the other wives. But it was

147

unnecessary, she saw that.

Sally said, 'What do you want us to do then, Claire?' Though there was nothing untoward in Sally's voice, there was a neutrality which hadn't been there before, and it was a neutrality which she detected in the group as a whole. It was like a shadow in their eyes, an invisible veil, and why not?

She said, 'When you hear gossip, or are asked, perhaps you could express my sorrow at my denial. Perhaps you could emphasize that I was taken by surprise, underline that I just couldn't grasp the situation, and that Anna had tried to warn me.'

Jo Franks agreed: 'I know I would react the same. I just know I would.' But her eyes expressed her doubt.

Sally shook her head. 'After twenty-five years who wouldn't panic at a bolt out of the blue, for goodness sake? Thank God Mark already knows, or it could have been a nightmare.' There was less reserve in her voice now and for five minutes or so Claire let them convince themselves and hated herself for the manipulative woman that Liz had been right to call her.

At 8.45 she directed the meeting towards the pantomime schedule that Jo had copied up, and as though from a great distance Claire heard the group agree that at next week's meeting they would concentrate on defining jobs. Auditions and readings would take place over the following two weeks. In the third week they would finalize the cast, and the scenery, lighting, sound effects and costume teams would be set up.

December and January would consist of rehearsals, with a complete set of understudies to cover R & R. 'That means leave,' Jo explained to

148

the vicar. 'Most of those on the patch will disappear for the ten days or so. If it falls over the performance week we could lose our stars. Claire and I decided this afternoon that ideally we'd like a complete understudy team. It'll involve more people and from the initial response it looks as though it should be possible, though we'll be hard put to double up on Uglies.'

Sally volunteered, 'You spoke to Rob this afternoon didn't you Claire? He's going to be one of the Uglies, and the Reverend Masters the other'—she shot a smile at the vicar—'with the warden the stepmother, isn't that right? If they bear the production dates in mind we shouldn't need "spares".'

The vicar laughed softly. 'You can count on us, m'dear.'

Claire nodded. 'Rob was only too relieved. He was worried he'd be the chicken.'

In fact Rob had offered more than reliability as an Ugly, he'd offered to support her personally. His concern had been totally non-judgemental and had carried Claire through until now.

Jo was reading from the schedule. 'Rehearsal will take us through to the Christmas break, and through January too. By early February we should be ready for a complete run-through, then the dress rehearsal.' She checked with Claire, who took up the proceedings, her eyes on the schedule. 'The performances will be in the second week of February, on Wednesday, Thursday, Friday and Saturday. The venue is to be the Garrison Theatre, which we've chosen with the full agreement of Reverend Masters, as the village hall is not as large, and,' she looked round, 'we're aiming for big audiences, everyone.'

There were boos to her left, and hisses from her right. The atmosphere was almost as it should have been.

It was when loose ends were being tied that the doorbell rang, and Claire rushed to open the door, her smile ready for Liz. But it was Muriel who bounded in with a large envelope under her arm. She smacked a kiss in the region of Claire's cheek, and tore on into the sitting room, bellowing hello towards the vicar, and a general 'Evening gals' to the others.

She waggled the photographs in the air. 'As young Liz couldn't make it—a real surgery meeting tonight just for once—I thought I'd better pick up the photos I'd left with her and pop them in myself. Mind you Claire, I could do with a coffee, and so could the rest, from the look of the tongues hanging out.'

Instant coffee was all Claire could summon the energy to make, especially as Mollie insisted on helping. Sally, however, joined them, squeezing Claire's arm, her whispers unheard by Mollie who was busy tipping more bourbons on to plates. 'It'll be fine. We understand. The women won't forget what you've done. Poor Claire, all these years— how it must have hurt.'

They carried the coffee in. Muriel had firmly taken Mollie's place on the sofa and now tapped the cushion next to her. 'Come on, slap that naughty backside down here, Claire Baird.' Mollie, who had rushed for the space back-pedalled, smiling weakly as Claire sat on the sofa. Muriel's smile was terrifyingly broad as she instructed Mollie to bring through another chair from the

150

dining room for herself.

The women were sharing out the photos. 'Who will be involved in the costumes?' Muriel rattled on.

Jo gestured to Mollie, who was shifting her chair to the other side of Muriel. 'Mollie offered. She has experience.'

Muriel peered at Mollie. 'Jolly good. Idle fingers lead to mischievous hands.' She shut her mouth as though it were a trap. Claire winced. Muriel smiled that smile again, then reached forward and grabbed a biscuit. She said, her voice loud, 'Well, Claire, you almost made a hash of your daughter turning up.'

Claire slopped her coffee and the vicar looked as though he was about to pray, but Muriel carried on as though unaware: 'These things are an absolutely bloody nightmare if you're not on the ball, but how can you go through life forever on the alert in case the little soul takes it into her head to hunt you down? I'd have had the vapours, don't know how you held yourself together. I remember when my old dear told me that Mark had chatted to him about it just before he married you. God, seems like yesterday. Still you've got a good team behind you to help sweep up the mess.'

Muriel sucked coffee from her biscuit, ignoring Claire's look of surprise. Until now Claire hadn't known the senior officer had been Percy. Muriel's biscuit became soggy and fell into her coffee. Muriel stirred the coffee. 'Dunking's a disgusting habit, girls, but I thank my lucky stars I wasn't born an Eskimo. Out there, they put you out on an ice floe when you're old and decrepit and can't chew properly any more. Mark you, it's not bourbons they chew, but hides.'

151

The women were laughing. Sally who was a particular favourite of Muriel's said, her voice heavy with meaning, 'I doubt that you're past chewing a hide or two.'

'When necessary.' She looked at Mollie, gulped her coffee, then struggled to her feet, pushing Claire back down. 'You stay put and be thankful you've got these girls around you, though they're no more than you deserve after all you've done for them. You remember that, girls—you've had a good example set, so let's not be forgetting that.' Her voice was quiet now, and very serious, and her eyes flicked to Mollie again as she headed for the door.

By the time she reached the front door her voice was restored to full volume as she yelled, 'Carry on, carry on, and before you ask, Claire, no, I won't be the chicken. However ask my gardener, Roland. He *will* wear shorts in the summer and it isn't a pretty sight—even worse in tights I should imagine.'

With that she was gone, and a silence descended, as it invariably did after one of Muriel's forays. Eventually Jo spoke, her pencil poised over her clipboard. 'I take it that was an order?'

Claire laughed for the first time since last night.

CHAPTER ELEVEN

Mark hadn't phoned Claire; neither had he followed up on Perkins. He'd been too tired and had fallen into bed shortly after the patrol had arrived back, sleeping soundly through the night. Sleep was a knack the army taught them, along with a way of switching to automatic pilot to override emotion, and as his batman brought tea at 0600 hours Mark felt exasperation flood in. This bloody tour the pilot had been working overtime, and it looked as though it'd be needed again this morning. Bloody Perkins.

Once dressed and breakfasted, and after Formal Orders, he finally phoned Claire, perching on the corner of the desk, fiddling with his ballpoint, the one she had given him when the deployment was confirmed. That was something she always did—it was her idea of a talisman—and he smiled, his exasperation ebbing, missing Claire suddenly: her voice, the strength of her, the sameness of her. As he heard the phone ringing down the line he held his breath, wanting to speak to her, staring out at the hills, seeing the snow which had been heavy last night. Suddenly he felt lost and alone. What was the winter going to bring?

The receiver was picked up. Claire's voice was quiet. 'Claire Baird speaking.'

Mark smiled, relieved. 'It's me. I'm glad it's you, not the machine.'

Her voice was tired as she said nervously, 'I received your message but I thought you were phoning last night, I was . . .'

Mark felt his longing drain away and he threw down the pen, interrupting: 'For God's sake, we're not going to have a bloody fuss about that, are we? I'm on the damn thing now, aren't I, even though I'm in the middle of the equivalent of a war zone?'

'Worried,' she finished, her voice strangely subdued. 'I was worried, that's all.'

Shit, why did he go up in the air like that? He had to get a grip. He took a deep breath, sighing

153

wearily. 'Sorry, Claire. Look, I was knackered, had a difficult day to say the very least, talking "let's be reasonable" to people who are not living in a reasonable world and now I've got to conduct a guided tour for a cabinet minister. So, give me an update on Mollie v. the Colonel's wife before I see that ass Perkins. I hope it's sorted. I just don't need any more hassle.'

Claire said nothing. He snapped. 'Claire.' Slowly she spoke and he listened, barely understanding, making her repeat it. When she had finished he said nothing for a moment, just shook his head trying to clear it. He straightened, standing erect, the edge of the desk digging into his thighs. Through the window he saw it was still snowing, but the snow had done nothing to deaden the banging and clanging as the reinforcement update continued. In the distance seeming further away than usual were the mortars. Along the corridors a door slammed, hard heels rang on the floor, receded. Claire spoke again. 'Mark, I'm so sorry.'

Still groping and grasping for the sense of it all, just as he'd done when she'd first told him all those years ago, he said 'Sorry?'

His mouth felt dry. He brushed his forehead with his hand, staring at the sweat on the tips of his fingers. He'd forgotten all about it. Life had closed over. He shivered. Cold. Another door banged. 'Mark,' Claire's voice was loud. 'Are you there?'

'I'm here,' he replied and his voice was strong in the room. He repeated: 'I'm here.' He forced himself to perch on the desk again just as he forced his hand to loosen on the receiver, his shoulders to drop. A mortar thumped. A Land Rover horn sounded.

Everything was normal. He looked at the clock. Yes, everything was normal. The routine was set up. He must leave in ten minutes to greet the Minister. Before that he must phone Nigel. He was travelling with Miss Sevo. Ben would be in control here. Yes, everything was normal, in focus, and now his brain was active as it centred on today's schedule, and then he allowed it to click over and beyond that, restructuring Claire, embarking on a mission analysis of the situation, his eyes following the snow as it fell, much lighter now.

So the kid had turned up. It was a shame Claire hadn't seen her note in amongst the bills, it would have changed the whole thing. Anyway, it was done now and couldn't be changed. But there was still the patch and after all he'd done to try and get the regiment sorted—something had better be done there. His voice when he spoke was businesslike. 'OK, so what have you done to pull this round?' Even as he continued he knew that businesslike was slipping into—what? He swallowed, the sweat breaking out again. Why the hell did this have to happen after all these years? Why the hell now? Yes, that was it. It was rage he was feeling. Why now, when he was up to his armpits in shit? 'Why now?' he yelled, 'and for God's sake, why deny it? I could understand if I didn't know about it, but why do that? Why add to my problems?'

He walked the length of the desk, then back as Claire repeated, 'I'm sorry . . .'

'Shut up, Claire. Just shut up. "Sorry" is no damn good. Whatever possessed you to do that in front of the women—have you any idea of the consequences?'

She protested, 'I didn't do it deliberately. It was

155

the shock. I'm sorry, I've said I'm sorry and I've contained the consequences, or I'm on the way to doing so.' She was crying, but she never cried. He stopped walking, gripped the phone lead and said, his voice low and urgent, 'OK, OK Claire. Now pull yourself together. I know it must be hard, but there are worse things, believe me. God almighty, you should be out here then you'd really be stretched. Look you've just got to keep calm, get the whole thing into perspective.'

There was a tap on the door but they could damn well wait. He continued desperately: 'For God's sake, Claire, I need you strong. Come on, buck up, get a grip.'

She stammered. 'I'm so sorry, and I'm so wretched.'

There was a cough. Ben stood in the doorway. How the hell long had he been there? Ben pointed to his watch and flashed a look at the clock. Five minutes to go. Mark nodded and mouthed, 'OK, be with you in a minute.'

Ben looked at him, his face expressionless, then left the room.

Mark turned back to the phone, seeing his ballpoint on the floor. He crouched and retrieved it, half grunting as he said, 'OK Claire it's difficult, but it's happened and we can't change that, so what have you done about it?'

Her voice was calmer as she said, 'I've rung Anna—'

'No, what have you done about the patch?' He checked the clock. The big hand lurched. Four minutes.

Her voice shook a little. 'Oh, I've spoken to Mollie. The others on the committee understand,

156

Muriel too. She came last night.'

'Thank God for that. So, this'll spread out to the rest and it'll be as good as new in no time. just keep me informed, all the way along the line, got it?'

Her voice was little more than a whisper. 'Yes, I'm so sorry Mark, I'll make sure everything is fine. Please, don't worry, you must concentrate, be careful. I didn't mean you to know until you came home. I'm so sorry.'

'It's all a bit late for that now, isn't it.' He slammed down the phone, then hesitated, checking the clock. Three minutes. He picked up the receiver again and was connected with Perkins. Brushing aside Nigel's greeting Mark said, 'Never mind that. Now, for your information my wife's child has returned. It is a child I had full knowledge of but because of the inappropriate way this child chose to announce her presence, my wife was startled, shocked, and spurred into a denial. It was a misunderstanding that Mollie has probably already informed you of, given her usual alacrity and attention to detail in these matters.'

Perkins said, 'Oh, I say . . .'

Mark overrode him. 'No, don't say anything, just do a bloody good job from now on, because you've ground to make up. Believe me, we're in a shifting sea right now and Christ knows where the next bloody fracas is going to break out. We need to be on our toes, concentrating, not listening to a lot of bloody natter. Do I make myself clear?'

'Abundantly, Colonel.'

'Our estimated time of arrival is 1000 hours. We'll brief the Minister *in situ* before bringing him into our area proper.' With that, he slammed down the phone and rocketed out of the door, almost

157

barging into Ben who was waiting in the corridor. They walked out of the school door and down the steps together, coughing as the cold air hit them. By Mark's Land Rover they checked final details together and Mark was just about to climb into the Land Rover, where Gordana Sevo already sat, when Ben asked, 'All well at home, Colonel?'

Mark stepped away from the vehicle, ignoring the revving of the others in the convoy as they waited less than patiently. Lowering his voice, he filled Ben in on the news. unaware that his 2IC already knew, finishing: 'Bloody women. They choose their times to throw a wobbler, don't they?'

Ben's tone was sympathetic. 'Well, I'm not surprised, it's a lot to take in, a lot to deal with. Good grief, she's just seen a daughter she gave away. What's the girl like?'

Mark shrugged, as the air filled with diesel fumes from the revving engines. 'How should I know?'

'Well, when's she seeing her?'

Mark swung back to the Land Rover, walking away from Ben, his voice low and irritated as he threw back over his shoulder, 'For God's sake, Ben, if you want the answers perhaps you'd better ring her yourself.'

Ben stared at Mark's retreating back, and murmured, 'Yes, Colonel.' Then he turned on his heel, and made his way back to the Ops Room.

* * *

Was the road unusually busy or was it just that already it had been such a pig of a morning that he couldn't think straight? Mark wondered, pressing himself back into the seat, scanning Miss Sevo's briefings and the additional information that she had gleaned over the past twelve hours. 'You've passed this to the Intelligence Cell in the Operations Room?' he barked.

She nodded, saying nothing. As he read, Claire's voice kept breaking through, and the tears in it; his stomach twisted. He should have asked about the girl, but he'd do that tonight. He'd phone. Poor Claire, poor little Claire, she must have been shocked to lose it like that, to actually deny her. But it figured. After all, shock could turn the world on its head, you just had to look at some of the sights he had witnessed over the years to realize that. He stared at the notes which danced, made no sense, and he wished to God he hadn't flown off the handle. Damn it.

He tossed the notebook to Miss Sevo and stared out of the window, remembering it all, remembering her telling him, way back in those early days, remembering the awful . . . He slammed shut the door on memory. There. Finished. Forgotten. It was so long ago. The girl had come. So what.

'Checkpoint,' Miss Sevo called. The Land Rover halted behind a horse and cart. Almost with relief Mark approached the checkpoint, glad to be occupied. Beside him Miss Sevo said nothing but when they reached the Muslim local forces she took out her cigarettes, and Mark found himself slipping into the negotiating routine as easily as he'd ever done.

Permission was granted, and beneath the light covering of snow the pebbles turned beneath his boots as they walked back to the Land Rover.

Mission accomplished, progress made, so far. The doors of the Land Rover clicked shut satisfactorily, the heater hummed. He half saluted the checkpoint guards as they drove past. Their cigarettes glowed.

There were three other checkpoints, all of which were as effortless, and as the road wound higher to the top of the valley and they passed chalets perched above them he allowed himself to notice the crisp blue sky. Miss Sevo said quietly, 'I have skiied here.' Now the chalets registered properly and he saw the washing hung on makeshift lines, and the refugees who stood in groups watching them, their faces registering no emotion. There was nothing to say because he'd seen it a thousand times. Nonetheless he looked at them, and at the hills, the birds, anything, wanting to fill his mind.

Arriving at Gornji Vakuf he snatched a look round the compound, resenting the need to double check Perkins, then hurried in to find Perkins and the Brigadier entertaining the Minister to coffee in the mess, and the press nuzzling at the group, eager for titbits.

Mark and Miss Sevo were handed coffee. It was hot and bitter and good.

'Good trip?' the Brigadier asked Mark.

'Fine thank you, Brigadier. Trouble-free checkpoints and today no alarms whatsoever.'

The Minister was listening and now he smiled. 'Bodes well for our little tour.'

Mark smiled. 'Indeed, sir.' There was a steady murmur of conversation all around but Charlie Bennet's voice was audible over everyone's as he bemoaned the snow and the cold and the fact that the sun wasn't over the yard-arm so rum wasn't yet on offer.

160

'If you're ready, gentlemen?' Nigel Perkins asked. He led them through to his office, leaving the press behind to tread water. Mark concentrated on every word, every gesture of the briefing as he'd never done before and it seemed just a matter of seconds before Perkins was leading the way to the Ops Room. As Mark shouldered past a fire extinguisher the Brigadier dropped back, remarking, 'All well with you, Mark? Any problems?'

Mark searched the tone of the question, looking for meanings, trying to glean what he meant. Staring at Nigel Perkins's back he said, 'No more than usual, sir.'

As they walked on the Brigadier said, 'This is a difficult job, Mark, a sensitive one and needs full-on focus. I gather there's been a bit of a hiatus at home? Remember I'm not just a pretty face, I'm here to support.'

Mark smiled, forcing reassurance into his voice. Hiatus? Yes, that's all it was, just a hiatus. 'Everything's under control. The child is one I knew of, and Claire always copes with everything beautifully. There's no problem, I can assure you.'

His automatic pilot was struggling as they reached the Ops Room, but almost immediately he heard, in the silence that had fallen, the urgent barked commands that were coming in over the crackling radio from Lt. Andrews as his patrol came under fire. He forced his way forward, his focus where it should be: on his men. It was a local argument, one that the patrol had stumbled into, but even as Mark tracked the action, his shoulders rigid, hearing firing, listening to Bob Andrews's commands, it was one they stumbled out of, just as quickly.

He caught sight of the Minister and now Mark let his anger flare again, but this time it was directed at a government that was asking too much of its reduced and pressurized army. It was an easier anger, one he could recognize and handle, and he finally let it drive out the other which was complicated, not quite anger but something that hurt, something that mustn't be allowed to take hold.

During lunch the conversation flowed, and by coffee his head was empty of everything but Bosnia. The relief had made him good company, so much so that the Brigadier's voice had been especially warm as Mark and the Minister left to head back to base. But so had the Minister's, as he requested that Miss Sevo join them in Mark's Land Rover, saying, 'I'm here to gain hands-on atmosphere, so let's be hearing everyone's views.'

At this Mark nearly stopped dead, but somehow managed to keep going, heading for the Land Rover. He ushered Miss Sevo into the rear seat while he swung up into the front, hearing the Minister settle himself beside her. 'Keep your eyes on the road, Corporal,' he murmured as he felt Simms's glance flicker to him.

They travelled with the press in tow, whilst the Minister gazed from the window, issuing platitudes, chatting easily of his time here as a tourist before Tito's death, though Mark had difficulty hearing because of the inadequate heater which was rumbling and huffing—all talk and no go. What the hell—just so long as it was the Minister talking non-stop, waiting only for brief replies, allowing Miss Sevo no time to launch herself on an in-depth discussion on UN lack of involvement.

At the first checkpoint the Croats came to the Land Rover window before Mark had a chance to get out, signalling them straight through with flamboyant arm movements. Amazed, Mark turned to Miss Sevo.

The Minister remarked, 'That seemed pretty trouble free.'

'Not always so,' Miss Sevo said. Mark's smile became fixed, and the muscles in his neck tensed as they had done every time she had spoken. She continued: 'Colonel Baird is firm, but diplomatic. They respect him, those that have met him.'

Again Mark felt Simms's eyes flicker towards him and this time he grinned at the Corporal, whose lips were pursed in a whistle of relief.

The Minister then leaned forward. 'So, Corporal. How does your wife handle the separations?'

The Corporal looked into the rearview mirror. 'Always glad to see me back, sir.'

Mark's smile had faded at the question and now he braced himself as the Minister traversed and aimed at him. Mark replied, 'My wife has a lot to cope with, and she does it admirably.' There was an awkwardness in his reply and he stumbled on: 'Of course, she has a great deal of responsibility.'

Corporal Simms interrupted. 'Very highly thought of, is Mrs Baird, if I might just say, sir.'

The Minister settled back into his corner and Mark knew he should be talking, entertaining, giving the guided tour, but there were no words. He wiped his mouth, saw Simms flash him a look, but then they both heard Miss Sevo's voice drawing the Minister's attention to the village they were

163

passing, explaining the difficulties of partitioning communities, should it ever come to that, '. . . because within some villages live a mixture of all races'.

The Minister was looking closely at some damaged houses which were still smouldering, craning his neck to keep them in view for as long as he could, then pointing to the crags and forest line. 'Have you skied here, Miss Sevo? I noticed a skiing resort back a short way.'

Mark was back with them now, listening properly. 'Sometimes,' she said.

The Minister continued, 'It's so beautiful, but it seems somehow incorrect to make that comment when you consider the tragedy that is unfolding. But the UN is doing all that it can.'

Mark tensed, but Miss Sevo merely smiled. 'Yes, without Colonel Baird and his men and all the other UN battalions I dread to think what would happen to Bosnia.' Her tone was appreciative.

She then swept on, telling the Minister of the legendary creation of Bosnia from the Muslim perspective, explaining how Allah the Merciful and Compassionate had created the world, making it as smooth as the finest porcelain. This had so inflamed the devil that he gouged God's earth with his huge nails. She pointed to the ravines and rivers, and the crags. 'The gouges divided one district from another and kept men apart. God in his pity sent angels to spread their wings, thereby teaching men to build bridges to span the divisions. I think perhaps we need those angels again.'

No one spoke. There was just the swishing of the tyres, which changed to a thud when they met a pothole. At the next checkpoint there was to be no quick wave through, for a convoy had been halted. Miss Sevo and Mark walked to the head of it and negotiated passage for them all, and while the lorries roared and geared past them he said, 'Thank you for taking some of the load on this journey.'

Miss Sevo turned up the collar of her jacket against the wind. 'For . . . ?' she queried, stepping further back towards the verge. He grabbed her arm. 'Careful—*never* step near the verge.' She tensed with shock, then relaxed, half laughing. 'How silly. How stupid. A moment's thoughtlessness and . . . Thank you, Colonel Baird.' Her face when she turned to him was grateful, her smile genuine, the sun lines deep. She repeated, 'You were thanking me for . . . ?'

He said as one lorry came too close and spattered them both with snow and mud, 'For taking the load, finding things to say, you know, not making waves.'

She appeared to be struggling to comprehend. 'Taking the load, not making waves?'

He grinned because he was being teased by someone whose grasp of colloquial English was excellent when she felt like it. He said deliberately, 'For not going ballistic, for not being critical.'

She smiled again, nodding. 'Ah.' He knew he had just been made to ice the cake three times and shook his head in mock exasperation.

Miss Sevo's smile faded as the last of the lorries passed and the Land Rover convoy trundled up to the checkpoint. She said quickly, 'Well, you look worried. I'm not an ogre, Colonel Baird. I am capable of cooperation. I do not like to see disquiet, however well it is disguised.' Her face and voice were concerned.

165

Mark looked at her, not at the Land Rover whose wheels were spinning on the mud and snow as it approached. He hesitated, comforted by the kindness in her voice, and before he knew it he was saying, 'Well, thank you for not being an ogre, Gordana, if I may call you that. You see, my wife's daughter who was adopted twenty-five years ago has reappeared.' He stopped abruptly. Was he stark staring bonkers to be telling this girl?

The Land Rover was almost on a level with them as she said carefully, 'I see. That is good news, but difficult.' That was all: no sarcasm, no ridicule.

'Yes, it is rather,' he muttered.

The Land Rover stopped abreast of them. Mark reached for the door. As he swung it open she said softly, 'So, I am glad I have not gone ballistic, today of all days, Colonel Baird.'

She kicked her boots against the rear wheel, just as Claire did. He said, so that the others did not hear, 'Perhaps you should call me Mark?' He was astonished at himself but for a moment he had felt very alone.

The mud dispatched, she tucked the usual loose strand of hair behind her ear, shaking her head, saying firmly, 'I think not, Colonel Baird. It would not be proper, and the English are proper, no matter what.'

She climbed into the Land Rover, and he took his place in the front passenger seat, his mind back with Claire, knowing that perhaps this particular Englishman was not always proper, that this morning he had behaved rather badly, and he was swept with guilt.

Tonight he would find the time to phone Claire and ask about her daughter.

CHAPTER TWELVE

It was 9.30 on Saturday morning, and in her Well Woman consulting room Liz could hear little from the waiting room—but that was hardly surprising as it was only an emergency surgery. Even if it had been bulging it wouldn't have been her problem because Dr Smythe had pulled the Saturday duty short straw. Liz lit up her cigarette. She'd been here yesterday too, hiding. Muriel had found her, though.

Liz swallowed, pushing her cigarette packet around the desk. God, that woman had a mouth on her. What a rollicking, what a bloody cheek when the old charger didn't know about the photo, didn't know 'owt about nowt'. How dare Muriel accuse her of disloyalty. How dare she throw Claire's unfailing support in her face. How dare . . .

She swung round as the receptionist entered, sniffing the air like a tracker dog, fixing her eyes on the red NO SMOKING sign. Make my day, Liz begged silently, say something and make my day.

Clearly Mrs Brown knew all about self-preservation, and merely placed the cup of coffee near the pile of patients' notes Liz had taken from the office.

'We don't usually see you on a Saturday,' Mrs Brown said, as Liz tore open the sachet of sugar, licking her finger, dipping it in, then sucking it.

Liz patted the files. 'Admin. Thanks for the coffee.'

Mrs Brown said, 'It's decaffeinated.'

Liz murmured, 'Well, you can't win 'em all.'

Mrs Brown slammed the door as she left. 'Damn,' Liz said aloud. 'Damn you and your mouth, Liz Gibbons.'

That was virtually what Muriel had said, though there had been more: all about Liz choosing to blather endlessly about everything, whilst Claire kept problems to herself, a totally reasonable choice. 'Blather?' Liz muttered, stubbing her cigarette out in the lid of the jam jar that she kept for the purpose. She stared at the cigarette ends which half filled the jam jar, and lit another.

'This is only the beginning,' Muriel had said. 'There are other Mollies, other jealous, bored women who will stir. Put your self-centred concerns to one side just this once and support the best friend you will ever have.'

Liz fingered the files. At first nothing had made any sense. The lie about the photograph, the denial. It was not the behaviour of her Claire, the Claire who loved children, who worked so hard to get the playgroup off the ground, who ran it though it was not usually the job of the CO's wife to do so. Claire who helped set up the Mother and Toddler Group, using this avenue to reach out to young mothers, Claire who did her utmost to make sure no one felt alone. Claire who was over-protective of Leah, panicking unnecessarily every time the girl was late. Claire who had underpinned Mark and was too mild, too eager to please, who seldom permitted herself the luxury of expressing anger. Claire who was, she now guessed, still doing a sort of misguided penance, not just for the sin of bearing a child, but for being in the wrong place at the wrong time.

She stubbed out her cigarette half finished,

drank the coffee, tipped what was left of the sugar into her hand, dipping in her finger. She could taste the nicotine alongside the sweetness. Lord, she was revolting.

She heard Claire's voice again, out in the darkness, facing her daughter. 'Please, you must go. For your own sake, you must go.' She heard the anguish, the longing, and knew that she would visit her friend very soon.

She washed her hands in the corner basin, dried them on a paper towel, catching sight of herself in the mirror, seeing the signs of too many cigarettes. She tossed the soggy towel in the bin, ashamed of the person she had allowed herself to become. The old charger, Muriel was right: she had lost it recently. It was the partnership, the last-chance corral for a middle-aged old bag. But it still shouldn't have happened. Her eyes were on the files.

Yes, she would go to Claire, but she needed confirmation of her suspicions if she was to be as steadfast and as expert as Claire might one day need her to be. Suspicions which any good doctor would have picked up on when Anna appeared. She returned to the desk. Mrs Brown tapped on the door, and entered. 'The surgery is closing now and Dr Smythe has just left.' She took the cup that Liz proffered. 'Will you set the alarms?'

'Of course, Mrs Brown. I'm sorry I was flippant earlier on.'

Mrs Brown's smile was cold. 'That's quite all right.' She left. It clearly wasn't, but then nothing was all right with Frau Tight Lips.

Liz had always thought Mrs Brown had a look of Claire's mother about her. The same cold correctness. Did Mrs Brown heap the same expectations on to her daughter as Mrs Riddick had on Claire? Was it her resemblance to Mrs Riddick that repelled Liz? Probably.

She remembered how Claire's father had somehow faded with each year, stuck as a clerk in Turnbull, Turnbull and Watkins's solicitor's office, and how Mrs Riddick had decided in her disappointment that her daughter would be the achiever. Liz and Claire had passed the eleven-plus well enough to gain a scholarship to the independent girls' school, travelling into Guildford together from the bus stop between their roads.

Their home-made uniforms had never been quite the right shape or shade of blue but Claire hadn't minded. Tossing aside the glances she would drag Liz off to mischief, making Liz not mind either. Liz remembered the giggling, the chatting and the plans. She remembered the detentions that Claire's mother thought were hockey practice.

She remembered the tennis club, the dance lessons shared with the grammar school boys, the long summer days when they'd lolled in the heat, especially that last summer before they each went on holiday. There had been no mention of a boy, and no time when they were not together, sleeping over with one another more often than not.

In August Liz had gone on holiday to Bude in the West Country. She winced now at the memory of the salt-water swimming pool on the beach, and smiled at the thought of hot Horlicks in those special mugs at the café on the clifflop. Claire had gone to West Wittering and had been pale, quiet and withdrawn on her return. There had been no fun, no mischief, none of the spirit. Then had come the supposed TB and with it Liz's long loneliness which had really only ended when they met again by chance at a Sandhurst Military Academy ball.

Liz reached for the cigarettes, then drew back. No. But her resolve weakened and she lit up, going to the window that looked out on to the car park. The air was frantic with leaves snatched by the wind from the horse chestnuts dividing the surgery from the road. Lordy Lordy, Mrs Brown would be cross. Leaves in corners equated to unfiled records.

Claire had never returned to her house near Liz. Her family had sold up and moved to Camberley and it was to here that Claire had returned from the sanatorium. Of course the girls had written, but by then Liz had her A levels and was off to medical school and their friendship had been lost, but not forgotten. Never that.

A flurry of wind brought down more leaves just as Mrs Brown cycled from the car park, all outraged bust and thrust, but Liz hardly registered this as she heard Claire's voice, saw her face as she said, 'They promised me she would never be able to find me.'

Liz returned to her desk, and taking a deep breath eased Claire's medical records from the pile. Claire was not her patient, therefore she had no right to invade her privacy. If Mrs Brown had seen her the partnership would never have been hers. But sod that. It was Claire that mattered.

She pulled the notes from the buff wallet and braced herself, needing to know but dreading it. She rubbed her neck, eased her head from side to side, laid the notes down on the desk and swiftly worked her way back from the most recent entry to the birth of Anna.

A Leeds hospital doctor reported a straightforward delivery. Further back she went, scanning the minimal antenatal notes, finding only quite ordinary observations. Back she went, searching for an August or September date.

It was there—1 September. She took time out. lighting another cigarette, inhaling, exhaling, easing her neck again, then reading on, slowly, very slowly. Fearing what she would find. She read that Claire had been treated for cystitis. In addition the doctor had noted profound bruising to thighs and arms *attributable to a horse-riding accident*. Liz sat back: attributable to a horse-riding accident. Oh Claire.

There it was, such a small observation, but it was enough. More than enough—because Claire was allergic to horses. She never rode. Even if she was close to one she broke out in hives and had done for as long as Liz had known her. Liz checked—there was no note of any hives.

Liz tried to read it through a second time but had to stop, defeated, the words a blur. So that's when the lies started, my poor little Claire. She felt a great rage at the doctor who had not pursued the matter. But maybe he had. Maybe he'd said, 'Cystitis can be the result of energetic sex. Bruises can occur as a result of rape.' Did he, Claire?

Why didn't you tell him, or your mother? Why didn't you tell me, tell anyone. But no, you assumed that somehow you were guilty too as so many victims do. No wonder you haven't told Mark. It's something you've hidden away as though it never happened, it's something you've tried to deny every day of your life. But it did happen, Claire. Oh Claire, how can you ever accept

172

someone who is half him? For a moment she could only sit and stare sightless, that question repeating itself over and over, but she knew the answer all the time, for Claire would accept the child, would love her. That was Claire.

She stuffed the notes back, walked through to the office and filed the wallets, feeling very tired. What was it Descartes had said, something about God having the power to change things that had happened in the past, even to cancel them? Well, she wished he'd do that right now, for how did you tell a child she was the product of an act of violence, not love, and that in her dwelt a rapist's genes? It was a question she'd never been able to help her patients answer and she wasn't sure how successful the counsellors she had sent them on to had been either. No wonder Claire had backed away from her child, her child who had her father's eyes.

*　　　*　　　*

At Claire's house Jo, the co-producer held up the calendar. She had called ten minutes before, insisting that she and Claire 'talk panto'. Now she underlined the last night's performance in red. 'That's when Colonel Baird is scheduled for R & R isn't it? It would be great to have him there.'

Claire agreed, aware that Jo was making sure she was not alone this morning, of all mornings, and more grateful than she could say. 'He'd better be, since he's the *éminence grise* in all of this. If he was here I'd insist he took the part of the chook.'

Jo smiled. 'Ah well, the sight of the Colonel's legs has so far been denied me.'

173

'Keep it that way.' The banter was light but it was 10.15 a.m. and the playgroup celebration was only three-quarters of an hour away. Claire wiped her hands down her Laura Ashley skirt. It would be her first outing since everything had begun.

The phone rang and she left the answer machine to cope as she had done all morning; nonetheless she held up her hand for silence, checking that it wasn't an emergency. It was the Families Officer, Rob, wishing her luck and saying he'd meet her there, Rob who'd been wonderful and fielded practically all her visits to those wives in need. Those that he couldn't, she had done, ignoring the reserve, the questioning glances, and grateful when there were none. But then most of these women were more concerned with their own problems and one had even grinned and said she was glad that Claire had boobed, it made her easier to talk to.

Jo pointed out that the first read-through had been rescheduled for Monday. 'We've got easily enough people to start casting already.'

'But the script?'

Jo grinned. 'No probs, already up to scratch, and believe me the read-through and rehearsals will produce some ad libs we can incorporate. Oh damn, I haven't checked with the dance schools on base and the village.'

Claire said, 'I will, this afternoon, after the anniversary.'

Jo wrote that in her notebook. 'Apparently the Saddle Club have a Shetland pony that could pull the coach.'

Claire murmured, 'Oh dear.'

Jo snapped the elastic band she had used as a bookmark. 'Yes, I rather agree. It'll end in plops which will bring the house down, and rattle the stage-hands no end.'

Claire laughed gently. Jo was staring at the fireplace, deep in thought. 'Well, why don't we go for something quite different? It is our panto.'

Claire sat opposite. 'What do you mean, like a Warrior or something?'

Jo shook her head in admiration, her short bob shiny enough for an advertisement. 'Excellent. We could have the witch and her witchlets on missiles . . .'

The conversation clipped along as they divided the cast into Groups A, B and C for small group rehearsal purposes; the Uglies and stepmother together with the father and Buttons would make up one, the witches another, and so on. The Garrison Theatre had been booked for the reading on Monday, and the village hall for a reading on Thursday to encourage the villagers. Every time Claire checked the clock, Jo stepped in with a further suggestion, demanding attention, demanding concentration, just as she and Sally had decided.

At 10.35 the phone rang again. They both listened to the message. It was Clarissa, confirming that the celebration arrangements were bang on schedule; all that remained was for Claire to arrive, and the mayor, and the press.

Claire felt sick.

Jo pulled her back to the panto but then there was the sound of a car on the gravel and they watched Liz park next to Claire's Volvo. The sickness increased. Liz waved and pointed to the back door.

'Shall I?' Jo asked Claire.

175

'No, it must be me.' Jo was about to protest but Claire was already on her feet and had almost reached the back door when it opened and Liz entered. For a moment both women stood quite still, looking at one another. Then Liz touched her jazzy earrings, the ones she always wore for good luck purposes, and grinned. 'I ain't got a coach, you old slapper, so you'll have to make do with an old Citroën to rise up and take you to the ball. Well, for ball read playgroup.'

Claire kept her voice even. 'We're not having a coach and pony, we're having a Warrior.'

Liz smiled. 'Trust you to be different, but then it's common sense—horses bring you out in hives, don't they?' She grew serious. 'Always have, always will.'

Jo called from the sitting room, her voice tense. 'Time's getting on. We should be going, Claire. Is everything all right?'

Liz called, 'Everything's fine. Get her coat, there's a dear, Jo. I just need a quick word then. we'll tip the old bag into my car and whisk her away.'

Jo laughed with relief but Liz's attention was back on Claire. 'I'm sorry I let you down. I'm such a selfish idiot and I seldom think further than my own damn navel. I dump on you all the time and I felt slighted when I realized you hadn't done the same. I felt betrayed; all those letters from the sanatorium, all those carefully planned lies, the years of them, but then I'm a selfish tart who's a doctor and should have known better. But Claire, I'm here, if ever you need to talk.' She reached for Claire's hand, gripping it hard. 'Just remember that—I'm here. Sometimes it's best to talk about

176

things that have happened, to understand that *you* are not to blame. Do you understand me, Claire?'

Liz's hands were still gripping hers hard. Claire shook them slightly. 'But it was a stupid thing to do, turning her away. A cruel and foolish thing and there is nothing to talk about except that Anna is coming tomorrow, and that you are here.'

Jo called, 'We should go.'

Liz bit her lip. 'Talk to me, Claire, whenever you need to, about the past, and please remember that Anna will have been counselled to be ready for anything—even the truth.'

For a moment the two women looked at one another, and Liz thought she saw an acknowledgement of that truth in Claire's eyes, but then it was gone. Completely gone. Liz reiterated. 'I'm here, for you.' There was nothing else she could do.

Claire was brisk now. 'It'll be all right when I've got through this, and come to know Anna again. It'll be all right.' Liz's grip was still tight, so tight that she hurt. Claire said. 'Help me through this, and you can be Cinders.' Near them the central heating boiler cut out.

Liz smiled, laughed, relaxing her grip. 'What we need is a gin.' She quick-marched her friend back into the sitting room, frustrated, but Muriel had been right, Claire did keep her problems to herself and she had the right to do that, for as long as she could. But the mud had been stirred by Anna, and who knew if it would settle again or . . .

Claire protested, 'We haven't time for booze.'

Liz found the gin, longing for a drink herself but shoving one at Claire and Jo instead. 'Doctor's orders. Get that down you. I shall sacrifice my own personal pleasure and drive you both. You, however, Mrs Baird, owe me. Jo is a witness.'

Somehow they were all laughing, though it was a high, almost hysterical laugh.

Jo had slung Claire's coat over the sofa, and now downed the gin neat. Claire looked at the glass she held. 'Where's the tonic?'

'No time, and stop being picky.' Liz had grabbed the coat, and was guiding Claire's free arm into the sleeve. 'Come on, get on with it, change hands.'

Claire did so and felt Liz guide her arm down the second sleeve and it was almost like being a child again when the sun shone, and the sea was for paddling and the sand for buckets and spades. She felt a tremble begin, but caught it before it could grow.

Liz let Claire lead the way to the Citroën, catching hold of Jo's arm, whispering, 'How's the temperature on the patch?'

'Bit dodgy—a lot of curiosity, some shock, some giggling—the usual sort of thing. Some are disappointed in her, feel she's let them down. If Mollie hadn't got the denial going round at top speed it would have been fine. I have to say there's been a bit of bad-mouthing.'

Liz hurried to the driver's seat as Jo climbed into the back. She reversed too fast as always, but this time Claire relished her friend's driving, the normality of it making her feel safe.

*　　　*　　　*

Bunting hung outside the Coffee Shop, and inside children milled in the play area whilst their mothers sat at tables, and others stood along the side and in every other available space. There was a momentary hush as Claire entered, flanked by Jo and Liz. Rob hurried over from the dais that had been set up, squeezing his way between the women, apologizing until he reached Claire. 'We'll wait at the entrance for Sid.' His smile was wide and Sally waved from behind the lectern where she was setting up a jug of water. Claire looked round at the wives. Many avoided her eyes and shuffled, but at that moment the mayor arrived, in his official car.

'Good old Sid Harris, he's pulling out all the stops,' Liz murmured, opening the door as he stepped on to the pavement, his chain glinting in the sunlight. She mused: 'You know, he really should be in the panto, preferably a Dame. He so loves dressing up.'

Standing next to her, Claire smiled. 'I'm glad you're back.'

Liz's grin faltered, and her eyes filled. She turned quickly away and now Claire felt her own throat thicken, but at that moment Sid swept in. 'Good morning, Your Worship,' Rob called as the children crowded around.

'Don't be so daft, Rob,' the mayor muttered. 'Sid'll do.'

He thrust out his hand towards Claire. 'Nice to see you again, m'dear. I have to say this is one of my more pleasant duties, and I hope you feel the same way about the bazaar, not to mention the fashion parade.'

The children were getting noisier, but the wives were still subdued as they parted to allow Liz and the mayor through. Claire kept talking, pointing out the new fireworks frieze, much of which

Clarissa had overseen this week. As they stepped on to the dais it was as though she saw faces quite clearly for the first time since she arrived, for now no one seemed shy of facing her, and all of them seemed like strangers.

She heard Sid ask Rob if the press had arrived. They had not, and Clarissa exchanged a glance with Claire. 'Start then, for God's sake,' Clarissa muttered.

Liz tapped her on the arm. 'No hurry,' she said loud enough for Claire to hear. 'I've a feeling they've been told it's cancelled.'

Claire knew that look of old and relaxed, knowing that no press would come. Liz had seen to that and again her poise was almost broken.

Rob introduced the mayor, who praised the efforts of them all, before taking the bouquet presented to him by Barry Nichols aged three and three-quarters, and Amanda Berry aged three and a half.

Though the women had listened, their eyes kept flicking to Claire. The mayor now stepped back to stand next to Rob.

As Claire delved into her pocket for the notes she had made there was activity at either side of the dais, and as she moved to the front the whole of the steering and Wives Club committees, including Mollie and Jean, crammed on to the platform behind her in support.

The roller-coaster of emotion took off again in Claire and she cleared her throat, lifted her eyes from her notes and somehow spoke of the hearty efforts made by everyone to set up the playgroup, of the support the playgroup gave their children, and of the few precious hours of freedom it gave to

180

the wives.

She talked of the need for mutual support, of the help the Mother and Toddler Group gave in that area, and the gratitude she felt to the volunteers, and to those involved in the Neighbourhood Network. She urged that this fellowship and support should extend to the whole patch, from neighbour to neighbour, especially now the Options for Change had brought extra pressures, not to mention Bosnia. 'We need to be alert to those who might not come forward but are in need of support. The biggest weapon we have to combat loneliness is one another.'

She spoke of the pantomime and the fun it would be, and the boost it would give the Bosnia Fund. She paused and saw a movement to the left as Bridget Murphy readied her son Johnny to present the bouquet. She continued quickly: 'While I am here I have to tell you that I'm also in need of your support.' Behind she heard Rob whispering to Sid, and then Sid's deeper voice. 'Really.' The surprise was evident.

She went on, stuffing her notes into her pocket. 'I had a daughter twenty-five years ago. In accordance with the practice of the time, she was adopted. A few nights ago she did me the great honour of finding me.' She stopped, unable to go on for a moment. As she stared helplessly out across the crowd she saw Audrey Wilt whose husband had lost his binoculars. Young Audrey's gaze didn't flick away from her; instead it beamed encouragement. Cheered, Claire began again. 'My daughter came and because I had not yet opened her letter of warning I was so shocked I mishandled the situation. We have since contacted one another,

181

and she is coming back tomorrow. What I did was inexcusable but I want you to know that I'm back on course, that I'm here for you all, just as much as I ever was.'

She stepped back, and from behind came applause, which was taken up by the wives and the children. Johnny, aged three and eight months, brought on his flowers and she kissed him, and buried her face in the chrysanthemums just as Corporal Staines's wife took a photograph for the *Army Wives Journal*. 'Mrs Baird, I need a full frontal.' Claire smiled at her, as laughter broke out. The flash went again and everyone left the dais, including Claire, who handed the bouquet to Liz, before threading her way through the crowd towards Audrey Wilt.

As she arrived a voice from behind Audrey said quite clearly, 'I don't care how you wrap it, she shouldn't be here, swanning round our kids, when she turned her own away.'

As Claire stalled, Audrey turned, her child on her left hip, and hissed, 'Why don't you put a sock in it, Angie Neaves. You heard her. We all make mistakes, and you've made a bloody bucketful.'

Suddenly Sally was with Claire, then passing her. She reached Audrey and the other young woman, whose voice was ugly as she responded: 'Well, look who's talking. Binoculars, wasn't it. I thought you were going, couldn't hack it.' Around them other wives were murmuring to one another.

As Sally led Angie Neaves to one side, Claire remembered how Angie had been christened Turbogob by the Mother and Toddler Group when she first started coming. Audrey's face was red and shiny as Claire said quietly, 'Thank you, but please

182

don't get involved. You've more than enough to cope with.'

Audrey shrugged, hoisting Julie on to her other hip. 'You can't help getting involved with her, she's got such a mouth on her they could run a train through it.' Another young wife, Annie Bates whose husband had had the slight shrapnel wound, added her agreement, but from somewhere further back Claire heard 'She's got a point, that Turbogob has, you know.'

Rob was beside Claire now. He said loudly, 'Sorry to rush you off, Claire, but we're already late for the meeting.'

She looked askance, then caught his whisper as he led her to the door. 'Come on, strategic withdrawal, let them have their gossip and it'll all be flushed away by tomorrow.'

Jo was heading firmly towards Sally, talking swiftly, leading Turbogob to a table. Rob urged Claire out of the door. 'Jo sees potential in Turbogob's voice—she'd make an excellent 'Orrible Oracle, and we'd rather have her on our side than not. Besides, learning the lines will keep her busy.'

Liz caught up with them outside. Chatting away, she walked towards the car, her arm linked in Claire's, the scent of the russet chrysanthemums she still carried evocative of peaceful autumns.

'I'm not an invalid,' Claire reminded her.

'I know that, I'm the doctor, remember. I'm just going to order you to take time, all the time you need to get to know Anna. All the time you need to adjust, isn't that right Rob?' Rob had taken the keys from Liz and was unlocking the Citroën for them. He nodded. 'You've built up a good team.

183

Use it.'

Liz walked with Claire to the passenger's door. 'Just a couple more things. Remember I'm here for you, always.' She handed over the bouquet, touching the petals, saying quietly, 'I never saw a photo.' She pulled back, her voice insistent. 'Mark will be home before you know it and until then you're not alone. You'll never be alone again whatever happens. It's Saturday, talk to him when he rings. Talk to him, Claire. Now let's get home.'

Claire ignored the meaning in her voice, though suddenly found she was clutching the flowers too tightly.

*   *   *

On Sunday morning Anna drove through the patch. It was easier in the daylight and was shabbier than she had first thought. All these rows of similar houses. All these women walking along with kids, or just kids cycling or skateboarding, and so few men, if any. For the first time the reality of the army situation dawned on her.

At a T junction she stopped, looked both ways, turned left and all the time her confidence was ebbing. This was another world aeons from her own and she, Anna Weaver, had burst her way into it. She took a right turn at the phone box, and then the next left. Claire's house came into view. It was on its own, just beyond a street of big neat houses and in daylight the hedge was clearly beech, the lines of the house were sharper, its bricks surprisingly red. She felt the wetness of the laurel, remembered the awful stupidity of her actions, Claire Baird's desperation, her shock, the other

184

women. 'How could I?' she murmured. 'How could I have done anything so stupid, so cruel.'

She drew the car into the side of the road and sat motionless. Perhaps she should turn back? Perhaps she should never have contacted the adoption agency?

As she stared at the house a figure appeared and set off up the drive, coming to a halt at the entrance. It was Claire Baird and she was waving to her, to Anna her daughter.

*   *   *

Claire waited for Anna to approach, glancing quickly at Liz's house, nodding slightly to the figure who watched from the bedroom. It was Liz who had phoned to tell her Anna had drawn up near the house asking, 'Shall I go out to her?' Claire had replied, 'No, I will,' her heart thumping at the news, because her daughter was late, and she had thought she might not come after all, and she hadn't known whether to be heartbroken or relieved.

Claire watched as Anna flashed her lights. She returned to the house, hearing the crunch of gravel as the car crept along behind her. She thought her heart would burst out of her chest as she waited by the laurel for Anna to park but before Anna did so she wound down the window and called: 'Does it matter where?'

'Anywhere, but if you back towards the garage you'll be facing the right way when you come to leave.' Claire stopped. Oh God, she was talking of leaving the moment Anna had arrived. She stammered, 'I mean, if it makes it any easier for

185

you. It's what I usually say to guests ...' She stopped again. 'I mean ... of course you're not a guest ...'

Anna smiled. 'I know what you mean.' Her voice was calm, certain. 'I'll back, then.' Claire nodded, her heart still thudding somewhere in her throat, as Anna backed, stopped, took her foot off the clutch before she had disengaged the gears. The car kangaroo jumped, stalled. There was silence.

The car door opened, and Anna got out, slammed it shut. Claire walked to meet her, her eyes never leaving her daughter, her daughter's never leaving her. Within touching distance they stopped. Anna half smiled and looked away, then back again, at the ground. She slapped her raincoat pockets. Her keys were still in her hand. She said, her voice shaking, 'Sorry about the stall. Bit nervous.'

In the daylight her daughter was so familiar, so like Leah, so beautiful though her hair was much shorter and a bit lighter, Claire's colour. She wouldn't think about the eyes. Claire pressed her throat, trying to get words past the crazy pulse. In the distance she heard the revving of a car, the laughter of a child.

At last she spoke. 'I'm so glad you came. So very, very glad.' Tentatively she reached out and took her daughter's hands and kissed her cheek. Anna allowed her to do so, and again there was the scent of apple, but it was from her hair—so it was shampoo, not perfume. She felt the softness of her daughter's skin. Anna stood passively, but squeezed her hands as Claire drew back, whispering, 'I'm really so glad I'm here.'

For a moment they stood like that, but then a car

backfired in the road outside and the moment passed, and both women half smiled, and turned to walk side by side into the house. In the hall Claire took her daughter's coat, listening to the cadence of Anna's voice as she explained that the traffic had been hopeless, and the time had ticked away, and though it did not have the cultured accent of Leah's, underneath it was the same.

She stepped back from the coat rack and smiled though it felt as if her heart was in a vice. 'Yes, traffic is the one thing it's difficult to predict,' she agreed, though what she wanted to say was how she had missed her, how she had never stopped loving her, how she could hardly bear to be faced with the stranger that the years had made of the baby she had borne.

She led Anna towards the kitchen. Anna saw the mirror. 'That's stunning,' she said.

Claire smiled at Anna's reflection. 'My husband chose it. He'll be delighted you approve.' What she wanted to say was, it's you who are stunning, and somehow I must protect you.

The phone rang as Claire ushered her daughter into the kitchen. Anna stopped. Claire said, 'No, no, don't worry. It rings incessantly and the answer machine will cope. Coffee?' She listened, however, in case it was the headmistress, though the deputy head had said that if she did not return her call before midday it would be the evening.

Leah had told her that she would not be coming home this Sunday after all because of a hockey match but Claire knew very well that Leah loathed hockey and made it her life's work to avoid it. She wanted to ask the headmistress to support her daughter, to phone the moment Leah seemed

187

unhappy, the moment she might want to become a day pupil, though this morning she had refused the offer. She wanted to make everything all right for her again.

She also listened in case it was Mark, for he had not rung as he always did on a Saturday evening; but then why should he, when they had spoken so recently? No reason, absolutely no reason, and she had told herself that it was absurd to expect it of him under the circumstances.

In the kitchen Anna leaned on the breakfast bar while Claire boiled the kettle for the fourth time since 11.15, Anna's expected time of arrival. It was now nearly midday, but it had been the traffic, that was all, not second thoughts. Claire poured the water into the cafetière. 'Belle, Mark's mother, sends this coffee over from Italy where she has a vineyard. It's delicious of course, but a pain to squidge down.' The words were banal, but what else did one say?

She carried the tray through into the sitting room. 'Do take the sofa, Anna. Leah likes it best, says it's the most comfortable of the lot.'

Anna took the sofa and sat upright. Claire sat adjacent in the armchair and poured coffee. 'Cream?'

'Yes, but no sugar.'

How many mothers did not know whether their daughters took cream? Claire passed the mug to Anna. Or should she have used the best cups? Would her daughter feel slighted? Her daughter. This woman sitting here was her daughter. Claire still couldn't believe that any of this was happening.

Anna clutched the mug with both hands. The steam rose. Claire sat back and now there was only

188

awkwardness between them, a silence that ached. She rubbed her forehead. What did one say when there was so much to say? What were the rules? But there were no rules.

They both spoke together, Anna remarking on the sofa, Claire remembering that Anna's hair had been fair. They both fell silent. 'You go on,' Anna said. 'No, please, you first,' Claire insisted.

Anna ducked her head and stared at her coffee. 'I like the sofa. Mine's whitish too, matches the cat.'

Claire half laughed. 'We'd like a cat, Leah and I, but it would mean quarantine when we're posted abroad. Leah's sorry she can't be here today, she has a hockey match.'

Again there was a silence. Again they both started to speak together, but this time Anna rollered on. 'How is your husband getting on in Bosnia?'

'As well as can be expected, I think is all that can be said. It's a bit of a mess, really.' There was a pause, then Claire continued as Anna sipped her coffee: 'Much like the pig's ear I've made of all of this.' There, it was said. Anna placed her coffee on the table in front of the sofa and looked at her hands which were clasped together. 'I'm sorry, Mrs Baird, it's not your fault, I did it all wrong.' Now she was looking at Claire. 'It all happened too quickly when it happened, if you know what I mean.

Claire leaned forward, her voice urgent. 'I know exactly what you mean, and it wasn't your fault. I want you to understand that absolutely. Nothing of this is your fault.' Mrs Baird. She called me Mrs Baird. Her coffee slopped but she ignored it,

189

though Anna didn't. She drew a clean tissue from her sleeve and passed it to Claire, who half laughed. 'How unlike your sister you are, she never has a tissue when she needs it. And please, if you can't call me Mum, call me Claire.'

As Claire dabbed at her skirt, Anna thought as she had done that dark night how much smaller her mother had looked than on the television. Now however she could also see how good her skin was, much like her own. How fine her hands, again much like her own. Her other mother was stockier, her skin a different tone. It was all too much. The confusion was too much.

Behind on the old oak side table were photographs. She hurried over to them, wanting to be in the clifftop cottage, but wanting to be here too. She stood staring at the photos for a moment, trying to get a grip, but suddenly rage shook her, rage at this woman who had given her away, who had left her with the feeling that something was missing, that although she loved her parents she didn't really *belong* to them, that somewhere there was a past, a place in which she could set herself, somewhere there was a woman as slight as she, a woman . . .

She picked up two photographs, each of an elderly couple. Claire's voice followed her, pointing out Mark's parents, her own. Anna examined the one of Claire's parents and now the rage was ebbing, as she saw herself in the elderly man. This was her past, this was who she was, all this. Her voice was quiet as she asked, 'Are they still alive? Would they meet me?'

'Sadly no, they died some years ago. Your grandfather first, then your grandmother. But yes,

190

they would have met you and loved you.'

Anna was facing away and could not see the lie in Claire's eyes, or detect it in her voice, for though her father would have, her mother would not. Anna was evidence of the disgrace Claire had brought upon the family.

Carefully Anna replaced the sombre figures in the silver frame, hearing Claire say, 'Leah is in the one next to it, with her father.' Anna stared at the child who was so like her, except for the eyes and perhaps the chin.

She looked again at the photograph of Mark's parents, and Mark himself, not turning. 'Colonel Baird isn't my father, then? I thought perhaps he was, that his mum or dad had my eyes. I've been taping him, looking, just in case.'

Claire's voice was calm, slightly detached as she said, 'No, he's not your father.'

Anna came back to the sofa and sat down, leaning back now, her eyes fixed on Claire, her eagerness obvious. 'Who was then?'

Claire's coffee was cooling on the table, and she reached for it, holding it carefully. 'I was seventeen and he was a bit older.'

Anna waited as Claire paused, then continued in a rush. 'He had just finished law school. His name was Adam.'

Anna shook her head slightly. Her father was a solicitor. A solicitor with dark eyes. She'd been interested in doing law at school, but hairdressing had been more sensible, with the salon there and all that. Yes, that fitted, that really fitted.

She said, 'Was he nice? Why didn't you marry him? Why did you . . .' She wanted to ask that question, but faced by this woman who looked

191

tired, and strained, and so like her, she couldn't.

Claire searched her daughter's face, seeing the tension, the fearful expectancy and said what she'd prepared. 'Yes, he was nice but he went to Australia. We were . . .' she hesitated, 'foolish at a farewell party for him and he was long gone by the time I knew I was pregnant and he didn't contact me once he was there. There was no reason for him to. We weren't a couple, just two young people attracted to one another and swept away by the moment. The whole family emigrated, you see.'

Anna was nodding slowly, sinking back into the sofa, almost laughing in her relief. 'I'm so glad. It sounds silly but I didn't know it would matter so much. You see, the counsellor said I must be ready for anything, but I was hoping it'd be OK, that there wasn't something . . . D'you know what I mean?'

Claire affirmed, 'He was OK.'

Anna leaned forward, still wanting to ask the question, needing to. 'But that must have been hard for you. All alone when you found out, and him not there. That's why you had me adopted, is it?' There, she'd said it. 'Couldn't you have kept me?'

Claire's coffee was too cold to drink. She replaced it on the tray, her hands trembling. 'If it had been today, I could have kept you, it would have been so much easier.' There was momentary contempt in Anna's eyes and Claire shook her head. 'No, no, not just for me, but for you too. Please understand that to give you up for adoption was the only course for girls like me. We weren't considered "appropriate". The life we could give our children would not have been "appropriate".

192

You would have been branded in a thousand little ways. You see, girls who got into trouble were seen as unclean and unfit to be mothers. The only way we could pay our dues was to give our children a chance away from us, free of the taint of us, whatever it cost in terms of our anguish.'

Anna was staring at Claire's hands, which twisted and pulled at her skirt, just as her words tore into Anna's life. She wanted to put up a hand to stop her, but half of her wanted her mother to suffer because it proved that there had once been love, when now there was . . . Well, what was there? It was almost too much, too strange, too many doors were opening.

Claire had fallen silent; her hands were still. Anna wanted to leave, wanted to stay, wanted her mother. Not this one, but the real one, the one whose every gesture she knew, the one who had cottage furniture, not this large stuff, with a gilt mirror in the hall chosen by a man she didn't know.

Claire was speaking. 'Your mother was kind to me. She sent a photograph of you at three months. It's upstairs, in my special box. I wrote asking her never to send me any more, though I was so grateful for that one. I couldn't bear it, you see. I knew I couldn't bear to see you at one year, two years; growing up without me. I told myself I must let the memory of you fade, allow my grief to die. But you have never faded and it has never died.' She whispered: 'It must sound absurd but whenever there has been a train crash, a plane disaster, anything, I have wondered if it involved you, and even if it did, I knew I would never know. I had no right to know.'

The ensuing silence lasted for several minutes

193

but eventually Claire roused herself and noticed that Anna's coffee was untouched. 'You don't like coffee, do you? You'd prefer tea, wouldn't you? You should have said.' Claire was gathering up the mugs.

Anna walked with her to the kitchen. 'I didn't like to.'

As Claire filled the kettle she closed her eyes. Oh God, oh God, I didn't even know that my own daughter prefers tea. Plugging in the kettle she asked, 'Have you always wanted to find me?' The words had been in her head, she hadn't meant them to spill out, but there they were now, out there hanging between them.

'Only recently, really.' It sounded bald, almost heartless and Claire shrank a little inside, but Anna was unaware as she told of her own mother's adoption, which had probably helped establish total honesty and understanding in their home, of a curiosity which had not become a driving need until Anna's friend had married and borne a son. 'Seeing the grandparents at the christening I wanted to know who I was. I wanted to be able to set myself in that world, I wanted to know who my aunts and cousins were, my sisters and brothers. Where my people came from, you know?'

As Claire poured the water into the teapot Anna leaned on the breakfast bar just as Leah did, pulling at her lip. The water caught the rim of the teapot and splashed on Claire's hand. It stung and reddened her skin but it was something to focus on, something with which to steady herself as her daughter continued: 'My mum understands all of that. That's why she kept the name you gave me. Her own adoptive mother didn't and she felt the

194

new name took away part of herself. She kept the clothes you knitted me too.'

Claire put down the kettle abruptly, pressed her hand to her mouth, and walked to the sitting room and it was Anna who carried the tea tray to the table while Claire stood at the window with her back to the room.

Anna poured and placed the mug on the coaster in front of Claire's chair. 'I'm sorry, I shouldn't have gone on. Look, tea's up. Have a cuppa.'

Claire stayed by the window remembering the start of her grief. It was when she had gone into labour and knew that the process by which she would lose this baby had begun. This baby who had kicked and moved and been her companion—every minute of every day and night, this baby who had turned her hate into love, this baby who had made her strong in the face of her mother's contempt.

She said desperately to Anna, though still looking out at the shining day, 'I didn't want to lose you. I fought the labour. I tried to stop it happening but I couldn't even control that. You were born at eleven at night and were so beautiful, and it broke my heart. I held you. I made them give you to me, though they didn't want to. God what a fuss I made. Even then the doctor wouldn't talk directly to me, but informed me through the midwife that I might hold you for a moment before you were taken to the nursery, careful to remind me in words of one syllable that I must not ever forget that in six weeks you would be gone.'

Anna lifted Claire's mug and held it up to her. 'Please, Claire, you don't have to.'

Claire gestured the tea away, and Anna replaced it on the tray. Claire waited a moment before continuing, her voice little more than a monotone. 'But I do have to because I want you to understand how I longed to keep you. How very much I loved you, but how impossible it was, what a life of condemnation you would suffer because they considered you part of something sinful. How could I possibly inflict that on you? You know, not one single nurse said "congratulations", no one commented on your beauty, and you were so very beautiful. Your hair was fair then, your skin so perfect, your tiny fingers . . . No one phoned my parents, but that was normal. I had to write and get another girl from the home to post it.'

Now she turned, and at last saw a dawning understanding in Anna, a realization of the world as it was then. She whispered, 'But you must not think for a moment you were not loved. You were, so much.'

She told her then of her return to the home after the birth, of the nursery where the babies were placed, of the precious times between duties when she breast-fed though this was against the matron's wishes because it made it harder for the mother when the separation occurred. 'But I wanted to prove to you, young as you were, that you were as loved by your mother as any other baby was.'

'Duties?' Anna's voice was muted.

'Mine included scrubbing the back steps, and the laundry and kitchen floors.'

Anna was shocked. This woman scrubbing floors? 'Somehow I always thought of you as a colonel's wife, of someone with it all.'

'Please don't misunderstand, they were kind at the home. It was in Lancashire, by the way. As far from my home territory as my mother could

196

arrange. The contempt felt by the rest of the world didn't enter here. There was a ritual, a schedule by which we lived. It was comforting. It still is, though it drives my friends and family bonkers.' Claire laughed shakily.

Anna didn't, couldn't, because in her mind was a cradle in which she slept, and a mother who came to her, a mother who fed her and loved her. She wanted to examine Claire again, closely, to somehow picture the lost years which had separated her so completely from this stranger in whose belly she had been, in whose arms she had lain, who had loved her, but let her go. Could you *really* love someone and let them go?

Claire was still talking. 'We even had friends. We laughed together, joked, supported one another, but all the time we knew what was going to happen.'

'Are they still your friends?' Her voice was little more than a whisper.

'No. Any continuing friendship would have brought too much along with it.' Claire was still by the window, still needing to see the trees, the sky, the sun. There was puzzlement in her voice now. 'I was in the home six weeks before you were born and somehow I seemed to be outside myself, watching the days pass, but not really there.'

Anna said nothing, just reached for her tissue and wiped her eyes quickly, but Claire didn't see, she was concentrating on running her finger along the sill. Backwards and forwards, backwards and forwards, as though Anna wasn't there any more. Then she straightened and her voice became brisk. 'We were locked in at 6 p.m. Did they expect us to run riot with the local youth in our condition? We

197

used to laugh about it.' She had turned.

Anna smiled but it didn't reach her reddened eyes, any more than it reached Claire's. 'We wore Woolworth wedding rings and polished them on Saturday night to stop them looking tarnished when we went to church.' Now Claire really was smiling, almost laughing. 'We used to walk in a crocodile, all these girls waddling along, trying to time it so the congregation were settled before slipping in the back. The vicar liked us to leave before them too, lest we offend the delicate sensibilities of those who had not transgressed.' The laughter had not lasted.

'I would push your pram in the park. I would take you from the pram and hold you. Just hold you, thinking only of you, nothing else. We mothers ate at one big table. There were twelve of us. As people left we were moved one place closer to the head of the table, and had to move your cradles one place closer to the door so we could never forget that we had to live a lifetime with our babies in just six short weeks. I couldn't accept it. I bought *The Lady* and phoned for housekeeping jobs. None would take me, with you. It was a Sunday on the day I reached the head of the table and your cradle reached the door. The hymn that day in church was "The day thou gavest Lord, has ended".' Anna could hardly breathe as she listened. Claire's voice was high pitched and almost singsong, and it was a shock after the monotone which had preceded it.

'Your mother and father came for you on Tuesday, Anna. I didn't see them: at least I was spared that. All the girls were spared that. I dressed you in the matinée jacket and bonnet I had knitted. I'm not a knitter but how I worked on that

198

jacket, pulling it out, starting again, pulling out, and that was even before I reached the armholes.' Claire laughed suddenly. Anna too, and it was a real laugh from them both. They looked at one another in surprise. But that didn't last either because Claire had more to say, more to explain.

'I made up your feed because by now you were weaned but at least I'd done the best for you while I could. I placed you in the cot . . .' She stopped, swallowed, looked over at Anna whose clenched hands were in her lap. 'I placed you in the cot in Matron's office. I went into the grounds with the deputy matron. This was the routine, you see.' Claire checked that Anna understood, but why bother her with the detail? Because Anna must know as much as possible, however much it hurt Claire to remember.

'We walked. It was a late spring, the blossom was almost over, the new leaves were the palest green. It was still quite chilly so I was glad I'd knitted your bonnet.' Claire's voice was strained, almost hoarse, but it all had to be said, for the first time ever.

'The bell was rung, as it always was, to say the baby had gone and we could return. Your mother and father had taken you into their care. I walked back out of the sunlight into the darkness of the side passage. I entered the study. I had to see the cot. I had to see for myself that it was empty. It was, but there was still the sunken imprint of you on the mattress, your baby scent on the sheet. Matron allowed me to lift to my face and hold for a moment. She then took it from me, dragged it really, and led me to the door and up the stairs to the bedroom where I packed my case. I took a bus to the station. A train, and then another to my

199

home. They wouldn't let me keep the sheet but I had your wristband. I still have your wristband.' Claire pointed vaguely to the stairs. 'I still have your . . .' She could not go on.

The room was dreadfully quiet as Claire returned to her chair, lifted her mug and drank, as though she had been in a desert. All the time Anna stared at her as though memorizing every feature. Claire said, 'I thought I would never hear your voice, or see your smile.'

For a long while they sat quietly, as though both were exhausted. Eventually it was Anna who roused herself, thanking her mother, allowing herself to believe that her mother had loved her, but not sure what she, the daughter, now felt.

Throughout a lunch of moussaka which both only picked at, they talked of the years in between, building up a picture of each of their lives and however sketchy and anecdotal it served to build a bridge. It served to allow them to walk together around the garden, even laughing at the laurel bush. It served to allow Claire to kiss Anna farewell, though Anna still did not return it, because though this woman had loved her she had let her go. Though she declared she had missed her, grieved for her, thought of her each and every morning on waking, Claire had still turned her away when she came that night.

As she climbed into the car she knew that Claire was waiting for her to say she was coming again, but she didn't know whether she would. She didn't know anything, it was all too much and she wanted her mother, her real one. But then, that mother wasn't her real one, was she?

CHAPTER THIRTEEN

The Serbs were causing more chaos than usual in the northwest and Mark stared out at the refugees pouring along the road heading for Zenica, some with children dragging at their hands as they trudged along, some lucky ones riding on top of their heaped carts. As usual he felt furious, helpless, in fact a total fool, as Corporal Simms eased out, heading for the Refugee Centre in Travnik. As the Land Rover forced its way along their ranks, people turned towards the car, and many shouted, their faces contorted with desperation, grief and rage. Mark turned to Gordana, mortified. 'Translate for me, if you can pick out anything that makes sense, but I dare say an expletive will do.'

Impassively Gordana pointed to one youngish man. 'He says, *In the name of humanity, help us.*' She pointed to a mother carrying a baby, a shawl wrapped around both of them. 'She says, *You come, you stop nothing.*'

Mark looked back, checking that the rest of the patrol were with them. 'I think I've got the gist, thank you, Gordana.'

He settled back, resigning himself all over again to the sight of misery, to the frustration. Christ, they should be able to do *something*, but of course they were. They had loaned a medic and were now loaning an interpreter, Gordana, they were meeting with the Croats and the Muslims in Turbe, they were trying to negotiate another cross-line talk with the Serbs. Well, big deal.

The convoy was slowing to allow the press vehicles time to lock in behind them. Then they picked up as much speed as they could, weaving round the overloaded carts, the children who straggled out into the road, the old people with their belongings tied in bundles on their backs.

He asked Gordana for the briefings, wanting to look at something else, anything but the children, because Leah was there, trailing along a road with them and that awful feeling was back, that mixture he couldn't understand.

Wordlessly Gordana passed over her notes, saying, 'More Muslim refugees mean more tension, the Croats will feel even more swamped by us. The fighting between us will get worse.'

'Us?' He spun round. 'Us? Is all this going to be a problem for you? I need a professional here, not someone who's going to think of *them* and *us*.' He buried himself in his notes again.

Gordana's voice was icy as she raised it above the shouts of a large group of refugees. 'They are saying *Home, we have no home. You should go back to yours for you come with tanks and guns but never fire them*. There, am I not professional? Do I not earn my Deutschmarks? Do I not prepare the briefs you are now reading? Oh, no, it will not be a problem for me, Colonel Baird, so do not accuse me, do not fire at me, when you can't attack those you wish.'

Lance Corporal Simms took care to keep his eyes firmly fixed on the road, and a good job too, Mark thought, wiping his mouth with the back of his hand. He returned to the notes, reading these again and again until they were forced to a halt by a stalled aid convoy around which the refugees

202

clamoured.

As Mark and Gordana approached on foot with their backup they could hear the effing and blinding of the lorry drivers as the refugees banged on the sides,- or was it the Croat soldiers? Mark could see them now, close up to the lorries, not where they should be, at the roadblock.

He watched as they brandished their weapons and forced the refugees back with curses and blows. Gordana whispered as they continued their approach, 'Croats. Maybe on their way to the front line, maybe leaving or maybe they've just had enough of checkpoint duty. But there are too many for that.' She was listening hard. 'Yes, that's it. Some are on their way back and some of the checkpoint crew are joining them, they're alarmed by the refugees, they want to protect their own villages, and I think they do not want to go empty-handed.' Ahead of them more Croats, not refugees, barred the lead lorry's way.

Mark said. 'Well, they're not heading home with this aid, so they can get that thought right out of their bonces. Fall back. I'll lead.'

She fell back, just a pace, talking quietly, briefing him on the accents she recognized, identifying the regions, piecing things together quickly as they arrived at the lead lorry, hearing the convoy foreman yelling 'Don't mess with me, sunshine, or I'll have your arse in a sling.'

Panting up behind Mark came Charlie Bennet, the journalist, who mumbled, 'Man after my own heart.' Mark snapped over his shoulder, 'Shut up, Charlie, or I'll order you back. That's a Kalashnikov the guy's brandishing, unless you missed the damn thing.' Ahead of them was a

Croat soldier, clearly the leader, his Kalashnikov readied for action, his eyes on their every move, just as Mark's were on his.

'OK, squire,' Charlie wheezed, the cold air getting to his chest.

The convoy foreman leaned out of his cab window, his face pale with tiredness, his scarf riding up over his mouth and muffling his words, so that he yanked it down and yelled: 'The schedule's all shot to hell, it's bloody cold, and I'm trying to get this to Travnik to help poor buggers like these. Whose side are these stupid buggers on, for pity's sake?'

The refugees were crowding now, shouting, and tussling. Mark's men flanked him tightly as he approached the deserters and Gordana was at his elbow, translating as the young man with the Kalashnikov, his face strained and dirty, shouted at them, jerking his head towards the lorries, then back to his men.

Gordana translated, and it was what she had thought, that some of the Croats wanted the food, and to hell with what happened to those who were waiting at the end of the line. As she spoke she brought out her cigarettes, offered one to Mark who took it, though he didn't smoke it. She handed them round to the Croats. Behind him there was a sudden rush, and howls of anguish rose higher. Mark felt a shiver of anxiety run up his back. Now there were yells from the Croats alongside the lorries.

At that moment the Croat leader shouted, and gestured. Mark's men took up positions and he greeted the leader, his voice loud and insistent. Totic—for that was his name Gordana

204

murmured—kept his eyes on the mêlée and barely looked at Mark. Gordana spoke more severely and now he turned his full attention on them. 'What's all this about?' Mark asked.

His tone was sharp, forceful, uncompromising. All the time he maintained eye contact, all the time he leaned slightly forward, his chin up, forcing himself to appear totally calm, totally in control, sufficiently angry, but not too angry. It was all play-acting but what else could it be? Damn it, he should be in the women's panto for all the teeth he had.

He gestured at the refugees who were crowding closer, their shouts raucous. Tussles began between some of the Croats and the refugees as they were forced back. 'If you open the lorries it is these people who will have everything, not you. What would you do, fire into unarmed people?'

The Croats behind Totic were fingering their weapons, their eyes flicking from left to right, trying to keep everyone in their sights. Their nervousness was palpable. Totic, though, was calm, his eyes fixed on Mark's. He spat on the ground, and jerked his head to the clamouring crowds. 'So, what are a few more dead Muslims? Less to worry about later.'

Gordana translated this without emotion whilst Mark felt his own fury growing, a fury he contained with difficulty. He took a step forward, wanting to smash this man to the ground. He said, 'But *we're* between you and them and may I remind you of our rules of engagement. We need to be fired upon first, we need a clear sight of the perpetrators. I rather think we have that.' Gordana's voice was firm, still emotionless. It was as though she was invisible. It was just between the Croat and himself.

His men had heard and took pains to be obviously at the ready. In the pause that followed, his eyes held the Croats, the cold dug in, the noise of the refugees, the lorries and the wind seemed to grow. To his left Gordana talked to the man who stood a little way from Totic, hailing him as though he were an old friend, throwing him a packet of cigarettes which he caught with one hand. She spoke again. He answered and there was an eagerness in his voice which Mark heard, but still his eyes didn't waver.

He heard Gordana laugh, and speak again and it was almost as though she was gossiping at a coffee morning, here, where the tension was like an overstretched lifeline. But then her voice grew intimate, almost secretive. On the periphery of his vision Mark saw the soldier grow more attentive, thoughtful, defensive, and finally he put up his hand, cutting her off. She stepped back, while the soldier moved across and spoke urgently to Totic, whose eyes at last flickered from Mark's as he inclined towards his second-in-command.

Gordana whispered to Mark, 'I told him I know his area well. I told him we used to camp there in the height of the summer. I told him his village is a delight. I told him you are a strong man, one who does not hesitate. I told him that we will be talking to a commander who also knows his village, but maybe I could forget to pass on what we've just witnessed, if they all go home now to their mothers, their wives, their families.'

Mark kept his eyes on his protagonist, but nodded, hardly daring to believe that the situation could be resolved, hardly daring to believe that he

206

would not have his bluff called.

Quite suddenly Totic shrugged, his voice hoarse and angry. Gesticulating to the lorries, he called his men off. 'Shall I translate?' Gordana asked quietly, a glimmer of amusement in her eyes.

'As I said before, I get the gist, and thank you, Gordana.' This time his tone was grateful and as they had done at a previous roadblock they waited as the lorries revved past them and the mud splattered. This time Gordana did not step back on to the verge where mines might be, but stood her ground. 'See, I learn,' she said smiling.

'It takes us all a little time, including me.'

*   *   *

In Travnik Mark and his team passed shrapnel-scored buildings and rubble, conscious always of the Serbs overlooking the area from the mountainous Vlassic Feature. He craned his head and saw the skiing village they had taken as a headquarters and the TV tower perched high on the huge mountain. It seemed ironic to see the two together, but perhaps it summed up the whole damn thing.

Once at the Refugee Centre they hurried in and were caught up in a swarm of people pouring through the door. People who were tired and bewildered. Some were mute in their misery, some strident. Children cried. Mark grabbed Gordana's arm as an International Committee of the Red Cross representative with a clipboard made her way towards them. 'Look, over there.' Gordana waved at the woman but turned back to Mark, perturbed. 'But Jeremy isn't here. What if he
207

doesn't come? Who will handle the meeting?'

Mark pushed her into the flow as the ICRC girl held up her clipboard and waved it. He shouted after her, 'He'll come. Pick you up at 1500 hours.' Her reply was lost as Mark stood pinned against the wall, stunned by the noise, and the chaos, and the people. At his elbow was Charlie Bennet, silent for once.

He heard a shout, and at the same moment that Jeremy appeared Charlie dug him in the ribs. 'Sunshine and light is upon us, squire.'

Mark squeezed through the throng, heading towards the door. Outside he gulped in great lungfuls of fresh air, but only for a moment for immediately he and Jeremy and the convoy continued on to Turbe, a good seven kilometres away. 'And a bloody dangerous seven kilometres at that,' Mark grunted to Jeremy as the sounds of artillery and small arms fire grew louder and evidence of shell damage grew greater.

The Muslim commander in Turbe was tense—but what else could he be in the face of yet another sustained Serb attack?—and while the sound of war continued and dust trickled from the ceiling they discussed the pressure that the Serbs were putting on the north and ways of damping down the interracial tension, of the need to keep local troops under control, of the need, now more than ever, to keep the convoys rolling with winter coming, and all the time in the back of Mark's mind was the Refugee Centre, the stricken towns and villages, the pulverized hospitals. He put up his hand to refuse more slivovitz, but hell, he needed a drink. He tossed it down. If he smoked, he'd have needed a cigarette, he told Jeremy, who smiled, but it was a tight smile.

Back at Travnik they tackled the Croats but Mark did not finger the Croat deserters. Already briefed, Jeremy Baines looked at him in surprise and queried urgently, 'Sir?'

Mark insisted, his voice low, 'Move on, Jeremy. We'll leave out specifics. Miss Sevo gave her word and we will respect that. For heaven's sake, hers is a dangerous job at the best of times, we don't want anyone settling a score.' At this, Jeremy's surprise was even more marked.

By early afternoon they were back again at the Refugee Centre and while Jeremy slipped across to the surgery Mark waited in the lobby, pressed against the wall again. He checked his watch. He'd told Gordana 1500 hours and it was that now, for Pete's sake. He waited another ten minutes, then went in search of her, pushing his way through the milling throng, moving from one room to the next until he spotted her in the distance, across a large room. A room in which the stench of unwashed bodies was appalling.

There were beds and mattresses either side of the room, whole families sitting on them, or on the floor, shocked and tormented. Some were silent, some wept, some just talked incessantly.

As he made his way across to his interpreter he saw her sit on a mattress alongside an old man with a worn, exhausted white-stubbled face, down which tears streamed. In her hand was her notebook but she wrote little. Instead she put her arm around the thin bowed shoulders, murmuring—what? Words of comfort? Mark looked from left to right and saw the children. What comfort could anyone bring? He stared down at his uniform. God almighty, what

209

comfort could anyone bring?

He backed, then turned, forcing his way through groups, and over those who sat, forcing his way outside, hearing the mortars, sucking in the fresh air. Charlie Bennet said behind him, his voice weary and flat, 'I always come away thinking it's such a crazy stinking bloody business.'

*　　　*　　　*

Much later that day he toured all the messes at Vitez, chatting to his men, anxious about their morale, acknowledging their eternal frustration, letting them know that he shared it, but that they were here to do a job, and would do just that, and for now they must forget it, they must relax. He retired to the Ops Room where Ben was staring out of the window. Together they watched the flashes against the night sky and the dark shape of the Vlassic Feature in the distance. 'What a bloody mess,' Mark breathed.

Ben uncrossed his arms and said quietly, 'You've just been telling everyone else to switch off. Now it's your turn. Let's go to the mess.'

Mark had an image of the coffee and slivovitz, the mortars, the dust falling, and going to the mess seemed inappropriate. The radio nets were crackling, messages were coming in, but nothing dramatic. Mark said, 'So, Liz's partnership's in abeyance, that's good.'

Ben eased his foot, balancing on the walking stick he had progressed to. 'We've given ourselves until the end of R & R to think it over. Talking of R & R, I gather the wives have arranged the schedule so that your first night back is the last night

210

of the pantomime. Now you're not to go leaping on stage when they ask for kids to play the games.'

Mark smiled briefly. 'I'll try to contain myself.' He stared out at the sky and said what had been in his mind all day, dragging at him, turning him inside out. 'You know, I was looking at those kids on the road today, and at the Centre and I couldn't stop thinking of Leah, thinking how I'd never turn a kid of mine away.'

Ben was alarmed at the confusion in his friend's voice and said quietly, 'You don't know that, you haven't had it happen to you. She was shocked . . .'

Mark interrupted quietly. 'True, but does anyone ever really know anyone else?'

He was still looking out of the window, feeling lonely, distressed, off balance. Home seemed further away than ever.

Ben touched his arm. 'Come on, snap out of it, you'll be sitting on the mountain top meditating next. How's everything working out anyway?'

Mark rubbed his forehead as the radios burst into life, but again it was routine and only from Split, and as he thought of Gordana Sevo he felt sparked up, relieved. Jamming his hands in his pockets he said, 'Fine, just fine. Jeremy's got excellent recruitment skills. Gordana's exceptional, she keeps her head, wheels and deals. It's bloody amazing when you think what she's been through. She was even making notes in the Refugee Centre, I saw her at it. Quite incredible. The Intelligence Cell will be getting up-to-date information from her tomorrow, you mark my words.'

But Ben was just looking at him, waiting for him to finish. 'I meant, how's everything with Claire and her daughter?' he said.

211

CHAPTER FOURTEEN

As Claire heaved a box of fireworks into the boot of her car on a Friday afternoon two weeks later, Liz swished down the drive, hooting. She skidded to a stop outside the open garage, firing gravel in all directions. Claire slammed the boot. 'OK, where's the fire?' she queried, dusting off her hands.

Liz lowered her window and grinned. 'That little delight awaits us behind the recreation ground tomorrow night, doesn't it? Hopefully we have no guy and can perch Mollie or Turbogob on the bonfire. You're all set to light the wick of Rob's very biggest rocket, are you? Hey, that sounds as though Jo should include it in the script.'

Claire walked to her friend's car, leaned down and peered at Liz. 'Don't you dare mention wicks ever again, there was more than enough silliness concerning the subject on the Wives Club coach, thanks to you.'

Liz grimaced. 'Well, it was such a gruesome evening. I mean to say, Lower Bedley Amateur Dramatic Group's wild rush into *Showboat* is not my idea of a night out. Was there a sound eardrum left amongst the lot of us?'

Claire grinned. 'We are borrowing some of their sets for the panto, not to mention their sound-effect tapes, so, as panto stage manager, Barbs felt we simply had to. Anyway that cacophony was preferable to my experience on the trip back.'

Liz pulled even more of a face. Waving Claire aside, she clambered out. 'Yep, I saw Mollie nobble you.' Her wild red scarf almost but not quite clashed with her coat. The effect was wonderful. 'Come on, you can make me a coffee and tell me all about your *tête-à-tête*. By the way, how're you sleeping? You looked tired at the show, and you look no more rested this morning.'

The two women walked to the garage and squeezed down the side of the Volvo and into the kitchen. Claire shrugged out of her anorak, tossing it on to the table, and filled the kettle, raising her voice above the gushing water. 'I'm fine, just as I was when you asked two days ago, and two days before that, you wally. But OK, today I'm a bit fraught, though we can put that down to the effects of Mollie's "Muriel-induced virtuousness". Her "I'm here, lean on me" attitude at every given moment means the whole incident is still alive and kicking, instead of lying on the ground defeated.'

Liz spooned instant coffee into two mugs, her voice neutral. 'So no general sleep problems?' she repeated, taking in the dark circles under Claire's eyes, the deep lines around her mouth, and cursing Mark for not keeping to his phone schedule. Damn it, when he needed his routine everyone had to jump, but blow Claire. Couldn't he see that what she needed right now was support from all directions? Sure, it was busy out there, but come on.

Claire's voice was muffled as she reached into the fridge for the milk. 'No, no not at all, just lots of rushing around. I had to pick up the mayor's donation of fireworks after nipping straight from playgroup to support that kid from C Company who's leaving the marital home today.' She plonked the new carton of milk on the breakfast bar, tried

213

to tear it open, cursed, held out her hand to Liz. 'Scalpel,' she ordered.

Liz laughed and brought the scissors, saying, 'Remind me never to come to you for an operation.'

The women drank their coffee at the kitchen table, and running her finger round the top of the mug Claire mused, 'Poor little kid, the one from C Company. There she was, her friend with her, the kids at a neighbour's, waiting for the Marchout. God, as though it's not bad enough making that sort of decision without having that lot running their fingers round the back of the oven and working out how much they're going to fine you.'

Liz pressed Claire again. 'Enough about everyone else. How are things going? Do you need to talk?'

Claire smiled tiredly. 'What d'you want to hear?' She ticked off her fingers as she continued. 'The C I achieved for my History essay, the long face the English lecturer pulled when he tried unsuccessfully to talk me yet again into continuing his subject, the leaves we painted in playgroup this morning, the visits I've made to problems on patch, the mayor's fashion show which we're rehearsing, the mayor's bazaar, the panto costume department under the umbrellaship of the illustrious Mollie, who quotes her WI experience at every given opportunity? Pay your money and take your pick, Liz.' Suddenly the smile was gone. She looked at Liz and knew she was waiting, and before she could stop the words were coming, different words, a different world, a different voice, one that was slow, feeling its way.

'You see, I've got so much swishing around in

214

me. Here's my daughter, back again. She phones me, we talk, we fill in gaps and I have this great well of joy. It hurts, Liz.' She was clutching her chest. 'I feel I could burst. I feel I want to take days and days just to think and feel and hold that to me. She's here, my child is here and she wants to know me, she doesn't hate me. My child is back . . .' The phone rang and Claire slammed her hand down on the table. 'Then that happens, or the door goes, or dawn comes and life gets going again. There's no space, no time to feel, to hold it, sort it out, for more than a split second.'

Liz reached across and covered her hand as the answer machine coped. 'Make the time, go AWOL.' Claire just shook her head once, because both of them knew it didn't work like that. Liz sat back. 'I wish I could do more.'

'You're here, that's everything.' The phone rang again and they looked at one another and groaned, and Claire heard herself laugh, but not inside. She watched Liz peering into her coffee, grimacing, stirring, and the bubbles collected in the centre. Absently Claire listened to Sally's message, but then Liz was speaking over it. 'So, it's the big meeting between Leah and Anna tonight, is it?'

The bubbles clumped, Liz licked her spoon but even these familiar habits couldn't calm Claire's rush of nerves. She strove to sound calm. 'Yes. I pick Leah up at six from the station so I'll tote your girls home too.'

Liz shook her head saying firmly, while Claire finished her coffee, 'Nope. I'll pick them up while you create miracles with soya. I gather Leah's gone veggie.' She tapped her spoon on the mug. 'Are you nervous? I would be. But then she seemed keen,

215

didn't she?'

'Yes, she said she was looking forward to it. I just hope . . . I just want them to like one another but that sounds so damn silly, doesn't it? Please will you two sisters like one another.'

'It sounds pretty normal to me. Well, normal in the circumstances, that is. But talking of circumstances, Claire, *things* are bound to get stirred up. You must be prepared for that.' Her voice was full of meaning.

Claire took the mugs to the dishwasher holding them too tight, wanting to tell her to stop, she'd had enough now, she must leave it alone, stop reminding her. She said instead, 'I'm fine, the only problem is space.' Claire shut the dishwasher door and faced Liz. 'Anyway I've bored you with all this before.'

Liz was smiling, but there was still a question in her eyes. Claire put the coffee jar away, her mind racing: she could hear the sea, and sense the darkness.

Liz looked at the clock and stood up. She wanted the dark circles to go, the past to disappear, she wanted her friend's biggest concern to really be whether her two daughters became sisters.

But all she said was, 'No reason why they shouldn't grow together. As I say, I'll pick them up, and on the way back gee them up about the Youth Club dance rehearsal on Sunday. The message I've come hot-foot to bring you is that the choreography is finished. Captain Jenkins's wife, Zoë, has done a belting job, you know. She says she was a dance teacher, but judging from those hip thrusts she showed us at the audition the other night, I have my doubts. I can see her in the buff,

216

draped in a couple of diaphanous veils, gyrating . . .' Claire forced a laugh, and tossed a tea towel at her. 'Rubbish.'

Liz shook her head sorrowfully. 'I dare say you're right, but it would be so much more exciting.' She opened the back door. 'See you later.'

Claire put out her hand to catch her attention. 'Let me fetch the girls as arranged. I want Leah to understand that nothing has altered between us, that she is still my very precious daughter.' Yes, she would concentrate on that because nothing was more important, and with that thought she grew strong again.

                    *   *   *

At 5.30, when Claire was just about to leave for the station, the phone rang and she let the answer machine click in. Dragging on her gloves, she was already halfway to the back door but at the sound of Leah's voice she rushed back, and picked up the receiver.

'Was the train early? I'm on my way.' Claire was about to put the receiver down when Leah blurted, 'That's why I'm ringing. You see I won't be at the station, I'm at Natasha's instead.'

Claire couldn't quite grasp what Leah was saying. 'What?' she said. 'What?'

Leah's voice was rude and defensive. 'I'm at Natasha's, she's invited me to a party. She needs my help.'

Claire slammed her handbag down. 'How dare you go to a friend's house just like that, without asking permission? How dare you, Leah?'

217

'Oh Mum, don't make a fuss.'

'And don't you dare speak to me like that. It's your exeat, the school had no right to let you go off with someone else. You had no right. You always come home. I've been looking forward to it and you know very well Anna is leaving early on her busiest day. She's been looking forward to it. I've—'

'Don't hassle me, Mum,' Leah interrupted, her voice quiet, urgent. 'For heaven's sake, it's only a weekend.'

Claire closed her eyes, picturing her daughter cupping her hand over the mouthpiece, not wanting Natasha to know she had not asked permission, not wanting Natasha's parents to know. But damn it, the mother should have contacted her, what was the matter with the woman? She tried to picture Natasha, and groped towards a girl with black permed hair and ridiculously slim figure. Leah repeated, her voice even lower, 'Don't hassle, Mum.'

Claire spoke slowly, trying to beat back the anger and disappointment. 'Leah, I'm not hassling, but there are some things you don't do, and going to someone else's house at exeat is one of them. I want to see you, don't you understand?'

'Oh Mum, that's emotional blackmail. Look it's only a party . . .'

Claire interrupted her. 'Leah, if it's because Anna's coming I'll phone her, put her off. This is *your* home. I only asked her because you said you wanted to meet her when I took you for lunch last Sunday. Leah, you'll miss the run-through of the dance. Sarah and Louise are coming home too.' She checked her watch. God, she needed to leave,

218

or phone Liz. 'Look, let me speak to Mrs Markham.'

Leah's whisper was frantic. 'Mum, don't do this to me. Natasha needs my help, I told Mrs Markham you'd agreed. Look, I've changed my mind, can't you see that, I just don't want to meet Anna, I don't want to come back to the patch. I don't want to walk into the Youth Club and hear everyone tittering, I just want to get away from it all for a bit. Let the others come home and if it's calmed down like you say then it'll shut Mollie's girls up, and I'll meet Anna some other time. Mum, are you listening? Mum?'

Claire nodded slowly to herself, her heart sinking as guilt and pity competed, then joined forces, defeating her, and her voice was subdued as she said, 'Yes, I'm listening, Leah, and I do understand. Believe me, darling, it has quietened down. It really has, I thought I'd made you realize that last Sunday, but put Mrs Markham on, quickly. I won't say anything, I'll just thank her.'

Claire's hand was shaking as she replaced the receiver. She wanted to cry, to hurl the phone at the wall, to walk away because now there was all this when, Goddamn it, there wasn't even enough time to sort herself. She leaned back against the wall, pressing her hand to her mouth, harder. Shut up, shut up. The tears came and they were for them all, but the blame in the end was directed at herself.

*　　　*　　　*

Claire drove to the station to collect Liz's girls since that was quicker than phoning Liz who would

219

have to rush around finding her car keys. The train had been on time, and Sarah and Louise were just about to find their way to the phone box to check up on the lift situation when Claire swung into the car park and pulled up sharply outside the station entrance.

The girls slung their grips into the boot. 'Don't slam,' called Claire automatically but they already had. Quickly they slid into the back seat, leaning forward and tapping her lightly on the head as they always did. 'Hi, Aunt Claire, got the message from the idiot daughter, did you?'

As they clicked themselves into their belts, Claire checked the rear mirror and drove out of the car park. 'Indeed I did, some party. Obviously a bit of talent on display.'

The girls laughed, relieved because they had been prepared to be embarrassed by an Aunt Claire who had somehow changed, who had become this person who was not quite who they'd always known, someone who'd been proved to have had sex, who had transgressed, who was a person with a past, not just their mother's friend.

Claire let them chat away in the back, responding when required, laughing too, telling them of the dance rehearsal on Sunday, her voice almost normal until she dropped them outside their house, driving on straight away to her own, waiting by the phone, which she knew would ring once the girls told Liz.

It rang. She picked it up. It was a patch problem. She sorted it. It rang again. Liz said without preamble, 'The little trollop.'

Claire said quietly, 'Not really, there's still talk at school, though I thought it had blown over.'

Liz snapped, 'Sarah tells me it's only Mollie's girls, the delightful Monica and Deborah, so after this weekend that should be sorted out by the virtuous one. If not, we'll set Muriel on to them. Meanwhile, back at the ranch, you and Anna will come to supper with us, it's only pizza, but loads of it. Bring a bottle, then the grown-ups can get pickled while Sarah and Louise go to the club, and get hauled over the choreographic tiles by Zoë Jenkins.'

*   *   *

When Anna arrived, Claire met her in the drive, her coat already on, a bottle under her arm, totally in control. 'Park anywhere,' she called. Anna parked where she had before, and again walked towards her mother, but this time their hours of talking had eased the way. This time, when Claire reached forward Anna leaned into the kiss. Again there was the scent of shampoo. Again Anna did not hold her mother but her smile was warm in the light from the porch lamp as Claire stood back.

'How are you, Claire?' Anna asked. Her voice was firm, confident and warm.

'Disappointed, I'm afraid. At the last minute Leah felt she had to go to Natasha's house.' She explained that Natasha was a friend whose birthday it was, a birthday that required a party, a party that required Leah. 'She's very disappointed not to be here.'

Anna wasn't looking at Claire, but at the ground between them. Claire reiterated. 'She really is very disappointed.'

Anna was laughing as she at last met Claire's

eyes. 'I remember that, don't you, being asked to a party, knowing there was a boy you really wanted to see, and having to give it up because the relatives are coming. Hey, I don't mind, but you must, and I'm sorry for that.'

Claire didn't remember. She'd had no boyfriend before Mark, except . . .

She blocked out the thought, and pointed towards Liz's house. 'We're having our own small party. You really should meet Liz, I love her very much.' Her voice sounded strained to her own ears but Anna seemed to notice nothing, and together they walked towards the brightly lit house.

Supper was laid in the dining room. Liz placed Sarah and Louise next to one another, Claire and Anna opposite. She herself sat at the end next to Claire, pouring mineral water for Anna, who had to drive, and wine for Claire and herself. 'Because, glory be, we have not,' Liz crowed, holding her glass up towards Claire and Anna. 'To you two.'

'That's not fair,' Sarah chimed in. 'We want to toast them, and how can we do that with Coke?'

Claire and Anna exchanged an amused knowing look, and each saw themselves in the other. For a long moment the expressions talked of more than amusement. It was at last a spontaneous recognition.

Liz saw and quietly hooked two wine glasses from the sideboard behind her, poured a little for Sarah and Louise, giving her friend that moment before raising her glass again. 'To you two,' she repeated, 'and to absent friends and husbands.'

Sarah turned to Anna. 'Mum always says that when Dad's away, it's a sort of ritual.'

As Sarah and Anna talked Claire sipped her

222

wine, and felt the pressure of Liz's foot under the table. She returned her smile, knowing that her friend understood that something had begun to settle in Claire, and that somehow it was reciprocated by Anna.

For the next hour they talked, all of them, discussing the pantomime, the girls' dorm, and hearing of Anna's work on a cruise ship, which had led to her hairdressing on film sets.

'Oh God, tell me you've worked on Tom Cruise, just tell me that,' begged Sarah.

'I w-i-s-h,' crooned Anna. 'I wouldn't have washed my hands, ever. I'd have mounted my scissors in a glass case. I'd have—'

Claire interrupted, her laughter as loud as any of theirs. 'I think we've got the picture.'

As neighbours walked past the uncurtained window Claire knew that they too had got the picture, and knew too that Liz had deliberately left the curtains open. This time it was she who lifted her glass silently to her friend. 'To you,' she mouthed, as Sarah and Louise dragged Anna to her feet, making her show them some of the dance steps that had gained her free admission to night clubs.

Liz sipped and watched, then said to Claire, 'She dances like Leah—it's your genes.'

Claire coloured with pleasure, but Anna said, returning to the table, her voice sharp and defensive, 'My mum made me go to ballet, said it'd give me good posture and a sense of rhythm.' For she had heard Liz, and how dare she brush aside her past, her mother, and how dare she compare her to a sister who hadn't bothered to turn up when she'd left work early, when she'd put herself out.

223

Just because they had big houses, important husbands, it was all right was it to expect her not to mind, to be grateful? She sipped from her glass, her colour high.

The words had jolted Claire though she continued to smile, and she was engulfed by the other emotion that she had failed to explain to Liz: the pain of loss which accompanied the joy, the loss of the years which a chance remark threw up, the fear that she would lose Anna again and now she could do nothing other than allow Liz to take up the reins because her own voice would betray her. Liz rattled on, talking of her own childhood experiences at dance class '... an unmitigated disaster. Two left feet.'

Anna listened and as she did so she saw Claire's pain, and noticed the much deeper lines of tiredness on her face, the tension. She fumbled with her napkin, God, it was all so difficult. It was never going to work, she'd just walk away, leave them all to it, let them get on with their lives, get on with her own.

The doorbell rang and Louise dived to the door. She dragged Mollie's girls back into the dining room, as Liz was threatening to stand up and bop. Anna was pulled to her feet and made to dance and tell Monica and Deborah of her hairdressing for the stars; Sarah grabbed a last piece of pizza while Deborah's eyes widened as they spelt out the famous names. But by now Sarah was dragging Deborah out of the room. 'Come on, we'll be late. See you next time, Anna.' Sarah waved her last half-eaten slice of pepperoni. Then the girls were gone.

Anna turned to Claire and Liz and winced.

224

'They make me feel old.'

Liz and Claire groaned together. 'Then there's no hope for us—bring on the zimmer frames!' All three laughed and Claire knew that this is what it would be like for a long while to come. Advances, withdrawals, defensive positions taken up, laid aside, glances shared, retracted, but please God, they'd always progress.

*   *   *

On Sunday afternoon at the Garrison Theatre Claire and Liz were getting cups out in the kitchen whilst Jo sat behind the table in front of the stage. Around her those auditioning gathered in small groups, some breaking off to ease chairs from the piles stacked at the sides of the hall, for the theatre had no fixed seating. Children were running around, while at the back both the village and the Garrison Youth Club were being taken through their steps once again.

Claire could still smell the fireworks on her skin from the night before, though she had showered both evening and morning. Liz asked, 'Did he phone?'

Claire was filling the urn with pans of water. 'Not yet.'

'So you rushed back again last night for nothing.' Liz's voice was sharp.

Claire peered into the urn. She had no intention of putting into words what she felt, because why should Mark want to phone, she'd messed up hadn't she? 'Quit going on. I was more than ready to leave the hot dogs to you lot. Is this enough water, do you think?'

225

Liz joined her, grizzling, 'I'd rather perform an appendectomy than deal with this darn thing.' She peered in. 'Well, it matches the line so let's go for it.'

Claire muttered, 'Thank God for that. I had no idea being a producer meant this.' She slammed on the lid, just as Mollie rushed into the kitchen from the car park, whipping off her headscarf, stuffing it into the pocket of her fur coat, zoning in on Claire, bringing the cold with her. She gasped, 'So sorry to be late. Unforgivable but mother had cooked Yorkshire puds and I do the washing up afterwards. Yorkies stick to the pan so.'

'Not unless they're burnt,' Liz offered sweetly.

Mollie ignored her. Heaving off her coat, she handed it to Liz, who stared at it as though it was something released from a trap. She dropped it on to the draining board. Mollie glared and rescued it, stroking the drips of water from it, her smile as huge as it always was these days. 'I know you need me, Claire. I feel I've let you down. Now, what can I do?'

Liz mouthed. 'Hara-kari, I beg of you.'

Claire sidled away and hurried back into the hall, hearing Mollie coming full tilt behind her. She flung desperately over her shoulder, 'I think the costumes the vicar's brought over could do with assessment. Costumes are your province aren't they, Mollie?' She waved towards the black bin bags heaped in the corner, continuing, 'I'll pop over in due course, but right now Jo needs me. Rather a lot to do this afternoon.' Her voice was loud enough for Jo to hear, and respond to, which she did, calling, 'Come on, Claire.'

Mollie followed her to the table, however, while

226

Jo made space for Claire, tipping the hats that might do for the Uglies on to the floor. She pointed out to Claire where Turbogob had reached in the script. On stage the Uglies and Tom Smith, the stepmother, were reading. The witchlets were failing to come in on cue, and were wooden when they finally arrived. Jo whispered, 'Rob, the Reverend Masters and his warden are marvellous, such talent, and the chook has got to be Roland, Muriel's gardener. Such legs! We've got to try out a few more youngsters for the witchlets though. Buttons is a problem too, though that guy Frank, the village postman is pretty good.'

Claire nodded, trying to follow Turbogob, but Mollie was whispering, hot and breathy in her ear, 'I hear Leah's let you down, such a shame, a mother needs support, you know. I do so wish I'd been here.'

Claire leaned away, her finger tracing Reverend Masters's words. He was Dunny, the older of the Ugly Sisters, and it suited him to a tee because he'd come over from Australia years ago. Rob was Potty, so called, Turbogob was explaining in a ringing voice to the supposed audience, because he could often be found under the bed, looking for his shoes. Jo made notes on the witchlets, while Claire tried to deal with Mollie. 'Leah had a previous engagement, that's all, but thanks for your concern,' she explained.

Mollie's hot breath was in Claire's ear again. 'Yes, but I hear that Anna came. Very awkward. Could it be that she thought Anna was trying—'

Exasperated, Claire rounded on Mollie. 'She knows the situation, there is no *think* about it. She wanted to go to the party; I allowed her. It's a
227

tricky time but we're coping, Mollie.'

Thick skinned to the last, Mollie was solicitous. 'I gather from Monica and Deborah that she's a . . .' she paused and looked around, then mouthed, as though it equated to a transvestite or something equally out of the ordinary— 'hairdresser.'

Claire clenched her hands but before she could speak Jo swung round. 'A hairdresser. I heard that—brilliant. We could really do with her, Claire, any chance, do you think? The wigs will need styling, not to mention all the makeup on the night.'

Claire smiled warmly at Jo. 'I'd have to run it past Leah first, then Anna.' Her smile struggled to retain that warmth when she turned to Mollie. 'Perhaps you'd allow me to talk to Leah about it, before you mention it to your girls, Mollie. There seems to have been rather a lot whirling around in the wind at school, as well as on the patch, not to mention Bosnia.' Mollie was flushing, patting not one but two strings of pearls, but of course, it had been lunch with Mother, Claire thought. Mollie said, 'I wouldn't dream of it.'

Claire patted her arm. 'I'm so glad.'

Jo hissed, 'Can we have less noise.'

Mollie tutted, outraged. 'Well really. Claire is the Colonel's wife and I am a company—'

'Old enough to start behaving with some sense then, Mollie,' Claire snapped, returning to the script. At that point Liz called: 'Come on, Mollie, get stuck in here, I don't know what the hell I'm doing.' She was marching across the hall, leaving behind a heap of clothes she'd tipped out of bags. Mollie tutted again as she hurried off. 'Well, really.'

Squatting next to Claire, Liz whispered, 'Did I

hear you getting stroppy with the old bag? Well, not before time. I thought I'd get over to that lot in case I needed to create a diversion. It should keep her occupied for a while.'

Jo nudged Claire. 'Can you get up on stage and read through Buttons's part.' Claire grabbed the script and headed for the steps, seeing Turbogob making her way back to the cauldron which was centre stage. She hesitated. Jo hissed, 'Go on, all you need to do is get to know one another. She'll be defused by the third week of rehearsals. Trust me.'

Claire said faintly, 'Third week.'

Jo shook her head. 'Either that or she'll have your guts for garters.'

Liz laughed. Claire didn't but made her way to her position, listening to Jo's stage instructions, laying her hand on Turbogob's shoulder, saying as the script demanded, 'But you're not really a witch, are you Morticia?'

'Oh yes I am,' cackled Morticia, with more venom than necessary.

*   *   *

Claire arrived home just as Mark rang. She checked her watch. It was 1800 hours. Relief vied with alarm. 'How are you?' she asked over the crackling line. She held her hand to her other ear, straining to hear.

His voice sounded disembodied. 'Look, this is a brief call. Any more probs?'

'Just damp fireworks last night. And with you? I've been worried, it seems so long since you phoned. It must have—'

'Oh for God's sake, Claire, I was up to my eyes

229

in it.'

'I didn't mean . . .' She was shouting, trying to force her voice through the static. 'This is a terrible . . .'

'No, I'm sorry, but refugees are still pouring in. The Serbs are pressing, the tensions are worse, the fracas multiplying. There was another patrol ambushed today. It's bloody chaos. You just think you're getting somewhere and it flares up along the line.'

'I know, I saw it on the news.'

She strained to hear again. He said, 'Oh, I see, so you know all about it do you? So why am I ringing the expert?' She saw through the anger to the strain, the exhaustion, the irritation at her for making it all worse.

She soothed. 'Oh Mark, you know I didn't mean that.'

She heard his sigh as the line magically cleared for a moment. 'I know. Sorry Claire. But look, how are things? It's exeat, isn't it? Did it go well?'

'She's at Natasha's. A party weekend, would you believe?'

Mark's chuckle was quite distinct, and Claire relaxed but then the line broke up again and almost obliterated his voice as he said, 'So, a bit of peace for you. Your letter said today was the final audition. Is Liz still being good, or has she gone back to whingeing?'

Claire shouted, 'She doesn't whinge, she's wonderful. We had dinner with her on Friday.' The line cleared again.

'We? Who d'you mean?'

She said nervously. 'Anna was here.'

There was a pause though the line was still

230

wonderfully clear and Claire waited for him to speak. Would he mind? But she'd written to him informing him of progress just as he'd asked, so if he'd minded he would have let her know. But it had been so bad out there he hadn't had a chance, he'd just said. She tried to damp down the panic, tried to stop the roller-coaster which swept in so often, but he was talking, saying, 'Oh, right, I remember that now. I suppose Leah let you know too late to postpone. Are you sure it was a party, not just an excuse? Is this all a problem to her? I mean, what are we getting into?' His voice was rising.

Claire watched herself nodding in the mirror, just as the Uglies had done in their mirror scene, looking as vacuous as they had done. Suddenly tiredness was drenching her. Mark said, 'Claire, are you there?'

'I'm here,' she said. 'Yes, it was a last-minute party. No, there isn't a problem, we're not getting ourselves into anything. And it didn't seem necessary to cancel Anna just because Leah can't make it. After all . . .' She stopped. No, she mustn't get angry.

The line was crackling again. 'OK, I didn't mean that, no need to go on,' he said.

There was silence from them both, then Mark spoke again. 'Look, I'm sorry. So tell me what she's like, this Anna of yours.'

Claire sagged with relief and she found herself smiling into the mirror. 'Oh Mark, thank you.' He said nothing and so she continued: 'She's a lovely girl. She liked your mirror, you know. It was almost the first thing she said. Did I tell you that in the letter?' She knew she had.

There was another pause. 'So, she's like you, and
231

Leah?' She'd told him that too.

'Yes, but this weekend I could see my father in her too.'

The line was breaking down further. Mark's voice was intermittent as he said, 'Right. Good. Look, got to go. Take care.'

'Love you,' she shouted, for this was her ritual, but also the truth.

'Back,' she heard through the static.

*   *   *

In the dorm Leah was leaning back against her pillows, watching Sarah unpack, listening to Louise as she lolled in the doorway. 'Well, she's got this auburn tint. It'd suit you too, Leah. Bet if you asked her she'd do it for you—and what a dancer! She gets into clubs free you know, cos she gets the others going. Mind, she said she was getting too old for it. 'Spose she is, really. Twenty-five is pretty ancient.'

Sarah slung her grip into the top of the wardrobe, then tossed gum to Leah, coming over to sit on her bed. She reached across, put a Madonna tape into the cassette player on the bedside cabinet and pressed play, lifting her voice above the music. 'Anyway, don't know what you're doing slugging it on the bed. You missed the run-through, so we've got to teach you. Won't do to mess up if your dad's going to be there on the last night.'

Leah smiled to herself, hugging her knees. Yes, he was going to be here, and he was hers, not Anna's, not anybody else's. She asked, 'So, she's like me, is she?'

'Except for the eyes. They're very dark. Very,
232

very dark.'

The girls chattered on, and more came into the room, some of whom had been to Natasha's party. While they told the others about being totally trolleyed from the punch, and giggled about the boys they had met, Leah thought of those eyes. They must belong to the father, so would Anna bring him springing from behind the laurel bush into the bosom of the family? She'd asked her mother that, and her mother had said no, the father was in Australia, and Anna didn't appear to be interested.

Damn girl, wasn't it enough that she had given her mother the fright of her life, not checking to see if she'd received the letter before jumping out? Oh no, now she had to go meeting Leah's friends, including Mollie's girls, so she'd have to deal with all that fallout tomorrow. But isn't that what she'd wanted? She cringed just as a pillow hit her, thrown by Louise, who burst out laughing.

Leah jerked around, preparing to throw it back, but she saw that Deborah Perkins was in the room, and braced herself, cursing Anna. But all Deborah did was to grab Sarah by the arm, shouting above Madonna, 'Come on, let's show Leah the way Anna danced.' She beckoned Louise into line as well, saying, 'Really Leah, she was great, really nice. Look.' The girls tried but broke up, laughing, and falling on to Sarah's bed. Deborah rolled over, grinning. 'You're lucky you know, Leah, you could have been landed with someone really dorky— Monica comes to mind.'

Sarah loped across to Leah, laughing. 'Come on, get on your feet. You dance just like her so you'll find it easy.' She pulled Leah from the bed, turning up the volume. Leah protested, but then slipped into line as the other girls joined them, and while the music pounded she copied Sarah, then Deborah, then Louise. And as the others talked more of the evening she realized that she wished she had been there.

CHAPTER FIFTEEN

Anna listened to Claire's message, then slumped on to the settee, her feet throbbing. She had not closed the door on the last cut and blow-dry until 6.30 and no, she didn't want to go to Lancashire to see where she'd been born. No, she didn't want to try and balance everything and everyone. OK, she knew who she was now, and that was enough.

Mabs jumped up on to her lap. 'Oh, for God's sake,' she yelled, knocking him off. She stormed through to the kitchen, and leaned on the sink which was full of dirty dishes. It's too difficult, that's what she'd said to her mother. No, not you, Claire, my other mother. She looked out into the darkness.

Out there was the garden and it was only because she had too much work to do that it wasn't immaculate. How could her parents expect her to do everything? She had the business to keep going, hadn't she, and what was more important, that or a bit of pruning and clump splitting? It had nothing to do with not finishing things. That's what she'd yelled down the phone to Cornwall yesterday. 'And what's the garden got to do with walking away from Claire Baird anyway. I mean, I wasn't the one who was bloody rude and didn't turn up when I'd driven for an hour and a half to be there, I wasn't the one making out Claire was responsible for everything I am. It's too difficult, that's all.'

Anna poked at one of the mugs, then took another from the cupboard, switching on the kettle, leaning against the sink again. It just wasn't fair, I mean, whose side was her mother on, telling her to grow up, telling her to remember what it was like when she was fourteen and a complete pain in the bum, telling her it was time she thought of everyone else in this? After all, Anna had started it, she had been told it would stir all sorts of emotions up in herself and she'd gone ahead knowing that.

At this her mother's voice had broken and she'd cried. Anna turned the mug round and round in her hand. She'd never heard that sound before. Her father had taken the phone. 'Anna, come on lass, get stuck in and stop looking for excuses to give up. Your mother's right, no one said it would be easy so pull yourself together. It's hard for everyone, but wonderful too—don't forget that.'

The kettle had boiled but still Anna stood there, turning her mug in her hands because in finding her mother she knew even less who she was and she was frightened, and wanted to go back to things as they'd been before.

CHAPTER SIXTEEN

On the first Sunday evening in December Mark sat in his office listening to the ringing tones begin, swivelling his desk lamp away so the glare fell on to the phone, not his face. He pressed the bridge of his nose, tapping with the fingers of his other hand on the mouthpiece, anxiety clawing at him. If it was the answering machine again he'd phone Liz.

There was a click, and it was a living, breathing Claire who answered. 'Hello, Claire Baird here.'

'Thank God,' he said. 'I tried to phone last night. I imagined you splattered all over the road somewhere.' He pushed the lamp even further away and it lit the two extra chairs and the coat stand as she replied, her voice as anxious as he had felt now she was safe, he just felt exasperated. Where the hell had she been? Saturday was their night. She was saying. 'Mark, you're all right?'

Through the frosted window the night sky was lit by a distant flash. 'Fine. Where were you?' His voice was cool, he knew it, but he couldn't change it because suddenly it was how he felt, how he had been feeling in fits and starts since . . .

Claire said, 'I'm sorry, I was back a couple of minutes late. I was held up. But darling, you should have left a message, and rung again. Don't forget that I've been here by the phone every other Saturday, and on many of those you haven't rung.'

He pressed the bridge of his nose again. So it was all his fault now? He snapped, 'For God's sake Claire, I do my best.'

Immediately her voice was conciliatory, and so it damn well should be. 'I'm not criticizing, I'm just trying to explain.' The line was quite clear, unlike the previous time he had rung her. He said, his anger dying as quickly as it had come, 'It's crazy, I can phone home but just let me try to get through to my men on the radio in this godforsaken armpit and I'm asking for a miracle. I need to be able to count on something, Claire, while I'm here, I really do. I thought you knew that.'

'I do, and you can, darling. You know that.'

Mark sat back in his chair. 'It was rehearsals, I suppose. How's it going?'

She explained that today it had been the first complete read through, but that yesterday she had been in Lancashire. He was puzzled. 'Lancashire? Why, a problem with one of the wives' families?'

She was hesitant. 'No, nothing to do with the patch for once. I was visiting the home where I had Anna.' Now her voice was muted, almost tearful. 'Mark, we walked in the park where I pushed her, it had hardly changed at all. It was so strange, being there with her again. Did you get the photo I sent?'

He fiddled with the telephone cord. Lancashire. All day with the girl in Lancashire. First she denies her, then it's trips to Lancashire.

'Mark, Mark, are you there?'

He pressed his cheekbones now. Bloody hell, they were tender. It was the cold wind that had caught him as he was frigging around in the turret today. There was a clicking on the line and again there were flashes in the sky, the distant crump of mortars and at last the automatic pilot cut in, damping down this gut-churning sort of anger.

'Mark, are you there?'

He laughed, bitterly. 'Where else would I be? I can't go swanning off to . . .' He stopped. No. He talked instead of the refugees, of a tense Turbe meeting, of the snow which was falling and causing problems on the roads. She listened, sympathized, encouraged, then said, 'I didn't know whether to send the photo. I didn't know how much you wanted to know while you were up to your neck in

237

it, but you insisted I keep you informed and I don't want you to think you're being excluded. I think about you all the time, you know that, don't you?'

'Yes, I do know that.' He could picture her standing by the phone, in her cream blouse, her fingers playing with the paper knife, and for a moment he desperately wanted to be there, holding her. 'Well, did I make a mistake?' she asked.

'No, you didn't make a mistake,' he forced himself to say but he didn't want to know. Not about the girl, or the past. He'd never wanted to know, and he wanted to know even less now that he'd seen the photo because he couldn't deal with it here, none of it. He forced himself to say, 'Her chin is different to Leah's.'

Claire said quietly, 'Leah's chin is yours.'

The shadow of the filing cabinet fell on the heap of papers and maps on the table beneath the window which had been planked, but which still gave a view either side. That just left the eyes.

He saw flashes again but as though from a distance because he was asking himself what Anna's arrival meant to them. What it really meant.

Still as though from a distance he heard himself say, 'It's pretty hairy out here, but the men are holding up well. I'm proud of them.'

'As they are of you. As I am. You're doing a wonderful job, but I hope you're managing to remain as uninvolved as you can. Otherwise it'll tear you apart.' He could sense the anxiety.

'You've no idea, Claire. No bloody idea what it's like.' His voice was almost a whisper, and all the time her voice was getting closer and it was drawing this terrible anger towards her.

'I see it on the news, so I feel I can almost understand but—'

He exploded. 'Exactly. But you can't. You need to be amongst it.'

At her silence he pressed his hand against his forehead. What the hell was the matter with him? Quietly she spoke. 'Well, I can't be with you, though I would love to be. My job is here, and I'm doing all I can.'

There was a silence. 'I know, I know.' God, he was tired, too tired to think, to talk really, and he just wanted the world to stand still for a moment, just give him time, just . . . He said, 'Look, I've got staff, brass and press to circulate amongst, so I'd better get on with it, while I can get my eyes to stay open. Tell you what, why not put your news in your letters and that'll leave the phone free for a quick update on the patch and you and me. You take care now, Claire.' As he finished speaking he stood up. Yes, then he could skim-read, avoid, disregard, catch up when all this was over.

She said, 'I love you, be careful.'

'Back.' He clattered the receiver on to the cradle, then stood still for a moment, rubbing his face, listening to the firing in the hills, before striding from the room.

*   *   *

In the mess he ordered a Scotch, searching the room for Ben. He found him by the window talking to Gordana Sevo and three other interpreters. The Scotch came quickly, and he took a quick sip before strolling across to join them, acknowledging the greeting of Charlie and Arthur, asking 2nd Lt.

Williams if he had enjoyed his day, forcing a smile as the young man said, 'Patrolling in the snow and skidding on the ice beats a wet Sunday at Blackpool any day, sir.' There were no brass but it had been as good an excuse to end the call as any. He eased his shoulders.

When he reached the interpreters he asked Miss Nikola Martinovic if the water was back on in their flat. She and Gordana half laughed. Nikola groaned. 'If only it had a calling card, at least we could have our sponges, not to mention our kettle ready when it did finally pay us a visit.'

Ben and Mark grinned. Ben said quietly to Mark, 'Everything going well back home, Colonel? Is the pantomime on course?'

Gordana and Nikola looked puzzled, so Ben told them of *Cinderella*, and as he did so, Mark saw a look of total disbelief appear on Gordana's face. Ben saw it too, and finished lamely, 'It keeps up morale.'

Gordana's colour was high, and her eyes scanned the room as though she was looking for escape. Finding none she returned her attention to Ben and there was fury in her that surpassed all Mark had previously witnessed. 'Of course,' she almost spat. 'One must do that. One simply must take care of their morale, especially when their lives are so hard, poor, poor things.'

For the first time since they had arrived in Bosnia Ben allowed his control to snap, and he almost shouted, 'Yes, their lives are hard. They wait, they cope, they put their lives on hold. Sometimes, Miss Gordana, they have to grieve.'

Nikola had been twisting her glass of lemonade round and round in her hands, and now she tugged at Gordana's sleeve, speaking rapidly, and angrily in Serbo-Croat. Gordana pulled away, her eyes still with Ben, matching his rage. 'Whatever you say, Major Gibbons, but forgive me, I had no idea conditions were so very hard in England.' She turned on her heel, while Nikola held up her hands in apology and followed her friend as she cut a swathe through the unknowing mess.

Ben looked to Mark for support but Mark heard himself say 'For God's sake, Ben, you've got to take into account the experiences of these people. Who can blame her, I mean there's no bloody comparison is there?'

It was Ben's turn to stare in disbelief. 'Well, I'm sorry Colonel, but I don't think—'

Mark snapped, 'No, you don't seem to. Anyway, I'm going to bed. It's been a pig of a day.' He turned to leave but Ben grabbed his arm to stop him. Mark, astonished, jerked free, just as Gordana had done. For a moment there was a shocked impasse, but then Ben shook his head as though he was just waking. He stepped back, quite pale. 'God, I'm sorry, Mark, I mean Colonel.'

Mark walked away. He'd had just about enough for one bloody night and tomorrow there was Zagreb and the goodwill trip to a refugee hostel, courtesy of bloody Charlie, and Gordana, and with the Brigadier's approval. What did Ben expect him to do—put up with another sulking female all bloody day? Which is what would have happened if he'd leapt to the defence of the wives.

Besides, the long and short of it was that the girl did have a point.

*   *   *

The next day Mark entered the portals of the Transit Centre in Zagreb, Croatia, still trying to accommodate the sight of the clanking trams, and the big German cars speeding along the cobbles in this city, which was living and breathing again. It was a city which seemed heedless of the war on its borders, a city where pedestrians sauntered. In Vitez no one sauntered any more.

Charlie and his new photographer, Joe, were at his side as they forced a way through the dark, noisy, smelly hallway. It was Charlie who knew where he was going, and he greeted a woman who stood as though guarding the door marked OFFICE, or that was the translation of the Serbo-Croat above it. She clutched a clipboard and ticked off their names, shaking hands before directing them along the corridor, her Canadian accent apparent.

'Come on, squire,' Charlie directed. 'Onward and upward into bedlam.'

As they proceeded along the corridor to the stairs Mark could distinguish the racket of radios above the crying of babies, and the deeper resonance of male voices, and alongside him he could hear Charlie as he muttered darkly into a small tape recorder which he held almost up to his lips, like some inadequate pop star, a pencil stuck behind his ear.

Joe, the photographer caught Mark's eye and grinned. 'He uses the pencil for interviews, feels it makes him look as though he's taking their story seriously. Mind you, it'd be hard not to in this place.'

Mark felt the oppressive hopelessness all around as they squeezed their way up the stairs past small groups of refugees who sat or stood. Twice they stepped aside as others made their way down, and every so often he smelt the odour of Enver, the villager who had stopped his convoy what seemed like years ago.

Charlie was pulling a pack of cigarettes out of his breast pocket as he walked along the landing, fumbling one-handed, muttering all the time, and eventually handing the pack to Mark in exasperation. Mark raised his eyebrows at the photographer. The youngish red-haired man shook his head. 'Giving them up, or trying to.'

Mark lit one and handed it to Charlie, who stuck it in the corner of his mouth without missing a syllable of his commentary. They were on the first floor, and Charlie was counting the doorways with his finger, until he almost skidded to a halt in front of one. Now he clicked the tape recorder off. 'This is where we'll find the deadly duo.' His voice was noncommittal but his eyes told of a burning admiration.

'Duo?' Mark queried as Charlie directed the photographer to take several shots of the corridor. Charlie was peering into the room. 'Gordana and Stevo, her cousin. He's here most of the time, whilst she gets here once a month. On all other Sundays she's at the Travnik Centre. That's what's called a driven woman, my dear old sausage.'

Mark looked over Charlie's shoulder and the scene in the room was so like the Centre at Travnik that his heart failed. Why had he agreed to this? Everywhere there were desolate groups crouched, sprawled or sitting on mattresses, or just on the floor. He could smell Enver everywhere, but added to that was the stench of weeks of dirt accumulated as they trudged the road, the stench of deprivation

243

and panic. Where would they all go from here?

He must have spoken aloud for Charlie told him what he already knew. 'Onward passage to safe havens, or "civilized" Europe.' They eased their way into the room, and now there was a clatter of pans, and strangely, the laughter of a child.

Charlie prodded him in the chest, jerking his head towards the corner. 'There's our date.'

Gordana sat close to a weeping middle-aged woman. Mark felt like a spare part as he tripped along in Charlie's wake, listening to his resumed muttering into his recorder, a muttering which did not cease even when he arrived at the mattress on which Gordana was sitting, or even when he shook the hand of the young man who came across from the next mattress space. It was only when Gordana patted the woman and heaved herself to her feet, kissing Charlie, but virtually ignoring Mark, that Charlie clicked the machine off.

Abandoning Mark, Charlie moved with Gordana to the next bed. Mark stared after them as the sobs of the woman Gordana had left settled into a hopeless rhythm. At his side Joe was testing his light-meter, at the same time handing Mark some rolls of film. 'Hang on to these, stick with me, and hand them over as needed. No need to look any more surplus to requirements than you really are.' His grin took the sting from the words.

Stevo was hurrying to catch up with Gordana as she led Charlie from one refugee to another. Charlie, his pencil busy, squatted down near a young woman as Mark saw Gordana hand Stevo a sheaf of papers from her backpack, then flick through the pages of her notebook, the one she had written in at Tuzla, showing him material.

What the hell was she sharing with Stevo? Surreptitiously he studied the intent faces of the two young people, seeing the tiredness in them both. He looked around. Was there anyone who wasn't tired?

Gordana smiled at Stevo, and it was as though the sun had come out in this dark room. The usual strand of hair brushed her cheek, and Mark knew that in a moment she would try to tuck it behind her ear or up into that sort of bun.

At that moment Charlie peered over Stevo's shoulder but Gordana waved him away, smiling slightly. She said something to Stevo, who glanced towards Mark before folding the paper and putting it into the small rucksack he also carried. Only then did he approach Mark, shake him by the hand, and say, 'I've been delegated to give "the grand tour" to our esteemed visitor.'

Mark felt even more of a spare part.

For nearly two hours he was paraded before the face of misery until finally he reached saturation point, his emotions too numb to react to either the visual evidence of rape, violence, degradation, or to Stevo's running commentary. Like an automaton he continued the tour, handing out new film to the photographer, putting one foot in front of the other, but longing to be somewhere else,

When at last they were outside it was startling to draw in draughts of fresh air, and see the sky, hear the clanking of the trams, the rumble of the cars on the cobbles, and feel almost normal. The photographer said, taking the last film from Mark, his face thoughtful, 'It's strange how awfulness is made mundane by its repetitiveness. Rape, pillage, death, there's so much it loses its meaning, becomes nonsensical. Then you see something in the lens—a look, a scar, whatever—and you are reminded that these are not examples or exhibits, these are people just like us, or were like us. You know, like the girl who queues at the dole office back home, the woman who teaches our kids. Hell, this is just two hours flying time from the UK.'

Stevo was standing with them, squinting against the bright cold sun, the collar of his jacket turned up, his cap pulled down. Mark dug his hands into the pockets of his combat gear, and when he spoke his voice sounded as though he had not used it in years. 'It's a bloody disgrace,' he murmured. 'It's just a bloody disgrace.'

Stevo said, 'They rape to demean those they have conquered, they destroy homes to wipe out the past of those who lived there. They reduce us to nothing, to a limbo.' His voice was almost bored, but his eyes weren't.

He took them to a café full of smoke and young people, not to mention the press who sat in the far corner, their empty beer bottles and ashtrays taking every available inch of table space. The journalists waved to Mark and Joe as they followed Stevo to an empty table by a trellis fence set against the wall, and over which plastic vines hung.

Stevo gestured to the chairs around the table. 'Sit where you will.'

Joe unslung his bag, put it on the floor, but wound the strap round his ankle. 'They'll have to take me with it,' he remarked to Mark, shaking his head at Stevo who had sat down next to Joe, and was offering cigarette paper and tobacco. At that moment Charlie's voice could be heard loud and clear as he wove his way around the tables towards them with Gordana close behind: 'Come on then, squire, get the booze ordered. I'm not a bloody camel with my own supplies.' Guffaws came from the journalists' table, and it was echoed by the youngsters, who whistled, cat-called, and obviously knew and liked Charlie.

Stevo grinned and gave the order to the waiter, whose white apron was grimy. Charlie slumped, panting, into his chair next to Stevo, dragging out a handkerchief to mop his forehead, replacing it as the waiter brought a tray full of bottles. Gordana hung back, chatting to a girl at the table near them as Stevo acknowledged Mark's raised eyebrows at the sight of the two beer bottles that were placed before each of them. I thought we'd start with two—it's on Charlie's expenses. The beer is local, and cheap. Not bad though.'

Charlie had already poured his, and was gulping, pausing only to murmur, 'Bloody ambrosia, squire.' While he drank Joe turned to Gordana who had taken the only remaining empty seat, next to Mark. 'Tell me why you do all this. I mean, what drives you? If you're not here, you're at the Travnik Centre.'

Gordana was by now reaching for her beer. She brushed the glass aside and lifted the bottle to her mouth. 'Perhaps for my morale, as we do not have pantomimes in Bosnia?'

Mark looked away, but then felt the touch of her hand, heard her voice which was little more than a whisper: 'Colonel Baird, forgive me. That was cheap and unnecessary.'

Stevo interjected, pushing another bottle to Joe. 'She does it because she feels guilty that she was away in the "civilized" world when what was once

247

Yugoslavia decided to thrash itself to death. She does it because she feels even more guilty when she thinks that instead of heading for Sarajevo she should have been at home to be demeaned or destroyed, or perhaps both. Never mind that she thought her parents would be safe there. Never mind that in Sarajevo nothing was safe for her. Never mind that her mother wishes she would stay in Zagreb and just live as a girl of twenty-five should. Never mind that we all know her father is dead. Never mind . . .'

'Stevo, please,' Gordana protested.

Stevo's colour was high, his frustration obvious, but so was Gordana's, and with it was pain.

Charlie gestured to the waiter to bring another round of drinks, and as Gordana and Stevo quarrelled in Serbo-Croat Charlie said quietly to Mark, 'They do it to log atrocities which they then collate, tracking movements of forces to incidents, collecting as many eyewitness accounts of the same incident as they can. These they present to the powers that be, in the hope that one day a war crimes trial will be instigated. Others do this too, of course, but they perhaps do not have a father to find as well.'

Charlie poured the beer as soon as it arrived, then continued: 'It's amazing how personal loss and guilt drive a person on. Steve's right, she seeks confirmation of her father's death and until she has this she won't rest. So, at every roadblock she is working for you, but also for herself, asking, collating, trying to find him. You've noticed the green notebook into which everything is transcribed. Stevo helps, rather than let her do it alone. That's why we wanted you to take her on or

248

she'd have taken off with that damned freelancer. A right prat if ever there was one. Jeremy tried to tell you the whole story, but perhaps it's as well you cut him short.' His voice was dry. 'Maybe it would have counted against her, though now I think it will not.' The challenge was implicit, and Charlie's bloodshot eyes were cool and hard.

Gordana was pulling at his sleeve, the strand of hair swinging free again. 'Please Colonel Baird, Stevo is saying, as he always does, that the present UN stance reflects how little will be done to bring retribution. Please, what do you think?'

Mark looked around the table, hearing Charlie's heavy breathing, seeing him finish yet another beer, straight from the bottle this time also. He said, pouring his own into a glass, 'If it was up to me it would be done, every last bloody killer would be strung up. But, then, if it was up to me more would be done right now.'

He shrugged, lifted his glass and saw Stevo glance at Gordana, and then away, unimpressed. Gordana smiled at Mark, sadly. 'But it's not up to you.'

He lifted the glass. It left a ring of beer on the table. He said, 'No, this weekend more than any other I've realized I'm powerless, totally bloody powerless to do anything about virtually anything.'

CHAPTER SEVENTEEN

The journey from patch to school took longer than usual because of roadworks, but it was still only three-quarters of an hour. It took another fifteen minutes to reach the restaurant and as she and Leah made their way to the round table in the corner, Claire worried again that her directions would not be clear for Anna. Liz always said that the only thing reliable about Claire's sense of direction was that she had none.

The waiter left them with the menu and wine list, acknowledging Claire's request for sparkling mineral water, and a slimline tonic. Leah, neat in her school uniform, took care to take the seat which faced the restaurant, as she always did. 'I might miss something,' she'd told her father firmly some years ago. 'And what's happening in the rest of the room is far more interesting than listening to you and Mum.' He had roared with laughter, and squeezed Claire's thigh beneath the table but that had been during the good old days before his promotion. For a moment Claire's heart twisted and she knew that she loved him as much now as then.

Claire checked her watch discreetly. Anna was not yet late so perhaps the directions were all right. Behind Leah, Christmas garlands were already draped along the top of the prints and a laden Christmas tree stood in the corner, which was surely a bit early—it was only the second week of December. Leah said, 'They put them up on the first, it's good marketing.' Soft music played from the speakers in the corners and even they were garlanded. It all served to remind Claire of the mayor's bazaar, of the Christmas party for the patch which she and Rob had been planning during the week, of the toys that Sergeant Malloy had requested for the orphanage the battalion had 'adopted' in Bosnia, of the . . .

Leah gasped. 'Oh no.' She buried her head in the menu, muttering, 'Don't look round, just don't, Mum.'

Claire didn't. Instead she leaned forward, her lips hardly moving as she asked, 'Whatever's wrong?'

Leah dragged her hair, which she'd left unplaited, across her head, and ducked even lower. 'It's Annabel from school, at the bar with her parents.'

Claire shook her head slightly. 'Shall we go elsewhere when Anna arrives?'

There was an audible groan from Leah. 'For heaven's sake, that'd be even worse, all that getting up and going out. We'd have to pass them.' She looked as though she'd been caught in a car's headlight while taking a comfort stop behind a hedge.

Claire checked her watch again. Anna should have been here by now but thank God she wasn't, for Leah was still huddled behind the menu muttering.

Nervously Claire smoothed out the fold creases of the red tablecloth. 'Look, I didn't know it was a school haunt. Why didn't you tell me?'

Leah was peering round the side of the red leather-backed menu looking lost and angry and very like Mark. 'Oh for heaven's sake Mum, it seemed like a good idea at the time just because they come in, and now I've changed my mind, OK?' She looked as though she was explaining that A came after B for the millionth time to someone who should know better.

'But I don't understand.'

Leah looked embarrassed. 'I thought the bush

251

telegraph would pass the word that I'd finally met Anna, and it wouldn't be up to me to tell them.'

'Oh, Leah.' Claire reached forward, but Leah let the menu fall to the table, swishing her hair over again, glowering at her mother, then folding her arms. 'You've no idea how embarrassing the whole thing is. How would you feel if it was you, and Grandma had brought a half-sister to meet you?'

'Astonished. To think of my mother conceiving one child is hard enough. Two would have had to have been an immaculate conception.' Claire surprised herself, let alone Leah, but suddenly she'd had enough. 'Mum,' Leah exclaimed, sitting bolt upright, her arms dropping to her lap. Then she laughed before sobering, and reverting to a slump.

Claire said urgently, 'Leah, I'm doing my best, but there is no darn code of conduct for this situation, is there? Please believe that I'm trying to think of everyone here. You, your father, Anna.' She stopped as the waiter arrived with the drinks plus breadsticks. As he left Leah broke off a piece of stick, saying as she chewed it, her eyes challenging, 'Grandma was a tight-arsed nit-picker, wasn't she?'

Claire would have killed for a gin. Instead she sipped the tonic, avoiding the lemon which kept nudging her lips, her eyes meeting her daughter's, warily. God, when would it all begin to ease? She said, 'A somewhat indelicate description, but accurate.'

Again Leah looked surprised, and again she laughed, and poured mineral water into the larger of the two wine glasses set at her place, asking slowly, 'Was Grandma ever nice? She never seemed

252

to be.'

Claire traced a line through the condensation of her glass, just as John Mills had in *Ice Cold in Alex*. She wanted to say no, she was foul, I hated her, but somehow one never hated one's mother, one only longed for love. 'I think she was a frightened woman. She'd risen out of the blue-collar culture by marrying Dad, but had hoped for more. Poor old Dad was only ever going to be a solicitor's clerk, and what's wrong with that for goodness sake?' She stared at the Christmas decorations above Leah's head, aware of the increasing noise as the tables filled. 'I think she wanted him to metamorphose into a High Court judge, but it was I, of course, who really ruined her life.'

Leah had finished the breadstick and was starting on another, chewing her way through it like the lop-eared rabbit they had once had, the one they called Radar, because only one ear 'lopped' leaving the other as erect as a radio mast. Radar had been liberated by the hurricane which blew his run into the wide blue yonder, leaving him behind.

Leah said, 'Bet Grandma was glad when you landed Dad.'

Claire gritted her teeth. 'I think Belle was pleased when your father landed me.'

Leah was picking crumbs up from the red tablecloth and dropping them on to the side plate. 'But he took you on, even though he knew you'd had a bastard.' Her tone was offensive, deliberately so.

Claire touched her glass again. It was as cold as the wind had seemed as it rustled the marram grass, it was as cold as she now felt and as the darkness began to claim her, she fought it, pushing

253

back the panic, seizing her linen napkin, unfolding it, placing it on her thighs, feeling its texture, breathing slowly, deeply, until at last she could speak, and when she did her voice was calm but cool. 'Well done Leah, I think you can chalk that remark up as a victory.' She toasted her daughter, who had the grace to flush, and look away, mumbling, 'I didn't mean it. I just wish nothing had changed.'

Claire sipped, and replaced her glass on the table. Her voice was gentle, but had an authority which she did not in fact feel. 'I know, Leah and I'm going to say sorry just once more for making your life uncomfortable, but the past has happened and I don't want you being rude to Anna, because none of this is her fault, it is purely mine and it is not going to go away.'

'Do you want her to?'

Claire examined Leah's face, and saw that it was a real question. 'No, I don't want her to go away. I'm luckier than I deserve that she has come to find us and I desperately want you to like her.'

'Hi, Leah,' a girl's voice shouted from a nearby table. It was Annabel whose family had seated themselves a couple of tables away. Claire silently applauded Leah as she kept her smile steady and flicked a 'cool' hand in the girl's direction. 'Hi Annabel.'

Claire, in her turn, smiled as she turned to greet Steve and Gail Armstrong, who were as tanned as ever. Leah had told her they not only had their own sunbed, but a villa in Ibiza. They asked, 'How is everything?'

'Fine, thank you.' Claire's answer was bold, because she refused to see a double meaning in everything any more. For a moment they discussed Mark in Bosnia, and Steve in the City, and then the waiter brought Gail her cottage cheese salad, Steve his sizzling barbecue platter, and Annabel her scampi. Leaving them to it, Claire checked her watch again and started to speak to Leah. But Leah was staring, as though mesmerized, over Claire's shoulder.

Leah watched the young woman come into the restaurant and knew it was Anna, because she was Claire, but with different eyes, eyes which searched the restaurant, and finally found their table. Those eyes met hers, and for a moment they held, but then Leah looked away, feeling hot, sick, wanting to be anywhere but here.

She fumbled for a breadstick, as Claire repeated, 'Leah?'

By then the girl was almost at their table. A few paces more, and she stood just to Claire's left and said in a voice which was also like Claire's, except for the West Country accent, 'Claire.'

Leah watched her mother stand and turn and face Anna. She watched the flush of pleasure spread from her neck to her cheeks. She heard her say, 'You found us.'

Leah was surprised because her mother's voice was anxious, nervous, hesitant, and Leah hated this girl for reducing her mother to this, for making her vulnerable, which a mother should never be.

She watched her mother reach out and touch Anna's arm, saw the inclination of her mother's body and knew that she wanted to kiss the girl, but the girl ignored this, smiling instead, saying, 'Your directions were OK. I just got in a kind of tangle.' She was slipping out of her coat, hanging it on the coat hook on the wall beside them. She took the seat between Leah and Claire.

Leah could see the Armstrongs' sneaked looks and so she smiled at Anna, but really she wanted to shove her lookalike face down in the breadsticks: if Anna had come to find her mother, the least she could do was kiss her, not make a fool of her.

Anna took the menu that the waiter offered, and laid it down on the table because her hands were trembling so much. She heard Claire say 'Thank you, we'll have a quick look and call you back.' The waiter left.

Anna forced herself to smile at Leah, in spite of her nervousness, sensing the anger in the girl but ignoring it because her parents had been right, it was time to grow up. 'Leah, I'm so glad to meet you. Your mother never stops talking about you, and you're just as beautiful as she said.' She was amazed her voice didn't shake.

Leah said nothing. Claire rushed in. 'Let me order you a drink, Anna.'

Anna half laughed. 'What I'd really like is a vermouth and lemonade, but what I'll have is a mineral water if we're having wine. I've a long drive back.'

Leah saw that Annabel was looking so she smiled at Anna, saying, 'I like your hair, who cuts it?' Is this what you said to someone you'd never met who just happened to be your sister?

Anna touched her hair. 'My chief stylist, Cheryl, does it. The first time she was so nervous I'm surprised I had any ears left, but she settled down. I suppose she decided I wasn't such an ogre after all.'

Leah nodded, her anger visible again. 'We were just talking about an ogre, one *you* never met.'

256

The waiter arrived, his pad at the ready. Claire said firmly, 'Leah, concentrate on the menu. Now are you still off meat? If so there's aubergine *au gratin*, served with mangetout and broccoli.'

Leah shrugged. 'OK.'

Anna closed her menu. 'That sounds good, I'll have it as well.'

Leah sneered, taking the last of the breadsticks. 'Don't bust a gut to blend.'

Claire was aware of the waiter standing between the two girls, trying not to listen to any of this. 'Let's have three of those,' she said quickly, as anxious for him to go as he was to be gone. As he left she turned to Leah. 'That's quite enough.' To Anna she said, 'You don't have to have vegetarian.'

Anna thought for a moment but then took a deep breath. 'I'd rather. I'm veggie too, have been for years.'

Claire closed her eyes, thinking of the moussaka Anna had forced herself to eat on their first meeting, of the salami pizzas at Liz's. She protested weakly, 'You should have told me.'

Anna was placing her napkin on her knee. 'I didn't know how to, it was difficult enough without any extra complications, and anyway, it was great moussaka and I'm not totally off the wall about it. Sometimes I feel I need a bit of something, anyway.' Her voice was much calmer than she felt. Did it show that she was choosing every word, wanting very much for this to work?

Annabel was sneaking a look again, and Leah noticed. She leaned forward. 'Yes, that's right. I have Marmite. Maybe pickles, mustard, something sharp.' Annabel had returned to her scampi.

Anna answered quickly, relieved at Leah's smile

and enthusiasm, 'What about soya?'

Leah laughed. 'Mum should have that. It's supposed to boost your hormones, isn't it? It'd stop her being crabby when her oestrogen finally abandons ship.'

Anna burst out laughing, and it was only now that Leah remembered to check whether Annabel was taking it all in.

The waiter was back, asking about wine. Claire checked the wine list, looking dubiously at Anna. 'We're both driving, so half a bottle should do it?' Anna nodded, but said, 'I want to pay this part of it. But you'll have to choose. I don't know anything about wine. Ask me about lager and I can tell you the lot.'

Leah's answering stare was blank. Claire chose a Chardonnay, which was opened and placed in an ice bucket while somehow she navigated the conversation to the netball match that Leah had to play that afternoon, and the sports that Anna had enjoyed. Neither liked hockey. They talked of the GCSEs Leah would take in the summer, and the seven Anna had achieved. They talked of the A levels Leah would take, and the one Anna had taken at evening class, like Claire. They talked of the university degree Leah would take.

'Media Studies, that sounds great,' Anna said, tucking into the aubergine when it arrived. She waved her knife in the air. 'Hey, I'll do your makeup when you present your first programme.'

Claire smiled but wished Anna would stop waving her knife, then despised herself. Leah let the words sink in. So Anna would still be in their lives that far in the future? A big fat cuckoo in the nest. She lined her mat up with the edge of the table. Yes, she would be in their lives for ever, that's what all this was about. Her stomach turned over.

The waiter poured wine into Anna's glass and Claire's. Leah pushed her own glass into the arena. The waiter paused. Anna said to Claire, 'A bit wouldn't hurt, would it? She's got to get used to holding it.'

Leah said eagerly, enthusiastic again, 'That's what I keep saying. After all, you can go berserk if you're repressed.'

Claire faced her two daughters, both with the same expression, both on the same side, and a tentative hope took hold, but still she demurred. She murmured, 'This is a public place and you are in uniform.' She asked the waiter to replace the bottle in the bucket, holding her hand up to forestall Leah who she guessed was about to draw her attention to Annabel, who was sipping from a dangerously full glass. 'Just wait,' she ordered.

She had been right. Leah hissed, 'Annabel . . .'

'I said wait.' Claire was confident and firm, back to the mother who had always been in control, back to the mother Leah recognized and welcomed.

When the waiter had gone, Claire poured Leah's wine. 'It was coming, but not from him. It could cost him his job. You should think things through, Leah.'

Leah shrugged. 'It wasn't just me. It was her too.' She jerked her head towards Anna.

Claire took a deep breath. 'You should both have thought it through.' She looked from one to the other, and the looks on their faces were identical. Here we go, it said, and Claire laughed. Suddenly they were all laughing, and it was all right. Everything was all right, for the moment.

Anna eventually reached for her glass and raised it. 'To us all, and to Colonel Baird. May he be safe.'

Leah gulped her wine. Its dryness caught at the back of her throat, and she coughed, but not too much. Claire acknowledged Anna's toast and sipped her wine, then tackled the aubergine as Anna asked Leah if Annabel was at her school, saying, when Leah nodded, 'I hope this isn't difficult for you?'

Leah continued to cut up her food, saying without looking up, 'Of course it's difficult for me, but I wanted to get it over with. Anyway, Annabel is a motormouth and it'll save me having to spread the word that we've met. One part of the problem solved, wouldn't you say?'

Claire stared at Leah with what amounted almost to hatred but Anna seemed unconcerned, and just continued to eat, remarking, 'Good idea, but restaurants aren't as good as hair salons for gossip, you know.' Was it only Claire who noticed how Anna's grip had tightened on her knife and fork, how her knuckles had whitened?

Following Anna's lead, she said quickly, 'Neither are as good as the patch.' Though what she wanted to do was take Leah into the loos and scream at her to stop what she was doing, to give a little, just a little.

Leah sipped, listening, not joining in, because this Anna wasn't fighting back, she was calm, she was almost nice in spite of the fact that her knuckles had whitened. Suddenly she felt ashamed and poked at her meal as Anna said, 'Yes, I hadn't realized what a closed world the army is. I thought it was like outside, but it's not. I'd never have come like I did, if I'd known. But how do you do this right? Or don't you do it at all?' Her words were those she had rehearsed, hoping there would be a moment to say them, hoping it would be seen as the apology it was.

Leah took another sip of wine and no one spoke, though she wanted to say, You just don't come at people out of a bush. You don't do that to my mother. *Mine*, d'you understand? But though she thought it, somehow she didn't want to say it any more.

They ate on in silence and ordered ice-cream from the waiter, and now Claire talked of the party which would follow the first full rehearsal next week, and Leah said, sliding her teaspoon full of chocolate ice-cream in and out of her mouth, 'I'm surprised you haven't asked Anna to do the hair and makeup as well as supplying those wigs.'

Claire stopped with her spoon halfway to her mouth. 'I wasn't sure if you'd mind?'

Leah waved to Annabel as she passed them on her way to the loo. She hoped the girl had heard. She hoped it would be all around school that everything was fine, extremely, desperately fine. She allowed her voice to border on the surly again as she said, 'Why should I mind?'

Anna was looking from her to Claire, then drank a little wine. Leah mocked, 'Don't you even know you don't drink wine with dessert.'

Claire slammed down her hand on the table but before she could speak Anna replied, 'No, I didn't, but now I do and I'll remember, and while we're on the subject of self-improvement you shouldn't wear that blusher with your colouring. It's orange tones for us, Leah, or nothing.' It didn't matter that she'd

261

promised herself she would be calm, adult, understanding. This kid had had enough chances.

The two girls eyeballed one another, and Claire sat back. This was up to them, only them, and the tension which had been building in her fell away.

Leah was the first to break. Turning her attention to the ice-cream she finished it, as Anna finished hers. Only then did Leah pick up her wine, sensing Anna do the same. Together they drank, together they replaced their glasses. Leah toyed with the stem of hers, then asked, 'Orange you say?'

Anna grinned. 'Absolutely. The trick is to be subtle so it's there, but not obvious. Hey, come with me, we can have a quick try-out.' Leah hesitated, then said, 'I need to be back at 2.30. Maybe another time.'

Anna raised her eyebrows, saying evenly, 'Yes, another time would be fine.'

Claire checked her watch, beckoned for the bill, paid it with a credit card and added a cash tip, because she was never convinced that the credit card addition reached the staff. Outside it was still a crisp day. Anna hurried ahead of them to open the boot of her Fiesta which was parked near the entrance. 'The girls made a toy collection in the salon for Sergeant Malloy's orphanage.' As Claire unlocked her boot Anna struggled to lift the box while Leah did nothing. She just stood there with her hands in her pockets looking at the ground, but when Claire could bear it no longer and was about to shout at her, she moved, strolling to Anna, calling, 'Hang on, I'll give you a hand.'

Claire caught Anna's eye, and they both smiled. It was enough for now.

Once it was loaded Claire slammed the lid shut, then all three of them waited awkwardly for a moment. Anna dug into her bag, bringing out a £10 note and thrusting it at Claire. 'Please, I'd like to pay my share.'

Claire pushed the money away, wanting to say, I am your mother, you know. Instead she said, 'Thanks for coming all this way. You're welcome to come back for tea, rehearsals aren't until five.'

Anna smiled, but shook her head. 'No, Mum and Dad are expecting me. They're having a weekend break in Winchester and we're meeting for another meal.' She patted her stomach and laughed. 'I'll burst.'

Annabel and her parents came out then, and waved as they headed for a silver-grey BMW. Anna turned to Leah. 'Have a good match. Don't break any nails.'

Leah grimaced. 'Chance would be a fine thing. We have to cut them real short.'

'Really short,' corrected Claire automatically.

'Oh Mum,' complained Leah, then grizzled to Anna, 'She never stops nagging, you know.'

Anna laughed. 'My mum was just the same.' She adjusted the collar of her coat as the Armstrongs swept past them, hooting farewell. The car disappeared into the country lane. Anna smiled, hesitating before saying, 'Well, goodbye then.'

Claire moved towards her tentatively and this time Anna leaned forward and did what she had wanted to do when she entered the restaurant, but felt she shouldn't for Leah's sake. She kissed her mother, this mother who looked like her, whose mind seemed to work like hers, whose humour was the same, this mother who she felt sure now would

263

never deliberately want to take anything away from the ones who had nurtured and loved her, and always would.

Claire smelt the shampoo, felt her daughter's hands pulling her closer, and it healed the awful chasm that had opened at the words, 'My mum was just the same.'

Anna turned to Leah, noticing the closed expression. She touched her arm. 'Bye, Leah.'

Leah stood, uncertain again. Anna walked from them both to her car, and Claire felt a tightness in her chest as her elder daughter drove away.

After she and Leah had climbed into the Volvo, and were reversing to turn out of the car park, Leah said, picking fluff off her skirt, her voice deliberately nonchalant, 'It must be real hard to hear her say mum and dad.'

Claire put the car into first and drove out into the lane, driving along between the leafless hawthorn hedges. '*Really* hard,' she smiled, sounding more composed than she felt. 'They deserve it, they've brought her up, and I have you to call me mum.'

Leah insisted. 'It's still hard though.'

Claire reached the T junction, at which she turned left to go to the school. 'Yes, it's hard.'

Leah patted her arm. 'Poor Mum,' she whispered. 'Poor old Mum.'

Though there was a lot of traffic on the roads no one was doing anything stupid and Anna relaxed, turning on the radio, humming along to some Sixties song which she recognized but couldn't have named to save her life. She felt far too full and grinned to herself at the thought of meeting her parents for tea, and the scones that she would be

264

expected to force down. While she did so, she could at least tell them that she'd kept her cool, and that maybe Leah was sort of on the way to accepting her. But next time they met she must somehow get across to Leah that she wasn't going to take her mother from her, or impose herself too demandingly.

She slowed for a roundabout, changing gear, sliding into the flow of the traffic, accelerating out, keeping her eye on the signposts. The sky was grey and the wind quite fierce and she put her foot down harder, wondering if her parents were still admiring the cathedral. She laughed a little. Poor old Dad, he was probably dying for a cuppa. Her laugh died. She hoped they hadn't come across to Winchester just so they could balance her trip to Claire, just so they could remind her that they too existed. But then she shook free of the thought.

Of course not, they understood that her relationship with Claire would not affect how she felt for them, because Lynne Weaver seemed to understand everything about the situation. Not for the first time she realized how lucky she was. Imagine if all this had hurt them, or if she had to explain and reassure them all the time, or even fight them for the right to know who she was?

She grew thoughtful. Sometimes late at night she thought of herself in Claire's arms, just the two of them against the world together. How had she as a six-week-old baby felt, leaving those arms and being placed in a stranger's? Had she cried, had she been able to feed, had she lain awake, restless, knowing that things weren't as they should be? Had she pined, knowing something vital had gone from her life?

Just the thought of it made her want to cry now that she knew Claire, just the thought of it made her angry for them both. But even this she hadn't had to explain to Lynne Weaver, because she had felt the same about her mother. Would she one day explain it to Claire? Perhaps. Was this why she sometimes, inexplicably felt very alone? Or did everyone feel like that? Perhaps this was the question she would one day ask her sister, Leah. What did 'maybe' mean?

A signpost revealed that it was ten miles to Winchester and now Radio 1 was playing Simply Red. This one she *could* name.

*   *   *

Lynne and Harry Weaver stood back from the cathedral in Winchester, knowing they should be admiring the architecture and the tranquility of the environs, but they had a decision to take, and neither could quite make that final choice.

Lynne tucked her arm through her husband's. Anna would be leaving her biological mother now, and her biological sister, if she was to be in time for afternoon tea at the hotel. Sunday tea was a ritual in their house, especially since retirement. Good strong tea, half Earl Grey, half Assam, with scones or cakes, no rubbish about diets. It was the time when they would chat about the week. Perhaps the sprouts had come on, or—

Harry interrupted her thoughts. 'It would be the right thing to do.'

'Bugger the right thing.'

His arm squeezed hers. 'Come on, you don't mean that.'

266

But she did, for a wild ungovernable moment she did. Then she smiled at him. 'Oh, all right, I don't.' A Christmas cruise? Well, why not. It would mean new clothes, it would mean seasickness pills for the first three days. It would mean the first Christmas without Anna, and it wasn't fair, because Claire had Leah as well.

Harry and she walked in step, as they had always done, and at least she had that, not a husband who was stuck out in Bosnia, far away and in danger. Yes, at least she didn't have that and even as she thought it she knew she'd made up her mind. She said, 'Fine, we'll try and book up, but it's a bit late in the day to be absolutely sure we'll get a place, so no telling Anna, until it's certain.'

He agreed, and part of her was content because it was what her own adoptive mother had done: given her daughter her first Christmas with her real mother. It had meant on that occasion there had been no guilt on Lynne's part, no tearing of loyalty because her mother had said it was what she'd wanted for years, a Christmas in the sun, and that is what they'd say to Anna. It was what she'd say to Claire when she finally replied to the letter Claire had sent, thanking her for her generosity in letting their daughter find her.

Lynne rubbed her chest where the tight knot of fear seemed to live day in and day out. Her own two mothers had become good friends, travelling together when widowed, making wonderful grandmothers for Anna. Would she have the unselfishness to do likewise? Would Claire?

Harry said, quickening his pace, 'I know it's a wonderful piece of architecture and I know I'm a philistine, but all I want to do is put me feet up,

267

have a cuppa, and watch the television. How about you?'

Lynne laid her head on his shoulder as they walked along. 'Anything you say, my love.'

CHAPTER EIGHTEEN

Later that evening Mark stood with his back to the roaring fire in the sitting-cum-dining room of his house, just outside the Vitez base. Next to him Ben and Sven, the UNHCR representative, were sipping gin and tonic and talking of the appalling conditions the convoys were experiencing. Beyond them the candles flickered on the dining table, laid for seven. They were one man down courtesy of Major Stevens, who was stuck in Split.

Ben was shaking his head. 'We've tried chains on the Warriors, of course, but nothing is quite good enough. The roads are just so impacted with snow that it's practically ice. But then, I'm preaching to the converted.'

Sven said, 'Sometimes it's hard to imagine that the sun will come again. Did you ever holiday here, in the good old days?'

Ben shook his head. Mark noted the time. The others were late, but better that than early, Claire always said. But he didn't want to think about Claire, or her letters so loving and informative. It was the 'informative' he could do without, for God's sake. Ben was telling Sven of a canal holiday he'd had in the UK shortly before their deployment, and Sven laughed at the tales of Ben and Liz navigating via the pubs, and positively guffawed when Mark gave examples of Liz's obsession with fire escapes, and her need to check that there was one, even before she'd ordered a drink.

Ben protested, through his own laughter, 'She's not so bad now that the children are older.'

'We must be thankful for small mercies,' Mark said. 'Her highest point, Sven, was when she dragged that poor unsuspecting manager out of his pod at that rickety old theatre in Plymouth and made him prove that the fire exit was clear, only to light up a cigarette when the film started. I shall never forget that guy's face as he threw her out. Orgasmic satisfaction is the only word for it.'

Sven was beside himself. 'So, you missed the film?'

Ben and Mark exchanged a look. 'Certainly not, we all sat tight and she had to fill in two hours in the car park.' As they were laughing, Mark's batman, Wilkins showed in Charlie Bennet and Olga, another UNHCR representative. With them were Gordana and another interpreter, Irvana, a Croat who had moved into Gordana's flat in place of Nikola who had moved to Zagreb.

Mark, Ben and Sven fell into a stunned silence. The women were chic in cocktail dresses, dresses which clung to their bodies, bodies that the men had forgotten existed beneath the harsh weather gear the women always wore. Charlie cackled. 'Thought you'd think Christmas had come early, and so will I once I have a gin in my lily-white hand.'

Gordana laughed, looking glorious in her rich blue silk dress which made her greenish hazel eyes even more striking. 'Sometimes, if there is a very good fire, we are known to kick off our boots, climb out of our sweaters, and ...' Everyone laughed as Charlie pleaded with her to stop right there, or he'd have to take a cold shower, and what he really wanted was that drink. Mark and Ben had moved as one to greet their guests, and began to introduce Sven, only to find that everyone already knew everyone else.

Drinks were served by one of the civilians Mark had employed to take care of the house. He had particularly asked for the Muslim to be on duty tonight, and as the boy held out the tray to Irvana and Gordana they spoke quietly to him for a few moments, nodding and smiling, before Gordana excused herself, and made her way to Mark and Ben.

Mark was discussing the walking merits of the Bavarian countryside with Olga, who had lived in southern Germany during her teenage years, and widened the circle to include Gordana. She lifted her glass of sparkling white wine and toasted him. 'To you, for you have tried to employ an equal number of all factions here on your base, in spite of the high Croat population in this area. That is good.'

Mark sensed Ben's amusement, and knew that after the pantomime business he had expected his commanding officer to be at the blunt end of a heavy instrument again, instead of at the sharp point of a compliment. Mark smiled at her, glad that he had tried to ease her evening. 'It's common practice,' he said. Her smile was warm in return, her voice gentle as she murmured, 'Perhaps.'

Beside him Ben stirred as they heard Charlie call, 'Another robust gin, fragile on the tonic, if you

270

don't mind.'

*   *   *

Over dinner, which Mark had insisted should be a Bosnian lamb dish, the wine and conversation flowed easily, drifting from the Serb activity to the fighting between the Croats and Muslims, and on to the difficulty of maintaining regular aid convoys, finishing up at the battalion's R & R programme.

All the time Mark could smell the perfume of Gordana who sat on his right and the similar perfume on his left, which Irvana wore. It had a calming effect because it seemed to close the door on the outer world, all the outer world.

Gordana laid down her knife and fork, asking Ben, who sat next to Irvana. 'R & R, what is this?'

Ben explained. 'Rest and Recreation, aimed to remove us from the theatre of operations for a while.'

Gordana said nothing, just raised her eyes at Irvana, and reached for her glass of wine. As she did so, her short sleeve rode further up, and revealed the ugly shrapnel scar gouged into her upper arm.

Irvana said musingly. 'R & R. Yes, that will be refreshing for you all.' She proceeded to cut up her lamb, whilst Ben glanced, shamefaced at Mark.

Olga, the UNHCR representative, intervened sharply, 'But if, as you were saying, you did not have your leave last year because of pressure of work, Colonel Baird, then you must take care to take it. How can you think clearly when you are in the midst of chaos all the time? This is not your country, after all.'

271

By now Ben in confused embarrassment attempted to explain the problems R & R brought to their deployment, in the shape of a rotating shortfall of sixty men, not to mention the patch, where rehearsals could be messed up as the men took their wives away. On and on he wittered, and Mark wished to God he'd shut up.

So too, presumably did Charlie, who roared down the table, 'Nuff said about business. Tell us about Australia, Gordana, and if you feel you must wax lyrical about their wines, please do so. Even better if we were to have a wine tasting. How about that, my old fruit?' He peered at Mark. 'This will surprise you all, but I'm rather partial to a drop.' With a woeful expression he held up his empty glass.

Everyone leapt at the excuse to laugh, even Gordana and Irvana, though Irvana, who had a heavy cold, was looking pale and shivery. Sven poured red wine for his end of the table, because for this evening, unusually, Mark had sent the steward from the room, wanting relaxation above all else.

Somehow the conversation jigged round to the spring flowers of the Margaret River area of Western Australia, and the vineyards. Gordana explained how she had worked in the wine shop of one and had arranged for a case to be sent home. She paused. Mark almost closed his eyes, resigned to the blunt instrument, but all she said was, 'It is probably still there, at the dock.'

What she had the grace to not say was that there was no home. Instead she placed her knife and fork together, her appetite clearly ruined. Mark had never realized how slender her fingers were, and how graceful.

Opposite Sven, Ben was saying, 'You've heard that Mark knows all about vineyards, have you, Charlie?'

Charlie was holding his glass of wine up to the candle, his face thoughtful as he missed his cue, but Mark grabbed the subject and talked rapidly about his mother and father rejuvenating the Tuscany vineyard, his voice enthusiastic as he said of his mother, 'I swear she gives each vine a name, and has intimate chats on her daily rounds.'

Irvana smiled, her voice croaky, her eyes watery. 'Ah, so we have a wine expert sitting at our table. Do you prefer New or Old World wines? I know that Gordana favours the new, and in particular developed a taste for the Australian Chardonnays.'

Mark shrugged. 'Gordana and I will have to agree to disagree, I'm afraid.' He caught Ben's eye. So what's new, the look said.

Mark carried on regardless. 'Anyway, I have to support the Old World wines, don't I, or I'll get clobbered by Ma. As for being an expert?' He held up his hands in surrender. 'Not guilty I'm afraid, just wish I was. I should have listened more carefully as a child, but what with boarding school, and then Sandhurst . . .'

Gordana sipped at her wine sparingly, asking him over the top of the glass, 'So, how often do you return to help your parents, Colonel Baird?'

'Parent,' he said gently. 'My father died some years ago. My mother runs the business as though it is the easiest thing in the world. She never complains, just copes. She's a wonderful woman.'

Gordana was curious. 'So, you never go home, is this what you say?'

273

Mark finished the last of his lamb, wishing there was more, because the garlic and rosemary sauce had been delicious. Wiping his mouth on his white linen napkin he said, 'Oh no, I go home. I love it, I used to hate leaving it, I used to almost hate them for sending me away to school, it made me feel jealous, and excluded. My parents adored one another so much I sometimes wondered if they knew I was there half the time.' He stopped abruptly, embarrassed at himself. For God's sake, how much wine had he had?

He darted a glance round the table, but it was only Gordana who was listening to him. The others were chatting to one another. He said briskly, 'Yes, Gordana, I go back every two years. I enjoy walking, you see. I used to drag Claire along but it was never her scene really. She couldn't keep up in the heat, so now she and Leah sit round the pool and catch up on the gossip with my ma. There'll be no pool but certainly a lot of chat on the patch this Christmas as well. Mother comes every year. It's a sort of ritual.'

He fingered the ballpoint in his breast pocket, the one Claire had given him, and allowed Gordana to pour him more wine, though his thoughts were clearly becoming flabby, and it was more than time to stop. He tried to take the bottle from Gordana, saying, 'Please, allow me.' She waved him away, pouring more for herself, and trying to catch Irvana's attention, but she was deep in conversation with Ben. She replaced the wine in the cooler. 'It must be hard to be away at Christmas?'

'It always has been.' He was deep in thought for a moment.

'Perhaps this year it will be more than ever.' Yes, his mother's visit would ground him, it would prove that everything was normal, and as it had always been.

'I used to walk.' Gordana gestured towards the hill. 'These mountains are wonderful walking country, if you like a challenge.' The usual strand of hair had escaped from her bun, and Mark moved imperceptibly to brush it from her cheek, recovering himself just in time.

Oblivious, Gordana was telling him of Korcula, one of the Adriatic islands where she and her family had regularly taken their holiday. Now Irvana caught the name, and together they told of the slopes covered with pines, myrtle, juniper, rosemary. 'To me it is the scent of heaven,' Irvana said.

Gordana smiled and waggled a finger at Mark, and he realized that she too had drunk too much, 'On our little island we too make wine. It is *posip*. It is pale and white. One day you will try it, or perhaps one day, I might just bring you some. One day I might go back, and sail, and bathe and have some R & R.' There was no condemnation, no antagonism, just sadness in her voice, and it was in Irvana's also, as she added, 'Yes, one day, for our R & R.'

* * *

The dessert was fruit salad in a cognac syrup. Mark was mother, and ladled it into glass bowls, sending it down via a fire chain. When Charlie received his he held it to his nose, then bellowed, 'Try this, Irvana, it's powerful stuff. Got to be neat cognac—

it'll clear your sinuses at ten yards.'

Irvana would have none, and her cheeks were flushed, but she shook her head at Mark when he suggested a driver should take her to the flat. 'Please, it is so nice to be here where it is warm, so civilized.'

Half an hour later they retired to the sitting-room end of the room for liqueurs, and Ben and Mark had just poured brandy for them all when there was a tap on the door. It was Wilkins, Mark's batman. 'Excuse me, Colonel, but there's a message come through from the press house, for Mr Bennet. His presence is required. Apparently there's a query on his copy.'

Mark thanked him as Charlie lumbered to his feet, growling about the iniquities of jumped-up squirts nit-picking in their plate-glass offices back home. Mark grinned as Charlie downed his brandy in one fell swoop. 'Spelling all to pot, Charlie?'

Charlie shook hands all round, grunting to Mark as they moved towards the door, 'I half expected it, knew I was putting it a bit strong, not quite even-handed, if you know what I mean. This place gets to you.'

Irvana was on her feet, hurrying to join them, calling weakly, 'Please, Charlie, may I come with you? This cold, it really is too much after all.' As Gordana also stirred, Mark started to protest, but it was Charlie who waved her down. 'I'll take Irvana, but you stay. Mark'll see you get home, won't you old sport? Can't all be party poopers.' He patted Irvana hastily on the arm, reassuring her. 'Not that you are, my dear. You've done splendidly to stay the course. It's me and my pen, silly old fart that I am.' He was bustling from the

276

room as he spoke, and Irvana followed in his wake, with Mark bringing up the rear, to see them to the front door.

*   *   *

On his return he saw to his relief that Gordana had settled back on the sofa. She was chatting to Sven whilst Ben and Olga sat opposite, deep in conversation. Mark returned to his armchair in time to hear Sven ask Gordana if she still helped at the refugee transit centres, and as he did so he pulled out a pack of Marlboro cigarettes, and offered them around. Gordana refused. 'I don't smoke.'

She saw the surprise on Mark's face and half laughed, obviously realizing what was in his mind. 'I just keep them with me for the job,' she explained, then shrugged, her voice becoming a caricature of Marlene Dietrich. 'Well, my dears, it is one way to a man's heart. One way to smooth the path of a roadblock.'

The others laughed, but Mark protested. 'I didn't notice. Please, you must let me provide the cigarettes. You have so . . .' He stopped.

She swirled her brandy in her glass, speaking across Sven who was now talking to Olga about the front-line situation. 'So little?'

There was pain in her face, and anger, and frustration, and an awful, gaping emptiness. He said quietly, for her ears only, 'Yes, you have so little and I'm sorry to talk of holidays, of wine, of leave and a life beyond this. I'm sorry to talk of a future.' She sat back silently, and while the others, unknowing, continued to talk amongst themselves,

Mark too lapsed into silence.

At length Olga and Sven left to prepare for an early start, and a few moments later Ben checked the clock and announced that he needed to look in on the Ops Room. At this, Gordana rose, smoothing down her dress. Mark said, 'I'm so sorry, the driver won't have returned from taking Sven and Olga to their hotel, and even though it's a short distance we won't hear of you walking. Please, finish your brandy at the very least, Miss Gordana. It should only be about ten minutes, if that?' He checked this with Ben, who smiled as he took his leave of Gordana. 'Yes, not much longer I should say.' Mark walked to the door with Ben who said quietly, his grin wry, 'Shall I stay? Do you need reinforcing, Colonel?' Mark ushered him out into the cold hall, muttering, 'I dare say I can cope.' He opened the front door and the cold hit them both. Ben whispered, 'Send up a flare if she starts an attack.'

Mark stared out into the night. Ben didn't seem funny tonight, but he grinned, nonetheless. 'You can count on it.'

*   *   *

Back in the room he saw that Gordana had shaken off her dark blue shoes and curled her legs up beneath her. He sat opposite, offering her another brandy. She sighed and shook her head. 'Thank you, but I feel I should not have had the first one.'

Mark ran his hands through his hair. 'Feel much the same way myself. We'll suffer in the morning. Nine hundred hour start suit you, as usual?'

She nodded, as he knew she would, because this

girl, he had come to realize, could cope with anything, absolutely anything. She leaned against the cushions, letting her head tilt back until she was staring at the ceiling.

He followed her gaze. The light from the fire was flickering on the coving; all around was a scent of candles, perfume and cigarette smoke. The strand of hair lay against her cheek. He looked away, into the fire. There was just the ticking of the clock, the crackle of the fire, and in the distance . . . But no, not tonight, he wouldn't listen to it tonight.

He said softly, 'So, did you go to the Refugee Centre in Travnik today?'

She nodded. She still looked up at the ceiling.

Mark went on: 'The wives at home are raising funds for an aid lorry.' It sounded lame. Gordana nodded again, but nothing more. He continued: 'It doesn't sound much but they are doing all that they can.'

She murmured, her head still back, her eyes still on the ceiling. 'Of course they are. And your wife, she is well?'

As she spoke her throat moved, catching the firelight. Her skin gleamed.

'Yes, very,' he said, looking beyond her to the table, and the debris of the meal. The staff would be wanting to clear, but sod it.

'She's busy with the pantomime?' Gordana ventured.

'Yes, and other things.'

She lowered her gaze and looked at him, and there was concern in her eyes, a softening of her posture. 'The newly arrived daughter?'

Taken unawares, Mark found himself saying things that previously he had only thought, letting the words come in the jumble in which they chased one another round his head, explaining that the whole thing seemed to be larger than he'd thought, that it sneaked up on him at the most inappropriate moments. 'Stupid I suppose, but you just never get time to think here, time to sort yourself out, think things through.' He didn't look at her, couldn't look at her, because he felt this stupid ache in his throat, this awful need to swallow, to lower his head into his hands and blot it all out, to have a bloody good cry.

When Gordana spoke her voice was gentle. 'It is a bad time for this to have happened.'

Mark kept his eyes on the fire, and coughed, clasping his hands tightly together. 'No, she's glad, but any mother would be.'

They focused on the fire together. The scent of her perfume was stronger. 'No, I meant for you, because new allegiances are being formed that will change things. Nothing will be as it was, and that is a great shame. You know, when I was away in Australia I liked to think of my parents doing those things they had always done, looking at the same views, celebrating the same festivals in the same way. In sameness is security. It is like a comfort blanket.'

He shifted his gaze to her now, but he said nothing, because her words were still there, knocking away inside his head.

She was still looking at the fire. 'Sameness or a pattern, or is that the same thing? Anyway, it's what this chaos needs. A pattern. We'll have to wait for peace for that to happen. But I wonder if it will even then, or will this destruction just prove a breeding ground for even greater intolerance, primitivism, ignorance?'

Mark felt as though he could pin nothing down, as though it was all a jumbled mass; what was his life against all this?

There was a tap at the door. Wilkins entered. 'Miss Sevo's transport is ready, Colonel.'

*　　*　　*

They travelled the short distance in the Land Rover, with Lance-Corporal Simms driving, as usual. Mark accompanied Gordana to her flat upstairs which smelt of cat's pee and garbage. The beam of her torch picked out discarded cans and packets.

Outside her flat he held the torch, illuminating the keyhole for her. Before turning the key, she held out her hand. 'Thank you for a delightful evening, Colonel Baird.'

He shook it. 'Thank you for coming.' He smelt her perfume. She smiled, opened the door, then turned again. 'I feel for you, Colonel Baird, for whilst I seek my father, your wife's daughter will also be thinking of doing the same, or if she does not now, she must surely later.'

CHAPTER NINETEEN

Claire and Clarissa had crocodiled the playgroup down to the Garrison Theatre every morning for the last week, lugging Christmas decorations they had made and now, *voilà*, it was Christmas, though it was only mid-December. All around the hall maniacally grinning Santas were stuck up, alongside huge cardboard holly leaves complete with dyed polystyrene berries.

Jo grinned at Claire and Liz as all three sat at the producer's table they had set up in front of the fully lit stage on which several of the cast were checking through their lines, and preparing themselves for the ball dress 'fitting' scene. Jo said, looking round at the walls, 'Makes me feel quite sad I no longer believe Santa's going to plummet down my chimney.'

Claire grunted. 'I live in hope that at least he'll send one of his tall, dark and handsome helpers. It's been on my list for years.'

Liz leaned close. 'Much you know. The helpers are elves, and elves are short, fat and hairy.'

Claire raised her eyebrows. 'Well, OK, from this day forth I pass on the assistant.' Jo was laughing as she scanned the stage, pulling herself to order momentarily as Rob and the vicar sashayed from the wings in trousers, pullovers and wigs—one dyed bright blue by Anna, the other bright pink. At the sight of them a great roar of laughter went up from the other cast members dotted in small groups about the hall, some sitting, some standing, some rehearsing. The hilarity increased as Rob minced here and there while the vicar preened in front of the glassless mirror set dead centre.

Jo shouted above the clamour: 'Excellent, I knew the wigs would make you get the feel of the part.' In an aside to Claire she said, 'Thank Anna, won't you, Claire.'

Claire murmured to Liz: 'Though I dare say their wives are distinctly uneasy about their men's wholehearted approach to all this drag.'

282

Jo was clapping for order, calling over Claire's head to the groups behind them. 'OK everyone, you can work your way through your lines while we're doing this scene, but keep the noise down as much as you can.' She turned to Claire: 'You all set, Claire?' Claire stood by, ready to note Jo's stage directions and any script changes.

Already Jo was springing up the centre-stage steps, beckoning to the four youngsters chatting at the back of the stage. 'Now listen, you are the dressmaker's children, paid by her to admire the dresses, and to make out the two Uglies are the most wonderful sights since Kate Moss strutted her stuff down the catwalk. Let's get that across to Claire down there.'

Claire joined in the giggling as Rob more than strutted. Jo called, 'That's egging the pudding, Rob. Keep it for the march-past. The Colonel would love it—am I right, Claire?'

Claire gave a thumbs up. Rob peered down at her. 'Ah, so that's the route to promotion?'

Turbogob came up to the table, chewing gum, wearing flashing snowmen earrings and a witch's hat decorated with Christmas tinsel. She said, 'Or redundancy, if you're lucky, eh, Mrs Baird?' Claire smiled warily; she always expected a verbal attack from this woman, a repetition of the playgroup celebration. 'You could be right, Angie.'

Turbogob came closer to Claire, as Jo placed the youngsters to the left of the mirror, and the dressmaker to the right, telling them all to make sure they were in their positions, chalking on the floor so no mistakes would be made, Claire made a note on the script of the positions as Turbogob looked over her shoulder. Claire could hear her

283

chewing and braced herself, barely able to concentrate.

Liz, on the other side of Claire called. 'Come and check your schedule, will you Angie? I need to make sure you're OK for the group rehearsal on Wednesday.'

On stage Jo was concentrating on the Uglies. 'Come on, principals. That's right, Rob, swing around. Just remember that you'll have a crinoline on. Vicar, move away just a fraction, make the space, and *preen*, Vicar.' She called down to Claire: 'Claire, have you remembered Brigadier Fransten's wife is "dropping in" to see how we're getting on.'

Claire pretended not to hear the groan from all around, and waved an acknowledgement. As though she could forget. At that moment little Audrey Wilt walked past, and waved happily as Claire grinned in reply.

Audrey's husband had already been home for his R & R and though they had missed her from rehearsals the young couple seemed to have come to enough of an understanding to continue with the marriage, helped by an allotment on his earnings to repay his debts, including that of the binoculars.

On his return to Bosnia Audrey had continued to attend the Mother and Toddler Group, walking along with Bridget Murphy, the network rep for that part of the patch, and Claire had ceased to worry about her, though plenty of new cases had taken her place.

As she swung back to the script she heard Sal call: 'Liz, could you put the urn on? I'm just taking the mice through their scene in the dressing room.'

Instantly Turbogob called from her perch amongst the witchlets at the rear of the hall, 'The

284

urn doesn't suit her.' Amidst the groans Claire wrote it down, nodding confirmation as Jo caught her eye. Yes, that corny little gem would go in the script, somewhere.

While Liz sorted out the urn in the kitchen Claire checked her own schedule and saw that by now she should be taking a small crowd scene rehearsal at the back of the hall. Hurriedly she gestured young Annie Bates over to take her place at the table and made her way to the back, smiling at those of the cast who noticed her, stopping to answer queries and calm worries, picking up Sal, Bridget and Audrey from their territory near the wall heater, gathering several including the 'Orrible Oracle and the witchlets.

As they found their places for the crowd scenes in Act I, Scene iii, Audrey asked tentatively, 'Please, Mrs Baird, is there any news on Corporal Jennings?'

At once the group fell quiet, and Claire shook her head. 'No more than we already know, I'm afraid. Perhaps you heard that I drove Eva to her mother's in Hammersmith last night, the moment my husband rang with the news. John arrived at St Thomas's at 11 a.m., but he wasn't due to see the specialist until this afternoon. There might be a message on my answer machine, but she has Rob's mobile as well, so she knows she can ring here. Either way, the moment we hear we'll ring round the network leaders and they'll spread the word.' She turned to Bridget. 'Little Fleur's settled with you, has she?'

Bridget nodded, looking helpless. Claire shook her arm. 'You're doing a great job, all of you.'

The girls just shook their heads, for each one of

them knew that it could have been their husband who had stepped on to a mine at the checkpoint. Claire allowed them to brood for a moment, then said quietly, 'Are you all up to this?' She tapped her script, knowing that to keep busy was the best thing for them.

After working through the scene, Claire left them to rehearse it a second time. Making her way back to the table, she was intercepted by Mollie wearing two strings of pearls tonight because Heather Fransten was coming. 'I think we need a bit of help, if you wouldn't mind.' It wasn't a question.

'Problems?

Mollie sniffed in the direction of Roland, Muriel's gardener who had been volunteered for chicken duty. He was in the corner by the stage, arms crossed, with a face down to his knees. Ethel Mornament of Over Setton WI, and co-boss of the costume department with Mollie, was shaking her finger at him. Roland's wizened face grew even longer as he saw Claire approaching with Mollie. and before Claire could speak he shook his head. 'I ain't wearing that stuff. It's too bloody hot, and I don't care what Mrs Muriel says about it. I ain't wearing it.'

Mollie picked up the kapok lining they'd fitted inside the chicken outfit as Ethel snapped at Roland, 'Hush your noise.' Mollie's face was a picture of creative angst as she complained, 'He's right though, it's even hotter than the foam rubber.'

'Can't see why I just can't have the bloody material on its own and just stick in a few feathers,' Roland growled.

Mollie's tone was dismissive. 'You've got to have

286

padding as well as feathers. Isn't that right, Claire?' Her expression dared Claire to disagree but Claire had no intention of doing so. Mollie was quite right, and was, startlingly, doing a great job, so taking Roland to one side, she explained to him that the part of the chicken was crucial, it would woo children and adults alike and he needed to look plump and succulent. Mollie interrupted: 'Or else your skinny legs won't look half so ridiculous.'

Claire winced and laid her hand on Roland's arm. 'She means the costume wouldn't look half so ridiculous, and do remember this is for Bosnia, and we're all having to do things we might not normally do.'

Grudgingly Roland returned to face the tape measures, but he wasn't quite finished. He turned back to Claire. 'Except for Mrs Muriel, that is. Don't see her here in fishnet tights.'

Well, thought Claire, as she returned to the producer's table, we must indeed be thankful for small mercies.

At the back of the stage the dressmaker's children were not paying attention again, but this time, before Claire or Jo could sort it out, Turbogob rounded on them, her voice firm, but not vicious as she said, 'Come on, you lot, concentrate. Check the chalk markings and come through in the right place or you'll bust your noses barging through the wall when it's up. Bunch up, you've got to get used to it or you'll let us all down.'

Jo and Claire exchanged a surprised, appreciative look. Claire called, 'Well done, Angie. Thank you.'

Jo murmured, 'That's the first time you've been nice to her. I know it's because you're petrified of the woman, but she doesn't know that. Good going, ma'am.'

On stage Turbogob had flushed with pleasure, before burying her face in the script, as though unimpressed.

Jo continued quietly, 'While we're on the subject, Angie was a hairdresser. It might be an idea to get her to give Anna a hand with the wigs. I saw her having a look at Rob's a minute ago, telling him your daughter had done a good job.'

Claire looked at Jo in amazement, unable to believe that Angie had swung so far round. Jo shook her head in mock exasperation. 'You should try to believe that sometimes things work out, Claire.'

But how could she? Claire stared down at her script, suddenly cold. How could she, because last night, and the night before, and for as many nights as she could remember since Anna had returned she had floundered in her dreams between Mark, Leah and Anna and then the beach and her mother's voice, her own confusion, her own shame, and the anger which she must never allow to surface because, as her mother said, the only person who deserved it was her.

*   *   *

By nine o'clock they had reached Act II, and were putting the understudy Uglies—a farmer and his herdsman—through their paces when Liz called through the hatch: 'Tea's up, and Mrs Fransten's car's arrived. I'll bring through a cup for her.'

Claire hurried to the main entrance, with Mollie tripping along behind. At that moment Mrs

288

Fransten walked into the dark and freezing lobby, immaculate in her Jaeger suit and sensible court shoes. As Claire ushered her through into the hall she was horribly aware of her own grubby jeans, her ponytail which Liz had christened 'Rats', and her *Oh yes she did* T-shirt which Belle had sent from Italy, not to mention her trainers which seemed to squeak on the wooden floor with every step.

Mrs Fransten was graciously patronizing as always, taking the cup from Liz with every evidence of delight, but drinking germ-wise left-handedly as she viewed the activity all around her. 'Your little idea seems to be going very well, Claire.'

Mollie clung to Claire's side, her smile reflecting those of the blu-tacked Santas. Claire replied, 'Oh yes, everyone's working very hard. Mollie is doing a splendid job with the costumes, though we're having a bit of a struggle with the chicken's outfit. Kapok versus foam rubber.'

Mrs Fransten glazed over. 'Quite.'

From the stage the understudy Buttons, in the shape of the village carpenter, held out a marrow to Rob and bellowed, 'Where do you want this?'

Rob touched his bright blue wig and preened. 'Where do you think?' Mrs Fransten blanched. Mollie tutted. Claire, however, joined in the laughter which broke out all around, though it was self-conscious, and she knew that everyone here had half an eye on them. Mrs Fransten looked at her. 'I do so hate all this, it's so *silly*.'

Claire said firmly, 'Yes, it's just what's needed, especially after yesterday's bad news.'

Mrs Fransten handed her half-finished cup to Mollie, saying, 'So kind, do thank Liz.' Having satisfactorily dismissed Mollie Mrs Fransten adjusted her shoulder bag, crossed her arms and murmured, 'Yes, sad news. He's bound to lose the foot, isn't he? But I gather he wanted redundancy anyway so it's not such a loss.'

Claire somehow kept a smile fixed on her face, even when Mrs Fransten added, 'Could have been nasty, coming hot on the heels of that little incident of yours, but even that seems to have settled down.'

By now Liz was making her way towards them wearing Angie's flashing earrings, waving enthusiastically, saying the moment she arrived, 'So glad you could come, Mrs Fransten. Hasn't Claire done a marvellous job?'

Mrs Fransten was glued to the earrings, her smile all but gone. She recovered as Liz repeated, 'Hasn't Claire done a marvellous job?'

'Oh, yes, indeed she has.'

Liz charged on. 'We're expecting you on the last night along with Mark. There'll be *lots* of audience participation. Well, must get on.' She wafted off to a group to the left of them. Claire dug her hands into her jeans and stared fixedly at the stage, insisting to herself that she must not laugh.

Mrs Fransten cleared her throat. 'Well, I must shoot off too.' As Claire walked her to the door she saw Liz fire her finger, and mouth 'Bang.'

Mrs Fransten stopped as Claire opened the door for her, and drew out her diary.

'While I'm here, Claire, I must tell you that I've altered the usual New Year's Eve cocktail party this year. It's to be on the 23rd of December because I'm off to the house in Tenerife on Christmas Eve so obviously I won't be here on New Year's Eve.' Mrs Fransten's laugh was brittle. She continued:

290

'Short notice I know, but there are more wives staying on the patch this year, it seems their relatives are coming to them. Bring Leah.'

The door was heavy and the cold air from the lobby was penetrating Claire's T-shirt with consummate ease. She held the door half open behind her as she said, 'It's Leah's Youth Club disco that evening, Heather, but Anna, my adopted daughter, might be here for the evening.'

Mrs Fransten didn't respond for a moment, then she snapped shut her diary and made a great business of putting it back in her handbag, saying at last, her voice heavy with meaning, 'Oh, that *will* be nice for you, but you know Claire, I'm sure she wouldn't want to be sipping Manhattans with people she doesn't know. These young people would rather be out dancing the night away so naturally I wouldn't dream of expecting her to come to my little soirée. Why don't you just slip in yourself, for a few minutes? I'm sure Mark would prefer that.'

Claire felt the smile fade from her face. How stupid of her to be lulled by all of this. Her glance took in the room through the half-open door. How stupid when there were still the Heathers, Heathers who happen to be brigadiers' wives, brigadiers who happen to be important to Mark. Very deliberately she let the door swing shut behind them, finding her way in the dark to the front door, opening it heedless of the cold, her face set, her voice calm. She said, 'I'll check my diary, Heather. Thank you so much for sparing five minutes to see how we're getting on.'

Mrs Fransten, oblivious to the sarcasm in Claire's voice, issued a regal wave before leaving.

Claire did not see her to her car but let the door slam shut almost on her heels and stood for a moment in the cold darkness of the lobby. So, she was winning with Angie, but God Almighty, there was always something or someone else.

Through the closed door came the sound of laughter, the sound of singing, of clapping. She leaned back against the wall. She had to go to the cocktail party or it would be considered a snub, and that could damage Mark. But isn't a snub what that damned woman had just delivered to Anna? Anna who, like most of the people involved in this, was blameless.

She hugged herself, shivering, but it was only partly caused by the cold. She closed her eyes, then opened them as a burst of sound gushed into the lobby. She saw Liz standing at the open door, her earrings in full-flash mode. Liz grinned, stepped forward and let the door swing shut, flashing nicely in the dark. 'Thought I'd join you to see the full effect. One needs a darkened room for flashing, you know.'

Suddenly they were both laughing as though they'd never stop. Liz pulled out her cigarettes and lit one. Now there was a dull glow dead centre. 'It's Blackpool Tower for you,' Claire murmured.

Liz inhaled, and came to lean alongside Claire, who could still smell the sulphur of her match. Liz liked Swan Vestas. She said they took her back to their childhood when they'd go to the cinema together in Woking or Guildford and someone somewhere would light up. Liz said, 'I heard the bitch, you know. And she is a bitch because she'd got you over a barrel, quite deliberately, the narrow-minded idiot. But don't worry, I won't try and persuade you to invite her to take a running jump. One simply does not do that to a brigadier's wife, does one?'

Claire sighed, wishing that she smoked. Instead she dug her hands deep into her pockets. 'I can understand why she doesn't want Anna crashing into her world, there isn't a rule of behaviour in the manual for things like this, but it doesn't make it easier. I can't possibly go without her, it would be such a statement, but can I just not go? Think of the repercussions on top of everything.' She trailed off. 'I don't know, Liz, I keep thinking it's all working out, and then something like this happens, or Leah backpedals, or Mark . . .' She shrugged. 'It's like a yo-yo. The more I see Anna the more I regret the years I've lost, the more I regret those, the more I get this desperate joy that she's here, and then the more I want everyone to feel it . . .'

Liz's earrings were still flashing, and now Claire could see the litter on the floor, and the coats which the cast had hung, or flung, where they could. Frowning, Liz flicked her ash on to the litter, putting her arm round Claire and saying firmly, 'You must do a runner, go away, then you're not offending anyone, just giving yourselves the space you need, and the girls a chance to jockey for position away from the goldfish bowl.'

Claire relaxed against her friend. God, it would be perfect. She closed her eyes, seeing the three of them away from all of this, but even as she did so she knew it was hopeless. Quietly she said, 'But Mark likes us to be in whatever quarters we've been assigned, with Belle. He makes such a point of it every year and I don't want him upset. He's under such strain.'

293

Liz shook her. 'Don't be a silly tart. Everything in your life has always been for him, every bloody thing, and this would hardly be a crime. Go on, phone Belle, ask her if she minds a change of venue.' She paused. 'I know, go to Muriel's cottage in the grounds of that hotel, surely that'll solve Mark's problem. He can't possibly object because you've all stayed there so often it's just like home. He loves it, always blathering on about it being a second home. Anyway, I've always thought he was loopy to want to stick around the patch over Christmas.'

At 10.30 that night, Claire phoned Tuscany, stretching the cord of the phone to its utmost so that she could sit at the kitchen table and sip her cocoa at the same time. So far it had all proved amazingly easy. Muriel, Leah and Anna had all agreed, but would Belle?

Belle was surprised but pleased to hear from her, though when Claire mentioned the change of plan there was a hesitation, and Claire's heart sank. Belle's tone, however, was careful as she explained her relief, because she had very much hoped that Claire would take the girls off patch, and spend time with them, alone. 'It's not that I don't long to meet Anna, darling, but, I repeat, you all need this time together.'

Claire protested, 'But we want you with us.'

Belle laughed. 'Part of me wants to be there, but darling, the bigger part wants to stay here, just for one Christmas. It's been so long since I have, and I do hate leaving it. I've always come to you because I felt I should, but not this Christmas. This Christmas I really feel I can take advantage of the fact that I shouldn't. Come on, now, admit that it

294

would be better.'

Claire heard the earnestness in her voice, and she now realized what Muriel had been trying to tell her just a few moments ago when she had said that this would be a gift from the gods for Belle, who might well have her own plans.

Belle was hurrying on. 'Don't worry, darling, I know Mark's a bit set in his ways, but I'll write to him and explain. He'll understand both our points of view and, for heaven's sake, he really shouldn't need such patterns any longer. I'll come in the spring, or you will bring Anna to me. Promise. Remember I love you. I really love you.'

Claire knew she did.

Miraculously she slept and for the first time for so long there was no sound of Leah, or Mark, and not even the surging of the surf.

*   *   *

Belle set aside the parcels she was wrapping on the big table by the window, and looked over the slopes of the vineyard to Monte Vecchio, which was bathed in moonlight. There was not a cloud in the sky, and so there would be another frost tonight. She stretched. Tomorrow she would find a tree and decorate it now she didn't have to go to England. Whoopee!

She poured a second glass of wine. It was an indulgence she didn't usually allow herself but this was an excellent vintage, one of their best, and it *was* a special occasion. She raised her glass to the photo of Mark and his family, and then to the one of her husband. '*Salute.*' Her gaze fell on the painting she had been about to wrap. She must post it tomorrow now that she was not taking it. Yes, it would look good in that barn of a dining room.

Again she looked across the vineyard. Thank God she could stay at Chianciamo. She'd never liked to refuse to go before, because Mark was such a one for ritual. Why was that? Muriel said he'd felt marginalized by Belle and Clive's love for one another but Belle thought that was absurd, they had both adored Mark, but perhaps it was the hours they had to put into the vineyard in the early days—the end result was probably the same and amounted to neglect. The old guilt stirred.

In the huge fireplace the log burner was winding down and would need more fuel if she was to stay up much longer. She sipped again at her wine. No, she'd get to bed, just as she'd told Claire to do. Mark you, that's what she seemed to have spent her time saying to her since Anna had returned. 'Get to bed, you need to keep your strength up.' But there was always just one more patch effort to be tidied up.

There should be more she could do—but what? Claire hadn't wanted her to fly over, though she'd been more than prepared to. She loved that girl, very much. Restlessly she paced up and down before the window. When did you stop worrying about those you loved, regretting what you hadn't done, wondering what you should now do? Never, it seemed.

She'd felt the same when Mark had flown out just after Claire had originally told him of her illegitimate baby. Glory be, what a welter of rending of clothes and gnashing of teeth from the lad. It was plain jealousy, and insecurity, Clive had guessed, and so it had been. Mark had sat on the terrace with them the day after he had arrived that hot, hot summer and drank himself almost into a stupor before he had mumbled, 'Who is the father? Who the hell is the father? Did she love him more than me? Will he try and find the child, or Claire?'

'He can't search for the child,' she had said. 'It's not allowed, and even if he did, or if he looked up Claire, she wouldn't have him. Why on earth should she do that, when she left in the first place? Besides it wasn't a relationship, was it? It was a mistake—you've allowed her to tell us that much. I just wish you'd sit down and let her talk it through and stop being so stupid and jealous. But you won't, so you have to accept that it's all over, that she loves you. Or leave her. Whatever you decide you must stick to it.'

He wanted to know no more about it, he'd insisted. He'd returned to Claire, though, and put it behind him, never mentioned it again, nor allowed Claire to. In 1975, when the Adoption Act was passed and it became possible for children over eighteen to find their parents, he had said to Belle, 'If she comes, she comes. Claire has a right to know her child.'

Belle had been amazed, but realized that she shouldn't be, for Claire's self-denying love and gratitude, which had driven Belle mad at first though it was encouraged by her appalling mother, had worked the miracle. Mark had metamorphosed into a confident army officer and husband, until this final promotion, when he had crumbled, behaving like a petulant bad-tempered bully—out of fear of failure and the stress of the responsibility. Still Claire had supported him, beyond the call of duty, for God's sake. Damn it, why hadn't Anna come earlier, because from the tone of Mark's letters he wasn't handling this at all well.

Belle peered out across the valley, her breath misting the glass. Why the hell had he gone into the army in the first place? She and Clive had thought he would take over the vineyard. He was a natural, he loved it, it loved him. No one could handle vines like Mark. But it was because of the Gibbons boys, of course.

He'd brought that young Ben and his older brother Simon out for the first time when he was thirteen for the whole of the summer holidays. Those two boys were army brats, and destined for Sandhurst, though it was Simon who had been Mark's close friend. When he had died in a motorcycle accident, Ben had taken his place in Mark's affection, becoming more like a brother.

Mark had decided shortly after Simon's death that it was the army for him—Muriel had felt it was deeply Freudian, and so had Belle, but what could you do? At least it meant that he met Claire at a Sandhurst 'do', and what a love that had turned out to be. It was as great as his parents' for one another.

Belle felt the tears come, but pushed them back. Clive was gone, but memories weren't. She wouldn't be sad. Mustn't be sad. Again she looked across to Monte Vecchio, and asked herself what she could do.

Nothing. They were grown up people. All she could do was wait to see how this returning child really affected them.

CHAPTER TWENTY

The week before Christmas Mark felt he could die with weariness as he tumbled into the hotel bed in Tuzla, but once there sleep eluded him. He tried to relax from the toes up which some Radio 2 idiot had sworn was a good cure for insomnia but after he'd reached the top of his head for the second time he gave up, and just tossed and turned, listening to the creaks of the hotel, the thumps from outside, the sound of running water in the room next door. Gordana's room.

He turned over and faced the wall. So she wasn't asleep either. Where was her bed? Surely not on the other side of the adjoining wall, a wall which seemed as thin as plasterboard. God, he hoped he didn't snore. Claire said he didn't, but . . .

He sat upright, swinging his legs over the side, unable to put the phone call of last night to one side any more. How could she go away, how bloody could she? It would be almost the same, she'd said. How could it be the same for her to go to Muriel's cottage? They'd never been there at Christmas, for heaven's sake, so how could it be the same?

He pulled the blanket up round him. The sound of running water had stopped. Was that the creak of a bed? He didn't breathe, just listened. There it was again. Yes, the bed must run the length of the adjoining wall, parallel to his. He breathed lightly, listening and heard the click of the light, a soft cough. Yes, that was her cough. He'd noticed she had a cold today, but every second person had one, or something worse. That's why he had brought her. Irvana, who had been seconded to the Turbe region to support Liaison Officer Captain James Scaland, had gone down with pleurisy.

There it was again, and suddenly he didn't feel so threatened. He shook his head. For Christ's sake, Claire was turning him into a basket case. Threatened, what the hell was he talking about? Being here was being threatened. The meeting at Turbe today had been all about being threatened, not some bloody woman getting things in a bloody great mess just when he needed the support he was entitled to, for God's sake.

From next door came the creaking of the bed, then silence. Was she sleeping? Well, she damn well deserved to, she'd been bloody excellent and maybe some other people should come out here and feel the cold of the bedroom, hear the mortars, see how they'd cope with their first cross the lines meeting, especially when one of the Serbs might have been the one who took her father. Maybe then they'd stop whining about needing a bit of time to get adjusted. Adjusted, bloody hell.

Should he ask Claire if he should establish whether Miss Sevo had adjusted? He made himself stop, made himself relax, and heard another creak. Well, whether she'd adjusted or not she'd carried out her duties bloody brilliantly but he'd known she would, even when Ben was carrying on in the Ops Room about the risk of relying on Gordana being too great, that they needed someone with no axe to grind, that with the Liaison Officer and Jeremy there was no real need for her. That it was time for Mark to take up the reins at the base, to take up the overview position now Ben's ankle was A1. Bloody cheek, they might be old friends but that was just damned impertinence, and so he had told him.

Anyway, apart from telling his boss how to suck eggs what did the silly mug think Gordana was going to do—plunge a dagger into the nearest Chetnik heart? And what did he mean by saying Mark was depending too much on Gordana, that she was just another interpreter? 'Actually she's a bloody good interpreter,' Mark had said slowly and clearly in the privacy of his office, 'and haven't you heard of teamwork? Because that's what we are,' he'd stormed, 'a team, and it was you and Jeremy bleating on that made me take her on in the first place. What the hell are you going on about?'

Ben had apologized within half an hour, and so had Mark. It was the tension getting to them of course, and Claire's determination. How could it be the same, how could anything be the same? He wasn't there, and it was all slipping away, mixing up, reforming—without him.

He made himself listen to the mortars, to the opening and shutting of doors in the corridor where the rest of the patrol were booked in. He made himself recap on the day, on Charlie and Arthur, together with two other journalists locking their Land Rover in behind their patrol as they left Vitez.

He'd dropped them off in Turbe where he and Gordana had met up with Jeremy Baines, and James Sealand, and the official from the Prisoner Exchange Commission who had developed a regular programme of contact with the Serbs.

The ceasefire he'd arranged for the meeting was still holding, Jeremy had told him. They'd donned flak jackets, and he'd insisted that Gordana wore one too before taking the Land Rovers as close as possible to the apex of the front line. She'd been shivering with cold, but was it really the cold? She'd shivered as she'd helped interpret the Serbs' remarks throughout the meeting.

In the bedroom the windows were already frosted and the air seemed to almost crackle with the cold. He lay down, curled into a ball, two pairs of socks on, facing the wall. Was her window also frosting up, did she seem to hear it crackle? His water pipes were knocking. Were hers? Did it comfort her as much as it comforted him to know that there was a living, breathing colleague on the other side of the wall at the end of a day like this?

He'd turned over, dragging his blankets around his head, longing for some heat. There'd be heat in Claire's bedroom, there'd be wincingly hot water in the shower, there'd be soft lighting. There'd be heat at Muriel's cottage . . . He stopped himself. No, he mustn't dwell, he mustn't let it intrude because he couldn't understand Claire any more.

There was another soft cough, and another, but harsher this time. Then nothing. Was Gordana reaching for water? She carried a squash ball that served as a plug, as they all did. She carried a torch, mineral water and soap in her backpack. It was her survival kit. How would they like that, back home? Having to carry their own plug around, having to work with the people who had taken their father? How would they like to carry on when there had been such violence in their lives?

He heard the soft cough again, but it was controlled, just as controlled as her behaviour this afternoon. God almighty, how did she do it? How could she summon all that professionalism when later she had told him that at the back of the room she had recognized one man's insignia as belonging to the militia who had reportedly destroyed her village?

During the meeting they had discussed yet again the need to cease firing on aid convoys, to cease firing on residential towns, to ... Had progress been made? He didn't know. There might be a ceasefire, but for hours, or days? Would there be another meeting? Probably.

He heard another cough, picturing her cocooned as he was, the blanket over her head, trying to keep warm, and slowly his anger left him, slowly his breathing became regular, and soon there was nothing from next door, not even a cough and he was drifting, his limbs were heavy, his head just filled with the sounds of the night until he was asleep.

While he slept he dreamed of Christmas trees, and letters, and of notebooks, and Gordana's fragile hand writing, writing, writing.

*   *   *

In the morning he woke with a start from a dream in which Gordana's pen had become a hammer she was using to pound against a locked door. Pounding, pounding, pounding. He lay there in the darkness, his heart thudding, trying to place himself, trying to shrug off the dream but the pounding was still there. Now he heard Jeremy calling. 'Colonel Baird, we're down at breakfast. Are you awake, Colonel?' The door knob rattled.

He swore to himself, feeling a fool, realizing he hadn't set his alarm. 'Give me a minute, I was

303

working, just give me a minute.' He tore into his clothes, washed, sorted himself out, then hurried down to breakfast, snatching up some bread and gulping lukewarm tea from the buffet side table, whilst the others hung about waiting for him, but pretending not to.

He looked around, and saw that she wasn't there. Gordana wasn't there, and he was ridiculously comforted. So, they had both slept well and the tensions of yesterday were almost gone. He would phone Claire again, he would try and reason with her. He jerked his head towards the stairs, because the lifts weren't working. 'Better hook Miss Sevo out as well, Jeremy. We obviously had the quiet corridor. Charlie must have been on another floor.'

Charlie shook a finger at him, as Jeremy said, 'She's been up some while, and has nipped out to meet that freelancer she knows for breakfast at some café or other, or so she told Charlie.' Charlie verified this, pursing his lips. 'Bad news, that is, old sport. He's a veritable nutter. Just so long as it's only breakfast and she's not joining him on any hare-brained behind the lines story. Didn't know she still kept up with him.'

Suddenly Mark's bread tasted sad and dry, and he dropped it back on to the plate, pushing aside his half-cold tea, grabbing his grip and making his way with the team to their Land Rovers. The air was crisp and the sky was blue, and the light quite beautiful, but somehow it didn't touch him through the tension that had re-emerged, and along with it a violent irritation. God, how he hated this bloody country.

Approaching the vehicles he slowed. Beyond the

304

next building was Gordana with the long haired freelancer, and as he stared she reached up and kissed him, taking the present he gave her. He saw the look of delight on her face, and the second kiss, and turned away. He thought she'd have more sense. In fact, he hadn't thought of her with anyone, not while she was looking for her father, not whilst her country was falling to pieces, for heaven's sake. What the hell was the matter with all these damn women?

On the return journey they were held up again and again by checkpoints and village roadblocks. Again and again he and Gordana had to bargain, bluff, coerce and all the time irritation was building. At the fifth roadblock he and Gordana left their vehicle and approached the villagers and as they did so he burst out, 'This is an absolute bloody waste of time. They'll be doing this to the aid lorries all day too. Are they cretins or something?'

Gordana, who had been swinging her arms in an effort to keep warm turned on him. 'They're hungry, cold, frightened. They need some food. Perhaps they feel a lorry will give them some. That is why they do it. They think that the next village will attack, so they show strength. That is why they do it. You know that, Colonel Baird.'

He shouted at her: 'If you can't keep your allegiances to yourself, and maintain some detachment I suggest you return to the vehicle.'

She tightened her lips but said nothing, just walked on, silently, translating at the roadblock immaculately, her face and voice expressionless. As they returned to the Land Rover she said, 'These people are Croats as you well know. I am a Muslim.

305

This too you know. I was showing understanding, not allegiance.'

His anger continued for the length of the journey, and he was bloody glad of her silence, of Corporal Simms's silence, of everybody's bloody silence.

*   *   *

Back at base, after de-briefing, he slammed the door of his office behind him and sank into his chair, only then noticing the presents which had arrived from Claire in his absence. She had said they were on the way when she rang. She had said his mother would be sending an oil painting for the dining room. She had said his mother was grateful for the chance to have Christmas in Tuscany. She had said, as he was preparing to slam the receiver down, 'Mark, perhaps we could go there next year. Mark, surely you can't mind *this* much? It's absurd.'

'Yes, I do mind,' he'd yelled. 'That girl comes back and everything changes. I do bloody mind.'

There'd been a silence until Claire had finally said, 'I'm sorry Mark, but this year I've just got to do this, but nothing has changed between you and me. Nothing. I love you. I love you very much. Nothing has really changed.'

But it will, he'd wanted to say. It will, and I'm not there while it's happening and so where will I fit in when I get home? And will her father be the next one in our lives—until the end of our days?

He reached into his drawer for the bottle of Scotch, and poured a hefty one, slugging it back, enjoying the burn in his throat, enjoying the sensation as it hit his stomach, rubbing his eyes to try and clear his head, longing to feel less exhausted, longing for the world to stop.

At first he didn't hear the knock on the door, but when he did he barked 'Enter.'

It was Gordana. She stood just inside the door, her hands behind her back, her face paler than usual if that was possible, but why the hell should he care? He glared. She stepped forward, and held out the slim present she had been given by the freelancer. Mark didn't understand. She came nearer until she was just the other side of the desk. Still she held the package out. 'Please, it is for you. I asked André to bring it from Switzerland where he has been. It is a Christmas gift, though it is not a celebration for we Muslims, of course, and I would like you to have it early because today you seemed so sad. So angry, and so sad.'

Slowly Mark took it, staring first at it, then at her and he felt ashamed. She was always making him feel ashamed. She smiled. 'Please, you may open it.'

He shook his head, not knowing what to say. 'I can't, I really can't accept this.'

Gordana looked crushed. 'Please, I would like you to. Your wife, she would not mind?'

Mark looked again at the package, and then at Claire's gifts. He shook his head helplessly. 'No, it's not that, but on 200 Deutschmarks you should not, and I have bought nothing for you.'

She said, 'But I should, for it is your Christian celebration, and you should not, because you know that I am Muslim.'

He looked away from her face, away from the hair which had escaped as always. He rose, came round the desk, and shook hands. She smiled. 'A

Merry Christmas, an early Merry Christmas, Colonel Baird. You deserve one for even though your own life is difficult and full of uncertainty you care about Bosnia. Please, it is a gesture that is all.'

Slowly he raised his hand and moved back the strand of hair, and as he did so his fingers touched her cheek. Her skin was so soft, soft but firm. Her eyes were so huge, so unique, so lovely. Slowly she raised her own hand, and pressed his against her cheek. He said, 'How do you cope with your own uncertainty, Gordana?'

She pressed his hand harder still, and the collar of her waterproof brushed against their wrists. She whispered, 'I live just for today. I blank out all else. All the what-ifs, the maybes. I just live for the moment. It is how one survives, Mark. After all, it might be all that there is.' She brought his fingers to her lips and repeated, 'After all, it might be all that there is.' It was as though with each movement of her lips she was kissing him, and now he couldn't breathe, now nothing else existed except this woman who shared so much with him.

He brought her hand to his lips, and kissed her palm, and drew her close, and found her mouth, felt her tongue soft and gentle and probing and the desire that swept him almost buckled his legs.

At that moment there was a loud knock on the door, and he had to shake himself back into the room, back into the body that was Mark Baird, back to the sounds of the base. Gordana had stepped away. She sank down on to the chair, her cheeks flushed, her eyes anywhere but on him, and his anywhere but on her. God, was he mad?

The knock came again. Mark ran his hand through his hair, trying to collect himself. He

308

walked to the window, feeling as though he'd just run the mile. 'Enter,' he barked, turning nonchalantly as the door opened and Ben entered.

'A few points I need to clear, Colonel,' Ben said, then stopped when he noticed Gordana. 'I'm so sorry, I'll come back later.' His tone was suddenly cool.

Mark laughed, and even to himself it sounded false. 'No need, just a quick de-brief.' He strode swiftly to the desk, putting it between him and his second-in-command, and then he saw the present. He gestured to Miss Gordana. 'Miss Gordana was also bringing me a Christmas gift. Between colleagues, you know. I think it's a tie.' He was wittering. He must shut up. Ben just smiled. 'How kind. Claire's bound to find a shirt to go with it.'

Gordana had risen. She looked no higher than Mark's top button as they said goodbye, then slipped past Ben. Mark took the paper Ben held out, pointing to the chair Gordana had just vacated. 'Take a pew, Ben.'

By now Gordana was opening the door and Mark glanced at her, wanting her to go, wanting to apologize, wanting to make her stay, wanting to kiss her neck, wanting her to never come back again, oh God, just wanting to feel what he had just felt.

Gordana didn't look back as she left.

CHAPTER TWENTY-ONE

At Muriel's cottage, one of several in the grounds of a hotel, Claire placed the presents under the tree on Christmas Eve, working her way through

309

the cardboard boxes she and Leah had decanted from the boot of the Volvo. One box contained gifts from the playgroup children which Leah had fingered and sniffed, on the prowl for smellies that would suit her. It was an unwritten rule that these were shared between the two of them, though this year it would be between three.

As she finished Claire snatched a look at the clock: 6.10 p.m. Leah was at the hotel's indoor pool, and on a promise to be back no later than 6.15. Anna was on the road, held up, no doubt, by the seasonal traffic as everyone poured home.

Home. My children are coming home and here we'll have the peace to get it right.

She knelt before the tree, adjusting the silver beads which tended to slip into too much of a droop, enjoying the scent of pine, enjoying everything, especially now that Mark had snatched a moment to phone the day after their acrimonious conversation. 'It's a good idea to go away,' he'd said. 'Silly of me to object. Yes, you could all do with a break, so have a good time.' Then he'd gone, rushing to Gornji Vakuf and she'd loved him more than she'd ever done because he'd made it easy for her, after all.

Sitting back on her heels she hummed as the fire flickered, and the soft lamps lit this hidey-hole of Muriel's with its beams, its family photos, some of which were of Mark as a young boy; one or two even included Ben and his brother Simon. She eased herself to her feet, and peered at her favourite of Muriel and Belle with Mark at about Leah's age. She touched his image with her finger, wanting him here, wanting to hold him and thank him, and love him and tell him that everything

310

about this Christmas had started to work out.

Leah was in a good mood because she hadn't missed the Youth Club disco after all. It had been brought forward. Consequently Claire had been able to make plans to leave first thing on the 23rd, the day of the cocktail party, converting her non-attendance from a snub to an unavoidable change of plans. The Brigadier's wife had been politely disappointed when Claire had phoned her regrets but was probably dancing a jig the moment she replaced the receiver.

Moving now into the small kitchen which was thick with the steamy aroma of lentil soup, she checked the wine in the fridge. To follow the soup she'd bought *feuilleté* of mushrooms ready prepared from the supermarket, along with a packet of readywashed mixed salad. Champagne was also chilling but that was for the morning when she and Leah would introduce Anna to the decadence of the Baird Christmas breakfast.

As she shut the fridge door she heard feet pounding past the kitchen window, and Leah shouting. 'See you then.' Claire waited, grinning as Leah opened the front door and came hurtling straight into the living room. She called from the kitchen doorway, 'Well done, Leah, dead on time.'

Leah was rubbing her hair with a towel. Another was rolled up underneath her other arm and this contained her swimsuit. She was panting, and gasped, 'Anna's not here yet, then?'

Claire smiled gently, checking the clock. 'Not yet, but she rang to say she'll arrive just about now.'

'Oh.' Leah pulled a face and flicked the towel over her shoulder, shaking her hair much like a dog.

311

Claire walked over and took the towel. 'Look, you're cold, you should have dried your hair in the changing rooms, or did you want to walk, or should I say run, back with someone? I noticed there's rather a nice boy in the next cottage who was on his way to the pool at the same time as you.'

'Oh Mum.' Leah went to a vase which contained white chrysanthemums. She was no longer panting. Claire was envious. If she'd just swum Lord knows how many lengths and then run back she'd be flat on her face 'sucking carpet'. 'Nice of Dad to send us these, and to remember that we white-themed the decorations last year. He's got our phone number here?'

Claire reached out and touched the petals. Yes, it was nice, quite extraordinary in fact, and again she felt warmed. Leah repeated, 'Mum, has he got our phone number?'

Claire looked over the blooms at her daughter's anxious face. 'Calm down, we've stayed here often enough, and he had the address for the flowers.'

'But you gave it to him again?'

Claire laughed. 'Yes, I gave it to him again. Now sit by the fire, relax, and dry your hair.' Instead Leah stayed by the flowers as her mother put another log on the fire. Sparks showered and clung to the soot of the chimney. Claire pointed firmly to the armchair to the left of the fireplace. 'Sit. Dry.'

Leah jerked her thumb towards the kitchen. 'Is that soup? So we're definitely not eating in the restaurant?'

Claire was prodding the log with the poker, wondering whether it would be safe to try and balance another on top, and said, 'Yes it's soup, and we're eating here tonight, just as you

312

requested, madam.'

Leah was staring into the fire, then she headed for the stairs, saying over her shoulder, 'Good, she drank the wine with pud last time. I mean, p-l-e-a-s-e.'

Claire closed her eyes. Oh God. She called after her, 'Leah.' But Leah was stamping up the stairs, shouting, 'I hate all this, why do I have to have this idiot family? It's like some stupid game, up the ladder comes a sister, down the snake goes a father. Why can't we be normal?'

Claire started towards the stairs calling her back, telling her that next year would be. Leah yelled, 'Oh yes, hand on your heart, eh? Like this year? I mean, she'll be here for ever, won't she?'

At that moment a car drew up, a door slammed. After a pause there was a pounding, low down on the door, and a strangled call. 'Claire.'

Claire stood torn between the two, her head beginning to ache, her smile totally gone. 'Claire?' Anna called again. Claire made for the door, calling, 'You don't need to knock, just come in.' Had she sounded strained? Anna answered, 'I'm not knocking, I'm kicking and I can't come in, I don't have a spare hand.' There was a clatter. 'Oh shit, I have now.'

Claire pulled the door open, and there was Anna, laughing as she picked up the beautifully wrapped presents strewn over the frosted path. Claire forced a smile as she took some parcels, going before Anna into the living room, putting them beneath the tree, dodging the branches as she did so, branches which seemed determined to catch on everything they possibly could, precipitating a shower of pine needles.

Anna did the same, then stood back, gazing at the tree. 'This tree was made for me—white and cream,' she murmured appreciatively, slipping out of her red duffel coat, standing there in a cream roll-necked sweater and white jeans. Even with her Doc Martens Claire thought she looked wonderful and now her smile was soft, relaxed. But only for a moment, for then she turned and called up the stairs: 'Anna's here.' Could Anna hear the tension?

Leah yelled back, 'I'm washing my hair.'

Claire wanted to race up the stairs and make her come. Instead she said as she plumped cushions while Anna warmed herself by the fire, 'She's been swimming, she'll be down soon.'

The heat on Anna's back was a relief, but her eyes were on her mother, on those thin nervous hands, those tense shoulders, and half of her wanted to be cruising with her parents but the other half needed to be here. Damn it, this was her family too, even that horror who had just yelled down from the bathroom. She saw her vanity case by the door. Well, OK, if Miss Leah was already up there, maybe that was as good a place as any to get started.

She snatched up her vanity case and made for the stairs before she could change her mind, saying over her shoulder, 'Come on Claire, I've brought some tints. Might as well start the session now.' Raising her voice, she stood at the bottom of the stairs. 'Leah, as you're already under way, I'm coming up. Stand by for the new you.'

Leah's voice was muffled as though she was rubbing her hair dry. 'I don't need any help, if you don't mind. Just stay down there and talk to *my* mother.'

314

Claire, right behind Anna, said, 'Oh, I'm sorry, give her time. She's missing her father and if we had a cat she'd kick it.'

Anna kept her grin. 'Well, she can plant one on her sister instead. The holiday starts here.' She started up the stairs, saying quietly to Claire, 'Don't worry, I can understand where she's coming from, I was fourteen once, and I didn't have someone like me bursting into my life, but we've only got a couple of days, so let's not waste them.' Raising her voice again, she yelled, 'Hey Leah, can we all fit into the bathroom?' Anna was on the landing by now with Claire close behind her. 'Straight ahead,' Claire directed, feeling swept along, feeling that someone else at last had taken control.

As they reached the door they heard it being locked and bolted but Claire wasn't worried. She stood quietly as Anna rattled the handle. 'Come on, remember even the Bastille fell and I might not have a battering ram but I've got some great tints here, and no one likes a party pooper. Choose which one will go with the blusher you might have under the tree, and just happens to match the one I have upon my person, and which you can borrow until tomorrow. Later we can get tarted up for the midnight service. I told the lad in the cottage next door that we'd be going. Steve, I think he said his name was. Sixteen and pretty snoggable, I'd say. He helped me to get my stuff out of the car and said he'd see you in the back pew and no running out when the clock chimes twelve.' Anna rattled the handle again, and after a moment the bolt slid back and the door opened. Leah stood turbanned in a towel saying, 'I can't believe you got him to help you with your parcels. It's so embarrassing.'

315

Anna brushed past her, all business as she plonked her vanity case on the lavatory seat. 'Not at all, he wanted an excuse to talk about you. His hair was wet, been swimming too, I'd say. Nice cut. If you want my opinion, he's a bit smitten.'

From the doorway Claire watched Anna sorting out bottles, brushes and Lord knows what, reeling Leah in, and knew her smile was larger than any smile had a right to be.

Anna dragged on an overall, issuing orders left, right and centre until everything was as she wished, then she grinned across at Claire. 'Come on, there's no room for slackers, find a chair from somewhere, then this lass of yours can droop over a basin and we'll get cracking.' She was handing a tint card and blusher to Leah who sat on the edge of the bath, looking confused. 'Choose.'

Leah hesitated in the face of all this determination, then crossed her arms, shaking her head, obdurate. 'Anyway, Mum won't let me have a colour until I'm fifteen.'

Claire, on her way out for a chair said sharply, though her laughter kept breaking through, 'If you go on at this rate you won't have to bother about your hair at all, because your head will be out there on a pike. Choose, or I will for you.'

Leah tried to hide her grin as she bent her head to study the chart, whilst Claire and Anna shared a look. Leah chose an alarming orange which Anna talked her out of and they settled for auburn. Claire found a chair and soon Leah was settled at the basin, leaning over while Anna adjusted the temperature of the water spraying from the shower attachment.

Anna said to Leah, as she directed the water on

316

to her hair, 'I'll just give it another wash to make sure the chlorine is out and when you're finally done, you can set about mine. Then, my girl, we'll start on your mother. It's high time we sorted out that bird's nest and dragged her towards something approaching "chic".' Claire leaned against the door frame, hearing Leah's hysterical laughter, her shouted, 'Oh great, she puts rollers in it. I mean, rollers.' Claire wouldn't even ask herself how long this would last. She would just accept the joy.

*   *   *

Next morning breakfast in the cottage was late, and Leah and Anna voted to have their croissants in the living room as they opened the presents. Leah, in charge of the champagne, let the cork fly with suitable ferocity while Claire ducked her way to the Christmas tree to distribute the presents. Anna groaned. 'Cor, bet your dad could do with you out in Bosnia. Just the thought of you with a champagne bottle would be enough to bring everyone to their senses in no time at all.'

The champagne was spilling out of the bottle and Leah was laughing so hard that she missed the glass she was aiming for. Anna helped her steady it and between them three glasses were poured.

The girls pulled their chairs up closer to the tree and took the gifts as Claire called out the names. Soon all three of them were knee deep in wrapping paper, and a routine had been established, with Anna making a note of who gave what to whom, so thank-you letters would be on target, and Leah hurrying to and from the wine cooler topping up their glasses. While she was at it Claire noticed her

317

snatching quick looks at her new short cut and colour every time she passed the mirror. Mark you, Claire had taken a few quick looks at her own, which was considerably shorter than it had ever been, and with the highlights she did indeed look chic.

The last gifts she handed out were those she had selected for her daughters and she watched anxiously as they peeled back the paper from the small jewellery boxes from the jewellers. Inside each was a necklace which had belonged to her grandmother, and their plastic hospital birth bracelets.

Leah and Anna looked at one another, then at their mother. Anna said quietly, 'Thanks, Mum.' Mum, Claire thought, she called me Mum, but she hid her happiness because Leah was there, watching her, her eyes blank. After a moment Leah turned and fastened the clasp on Anna's necklace, and in turn, Anna fastened hers. Whilst Anna opened gifts from her parents Leah came to her mother and hugged her. 'Thanks, Mum,' she whispered. Claire had no idea what any of it meant.

Lunch was held in the hotel restaurant. It was a room which resembled a baronial hall right down to the minstrels' gallery and was completely over the top. Shields and stags' heads hung on the panelled walls. Claire loved it, but Liz would have loved it more.

As they entered Leah gawked at the stags which were wearing paper hats, and roared with laughter. Claire praised the heavens, and flashed a look at Anna, whose expression said, as clear as day, maybe we're winning.

They made their way to the huge refectory table

which did for all the guests, most of whom were already seated. But not Steve and his family. Claire touched Leah's arm. 'It's all right, they'll come.'

Leah stuck her head in the air and went to the opposite side of the table. but not before she insisted that she didn't know what Claire meant. Not half she didn't, thought Claire, settling herself down next to Anna, exchanging greetings with the other guests, putting on the paper hat they'd been presented with as they entered.

Last night, Steve had indeed waited for Leah in the porch of the church, and the two of them had slipped into the back pew, whilst Anna, practically dragged Claire to the front, murmuring, 'It's time for the wrinklies to know their place.'

'But he's sixteen and she's only fourteen,' Claire had protested, trying to look back. Anna was having none of it. 'Got to let go of the reins a little, or she'll flip later on.'

'But . . .' Claire had protested as they reached an empty pew. 'But what?' whispered Anna as she stood back to allow Claire to enter first. Claire looked at Anna's soft smile, her shining hair, her eyes which seemed no one else's any more. 'But nothing,' she said finally, sitting down in the pew, letting the scent of the candles, the sight of the nativity, the sound of the organ work their soft magic.

Now she stared at the seasonal candles which had been placed at regular intervals down the length of the dining table, their flames flickering. But nothing, she repeated to herself, as Mr and Mrs Simpson and Steve made an entrance and Leah suddenly started talking to Anna as though they'd been deep in discussion about the state of the world all morning.

Claire smiled because Leah had turned to Anna, and because Madge Simpson was so reminiscent of Liz as she positively glowed in her bright pink ensemble, and jingled with costume jewellery, the *tour de force* of which were the earrings that hung almost to her plump shoulders.

She called as she approached: 'Cooee, cooee, cooee.' Leah almost died and the rest of the table was stunned into silence as Mrs Simpson led the charge to their places alongside Claire's party, shooing the diminutive Henry Simpson and the rather dishy Steve to their places, while she took the head of the table. 'Merry Christmas, how lovely to have a chance for a proper chat. Church isn't the time, or the place, but of course, some didn't find that a problem.' She grinned at Leah, who was an interesting pink.

Anna murmured to Leah, 'Heaven spare us from mothers.' Leah sniggered and to Claire it was a magical moment.

Steve sat next to Leah, who had stopped laughing and was examining the candlestick rather too carefully instead. A waitress arrived with glasses of champagne for them all and this caused Madge to pat her chest, and slap Henry on the arm.

'Yum, hey Hens.' Mrs Simpson leaned forward. 'Henry and I were so glad Steve found a friend. So boring for the youngsters without someone of their own age. Come on, Hens, let's chuck this back. Might as well be hung for a sheep as for a lamb, we've already had a taster back at the cottage.' Her laugh was robust.

Leah said in a loud voice to her mother, 'Grandma Belle started our champagne breakfast idea, didn't she?' Claire knew that this was for Steve's benefit, because her daughter could not yet pluck up the courage to speak to him direct.

'Lord yes,' she answered, and spoke to Steve. 'I gather from your mother's remark that you've had a liquid breakfast too?' It was Steve's turn to blush, dragging his hand through his hair which was long on top, but short at the back. Claire persisted. 'Lots of presents? Leah did quite well.'

Smoked salmon was served at this point, with vegetable terrine for the vegetarians. Steve grimaced at Leah, whispering, 'God, I hate this stuff.'

Leah agreed. 'There are a few perks to being a veggie.' She paused a moment, catching Anna's eye and nodding slightly as some message was relayed. She said to Steve, 'You could try some of my terrine?'

Madge was putting on her paper hat, making Anna do likewise, and issuing instructions to Leah and Steve, while Henry filched the smoked salmon from his son's plate. Spurred and hatted, Leah shovelled across some terrine, still without making eye contact with the boy. Mrs Simpson placed her napkin on her lap, observing all that was going on. 'Now that we've sorted that little problem, let's start troughing.'

Claire saw Anna check to see which knife and fork Leah was using for the terrine and followed suit and soon all the guests were chatting to one another as though they'd grown up side by side. The most frequent sound Claire heard was laughter from her daughters as Madge orchestrated the ebb and flow of conversation. A wonderful CO's wife, Claire thought, relaxing into the luxury of being organized. Eventually the main course was cleared and she heard Leah say to Steve, 'My grandma lives in Tuscany, and my dad's a CO in Bosnia.'

Steve's reaction was as gratifying as Leah had obviously hoped. 'Blimey, that's high powered.'

Madge was instantly alert and launched into the torrent they were now familiar with. 'Oh my, how worrying, but how lucky you are to have the support of your two daughters, Claire. They're both like you, except for Leah's chin, and Anna's eyes. They're even both veggies. Strange how things run in families. It's your husband, is it, who doesn't eat meat? Or is it just something the girls have decided for themselves? I like a bit of meat, I must say. Yes, lovely to see you all together. You're a lucky woman. Anna still lives with you, does she?' Across the table Leah's silence was painful. Claire smiled gently at her, though her own shoulders had tightened. She said carefully to Madge, 'I am lucky, Madge. Very lucky indeed.' She left the questions unanswered.

Opposite her Leah began to return to her food but Madge wasn't finished. She spoke past Henry to Anna. 'I bet even at your age you miss your father, don't you?'

Claire wanted to say something, anything, but she'd frozen. Anna paused thoughtfully, quite composed in her cream silk dress. Looking at neither Claire or Leah, she said, 'Yes, of course, whenever he's away it's strange.' Even as she said it Anna wondered how she sounded so normal.

Leah swallowed, her hat slipping. God, wherever she went, the whole damn stupid set-up was always there, it always would be. Opposite her Claire said nothing. Come on, Leah shouted silently. This is your mess, do something.

Madge was looking from one to another, aware of a difficulty. Claire asked Anna, 'Was the nut roast as good as our turkey?'

Anna grinned at her empty plate. 'This tells the story.' She patted her non-existent stomach. 'Excellent. What about you, Leah?'

Leah stared at her, then at her mother and saw what looked like fear in her eyes, a sort of bracing, and suddenly she remembered her foul unloving grandmother; not Belle, who was all sunshine and light, but the other one. This was the look her mother had always had in her eyes when that woman came to stay, with her mouth never still, nothing ever right, and her mother had just taken it, never complaining, much as it had been with her father at his worst. Leah caught her hat as it fell, and it was she who felt like the bully, the spoilt child.

She realized everyone was waiting for her to speak. 'Mine was fine.' She turned to Madge, touching her new short, chic haircut. 'But Anna's father isn't away as often as mine. We only share a mother, you know. We're half-sisters, which is strange, because we are very alike.'

Claire stared, knowing what the public admission had cost her, knowing that she could have let it go, knowing that because she hadn't some sort of an acceptance had been signalled. Leah smiled at her, then at Anna, winking but now Claire was reaching for her handkerchief, fumbling with the catch of her handbag, making the tears stop before they started.

Madge slapped Henry on the arm so that he

323

slopped his wine. 'Oh, is that right? D'you hear that, Steve?' She waggled a finger at her son. 'I'm on my second marriage you know, Claire. Makes you realize the whole male race is much of a muchness, doesn't it, but let's not get into that now. Steve has an older sister. She's an air hostess, but has to be careful, you know. She puts on a bit of weight soon as look at a chocolate and I mean, she'd be out of a job wouldn't she, if she let rip. Can't waddle down the aisle knocking everyone's drinks all over the show, can she? Young Steve takes after Henry, eats what he likes and is still as thin as a rake.'

Soon the Madge road show was under way again but now Leah, Claire and Anna were working as a team and their humour was as strong as Madge's; Claire didn't feel things could get any better.

They all cheered when a huge Christmas pudding was brought in to the canned sound of bagpipes, and fully alight. It was all in such bad taste that Liz would have been almost insane with delight. At the same time a waiter brought round a dessert wine but before Anna could make the mistake of refusing, Leah leaned forward. 'This *dessert* wine is pretty good, isn't it, Anna? Don't you think Mum should let me have some as well?'

Anna brought back the hand she had been about to place over her glass and allowed the waiter to proceed, her smile warm as she silently acknowledged Leah's help, feeling suddenly exhausted with relief. OK, maybe they'd still go two forward and one back but they'd broken through, she absolutely knew that now. She said, 'I dare say, as it's Christmas, Mum will let you.'

Claire agreed, as though resigned, and watched

Anna raise her glass to her sister. 'To us, Leah,' she said. 'And to our mother.'

'To us, and Mum,' Leah agreed, sliding a look at her mother and grinning like the cat with the cream, but then she was. She'd never before been allowed dessert wine. And never before had Claire loved her as much, and truly *now* the day could not improve.

By four they were leaving the dining room, already breathless from the conga Madge had insisted on forming as luncheon was decreed 'over'. They'd been twice round the room, and now everyone was singing as she led the way out into the cold, along by the tennis courts, round the sunken garden, back to the hotel where they left the relieved hotel guests, then on to each cottage dropping off those who were staying in the grounds until there were just the Bairds and the Simpsons left. Long before this point Claire had made a mental note that she would never again willingly join a conga led by this irrepressible woman, at least not just after a Christmas meal.

As they approached their cottage at last, Steve yelled from his position at the rear of the line, 'Frisbee match next, yeah?' Claire groaned and shook her head, convinced she probably only had a few moments more to live. Leah however whooped just behind Claire. 'We'll smash you. Just smash you.'

At Claire's front door Madge disengaged, gasping and panting in the cold of the afternoon. 'You go ahead and smash, I'm going to crash. Come along, Henry.' She kissed Claire, patted the girls, and tottered off, calling, 'Frisbee all you like, my dears. I know my limitations.' She and Henry disappeared into the cottage beyond the hedge, and Claire groped for her keys, found them, then turned to Anna, but she wasn't there, she was chasing Leah around the shrubs while Steve collected the Frisbee from the back of his father's Cavalier.

Claire watched for a moment, the breath rasping in her lungs, her legs like jelly, then hearing the phone she hurried indoors. It was Belle, who wanted to talk to both girls. Claire called them in and built up the fire, wondering if anyone would notice if she measured her length and just slept for the next twelve years.

That call finished they rang Liz who had her mother to stay with her on the patch and while they chatted Claire checked her watch, hurrying her friend off the line because Mark had said he'd phone at 1630 hours. It was 1625. The moment the call to Liz was over the phone rang again. Leah grabbed it. 'Hi Dad.'

'You telepathic or something?' Mark laughed.

Leah shook her head, grinning at Claire and Anna. 'No, although your timing's been dodgy recently I knew you'd phone at the right time today.'

Mark hesitated for a moment. 'I try to keep in touch, it's not easy,' he said. 'Anyway, what are you up to?'

Leah told him of the conga, of the Simpsons, but not Steve, and Anna grinned and caught Claire's eye, then swung back to Leah as she heard her say, 'Say hello to Anna.' Anna waved a no. Leah held out the receiver. 'Come on, he won't bite.' She put it back to her ear, saying into the mouthpiece, 'You don't bite, do you, Dad?'

She held it out again. Claire pushed Anna forward. 'He's not known to like raw meat,' she murmured gleefully, safe in the knowledge that Mark had accepted Anna, for why else had he phoned to give her the green light about the cottage?

Anna took the receiver as though it was a primed grenade. Leah was giggling, and it was champagne, and dessert wine, and happiness as she pressed her ear against the outside of the earpiece. Anna said, 'Merry Christmas, Colonel Baird.'

Mark said, 'To you too, Anna.'

Leah shrieked. 'Call him Mark.' She snatched the phone. 'She should call you Mark, shouldn't she, Dad?'

'Yes, of course.'

Leah handed the phone back to Anna, who said, 'We've just had lunch in the hotel. It was good fun, *lots* of champagne.'

His laugh was wry. 'I rather gathered that and I'm glad it's going well. Your parents are on a cruise, I understand?'

'Yes.'

'Well, let's hope it's not too rough.' Anna smiled and said, 'Would you like to speak to Claire?' Outside Steve was calling them.

'Thank you,' Mark said. Anna handed the receiver across before being dragged out of the door by Leah. Claire called, 'Shut the door.' Anna ran back and did so, shouting, 'Keep your new hairdo on.'

Claire laughed into the phone. 'Merry Christmas, darling.'

Mark sounded weary. 'And to you. Look I can't stay on long, evening draws close and the usual

327

mess games are about to commence.'

Claire groaned. 'I've a feeling that just about sums up the rest of our afternoon here, but without the assault upon the person. Now, remember you're not as young as you were.'

He laughed. 'I'll dip out in good order, pretty damn smart.'

She said, 'I gather Ben's rung Liz and he's fine. Looking forward to getting home. It's only three days now.'

Mark said, 'I'll miss the old devil.'

'Not as much as we miss you. If you were here, it would be perfect. I really miss you so much but it's not much longer until February.' She waited. The line crackled, almost broke up. She said. 'Mark?'

He spoke. 'I miss you, too. But it sounds fun, even the conga.'

She laughed. 'After two months on a panto it's status normal.'

He said, almost as though he was thinking aloud, 'It's another world.'

Claire was silent for a moment, unsure of his mood. At last she said carefully, 'I know it is, darling. I wish I could do more for you.'

Again the line crackled. From outside Claire could hear kids shrieking. Leah, Anna and Steve had obviously been joined by others. Mark muttered, 'I know, I'm sorry.' He paused. 'Claire, I've got to ask, is she going to . . . ?' He stopped.

She ran her finger over the phone where the dust had settled. Open fires were the very devil. 'Going to what? And who do you mean?'

Mark said, 'Oh, Liz. Is she going to take the partnership?'

Claire soothed him. 'Look Mark, I thought you'd

328

stopped worrying for now. Ben will sort it out when he gets home, you just go and enjoy mess rugger and try and escape being hospitalized. Incidentally, I thought I'd book us ten days in the Canary Islands for R & R. We'll go off straight after the last night, how about it? Liz said she'd stage the after-panto bash, and take my place in playgroup. I just want to get you somewhere you can relax, where we can catch up, have some time together.'

Mark barked a laugh. 'Good God, the earth has obviously moved on its axis if Liz is entering the lions' den.'

Claire grinned. 'Actually, she's been wonderful, everyone has. It's been a difficult few months.'

The shrieks from outside were getting louder and now they were chanting 'Claire, Claire, Claire.' She laughed. 'Look, I've got to go. I love you.' She waited. He said, 'Claire.'

She waited. He said, at last, 'Oh it's nothing. I love you back.'

*   *   *

They played for another half-hour out in the darkness, and Claire ran until the air hurt her chest, until the fierce joy threatened to choke her as she, Leah, Steve, Henry and Anna took sides against the rest of the cottages. They were a team, they had time, they had tonight, tomorrow and the next day and if Mark had been here it would have been perfect, but as it was she had never been so happy. She watched the way Leah and Anna moved, laughed, talked and just were.

'Last five minutes,' Henry gasped at last.

Leah threw the Frisbee to Anna, who dashed to

catch it. It was too high. Claire raced to cover her, but missed it. Anna rushed past, foraging in the darkness, laughing as she searched. The others ran towards them, but Anna exclaimed, 'Found it.' She turned to Claire, brandishing the Frisbee, coming at her out of the night.

For a moment Claire was paralysed. For a moment all she could hear was the sound of the wind in the marram grass, the sound of the surf, but then Leah rushed up, dragging her mother back into the game, shrieking at Anna who had watched Claire recoil, without understanding why. Leah repeated: 'Throw the darn thing, or you'll take root and in the spring you'll get pruned by the gardener.'

She patted her mother on the shoulder. 'Hey, you've done well for a wrinkly.' Claire turned to see Anna rushing back into the fray. Outside their cottage the porch light glowed. Outside the hotel there were Christmas lights festooned all over the huge conifer that stood on the terrace. Near her, her children played, and giggled, and called. Now she laughed, calling for the Frisbee too. It was over. Surely it was.

CHAPTER TWENTY-TWO

OK, so it was Boxing Day, Mark thought, sitting at his desk, but just because of that the war, or rather the peace, didn't magically go away. No, sod's law said that in the season of peace and goodwill it would spur itself on to greater effort. He stared up at the distant hill where the skiers still patrolled, just as his own men had all over Christmas, then fiddled with the latest strategic withdrawal plans he was always being tasked to prepare, just in case policy was changed and his regiment withdrawn. What would that do to morale? What would it do to Gordana?

He flung his pen down, glad to be alone in his office, away from those who had interfered. He sank his head into his hands. Bloody Ben, how dare he send Gordana away to stand in for Irvana as interpreter in Gorniji Vakuf without his knowledge? He could have wiped that look off his second-in-command's face as he'd assumed a surprised expression at Mark's objections the day after Gordana had given him that present, the day after he had kissed her, the day after Ben had almost found them.

Oh shit. Surely Ben couldn't have noticed anything. Damn it, there was nothing to notice, just a bit of gratitude. He strode to the window, bored, restless, lonely. He and Gordana had made a good team, that was all. He thumped the sill. 'That's all,' he said aloud, but he wasn't convinced and again he felt that surge of desire, the touch of her lips.

He'd looked forward to seeing her all through Christmas Day when the interpreters had been invited to dinner, but Jasna had said she was still in Gorniji Vakuf. He rubbed his gut, feeling the knot which had been growing since she had left, since he had been using Jasna, aware that it was a knot that he hadn't realized had previously eased.

He turned his back to the mortar flashes, resting on the sill, his arms crossed, staring at the desk. It had been so strange to talk to Anna. She was there, he wasn't. To hear them laughing, all of them.

Didn't they care, didn't they . . . ?

He moved back to the desk. God almighty, he'd almost asked Claire if Anna was going to find her father, he'd almost told her about Gordana on the phone. Instead he'd smashed his fist down on the desk when he'd replaced the receiver.

Someone knocked. 'Enter,' he called.

Ben stuck his head round the door, looking wary. 'Patrol returned in one piece.'

Mark pointed to a chair. 'Well done, Ben. Sit you down.'

Ben looked relieved, and why not, Mark thought, he'd given him a hard time for the last week or so but he bloody deserved it, the interfering old woman.

Mark picked up his ballpoint and said, 'Been a bit off, haven't I?'

Ben looked at the pen, not at Mark, then out of the window. 'Well, we've all got a bit stretched on and off, Colonel.'

Mark nodded. 'That's what it is, that's all it is. I let everything get on top of me for a moment. You know, the domestic situation, the pressure here.'

Ben acknowledged this, concentrating on the map showing the front lines on the wall behind Mark saying, 'Well, at least we had a bit of fun yesterday.'

Mark stared at him in mock amazement. 'Fun, is that what you call it? I thought it was grievous bodily harm. I swear Samuel Williams had me in his sights the moment I got down in the ruck.'

Ben laughed, and it was real laughter, relieved laughter and now he looked square at Mark. 'You're absolutely right, I reckon. But you know, he's coming on, rising to the situation out here.

He's going to be the surprise of the sergeants' mess, rather than the Rupert. I rather like him.'

Mark seemed to be pondering this upturn, but actually he couldn't give a shit. He said, 'Could be you're right. So, it's to be more drinks tonight, but this time at the press house, eh?'

Ben groaned. 'Ten sharp, or so Charlie says and he's usually spot on where "refreshments" are concerned.' He became serious. 'It's as good an escape as any, I suppose. Apparently the mayor and others will be there by then, and the journalists want reinforcements, or our bottles.'

Mark asked the question which had been on his mind since he'd heard of the party. 'Everyone's invited, are they?'

Now Ben's face was wary again, and he shrugged. 'All I know is who's on the list from the mess, but I'm taking it easy tonight. I don't want the mother of all hangovers when I face Liz. That woman is a dab hand at guessing the exact ratio of booze to liver. Incidentally, she says we're both too old to play mess rugger, and if I'm back on crutches she'll sprain the other ankle personally.'

Mark laughed, though he was aware that he'd been drawn away from the guest list, but the interpreters were bound to have been asked. He worked the pen between his fingers. 'Age is a dastardly thing. Can't booze, can't play mess rugger, haven't the bodies to tempt other women. What's left?'

Ben looked further relieved, and grinned. 'Liz says it's dominoes.'

Mark tucked the pen in his pocket and put his hands behind his head. 'Well, hoo bloody ray. Got you a set waiting has she, all boxed up for your arrival.' They both laughed. Mark said slowly, serious now, 'You just make sure she arrives at the right decision about the partnership.'

Ben checked his watch as he got to his feet. 'It doesn't work like that for us. We'll talk it through until we get to the other side. After all, there's more than just my life to consider.'

Mark rubbed his face. 'Did you ever think that when we got to this age we'd have to be making such life-changing decisions? I remember my parents, set so solidly on their path, so sure of everything and themselves. No thought of anything changing, of saying balls to it all, of starting again.' He let his glance stray to the present wrapped beneath the small Christmas tree on the filing cabinet. He'd bought it in Zagreb, where they'd wrapped it beautifully.

Ben was also looking at the gift, knowing instinctively who it was for, and wanting to chuck it through the window out into the snow. Mark was mad, utterly bloody mad, but what could Ben do about it, any more than he already had? For a wild moment he thought of cancelling his R & R and staying put, like a bloody gooseberry. But in the next breath he changed his mind. It was enough that he had managed to get Gordana transferred to Gorniji Vakuf; the rest was up to Mark and his common sense.

*   *   *

The press house was a riot of talk and laughter, and paper chains hung all around the room, plus greenery tied in bunches to hang in each corner. It was eleven and Mark had been talking to the mayor for so long, courtesy of the press interpreter, that his gin and tonic had absorbed the warmth of his hand and needed to be put out of its misery, rather than find its way down anyone's throat, especially his.

He signalled surreptitiously for Jeremy Baines to take over, shaking hands with the mayor, thanking the interpreter, and forcing his way to the bar, feeling that as CO the waters should part before him, or so he told Charlie who came wheezing up behind him.

'Oh, Lordy Lordy, tell me about it, cock. A prophet has no honour in his own home, let alone easy access to a bar.' They replenished their drinks, and eased themselves to the edge of the throng, joining Arthur whose ponytail had progressed from rodent species to marsupial, according to Charlie. Arthur put it down to the slivovitz he'd been drinking in Gornji Vakuf yesterday. 'Reaches the part others don't,' Arthur slurred.

'Gornji Vakuf?' Mark queried. 'How did you find things there?'

Samuel Williams careered past, trying to catch a flying paper plate thrown by a Sea King crew member. 'Sorry, Colonel,' he gasped. Mark smiled. 'At least it's not full of quiche and for that I give thanks.' Second Lt. Williams's laugh was hearty.

Arthur sipped his wine tentatively. 'How did I find it? Pretty blurred after a day's devotion to alcohol, and noisy, like the rest of this cauldron. It was good to be amongst friends, though. Irvana joined Gordana and we made up a good little press party. Christmas is funny, people cling, if you know what I mean.'

Mark looked out across the mêlée. No, he didn't

bloody know. Cling. Who was clinging to whom? Arthur continued, 'Actually, I brought the girls back with me today. I thought they'd enjoy another little soirée, but maybe they've given it a miss. Faint livers, obviously.'

Charlie was weaving his way to the bar again but Mark hardly registered that fact as he said, 'You brought them back where? To their flat?'

'Yes, thought it'd be good for them to catch up with the old crowd. Gordana was looking a bit peaky, tired you know. She still hasn't found out anything definite about her old man and I think it must be getting her down rather more than usual. She's been distinctly crabby, sort of depressed.'

There was a stir by the bar and they heard Charlie bellowing, 'Irvana, light of my tired old life, come and seek out the mistletoe with me.'

A great roar of laughter went up and Charlie appeared, dragging a smiling Irvana by the hand. Mark was looking beyond the interpreter for Gordana but the ranks had closed behind them. Irvana shook Mark's hand. 'You have enjoyed your festive break, Colonel Baird?' Her voice was barely polite and her look was cool. Not waiting for an answer she panned round to Arthur, chatting to him about the day they had spent in the freelancer's flat yesterday.

Mark felt his gut twist even more. The freelancer who knew Gordana well enough to buy a gift for her at her request. Christ, so he was back on the scene, was he? Is that why she hadn't come tonight? Irvana was saying to Arthur, 'Goodness, it is as well such celebration only comes once a year.'

Mark cut across Arthur's reply. 'Gordana obviously feels the same if she wasn't able to make

336

it tonight. Can't stand the pace?'

Irvana turned to him. 'Gordana is not in festive mood, neither was she yesterday, but why should the poor girl be?'

Arthur looked into the far distance, and slid away from them as Mark grabbed the girl's elbow. 'What do you mean? Arthur said she'd had no more news of her father. Was he wrong?' Irvana jerked free. 'No, it is not that.' She examined her drink whilst the noise in the room increased, if that was possible, then looked up at him. 'She doubts her welcome, Colonel Baird. She has been deployed, isn't that the term? She has been deployed to Gorniji Vakuf, your rear stop, so she is not meeting those who could give her news. It was a cruel thing to do, Colonel Baird. She said something strange. She said that it is almost as though it is a punishment.'

Ben was calling to him, 'Colonel, Captain Saul wants information on dominoes. I know they await me, but the finer points are beyond me. Any info?'

Mark forced himself to laugh, shaking his head, 'I'll see what I can dig up.' He turned back to Irvana but she had made good her escape and was chatting to Lt. Andrews. Mark placed his half-empty glass on the sideboard and walked steadily from the room, taking his gift from his coat pocket and leaving the house. The night air was bitter and all around were the usual thuds, and flashes in the sky towards Sarajevo. The puddles at the edge of the road had iced over and splintered beneath his boots as he headed to the interpreters' building.

The stairs smelt of rotting vegetables and cats' pee, just as they had done the evening he had walked her to the door. It was the second floor,

337

second door along. He stopped, knocked. There was no sound, but a dim light was showing beneath the door. He persisted, calling softly, 'Gordana, it is Mark Baird.'

Eventually, just as he was turning to leave, chilled to the bone, he heard the rattle of a security chain being removed, and the door opened. Gordana stood wrapped in a blanket, the light from the oil lamp on the table behind casting her face into shadow. She said, 'Ah, Colonel Baird,' then stood aside, beckoning him to enter.

He did so. It was hardly any warmer in the dingy room which obviously served as kitchen and living room. He stood by the table as she shut the door. turned and leaned back against it, her face expressionless. He saw that her face was thinner, and her hands which held the blanket seemed even more fragile than when he had felt them press his own to her face. He sat on the chair, his legs weak at the thought.

He laid her present on the oilskin-covered table, and said, 'I've missed you.'

She turned away, staring out of the frosted window. Her notebooks lay before him, together with several biros, and two pencils. Her backpack lay unfastened on the drainer, a squash ball beside it. Several pans were heaped in the sink. She said, still not looking at him, 'I have done something to displease you?'

He stood now and walked tentatively towards her, stopping halfway. 'You have only pleased me, never anything else.'

Now she looked at him in anguish, her voice rising, her hands tightening on the blanket. 'Then why send me away to the rear where I could gain

338

no information? Why punish me? Why?'

He reached her in three strides. taking hold of her shoulders, feeling their thinness. 'It was a decision I didn't take. It's not one that is my direct responsibility, and I'm sorry. I'm sorry because I only thought of how it was affecting me, not you, not your search. I'm so sorry. I will rectify things. Trust me.'

She broke away, walking to the table, touching her notebooks, her voice quiet, strained and unnatural. 'I should not have given you a gift, I should not have kissed you. I'm sorry and it will not happen again. I am glad that you will allow me to resume my duties. I ask nothing else of you.'

He was so close that he could smell her skin. He said softly into her hair, 'Yes, you should have given me a gift, and on the table is mine for you.'

He leaned past her, his body brushing her arm and he felt the shock of desire almost take the breath from him. He trembled as he picked up the package and placed it in her hands. The blanket fell from her as she took it. In her shirt and sweater and her thick cord trousers still she shivered. As she opened the package the rustle of paper seemed very loud, ceasing only when it fell to the table. Slowly Gordana opened the jewel box. Inside was a gold bracelet. She said nothing, just looked at it, then at him, and he couldn't read her eyes. She said softly, 'It's beautiful, so beautiful.'

He took it from its velvet bed, and placed it over her wrist, fastening the clasp. Her skin was soft and so cold. He stooped and kissed where the blue veins gathered. She touched his hair, his face, tracing across to his mouth. 'I've missed you, my warrior. The man who makes me feel safe. It hasn't been the same without you. I have been lonely. there has been no laughter, no comfort.' She reached up and kissed his mouth and it was like before, and his arms were around her, holding her, moving against her. Her mouth opened, her hands were in his hair, and his in hers, and pins were falling, until her long black hair fell loose in a stream of curls, and he sank his face in them. 'Oh Gordana,' he murmured.

She took his hand and led him to the bedroom. He could not think of anything but her, he would not because she had turned to him, and was pulling him down to her lips, kissing his mouth, his eyes. They stepped away from one another, coming together again, knowing it was cold, but not feeling it. They struggled with boots, and trousers, everything, standing close together, skin to skin, and he was hot against her, huge against her.

Together they tumbled to the bed, scrabbling beneath the blankets and the thin rough sheet. She was on him, her lips wet on his face, her tongue strong in his mouth, on his throat, her hands urgent on his chest, on his belly, flicking down, right down, touching him, pulling, pushing, working him, then away again, up into his hair, her mouth on his, her breasts close, almost touching his chest. Almost. His hands found them, cupped their full tautness.

He broke free from her mouth, kissing her breasts, rearing up, turning her on to her back, kissing the length of her body, hearing her soft moan, but then she was dragging him back to her mouth and her hands were on his buttocks, on him, stroking him, abandoning him, rolling free, laughing up at him as he groaned. She in her turn pushed him down and he kissed the sun-deep lines,

340

he kissed the breasts she teased him with. On and on it went and it was a heedless, endless passion, one he could not remember feeling for far too long.

But no, just think of this moment, just this. Live for the moment, she'd said to him once. His mouth was on hers, his body on hers, and she told him what she liked, and he did it. He told her what he liked, and she did that and never had he been so strong, never so powerful, never had foreplay been like this. Never, and if it had he didn't want to remember.

She kissed him again and now he was done with all of this, it wasn't enough, he wanted to be in her, he wanted to thrust and know her, and mingle with her, make her his. He dragged her back as she rolled away from him, heaved himself on her, looking into her face, kissing her hair, her eyes, her mouth, her neck and slid his legs between hers, pushing her wide, raising himself. She gasped, 'Wait.'

He stared into her eyes, sweat from his forehead dripping on to her. 'I can't, not any longer.'

She was reaching for the side table, her eyes locked to his, her other hand stroking him until he could hardly breathe, unable to think of anything but her, of his need of her, of his desperation. Stroking him steadily, strongly, faster. He moaned. 'Oh God.' She ordered, 'Look at me.' He did, boring deep into her eyes, almost insane with pleasure, a pleasure which was heightening beyond belief.

She was groping one-handed in the drawer. 'Here,' she murmured, fully back beneath him now, tearing at the foil with her teeth, putting something into his hand, stroking, still stroking.

He bore his weight on one elbow as she waited, her hands on his back now, her eyes trying to hold him. 'We must,' she murmured. It was a condom. She took his face in her hands. 'Put it on, Mark,' she ordered.

He flicked a glance towards it. 'Look at me,' she commanded, stroking him again. 'Look at me.'

He did and she kissed him, her tongue active, her hands active but the condom sat in his hand like a question mark. Where did she think he'd been, for God's sake?

She said against his mouth, 'Put it on. We must, these days we must.'

God almighty. Her lips were on his, her eyes were on his, and now he found himself fiddling, struggling to keep his eyes on hers, knowing he was finished if he lost eye contact. He found himself, pushed, fumbled, dropped it. Bloody, sodding thing. He groped, looked down, found it. 'Look at me,' she said.

He did, and felt her hands take it from him, saw her glance flicker as her hands found him, but it was too late, his strength was leaving him. She kissed him again, stroked him, but all he felt was the cold as it seeped into his sweaty body. Desperate, he kissed her, but he saw her too clearly, heard the dull thud of distant mortars, the ticking of the clock. She tried to maintain his passion, her arms around him, murmuring, 'Don't worry. Don't worry. We can start again.'

He shook his head and as he did so he saw himself in the wardrobe mirror, bare-arsed, middle-aged, absurd, and he rolled off her, flinging his arm across his face. What the hell was he thinking of, what the hell was he doing here? Was

342

he a complete bloody idiot?

He lay with his eyes closed hearing the rustle of the sheet as she dragged it over them both. He said, without opening his eyes, 'I'm sorry, this should never have happened.'

They lay there, silent. Each sound seemed too clear. The bare bedroom was just visible in the shadowy light from the kitchen oil lamp. God, what had he done? What a bloody idiot he had made of himself. Where were his clothes? He was going to have to grope around naked. Oh God, what had he done. Oh Claire. What the hell have I done? He wanted to rush home, let her hold him, let her mould her soft body to his, a body as familiar, as worn, as his own.

Holding his stomach in, he edged from the bed, feeling with his feet for obstacles, making for the light which fell through the open door, peering for his clothes, picking up her shirt in error, laying it on the bed, glancing at her, but she didn't move. Was she asleep? God, he hoped so. At last he had them all, and dressed quickly, but his fingers were clumsy.

He started to leave, then said quietly, 'Gordana?'

She turned immediately, her face in the dim light lost, pale, cold. His heart twisted. He came to the bed and said, 'I'm sorry. Please don't think that you will remain at Gornji Vakuf. You will be reassigned to me. This was my mistake. It will not affect your position. I'm so sorry, this was unforgivable, I should have known better.'

She reached up and took his hand; the sheet clung to her breasts. 'I'm glad it happened. If we had been on my island where there is peace and

343

time, it would have worked. Don't be sorry, Mark. Please, do not be sorry. Do not have regrets. We must take our moments. Remember that. We are owed our moments, as long as they hurt no one.'

CHAPTER TWENTY-THREE

Leah placed a cup of coffee carefully on the shelf in front of Anna's customer, looking into the mirror and seeing Anna smiling back as she blow-dried Mrs Price's hair. It was New Year's Eve and tomorrow Anna would drive Leah halfway home, meeting up with Claire at the Forester's Arms. All three would then grab a snack before Claire took Leah straight to school to catch the coach that would take her class on the first leg of their skiing trip to Tignes.

Mrs Price said, 'Thank you Leah dear, just what I need to perk me up, though how I'm going to get through to midnight heaven only knows. My body clock gets ready for cocoa at 9.30 and sort of shuts down.'

Leah smiled, thinking how terrible it was to be so old. Mrs Price, who was fifty, asked Anna what she and Leah were doing to celebrate New Year. Before Anna could answer Cheryl called from behind the next chair, where Ethel was having a blue rinse. 'We're partying upstairs, so get your earplugs in if you're in the vicinity, Mrs Price.'

Ethel piped up. 'Can I come?'

Anna said firmly, 'Certainly not, you'll wear the rest of us out.'

Mrs Price handed the postcard she'd been

reading back to Leah. 'Well, your parents certainly had a wonderful time, Anna. Will they be going to this panto you two are involved with?'

Anna had finished blow-drying, and now took a mirror from her trolley, angling it so that Mrs Price could see the back of her hair. 'It depends on Claire. It's her production and we don't want any more strain than necessary, do we Leah?' She smiled encouragingly at Leah, nodding towards the cork board. 'You could pin it back up there for me Leah, if you wouldn't mind.'

As Leah made her way towards the board behind the reception desk she heard Anna telling Mrs Price and Ethel of the progress they were making with *Cinderella*, explaining that the first complete run-through two days ago had been as successful as it could be with the rotating R & R situation, but that the understudy cast had made everything possible.

Anna said, 'We've got some of the scenery in place so the movement of the cast is easier to choreograph, but the songs are still a bit tatty. The Youth Club jiving number is fantastic, though. Claire and Jo have them jiving down the centre aisle at the end of Act I, and performing in front of the stage. It gives the feeling of a huge party. The costumes are on the way to completion, and there's a young mum who's come in as Cinderella because the real one's gone home to Mum. What's her name, Leah?'

Leah, pinning the card on the board, called over her shoulder, 'Audrey Wilt.' Anna brushed Mrs Price down, removed her gown, and led the way to reception. While Mrs Price paid, Leah fetched her coat from the rack, waiting patiently as Mrs Price chattered on, finishing, 'It's learning the words that would bother me.'

Cheryl called across, 'I gather from Leah and Anna that's pretty common.'

Leah agreed, as she helped Mrs Price into her coat. 'Cheryl's right. It drives Jo mad, but Mum doesn't mind so much because she's hopeless at remembering anything. She just tells them to fake it.'

Ethel cackled. 'Well, let's face it, we women are used to doing that.'

Everyone laughed and Leah turned to Anna, puzzled. 'Yeah, that's what Mum said and Jo wrote it in the script. I still don't get it.'

Mrs Price pressed 50p into Leah's hand. 'There you are dear, thank you for being such a love.' Behind her Cheryl grinned. Leah blushed and tried to return the money. Mrs Price wouldn't hear of it, so Leah put it in the staff box, and held the door open. It was four o'clock and already dark; the heavy cloud layer didn't help.

Closing the door she found Anna at her side. 'Come on Leah, you didn't come here to work, you came to party, so go and have a break.' She scooted her through the salon to the lobby at the back. 'But I don't know what I'd have done without you. I'm glad you gave Steve your phone number too, it's just a shame he couldn't make the party, but there'll be other times.'

In the lobby it was dark, and already Leah missed the bustle and the hairdressing smells. She said quietly, 'Shall I put the supermarket platters on your own plates? Mum does that with paté. Buys it and puts it into bowls then melts butter on the top. Dad still thinks she makes the best paté in the world.' Anna laughed, and hugged her. 'You are just so fantastic. Yes, why not. I can cheat just as well as Claire Baird any day. Go for it, Leah, but have a bit of a relax first, promise me.'

Leah objected as Anna pointed up the stairs, as though she was directing traffic. 'But you're not going to have a chance today.' Anna shook her head, going back into the salon. 'I'm used to being on my feet. Now go on, put 'em up for a bit.'

Cheryl called, 'See you later, Leah.'

*   *   *

Upstairs, propped against the phone in the pale cream and white sitting room, was an envelope addressed to Leah. She opened it and saw the £10 note, together with the note Anna had written: 'Thanks.' She grinned, headed towards the sofa, took off her Doc Martens and sprawled alongside the cat. So what if she got covered in hairs?

She snatched the remote from the arm of the sofa and flicked from channel to channel, stopping at the news, seeing that Sarajevo was still under siege, that Mostar was still suffering, that no miracle had happened since the lunchtime news to end it all and bring her dad home. She flicked back to the cartoons, lying on her stomach, stroking the cat who had gravitated to the floor, humming to herself, thinking of Steve who had snogged her beside the pool on the day after Boxing Day. He'd smelt of chlorine.

She'd been embarrassed at first, sitting on the edge of the pool, wet with only her swimming togs on, he with his. Embarrassed and almost scared because they were alone, and all she'd ever done

347

with any boy was snog. What if Steve wanted more? What if letting him kiss her beside the pool, almost naked, would make him think she did, when she didn't? She grinned down at the cat. 'But it was OK wasn't it, little fur ball? Hey, he's a great kisser, and no pressure from him either.'

She rolled on to her back, stretching, thinking of him, smelling the chlorine as though she was back at the pool, feeling sad he hadn't been able to come to the party, but in a way relieved because he'd have had to stay, and there'd have been the hassle of getting him back in the morning. Still, maybe it would have been nice. The cat jumped up on to her midriff and clawed at her jumper. 'Hey,' Leah scolded, picking him up, easing snagged wool from one of his claws. He jumped down and headed for the kitchen.

'Relax, the woman said, weren't you listening, cat?' Leah grumbled as she padded in her socks to the kitchen after him. She found the tins of cat food but the tin opener wasn't in the cutlery drawer. She looked in the one below but it was full of tea-towels. She tried the one below that. No, that was full of letters. She was about to push it closed again when she recognized her mother's handwriting on a big brown envelope. She pulled it from the drawer, intrigued. She noted the postmark. It was dated a few days before Anna had hidden behind the bush. Not understanding, Leah peered into the envelope and saw what looked like a photo. She pulled it out. Paper-clipped to the photo was a note in her mother's handwriting. *I'm so sorry, but you are mistaken. However, please accept my best wishes for your future.'*

Anna's friends were due to start arriving at eight and in the meantime Leah hoovered, dusted, even cleaned the lav. She decanted the supermarket platters, she heated butter and poured it on to the pâté, she tossed the salad, she worked until she could have dropped, even though Anna came out of the shower saying, 'Enough, enough.'

But it wasn't enough. Her mother had lied. She'd sent this sister of hers away, and she'd lied. There was no warning letter that had been lost under a pile of bills. There'd been an envelope that had been opened and returned, and if that wasn't a warning, what was? Now she hated her, hated her, and she felt sick with the hate and couldn't believe that she'd ever felt sorry for her, ever felt that she was the one who took everything that was thrown at her without complaint.

Cheryl breezed in on the dot of eight, her arms full of crisps and wine bottles, kissing Anna and Leah, bringing the coldness of the evening with her. 'Get over there, by the fire,' Anna ordered. 'How's the punch, Leah?'

Leah and Anna had heaved the big preserving pan on to the top of the cooker where the gentlest of flames burned blue beneath it. Leah grinned. 'Fine. It should warm the cockles.' She scooted off to get some, answering the door on the way, letting in a horde of people, taking their coats and grinning. How could she grin? How could she talk, function, breathe even?

She filled glasses almost to the brim with punch and brought them in on a huge tray. She thought the smell of cinnamon would stay with her for ever.

349

But what was for ever? Who was she? What was she? Who was this woman who was her mother? Anna took a glass, concern on her face. 'Please, Leah, slow down. This party is for you too. I want to show my sister off, not work you into the ground.'

Leah grinned. 'I'm just going back for some for myself, is that all right?'

'Yes, but don't drink too much, you've a long trip tomorrow, and you are only fourteen.'

Clive, one of Anna's friends, called, 'Oh boy, just listen to big sister. You go for it, Leah.'

Anna reached forward and touched Leah's face. 'Leah's got more sense.'

Leah returned to the crowded kitchen and headed for the punch. She loaded the tray with empty glasses, and steadily filled them, concentrating on that, but it didn't help because her mind wouldn't shut up, wouldn't stand still but just kept replaying all that had happened, kept replaying all the words, the feelings, all the resentments against Anna for bursting into her life, for putting her mother on the spot, for not checking that the letter she had sent had arrived, the letter which had supposedly been hidden amongst the bills.

Now she understood. Now she knew she had a mother who was a liar, a mother who didn't mind rejecting her own child, who only accepted her after she had been bearded in public.

She passed the punch around the throng in the kitchen, then moved to the hall and the sitting room. Music was blaring, perfumes mingled with cinnamon, and she knew she was still smiling because she could feel the stiffness in her cheeks.

But why did Anna have to come like that? That wasn't fair either. Why did she have to leap out of a bush at her mother? If she'd waited, talked to her quietly, her mother might have still admitted it. But why send the photo back? The tray was heavy. Clive took it from her. 'My turn to be host. Big sister's orders.' Clive was blond, his smile was friendly, his eyes very blue. There was oil round his fingernails. He must be a mechanic. Clive winked. 'Go on, take a glass, you deserve it.'

The punch was warm, the glass sticky. As she gulped it down a piece of orange nudged her lips.

But then at Christmas Anna had made it clear she hadn't meant to jump out of a bush, she had only come forward after her mother had heard a twig break. Anna had told her that as they walked to the pool on Boxing Day morning but she hadn't said Claire had returned the photograph. No, she hadn't tried to hurt her mother as her mother had hurt her.

Leah drank more, but the sickness was still there, the rage, the hurt. She wanted to go home. But where was home? With this woman who had lied, who had only accepted her daughter because the embarrassment would be greater if she didn't. With this woman who made such a show of caring for everyone, of being such a big wheel on the patch, the perfect CO's wife.

Cheryl came up, grabbed her glass of punch and set it on the coaster-covered sideboard. 'You and me, babe,' she shouted above the music, 'you and me are going to show this lot how to boogie. Pelvic thrusts and me are like this.' She held up her hands and entwined her first and second fingers. Leah laughed, and danced, and hoped the throbbing

351

music would stop the tape in her mind, but it didn't.

Clive and Anna were pouring more wine and fruit juice into the preserving pan, dodging the steam as best they could, giggling as another friend, Sylvie, tipped too much cinnamon in. 'Oh dear,' said Clive. 'Looks like I'll have to put in more wine to absorb that. What a bummer.' He did so, then grew serious. 'She's a nice kid, your Leah, but a bit quiet.'

Anna looked concerned. 'She is tonight. Maybe I worked her too hard, or she's missing her mother or something.'

Clive stirred the brew. '*Her* mother?'

Anna was cutting up oranges at the side of the cooker. 'Slip of the tongue. I really do think of Claire as my mother. I've kind of sorted it all out now in my head. I've two mothers, and I don't feel awkward about it any more. I just feel more or less settled and I think Leah does too. Here, move aside, young man.' Clive stepped back as she tipped the oranges into the pan, then resumed his stirring. 'More or less? Are you still thinking of finding your father?'

'Shh.' Anna looked round to cheek that Leah was nowhere in the vicinity. 'I don't know. I don't want to upset anyone more than I have and it's not really that important. It'd be bound to complicate things for Claire and Leah, not to mention Mark, so it's best left alone, I think. Though Ethel has a friend who used to be a policeman and could probably help trace him if I ever wanted to. Australia's a big place though. Anyway, enough of me. How're you and Cheryl making out?'

Clive had spooned some punch out and was

352

blowing on it. He sipped. 'Excellent.' He held the ladle out to Anna who tasted it and gave it the thumbs-up. Clive looked behind him for glasses, which Anna hurriedly put on the tray and carried to him. He said, 'That's my girl, I shall now take the tray round again, and home in on Cheryl, and see just how we *are* making out.'

*   *   *

Claire missed Liz. She and Ben had taken off for the hills, or ridden into the sunset, or however you liked to put it, and it was only right that they should she thought as she and Clarissa Baines helped to clear up the Coffee Shop now most wives had gone after seeing the New Year in. She picked the remnants of a party popper off her dress, and dropped it on to the pile she had just swept up.

Clarissa leaned on her broom and said, 'Are they really using party popper fuses for the flashes in the panto?'

Claire nodded. 'According to Sparks. They've ordered flash powder from the theatrical suppliers and made up this sort of contraption that works wonders, or didn't you think so this afternoon when we did the transformation scene?'

Clarissa resumed her sweeping. 'Not half. I nearly jumped out of my skin, and let me tell you that never has a pumpkin been turned so effectively into a Warrior tank.'

Claire beckoned to Sally. 'Can you bring that dustpan someone's left on the table down this way when you come, Sally.'

Sally called, 'Angie and I just want to finish crating the empties down this end first.'

'No hurry.'

Clarissa smiled at Claire. 'I never thought I'd see Turbogob staying behind and helping at anything.'

Claire chuckled. 'Angie's OK. I really like her now I've got to know her.'

Clarissa propped the broom against the table, and perched herself up beside it. 'So, are Liz's girls up to speed for the skiing?'

Claire joined her on the table. Sarah and Louise were staying with her and it was her job to get all three girls on to the coach in time. She eased her neck. 'They most certainly are and I expect the staff are rushing around packing their Prozac right now. They must be saints, taking a crowd of adolescents anywhere near skiing instructors. Those poor men won't know what's hit them.'

They laughed together, tired but relaxed, watching as Sally bustled over with the dustpan and brush. Clarissa brushed the accumulated rubbish on to the dustpan which Sally then tipped into the bin bag Claire held. At last it was all finished and the women left in groups to walk home. The night was cold, the stars bright and as Clarissa strolled beside Claire she said, 'Strange how we could be in there tonight laughing and joking, talking of skiing trips when there's that mess over in Bosnia. Sometimes it doesn't seem real, it's as though there's a sort of parallel universe in operation. A universe in which our men are involved and all we can do is worry, and wait.'

Claire tucked her arm in the younger woman's. 'And cope. Which you do very well, I might add.'

They walked a little further until they reached Clarissa's house. Claire was about to walk on when Clarissa said, 'Happy New Year, Claire. I hope everything continues to work out for you. You deserve it. Good grief, if anyone knows about coping it's you.'

When Claire arrived home the answer machine was blinking. She played it back. All were New Year messages. The first was from Liz, the second from Audrey Wilt, the third from Belle, the next from Anna and Leah with sounds off-stage of a high old time, and the last was from Mark, wishing them a Happy New Year and hoping the patch party had gone well.

That night Claire lay in bed, listening to the sounds of the house as she relaxed into a contented sleep.

CHAPTER TWENTY-FOUR

It was January and things were just as chaotic. As he hurtled along in the Warrior with hatches down and weapons ready to fire, Mark reviewed his company commanders' actions, their projected actions, his troops' actions, his own, the Brigadier's, the whole bloody kit and caboodle until he thought his head would burst and his stomach tie itself into a knot any sailor would be proud of

Then he thought about Gordana, and that small tragedy seemed to mirror this ongoing one in a way that made both even more painful. On 28 December she had come across eyewitness confirmation at last of her father's murder and ever since it was as though she had been on automatic pilot.

He listened to the crackling of the radio, to the

reports coming from Samuel Williams in the north whose turn it was to return fire on Serb positions after being engaged by small arms and mortar fire whilst escorting an aid convoy.

He nodded to himself as 2nd Lt. Williams reported that though firing had ceased his troops were maintaining static over-watch positions from high ground above the road. He reiterated that all UN Rules of Engagement had been applied, and the aid convoy had been able to proceed. His reaction to the situation had been exemplary, textbook stuff, and though he'd had the wise head of Sgt. Malloy to support him the Rupert tag was gone for ever.

Mark smiled tiredly and rubbed his hand across his face, chastising himself. Textbook stuff, my arse. What was textbook about this situation? He winced as the Warrior bounced down and up, and then he felt the skid. Quickly he checked that seat belts were being used. Damn the snow, damn the fact that they couldn't effectively prevent the tracks from skidding, damn the whole bloody performance.

Gordana had come to his office at the end of the day on 28 December, a day that had been so cold the air had seemed to crack as they negotiated their way through checkpoints. Sure, he had noticed that she had fallen quiet at about midday, after their first post-Christmas meeting at the Muslim Command Centre in Turbe, and even quieter after they had called into the Travnik Refugee Centre on their way back to base, but he'd thought it was embarrassment about their abortive sexual encounter, an encounter that had not only brought him to his senses, but probably made him and the British seem even more absurd and ineffectual in her eyes.

On their return she had followed him into his office and shut the door behind her. He had braced himself as he had used to, preparing for a harangue about impotent soldiers when she said, her voice a hopeless monotone, 'He's dead. I have heard today, first at the checkpoint, then at the Refugee Centre that my father is dead. I heard how he died.' She'd slid to the floor, her back against the door and the sounds that had come from her had not been sobs, but an awful sort of moaning.

He'd gone to her, lifted her to her feet, and she'd been limp against him, all arms and legs and hard to handle, and all the time there had been those awful sounds. Somehow he'd managed to get her to his chair, and phone for the Medical Officer. The MO had seemed to take his bloody time, but he'd been panting when he'd arrived, so he must have run, but even here, above the noise of the Warrior, he could still hear those sounds, see her gaping face, the wetness of her shirt where her tears had streamed.

The MO had wanted her to go to the sick bay, or to the hospital, but she had refused. As an extreme measure the MO had insisted she spend the night in Mark's house, using one of the VIP rooms, joking, telling Mark that if the Brigadier arrived he could have the second-best room. Neither man had been laughing. He'd loaded her with Valium, or some such thing, and Irvana had moved into the same room to keep her company and pay homage to propriety.

When Mark had looked in on her Irvana had risen, excused herself and left for a moment. He had sat by Gordana's bed and taken her hand. Her hair had been spread on the pillow; then she had wept. He had held her and there had been no passion, just compassion, a great welling of distress for this girl who had endured enough. That night he had not slept but had lain on his side in his own room, remembering the way she had clung to his hand when he'd tried to leave and begged him to stay because her whole world was finally in ruins.

The next day she'd been back on the job, back in her flat, and there had been no tears, just a deadness, a control that was awe-inspiring, a painful thinness that seemed to come upon her overnight, but later as she had walked to a checkpoint with Mark he had seen the tremor begin in her and but for his hand beneath her elbow she would have fallen.

That evening he had insisted that Irvana and Gordana eat at his house, and had brought the MO into the office to back up his instructions. She had eaten a little. Consequently Gordana had eaten in his house every night, though she slept in her own room, joined by Irvana when possible, but it was only on an evening when Irvana was in Travnik that Gordana told him the facts, in a voice as dry as their lips at the end of a day on patrol.

She had brought out her notebook, the one she kept personal accounts in, the one that Stevo copied up into typewritten sheets. He remembered her hands, the skin almost translucent, too many veins visible, but wouldn't his be also if his father had been dragged from his vineyard because he was considered a village leader? If he had been led with fourteen others into the wood and forced to dig a pit which was to be their grave and then

358

suffered unspeakable indignities until released by a shot in the back of the head by Serb militia who called themselves soldiers? The next day she had hacked her hair short and it was this that had upset Mark most, because it reeked of self-mutilation, and mirrored Bosnia.

*　　*　　*

The fog was thickening as they drew closer to Gornji Vakuf and the Warrior column slowed, then stopped altogether at a Muslim checkpoint, but it was only as he and Gordana approached with their back-up that he saw it was now in the hands of Croats. As though it was nothing untoward Gordana distributed the endless cigarettes with an unfaltering smile, her calm never cracking.

They were allowed to proceed and Gordana thanked the soldier, who stared at her, his hostility barely veiled. Mark moved closer, eyeballing the bastard, wanting to snatch the cigarette from his mouth, wanting him to understand what this woman was going through. He felt her hand on his arm, restraining him. She spoke softly. 'We go, no. Perhaps his father was killed, his son, his brother. We go, Mark. Your Major Nigel Perkins is waiting, then we have to reach Turbe. It is a long day, Mark, and after that is another, and another.' With grief her fluency had lapsed.

She turned now, and walked to the rear of the Warrior. Mark caught her, swung her round. 'One day at a time. Remember what you told me. One day at a time and that is how to survive. Don't ever forget.'

She shook her head slightly, looking out into the

fog through which there was the hint of trees. 'That was then. That was when I had hope, that was when there was still a "maybe". Now there is nothing.'

Once in the suburbs they travelled fast, the press vehicles, one of which contained Arthur and a Reuters man, locked in tight behind. Inside the base they decanted and Mark resisted the temptation to check that Perkins's security measures were up to scratch, because he knew that at last they would be. Samuel Williams was not the only one who had grown into the job. Everyone had, and pride in his men swept everything aside for a precious moment.

Gordana did not accompany him as he hurried to the Operations Room with Nigel. He knew she would be given coffee, but would she eat? In the Ops Room, the Brigadier and the Commander-in-Chief United Kingdom Land Forces based in UK were already there. Nigel and he brought them up to date on the situation, explaining that, as so many times before, efforts to achieve ceasefires were never ending, as they were in other areas of Bosnia, that Warriors patrolled the area unceasingly, as they did in other areas of Bosnia, that somehow aid across the province was still being delivered. God almighty, it sounded like some sort of a mantra, Mark thought.

After showing them as much of the battalion group as possible, they drove on to Turbe, this time with Gordana, though she was in a follow-up Warrior with Lt. Ogard. While outside the sounds of war continued, inside minds were as usual busy with the ramifications of possibly decreasing British commitment, possibly withdrawing altogether, possibly continuing operations as they were, or somehow cobbling together a peace plan.

At Turbe they ducked into the Muslim headquarters alongside their own liaison officers, and Gordana interpreted as Mark's senior officers snatched coffee and slivovitz, all of them heedless of the dust showering from the cellar ceiling every time a mortar fell. On their return, the talk inside the Warrior was muted, the atmosphere thoughtful and disturbed, but what was new about that?

On their way back to Vitez after the Brigadier and the General had gone on to Split, they travelled with hatches half closed. In the moonlight Mark counted the latest additions to the destroyed houses forum, distant flashes, but soon lost heart and just stared, and it all looked like some surreal landscape he might find in one of Leah's art books. He wanted to vomit.

*   *   *

That evening while Gordana showered in his bathroom as a prelude to dinner, he sat on the sofa and sorted through his mail. There was the usual weekly one from Claire, which he put aside to scan-read later if he had the chance, along with Belle's. Then another from France addressed to him in Leah's handwriting. He was puzzled for a moment because his daughter was as bad a correspondent as he, but then he grinned: she must have managed to tackle a black run, and maybe the moguls successfully at last. Well, rather her than him. He rubbed his knees ruefully, and was about to open it when Arthur Pierce arrived.

Mark had invited him for a drink when he had

learned that today was his thirty-eighth birthday, and as he poured a Scotch he tried to persuade him to stay for dinner but Arthur had a more pressing appointment with his typewriter. 'Got to earn a living, Mark. Busy times, interesting times.' Sitting on the sofa opposite, Arthur fingered his ponytail and Mark wished to hell he'd cut it off. Damn silly effort for a grown man.

Suddenly Gordana's hacked hair came into his mind and he stared at the apology for a fire. Reaching down, he hurled more of the scarce fuel on to it. Sparks showered. Arthur laughed 'Feel better for that, do you? Not sure the fire does.'

Mark prodded with a poker but it still wasn't drawing well. 'Bloody thing.' He propped the poker against the fireplace, and raised his glass to Arthur. 'Happy birthday, many more of them.'

Arthur smiled. 'Thanks, squire. Don't know how many more there'll be after tonight. Charlie's taken it upon himself to celebrate with me when I've filed my piece.'

Mark grimaced. 'Got the order of service sorted out, have you? Cremation, or you might be lucky and get on the liver transplant . . .'

Arthur's burst of laughter cut him short and for a few moments they talked of the world they'd once known but then Arthur leaned forward rolling his glass between his hands. 'Charlie and I are worried about Gordana. She needs a break. Can you have a go at her, persuade her to get away? How about that island of hers? Maybe she can pick up her mother from Zagreb? We're fond of her at the press camp, you know. We've tried to persuade her, but she seems to feel she must do her share for Bosnia and you boys in blue berets, but our guess is

362

she'll snap if she goes on too long. Irvana was going to have another go at her tonight, but as you know she's with Ben in Novi Travnik. How is Ben by the way, did his leave go well?'

Mark didn't know. Ben was due back tomorrow. Was he trying for redundancy or staying in? What had Liz said? Well, at least there couldn't be chapter and verse from Ben once he knew Gordana was eating here, because Irvana had more often than not been on hand. He shifted uncomfortably, knowing that he'd feel embarrassed and guilty about the night in the flat until the day he popped his clogs, guessing that from her silence Gordana felt the same. Funny though, how at the same time it had made them easier together, as though they'd broken a barrier and bloody hell, they had most certainly done that.

Arthur and Mark talked for another ten minutes, then there was a light knock on the door and Gordana entered, her hair still wet from the shower. She wore the same clothes as she had done all day. Both men rose, but it was Arthur who walked to her, taking her elbow, leading her to the fire. 'Come on, stick your backside in front of that feeble flame. Give it something to roar about.' Gordana smiled, and the skin seemed to stretch painfully across her cheekbones. 'That's better,' Arthur said approvingly, handing his glass back to Mark, his eyes meaningful. 'Now, I'm off to work, and then to Charlie's ministrations. God help me.'

Again Gordana smiled and it almost reached her eyes. Mark started to walk the journalist to the door, but Arthur waved him back. 'No need, know my way and won't snatch the family silver on the way out.' He turned to Gordana. 'Eat well, little sparrow. There's always a tomorrow.' With that, he was gone, shutting the door quietly behind him.

Gordana had settled herself where Arthur had been and Mark returned to his seat opposite, knowing she would not accept a drink. Since her father's death she had ceased to drink alcohol, and Charlie had said it might have been as a sort of penance, a sort of reversion to the Muslim religion, or maybe it was because she simply couldn't bear the taste of anything any more.

Mark said quietly, 'Arthur's only thirty-eight and has seen so much, but is still a good man. Not cynical, not even angry, though you'd expect it.'

Gordana just nodded, as though speech was too much of an effort, but he was used to that, and most evenings it was he and Irvana who chatted, drawing her in when they could. He tried again. 'We were saying that Korcula must be nice, even at this time of year? Tell me about it again. The dinner party was so long ago I can barely remember what you told us.'

She dragged her gaze from the fire that was flickering as though it meant it now. She looked at him, and it almost seemed that she was bringing him into focus for the first time for a long while. 'You actually remember me telling you of Korcula?'

Mark smiled. 'Of course. I remember a great deal.' He hesitated, knowing that now he should speak of the night in her flat. 'I also remember I behaved badly in your flat. I abused my position, I was temporarily out of control, it was stupid, unforgivable.'

She held up her hand. 'Korcula is beautiful. Korcula is where one can relax, shut out the world,

364

be happy. I like to reach it by boat, landing at Korcula Town. It is a town that just seems to float on the sea. It is a town that was built for safety, moated on the landward side, massive walls, and corner towers. Yes, it is a town of safety, just as you are a man of safety.' Her voice trailed away.

He stared at the fire, the tremor in her voice stirring him to pity; he wanted to disabuse her of the image of him as a safe haven. Good God, he felt no safer than the next man, no more sure of himself or the job he was doing than a bloody milkman would have been. He said, 'It sounds wonderful, just what everyone needs at the moment. Just imagine, to step out of this madhouse for a week or so. Think of it Gordana, it would give you a respite, a time to recover. You don't owe this job your health, you know. No one expects all this of you. R & R is essential, even I feel that, and I'm the biggest worrier in the universe.'

She had bunched her hands into fists at his words, and now her eyes were almost fierce, and there was a slight colour in her cheeks. 'There are hills covered in pines, cypresses, and shrubs too; myrtle, juniper, rosemary. There are herbs like oregano and mountain sage. In the summer you can lie in bed and breathe in their scent. In winter you can dream of the promise of it. It is where I have been happy.'

'Then, come on, why not go again?'

She was on her feet, coming to him, kneeling at his feet. 'Shall we, shall we go? Shall we lie in bed and dream of the promise of it? Shall we live for each day, and just dream of the promise that life goes on.'

Her hands were grasping his, her face was lifted to him and he felt the panic sweep him, for that was not what he had meant. Oh God, that was not what he had meant at all. He withdrew his hands, and stroked her hair, her poor shorn hair. He said. 'You go, *you* go, it is what you need. Go with Irvana. I'm too old for you, you deserve so much more than me.' Is that what people said, people who were fools like him, who had taken advantage, who had dug themselves into damn great holes? She sat back on her heels, and silent tears began to stream down her cheeks while he stared at her helplessly, and the sobs began, loud enough to be heard beyond the door.

'Shhh.' He put his hands beneath her elbows, stood, pulling her up with him, feeling her sag against him and her body was so fragile as he held her and at last she quietened, and lifted her face to him and he kissed her forehead, but she dragged him to her mouth and he tasted the salt of her tears, and felt an echo of that same passion he had experienced before. She whispered against his mouth, 'Just a week of your leave. Is that too much to ask? Just a week out of your life? Just a moment of your time?'

The words cut through the passion, cut through the madness, and slowly he reached up and gently pulled her hands from his neck, kissing them, saying against her fingers, 'You're a lovely girl, and if things were different wild horses wouldn't stop me but there's Claire, and she wouldn't deserve that.' He looked at her now. 'But I want you to go to the island. You need to go. Collect your mother from Zagreb, take her, but go.'

She pulled her hands from him, her voice

shaking as she shouted: 'And me, what do I deserve? A meal, scraps from your table, from the table of the British.' She hit out at him, catching his mouth, bursting his lip. The pain was surprising, immobilizing him for a moment. He tasted blood, and dabbed at it with his handkerchief. Gordana was backing from him, staring at the blood on her hand, saying, 'I'm sorry. I'm so sorry. It is not what I meant. I'm just so sorry.' She turned and ran to the door. He was close behind her, calling her back. She pulled the door open. He caught it, caught her. 'It doesn't matter. It's nothing. I deserved it. It's nothing.'

She yanked free of him, snatched up her coat and headed out of the front door into the cold night and he stood and watched her go, half relieved, half not, not knowing what else to do, what else to feel.

Much later, when he'd discarded his meal and sat with his paperwork on his knee, trying to concentrate while his lip throbbed, he remembered Leah's letter. He found it on the occasional table and again he stared at the handwriting, wanting to be home, wanting to be with his family, wanting things to be as they had been, just the three of them, no Anna, no Gordana, no Bosnia. Perhaps they could be. Soon it would be R & R. He would be there for the pantomime, then it would be just Claire and he in Tenerife. He could rest, talk, walk and for once they'd have time for one another, and it would be like reaching a safe shore.

And after Bosnia there would be just the three of them; and Anna sometimes, which was all right. It would be all right even if she found her father, because nothing could touch him and Claire. She

367

was strong, she loved him, she was his partner, his comfort, his security, his age. She was his history.

He opened the envelope and looked at the view of Tignes, all blue skies and crisp snow. He smiled. Before they left for Tenerife he'd nip over to the school, beard the headmistress and demand that his daughter be released for a couple of hours, then he'd waltz the old sausage out for lunch, or breakfast, if that was the only time they had. He wondered what time the flight to Tenerife was. He turned the postcard over, preparing to wince at stories of black runs and moguls.

Instead he read the words:

Come home, Dad, I need you. You should be here with me, not out there. If you loved me, you'd come back. Mum knew all the time that Anna was her daughter because Anna sent her a photograph. Mum sent it back saying she was mistaken, then she sent her away when she came. She lied when she said she was shocked. Come back. Please come back. I just need you. I don't understand her any more.

CHAPTER TWENTY-FIVE

Claire listened to the six o'clock news on the car radio while she waited at the school for the return of the skiers' coach, hearing the details of another failed ceasefire. Well, no wonder Mark hadn't been able to phone yesterday, but she wished he had, because it was as hairy as ever out there and as worrying. She peered out into the darkness, seeing the interior lights in the other cars, and they probably had the heaters going full blast.

With her it was a question of radio or light, she didn't dare ask for both, and forget about the heater. Mark had always said that even using all three wouldn't run the battery down but about three years ago, before they'd bought the Volvo admittedly, it had done just that the moment he'd gone off to defend some country's virtue. Had he ever tried pushing the equivalent of a bloody great tank while 'the' daughter sat in the driving seat saying, 'I can't believe we're doing this, what if someone sees?'

She checked her watch again in the light from the lanterns which were strung around the car park. The coach was half an hour overdue, but no one expected perfection on these occasions. Yes, of course it would be nice, but there you go. She pulled up her scarf, knowing that in this cold she would by now resemble Rudolf. Why was her nose always the first thing to go?

Just then, a car stormed into the car park, taking the sleeping policemen at a rate of knots and even if she had not recognized Liz's Citroën she would have known it was her. Was that woman ever on time? But her grin had already begun, and with it came a great sense of relief that her friend was back from leave, not just in time to collect her girls, but to call her an old slapper, and give her a kiss. The Citroën skidded into a space across the car park and Claire switched off the radio and hurried to join her.

Liz was getting out of the car as she arrived. She flung her arms round Claire. 'Well, you old slapper, how is everything?' Her kiss was a smacker, her dangling earrings new. 'Wonderful,' Claire said. 'Anna gave me a photograph album of her life. It hurt to see the years pass like that, but it was wonderful too. She was beautiful, Liz, a tomboy with blonde hair until she was five.' Liz hugged her, tighter still, then whispered, 'Oh glory be, incoming fire.' Claire laughed and she didn't need to turn to know that Mollie was bearing down upon them, indignation in every breath.

'Really Liz, those humps in the road are there for a reason. Coming in at that speed you couldn't possibly stop should a child run in front of you.'

Claire whispered, before relinquishing Liz, 'One day I will allow you to administer the mother of all enemas to this woman. It can only do her good.' Liz laughed, then turned to Mollie. 'I hardly think there'll be any kids rushing across my path at this time of night, but just to put your mind at rest we'll have a re-run. You step out in front of me and we'll see what happens.'

Mollie tutted, but did she ever do anything else? Claire broke up the brewing battle by saying to Liz, 'So, you saw Ben off, and then had a good few days with your mother? Are they both well?'

Mollie interrupted: 'As you've been away I expect you've missed the latest Bosnian excitement.'

Liz's tone was dry. 'Hardly. There is TV at Mother's, and it is at the forefront of all our minds.' Firmly she walked Claire away, leaving Mollie puffed up but deflated at the same time, which was a quite extraordinary sight. Claire said quietly when she caught up with Liz, 'That was a bit hard. Nigel's been on TV after getting that convoy going again. We should allow her her bit of reflected glory.'

Liz stopped in the light of one of the lanterns, drawing up the collar of her red coat. 'Oh I know, but she chooses her bloody moments, doesn't she?'

Claire smiled sympathetically. 'You're a bit blue because the old man's gone back?'

'Got it in one.'

Claire pulled her friend's collar up even higher. 'Come on, tell me all. Any decisions?'

Liz wiped her eyes, her voice full. Claire found a clean tissue and Liz snatched it, saying, 'Damn the wind.' She blew her nose, then grinned and said, 'We talked, we still haven't quite decided, but 31 January is the deadline we've made and probably I'm not taking the partnership. Somehow I find I quite enjoy all this patch malarkey, now I'm actually having to do it.'

Claire groaned 'Darned fool,' before linking arms and beginning a slow march back to the main group. Liz asked: 'Have the girls had a good time on the slopes? My horrors didn't phone me in Goa but Mum had a call. Seems they were sound in mind and limb at that stage of the game.'

Claire frowned, her uneasiness returning because Leah hadn't rung at all. In fact from the moment of meeting up halfway with Anna after the New Year party she had seemed remote, disdainful, surly, though Anna had said quietly, 'The punch was a wee bit strong, Claire. She'll sleep it off on the coach.'

Liz was asking about the pantomime.

Claire turned her mind to practical matters. 'Rehearsal tonight. We had lighting and props run-through last week and everything is more or less as it should be with two weeks or so to go except that we've had to insert a "filler" at front of stage while we set up for the kitchen scene. Buttons is going to do some sort of competition with the kids, get a few up from the audience. Apart from that, the cast is almost word perfect, and most of them have shaken down beautifully into their roles. We're still fiddling a bit with the transformation scene. The pulley system to lift the pumpkin up and lower the Warrior down is not quite the smoothest thing you've ever seen.'

They were almost upon the small group of parents and lone patch mothers who were leaving their cars, and stamping their feet as they stood around. Liz said quietly, 'Any other problems on patch?' She was looking intently at Claire. Claire shrugged. 'Just the usual alarms and crises to keep me off the streets.' Liz smiled at her. 'But you're looking less tired now the girls have shaken down. You're sleeping better, aren't you?'

Claire squeezed her friend's arm. 'I've never been happier. Mark's been phoning regularly again at last so it's all wonderful.' At that moment the coach hove into sight. Liz called: 'OK everyone, peace is at an end, our little darlings are back.' Over the laughter Mollie's voice could be heard. 'I for one will be glad to see them, and if some are difficult, is it to be wondered at?'

Liz's whispered chant of 'Enema, Enema' wiped away Claire's irritation, and she waved along with the others as the coach eased its way up the circular drive, stopping at the entrance to the car park. In a moment the driver was down, opening the luggage bay, and soon the girls were streaming out.

In a few moments Leah was slouching along towards Claire, carrying her huge rucksack in front of her, her knees banging against it. As Claire kissed her, she averted her face keeping the rucksack between them, then headed for the boot of the Volvo. Claire tried to help her with it, saying, 'Leah, I've missed you so much. Have you had a great time?' 'Fine,' Leah answered, her voice flat.

Across the car park Liz was unlocking the boot as her girls lurched in her wake clutching their rucksacks, clumsily kissing their mother, then heaving in their gear. Liz called across as she was about to drive away: 'The girls will see Leah at Youth Club for the dance rehearsal, and I'll see you Claire, at the theatre. Eight-thirty, isn't it?' Claire nodded, and waved while Leah clambered into the car, sitting with her head back and her eyes closed as Claire started the engine. 'Put your belt on, Leah.'

Leah did so, her eyes still shut. Claire reached across and stroked her hair from her forehead. Leah recoiled. Claire said, 'Leah, what's wrong?'

'Oh for goodness sake, you know I always want to upchuck in a coach. Let's just get home.'

Claire started the engine. 'I thought you'd grown out of that.'

'Well, sorry to disappoint you. I can't do things to order, you know. Anyway I'm tired.'

Claire headed out in convoy with all the other cars. 'Perhaps you ought not to go to the Youth Club?'

'There's tired and tired, or were you going to sit by my bed and play mother?'

'I'm more likely to put you across my knee if this goes on.'

'But you haven't checked your schedule. Perhaps you're too busy even to do that.'

373

Claire spun round, taking her eyes off the narrow country road. Leah said, 'Yes, just kill the two of us, why don't you.'

Claire turned back to the road, wanting to screech to a stop and shake the child. Fuming, she drove on until she saw the lay-by she was searching for and pulled off while the other cars carried on past. One slowed and someone shouted: 'You OK?'

'Leah's a bit sick.' The car drove on.

She switched off the engine. Leah sighed dramatically and folded her arms, her eyes still closed. Claire shouted, 'What the hell is wrong with you; you've just been on a skiing holiday which cost the earth and this is the response? Now smarten up.'

Leah opened her eyes in shock. Her mother seldom shouted, and never at such close quarters. 'Go on, sit up, stop slouching and get a grip, or is there something really wrong?' Claire waited, tense. Surely it wasn't about Anna again?

Leah did as she was told, then shouted back: 'Like you've just told that guy, I felt sick. That's all, I just feel sick. Don't make a drama out of everything. I want to get home—is that too much to ask?'

They drove back in silence, Claire taking the bends slowly, but wanting to throw the car around, knowing that to do so would be as childish as Leah, but incredibly satisfying nonetheless. In the garage she handed Leah the keys. 'You let yourself in, I'll bring in your gear if you're out of sorts.'

Leah said. 'I'll do it. It's my stuff.'

It was the right gesture, but the tone was wrong. Claire opened the boot and Leah dragged out the rucksack. Lugging it to the back door she let

374

herself in, turning, her voice eager, 'Has Dad written?'

Claire shook her head, and saw the eagerness fade, and she could have kicked herself. Was it any wonder she was strained when her father was still out there? She called after Leah: 'We'd have heard if he was hurt. They're all being very careful.'

*   *   *

The rehearsal went well. The costumes were in their final stages, though the chicken's suit was still causing trouble because the feathers they'd collected from the chicken farm made the poor old creature look as though it had had too close a brush with fowl pest.

At nine o'clock, Muriel stuck her head round the door on one of her infrequent visits and suggested that playgroup might like to replace the feathers with shaped crèpe paper. This induced a prolonged discussion about whether it would ruin it for the children if they recognized their own handiwork. It was decided that it would, so before Muriel could make good her escape, Claire volunteered her for the job. To the sound of cheers Muriel was forced to accept, which brought a great grin to her gardener's face until she threatened to dock his wages for insubordination.

Angie, the 'Orrible Oracle, was word perfect, and had whipped her witchlets into line, Audrey's voice was growing in strength day by day, along with her confidence, and now she ran through the songs again. Claire and Jo listened with one ear while talking through the details of Cinders' transformation from waif to stunner in the meagre

375

thirty seconds they had for the costume change.

Jo sucked her pencil, finally agreeing that they'd need three dressers at least, including Anna who could deal with the wig. As Audrey finished, they clapped and Jo called across to the pianist: 'The Youth Club and the dance schools are putting the finishing touches to their routines over at the clubhouse now and we'll have a complete run-through with them on Thursday. Can you manage to be here, Trish?'

Trish could. Jo then swung back to Claire. 'I forgot to ask, so please tell me—none of the dancers came home in plaster?'

Claire laughed, and Liz called out from the producer's table: 'Not one, though I dare say the staff are lying in darkened rooms as we speak.'

Mollie called Claire to the costume corner, and as she hurried to the back of the theatre Angie and her witchlets and part of the chorus fell silent at her approach, before talking in loud voices of the costumes they would be wearing. Their smiles were too bright, their voices false. Claire ignored it as she'd been doing for the past few weeks, guessing that it was something to do with the producer's bouquet, reminding herself to make sure Liz dropped them the wink about ordering the larger bouquet for Jo, not the CO's wife.

*   *   *

By eleven they were through, and the theatre locked. They left in a group and it pleased Claire enormously that the main sound was of laughter and extraordinarily bad taste jokes. She wished that Muriel had stayed long enough to hear, because

376

she had been so very right. Somehow it was keeping them all afloat, giving them something to hang on to as the deployment reached its midway point.

She, Liz and Mollie quickened their pace to be home before the Youth Club devotees. Jo called, 'Hang on a minute, I'll walk with you and we can clear up a few remaining problems.' Claire called back, 'Oh no we won't.'

The group yelled, 'Look out, she's behind you.'

Claire raised her eyebrows at Liz, who roared with laughter. Mollie however was saying grimly, 'This isn't as it should be. An example should be set.'

Claire and Liz chanted as Jo caught them up: 'Oh no it shouldn't.'

Mollie did not join in their laughter, and soon their own died as they looked ahead and saw Leah walking towards them, just ahead of a group of others. She was smoking. Liz's girls were in the background, and Mollie's nowhere to be seen. Claire hurried forward; Liz and Mollie too. Leah met her mother, stared at her, then blew smoke in her face quite deliberately, and her breath smelt not just of nicotine, but of beer.

Claire fought to keep her voice calm. 'It's time to go home.' Behind her she could still hear the laughter of the group they had far outpaced.

Leah said, her eyes fixed on her mother's, 'Thought we'd go on to a club. We're phoning for a taxi, any objections?' Behind Leah the other teenagers looked embarrassed.

'Plenty. We're going home. You're too young. It's too late.' Claire looked past Leah to the others, her hands balled into fists in her pockets. 'It's time

377

you all went home. Come on James, you too Matthew, your mothers will be worried.' She could see their resolve weakening, their embarrassment growing. Leah turned to them. 'Come on, don't chicken out. Why shouldn't we go to a club?'

Liz started to speak, but her girls had already turned and were hurrying home. Claire gripped Leah's arm now, saying quietly, fiercely, 'You are too young, that's why.'

While Liz suggested to Mollie that she went home to her daughters and made sure she went, Leah's voice was quietly vicious. 'Don't worry, Mum, I won't make your mistake.'

Claire felt as though she'd been punched but before she could retaliate Liz turned on Leah. 'That's more than enough.' She moved over to the youngsters, shooing them home, whilst Leah stood her ground, half shouting at her mother. 'I know it's enough. It's more than bloody enough.'

Claire reached out helplessly. 'What's happened, what's the matter with you? For heaven's sake Leah, the other children are worried about their fathers too. There is no excuse for this.'

Leah was laughing now, and it was a dramatic over-play. 'Shocked, were you? Isn't that what you said? Too shocked and so you denied her.' She was stabbing her finger at her mother. 'What about the photo she sent, and the letter? You must have known she'd keep trying. Shock, how can it have been shock? Good God, it wasn't as though rejecting her was strange to you. You did that when she was born, you did it again with the photo. I hate you. I just hate you.'

For Claire everything was in slow motion, a million miles away, and it didn't alter when Liz grabbed Leah and frogmarched her away, and Jo took Claire's arm and made her walk on. Behind them were the wives, still unaware, talking and laughing. Ahead of them were the youngsters too far away to have heard. But it didn't matter. Nothing mattered. Nothing at all. Not even Leah stopping to vomit in the gutter, not Liz shouting at her: 'Serves you bloody well right, you little madam.' Not even the fact that at last the wives had fallen quiet behind them.

On they walked, Leah and Liz ahead, Jo and Claire behind, until Claire heard the gravel of her drive, but she also heard something else: the sound of the wind, of the surf, of crying, and she'd been a fool to think she could ever escape it, ever give it the slip, ever be free, ever be safe.

Jo led her into the sitting room. It was dark, horribly dark, the sounds were worse. 'The lights,' she gasped, her own voice strange to her. 'Put on the lights.' Jo did so, easing her coat from her, forcing her down on to the sofa, making her sit still just as Liz almost ran in, rolling down her sleeves, mouthing at Jo, 'You go, and thanks. But if you could call on my two? Any chance of staying all night? I can't leave here.'

Jo agreed, then hurried out, not voicing the questions she wanted to ask. Liz sat beside Claire. Taking her hand, she said, 'Stupid child, but the two pints of water I've poured down her throat will ease the situation though she's still going to feel as sick as a parrot in the morning.' She rubbed Claire's hand. 'You know I didn't tell her about the photo, I've told no one . . .'

Claire interrupted and it was as though it was a stranger's voice, as though her lips weren't hers. 'It

379

must have been Anna.'

Liz turned on the gas fire, then tucked a coat round Claire's knees but it didn't stop the trembling. 'It wasn't Anna. Leah's just told me that she found the envelope in the flat so I've tried to explain that the level of trauma involved in receiving the envelope created delayed shock, because you wouldn't deliberately hurt anyone.' Liz paused, looking intently at Claire, her eyes sympathetic but firm. 'Sounds a bit thin, doesn't it?'

Claire clutched the coat. Liz said gently, 'I think you should tell her the truth. It'll have to come to that in the end if you are ever to leave it behind.' The table lamp behind Claire was too bright. Liz switched it off.

Claire felt herself trembling, felt her mouth working, heard her voice which sounded high pitched, like a madwoman's. 'What is the truth? What is the damned truth?'

Again Liz took hold of Claire's hand but Claire didn't want anyone touching her. There had been too many people taking hold of her, grasping at her, too many people. She hit Liz away, but she came back, grabbing both her hands now, hushing her but she didn't want to be hushed, she just wanted her hands back. 'Let me go.'

'Tell her the truth,' Liz insisted. 'Tell her you were raped.'

Claire sank back, fighting for breath, pulling at her collar, feeling Liz's hands there helping. They were warm, gentle and now Claire gripped them, tighter, tighter, and she didn't stop, even when Liz winced. She whispered, 'Was I?' Her lips were stiff, and the trembling began again and now she felt Liz smoothing her hair and she wanted this, she

380

wanted to be touched, needed to be, needed to hear the words she'd never heard before and which were now coming as her friend said, 'Of course you were. I've seen your notes. Of course you were.'

But these weren't the words she needed to hear, because what were notes? The darkness was coming again, and the sound of the surf, the feel of those hands, and she pulled away again, pushing Liz's coat from her knees, pushing her friend away, not deserving anyone's kindness. 'There's no of course about it. It's not like you think, that's just the trouble, that's always been the trouble.' Her voice was a horrible wail and she clapped her hand to her mouth.

Gently Liz took her hand, but again Claire pulled free. 'Then tell me what happened. You must tell someone.'

Claire couldn't. Liz tried again. No, she couldn't. Liz shouted: 'You must. You have to. I insist that you do.' Claire had never thought she'd be able to, never thought she'd find the words, never thought she'd allow her mind to go back and remember it all, every minute, every second, every sight and sound, after so many years of desperate denial. But now here, with Liz shouting at her, catching at her when she tried to turn away, never leaving her in peace, she did, in a torrent of words that once started wouldn't stop, that tumbled from her, so quickly, so horribly quickly that it was as though they'd been building all these years, just for this moment.

She told Liz of lying on the sand at West Wittering with the clouds tumbling across the sun while her father read the *Daily Express* and her mother knitted, and of the boy who had passed

381

with his father, of her mother's delighted call: 'Mr Turnbull, what a lovely surprise.' Of her father's crestfallen expression which had altered to polite pleasure at this unexpected meeting with his boss and his son. She told of the torture of her mother's blatant angling for an invitation to the Turnbulls' house once she heard that they were having a barbecue that evening.

'We were invited. My father was furious but as always he didn't show it. We went. I was wearing those long white boots we both had. Do you remember?' Claire didn't wait for a reply. 'Long white boots and a short black skirt, just like all the other girls in the Turnbull garden that night. We all thought we were so unique, but we weren't. We all had black eyeliner, pale lips. It was a beautiful evening. We drank wine, chilled white wine and Mum kept steering me towards Alex, that was his name. Alex Turnbull. He was at university and due to join the firm in Woking. She kept telling him that I would be going to university too, that perhaps I would become a solicitor, just like him. That I was much more intelligent than my father. That I liked going to the cinema. Can you imagine that, Liz? Why the hell didn't she just put a price tag on me?'

She gave Liz no chance to answer, and all the time she didn't know where the words were coming from, the words that were spilling out into this room, with its hissing gas fire. 'I could see he was laughing at Mum and Dad. Laughing at me, I expect. I hated them all. I said I was leaving. It was eleven. I found Dad and told him. He was relieved. He wanted to leave with me. He said he'd walk me back. Why didn't he? Why didn't he insist? But he

382

didn't. Mum overheard. She said in as loud a voice as she could, right by Mr Turnbull and Alex. "I'm sure Alex will, he's such a gentleman." Alex did.'

Claire was rubbing her hands together as though she was washing them, over and over until Liz could bear it no longer and tried to stop her. Claire brushed her aside, her voice driving on relentlessly, the pitch high, strange, her throat dry, aching. No, no one must touch her, no one should want to touch her.

'We walked along the beach. The surf was driving in, my boots were digging into the sand. I remember thinking they'd get scuffed. The wind was strong, my hair was all over the place. He held my hand. I liked that. His hand was warm, his voice was cheerful. He smoked but his cigarette burned up too quickly in the wind. I could smell the wine on his breath as he turned and said "Sod it."

'He tossed the cigarette into the air. The wind carried it for a good yard. We stood and watched. He kissed my hand. I was surprised, but it felt nice out there with the wind and the surf. A bit magical, polite somehow. I smiled, he laughed and he kissed me properly and it was nice, even though I could taste wine and nicotine and the surf caught us. It bubbled over my boots. If I'd moved sooner maybe it wouldn't have . . . If I'd paid attention perhaps none of it would have happened. Maybe he wouldn't have grabbed my hand. Maybe he wouldn't have said "Come on, I know a way through the dunes, away from the surf." If it hadn't been for the boots perhaps I wouldn't have gone.

'We ran together Liz, into the dunes where the marram grass grew, and it was quieter here, the wind didn't matter, it just sang in the grass. He

383

stopped, pulled me to him. I bumped against him, and giggled. I was nervous, and so I giggled. If I hadn't giggled maybe he wouldn't have . . .

'He kissed me again and again and it was too much and I pulled away, tried to walk on. He dragged me back, laughing, saying that my mother would be thrilled that he was paying me so much attention.

'I laughed again, embarrassed, scared. I didn't know what to do. After all, this was the boss's son. Would it hurt if I let him kiss me just once more. even if I didn't want to? It was only a kiss, after all. But I didn't want to, so I kissed him on the cheek and said "It's time I was getting home." He staggered a bit. That's when I realized how much he'd been drinking.

'He grabbed me then, kissed me again. I sort of let him, for a moment. It seemed polite but then it went on, and his hands were all over me, and I struggled. I pushed him away. He came at me again. I hit out at him. He was bigger. He was so much bigger.'

She could hardly breathe and it was dark again and the wind and the surf were sweeping away the soft lights, the hissing gas.

Liz wanted to stop her, because she could hardly bear to hear this, to see the look of horror on Claire's face, to hear that strange awful voice. Instead she sat very still.

'I struggled, I promise I did, but one arm was round me, while the other was pulling up my skirt and I couldn't break away and my voice wouldn't come. It just wouldn't come. It couldn't be happening, that's what I kept thinking. This can't be happening. He got me on the ground, rolled on

384

top of me. I fought him off, it made him angry. He was too strong. I couldn't do anything. He hurt me, he hurt me. He pulled down my pants, they caught on my boots. He swore. I said "Please, please."

'He was kicking my pants down, he was sort of kneeling on my thighs. It hurt, it hurt so much. His hands were on my shoulders. His mouth was on mine, then he got my hands above my head. He held them. I remember the wind in the grass, the surf. I could hear the surf above his breathing. How could I do that? How could I have noticed that? Then I tried to scream when he pushed my legs apart with his knees. I tried to scream when he did . . . it.' She was silent for a moment because the sea was so loud, the scream in her mind so high that they took the words and drowned them in her throat. She reached for Liz's warm hands and they were pulling her back, they were letting the words escape. 'I tried to scream, but I couldn't. Why couldn't I? I remember feeling when I was being torn apart that I was choking, that my mouth was open but I was choking and I couldn't scream.'

Again she was silent, and felt as though she was gagging, smelt the nicotine on Leah's breath, felt the vomit rising. She swallowed, sweat breaking out on her forehead. She clung to her friend and the words were slower. 'He rolled off me. He didn't hold me any more, but I didn't move, I didn't go for him, I didn't run away. All I did was cry. I heard the wind, and myself crying. I heard him say. "Oh for God's sake, you're not going to make a fuss when you know you wanted it. You've been after it all evening."

'He was sitting there beside me, doing up his trousers, and I was just lying there crying. I said.

385

"But I didn't want it. Not that."

'He stood up. His feet were so close to my head. He was so close, so sort of looming. He wore plimsolls. There were spots of blood on them. My blood, I think. He shouted down at me. "Course you did, that's why you came here with me. Bloody hell, you ran into the dunes, then you said 'Please, please.' Now get up, and go home."

'I couldn't. I hurt, everything hurt, my legs were wet from him, and the blood. I tried to sit up, it hurt. I tried again. He said. "Everyone bleeds first time." So he knew it was my first time, Liz. He knew I didn't do this all the time. He kicked my pants over. Sand hit my face, went in my eyes. "Go on, get dressed." He lit a cigarette. I felt sick. I tried to sit up again and I did and I put my pants on, Liz. Can you believe that? I didn't run away, I just put my pants on over those white boots. My pants were full of sand, and rubbed me, and got into where he had torn me. He started to walk away. I said, "I don't know where I am. I don't know how to get home. You can't do this and just leave me." How could I say that Liz, to someone who'd just done that to me? He walked away, pointing to the left. "Home's down there."

'I crawled after him. "I'll tell Dad. He'll get the police," I said.

'He came at me then. He dragged me up and shook me so much it tore my blouse across the back and I felt sick again. He said. "You silly bitch, on what charge? Rape? You came up here with me, you never said no, you asked me to take you home afterwards. Rape? Are you crazy, you'd be laughed out of court, and your father would never work again. So keep your mouth shut and stop being

386

such a bloody fool." '

Now there were no more words. Her throat ached but it was all still there in her head, on her skin, in her body, all of it. She hunched over, drawing her hands away from Liz, clasping them tightly together, feeling a gentle stroking on her hair, so gentle it was barely there, and heard Liz ask why she hadn't told someone. She almost laughed, because she had. But she wasn't going to tell Liz that, she couldn't bear to. She said instead, her words almost painful in their slowness, 'I finally told the matron just before Anna was born, because I didn't want her to ever be able to find me. They could sort of block a search then. You see, I never wanted her to know she was born from a violent act, or what sort of a woman her mother was, going into the dunes with her father's boss's son.'

There was silence for a moment, and Claire stirred, her voice faster. 'I mean, why didn't I scream? What the hell sort of person am I?'

She heard Liz tell her in no uncertain terms what sort of a person she was, and Claire smiled at her words but it was as though they came from a great distance and meant nothing really. It was as though Liz knew that, because she forced her to sit up, gripped her chin and said it slowly again, and with great passion, and Claire at last began to feel that it might be true. But then Liz said slowly and clearly, 'You must tell Leah, and Anna. It's gone too far now, and you need to assimilate the rape, and I repeat that word. Assimilate it into your life, instead of denying it, recognizing his guilt, not yours, for you must feel none.'

But Liz didn't know what she was asking, and

387

wouldn't listen when Claire tried to tell her. She just eased her to her feet, led her to the bedroom then made cocoa, bringing it to her, sitting on the bed with her, heaping the pillows up behind them as they had done in the halcyon days before Alex Turnbull. Though it was not quite as it had been then, because now they didn't talk in the dark but had all the lights on as Claire insisted, just as she had always insisted to Mark when they made love. 'It made it easier for me. I even came to enjoy it eventually.' Now tears came, and more words, and so it went on throughout the night, and even when Claire slept it was fitful and nightmare filled, but every time she woke Liz was there and *she* hadn't turned her back, *she* hadn't looked on her with contempt. *She* had believed her.

*   *   *

Claire woke at nine, feeling drained and weary and unsure for a moment what had been nightmare and what had been fact, but then she saw the two cocoa mugs. She lay looking at the curtains that Mark had called wishy-washy, feeling detached, her limbs leaden. Liz spoke from the doorway. 'In case you're worrying, I'm going to playgroup in your place and I shall expect you to polish my halo on my return. That is, if I can leave you now? You've slept peacefully for two hours.' There was a question in her voice.

Claire rolled over on to her back, smiling weakly. Liz looked tired as she lolled in the doorway but, even so, she'd borrowed Claire's muted red-brown lipstick. It didn't do her any favours. Claire murmured, 'Go and slap on some of your own

388

warpaint first, mine makes you a shadow of your former self. Everyone will think you're having the vapours. Mark you, perhaps you will be.'

'It's only a few small children, for heaven's sake.'

Claire sat up, easing her neck and clasping her hands round her knees. 'I can never thank you enough.'

Liz laughed. 'I'm only doing this once, and I refuse to make Play-Doh creatures. It'll ruin my nails.'

Claire shook her head. 'You know what I mean.'

Liz was serious. 'Yes, I know. Ring me if you need me at all. Leah will most certainly have a humdinger of a headache, but tell her that is self-inflicted injury. But, Claire, tell her more than that. Tell her the truth, even though it means telling Anna too because it isn't just Anna you have to consider. Apart from anything else have you the right to keep that knowledge from the daughter of Alex Turnbull? It's part of her history, and she's been counselled, and I'm convinced after the way she handled Leah that she's grounded enough to cope. You really cannot assume responsibility for everyone any more. By the way, I've phoned Rob, he'll sort out any patch problems, so pass phone calls through to him, got it?'

Claire nodded. Liz stared at her for a moment, and repeated, 'Got it?'

'I've got it,' Claire agreed and only then did Liz leave.

For a few moments Claire stared after her, knowing she was right but still she didn't move. She allowed herself to think and notice only the sounds of the house until, taking a deep breath, she showered and dressed, then walked to Leah's room

389

and peered in. Her daughter was groaning slightly and still lying on her stomach. She made her way downstairs, snatching up the phone as it rang, anxious that Leah should sleep as long as possible. It was the RSM's wife, Sally, who asked, 'All well?'

Claire brushed her hair back from her face, checking the darkness beneath her eyes in the mirror, struggling to compose herself. 'Rumour mill working well, I take it?'

Sally sounded surprised. 'What rumour?'

Claire sighed. 'So, there's more than one. Leah going ape yesterday evening, of course.'

'Oh that. Yes, there was a bit of nitter-natter, but it was relief mainly, because it could have been their own sprog coming to the front and making a fool of herself. They were all in it together, except for the sainted Mollie's. I don't know what they all thought they were doing, and as for going off to a club, heaven help us. We think the skiers fixed it up on the coach coming back, then rang round the patch getting others to raid their drinks cupboards as well. Incidentally, you'd better check yours. Mark you, this'll be the last time it happens for a while if the groans from Lance's bedroom are anything to go by. No, I was phoning to see if you would be at the Wives Club "do" at the swimming pool tonight. The dratted Mollie has managed to get us a cancelled booking.'

Claire refused, claiming pressure of work, which Sally accepted and just wished she could plead the same cause. As Claire replaced the receiver the letterbox clattered. She pressed her hand to her forehead as a headache began and a return to bed seemed imperative. Feeling guilty, she picked up the letters and made her way upstairs again. Sitting on the edge of the bed, she leafed through them, spotting one from Mark. She could have wept, because he'd been so wonderful recently, so accommodating, and now on this particular morning, there was the bonus of a letter.

She eased the flap open and read it, trying to absorb words which surely she must have misread, words which sent her icy cold, words which took the strength from her arms and hands so that she dropped the letter. She scrabbled on the floor for it, making her fingers grip it, forcing herself to read it a second time. The words were the same.

I'm not returning for R & R and you can hardly be surprised given the circumstances. I need to think, to clear my head. I've had enough, Claire. The last thing I need is to have a letter from my daughter asking me to drop everything and come home, because she has no confidence in her mother. How could you lose the plot so much, just when you know I need to concentrate, when I need all the support I can get, when there is such misery all around us? For God's sake, not only have I had to face all these changes in our life, but I'm left wondering what sort of a person is warned by a photo and still rejects their daughter. In the second week of my R & R I will be at the vineyard and will phone Leah from there. In the first I will be walking and out of touch.

CHAPTER TWENTY-SIX

It seemed impossible to believe that there would ever be a day when neither he nor Ben, nor one of his Warrior patrols, would be storming along one of these roads, trying to keep the show on the road. The snow was causing more problems of course, but the wheels were still turning.

He and Gordana had talked to the Muslim regional commander in the north of Bosnia this morning and arranged that Mark's soldiers should man a crucial checkpoint, rather than leave it to the Muslims on the ground. That would mean that at least all UN, UNHCR and ICRC vehicles would be allowed to pass unimpeded through the area. Gordana had said as they'd left Muslim HQ that it underlined the respect in which he, her warrior, was held.

Now, as they headed off with some escort Warriors he felt awkward as he had then. Why the hell had he gone to her flat after reading Leah's letter? Why hadn't he calmed down, rung Claire. He mimicked in his mind his words as he stood there at her doorway, she wrapped in a blanket, he freezing because he'd failed to sling on outdoor gear in his rage: 'Fine,' he'd said. 'Let's do it, let's go to your island, just for a week, and sod the lot of them.'

He'd turned on his heel and strode off. Who the hell had he thought he was, some knight on a white charger? The Warrior was throttling down as they approached the bridge at the junction. No sign of mines. The Muslims—and there were a hell of a lot of them—waved them through and he was glad, because he didn't want to have to be arguing the toss with them through Gordana at this precise moment, and it was all his own fault, none of it was hers.

The cold was bitter, and they were pretty close to a fracas that had just erupted between local Muslims and Croats. The tension was almost palpable. He ducked involuntarily as a mortar sounded, but it was nowhere near, though in the distance off to the left he could see smoke. He used his binoculars to focus in.

On they went, heading for another bridge, seeing that though there was a Croat position just behind, there were no mines. Fifty yards over the bridge, however, was a burnt-out Mercedes, plus a Citroën slewed across the road. Well, hoo bloody ray, and how were aid convoys to get past that lot?

Once over the bridge he used his binoculars again, checking the cars and approaches for mines or booby traps. It seemed clear.

His Warrior moved close in and he dismounted with CSM Franks to examine the vehicle more closely and was joined by Gordana. He ordered her to return to her place in the back of the Warrior, ignoring her expression, praying that she didn't say 'Be careful', that she didn't in any way betray what she thought their relationship had become. For a moment his concentration slipped.

Why hadn't he just done nothing, and gone home for R & R and sorted it all out then? Why dig himself into a situation there was no getting out of now? Maybe that was why. Maybe he'd wanted to do something he couldn't go back on. He turned to watch her as she walked from him, and his heart twisted with pity, but then he thought of Claire and there was a deeper ache. But why had she done what she'd done? Shock he could understand—but this? Again he felt the anger, the disappointment, the confusion.

'Colonel.' CSM Franks's voice was sharp. Suddenly he was back here, on this road, in the cold, with two bloody great cars blocking their path, a ruined one-pump petrol station on one side, a ruined café on the other. He adjusted his flak jacket, and they approached the cars, inspecting them close up, declaring the all-clear.

Mark ordered RSM Coates to move the Warrior up and push the vehicles clear, and as it ground forward the escort Warriors remained in position. At that moment the Croats emerged, gesticulating, and firing into the air.

At this something in Mark broke, and he stormed towards them. Now they pointed their guns at him. He took no notice, but barged right up to the leader. 'Get your bloody guns out of my face, out of my life, and off this damned road.' He heard CSM Franks close up tight next to him. The Croat leader was a man of about forty. Mortars were still firing in the distance. Gordana was running up, calling, 'I will translate. I will—'

Mark didn't take his eyes off the Croat as he bellowed at her: 'Get back to the Warrior, and you'—he shouted at the Croat—'Get your men and your bloody guns back to your own position.' He pointed. Behind him he heard the turret gun traversing. He yelled again as he saw indecision flick across the man's face. 'We are moving these obstructions. We are not your enemy, we are just carrying out our mandate, and in order to do that

394

we will take what measures are necessary. Please believe me most sincerely when I say that.' His voice was taut with rage, with a fury which had been building for days.

For a moment there was an impasse, but then the Croat ordered his men to their positions, his face like thunder, but so what, thought Mark, as he strode over to stand ankle deep in filthy snow at the edge of the road near, but not on, the verge as his Warrior shoved one car and then the other into the ruins of the café. They tumbled in turn on to a pile of snow-covered bricks, wheels spinning. All that remained of a side wall collapsed, dust flew up. The sound of metal on metal had been worse than any chalk on a blackboard, and over it had been the sound of mortars.

As Mark watched he knew he had just acted inappropriately, unwisely, and endangered CSM Franks. The Warrior reversed. The Mercedes slid a foot down the pile of bricks, then stopped. The Warrior took up position at the head of the column and waited. Behind, the escort Warriors waited. He stared at the ruins, not seeing them, not smelling the dust, just knowing that by now Claire would have received his letter, and that Leah would have read it, and he wanted to phone them, but it was too late. It was all too late.

CHAPTER TWENTY-SEVEN

Claire was kneading dough when Leah slouched into the kitchen at about eleven wearing jeans and an old black sweater. Her hair was unbrushed, last night's mascara smeared her cheekbones and she was pale. Claire dusted the dough with flour and started to knead it again. Leah propped herself against the breakfast bar and watched her. Claire said, her eyes fixed on the dough, 'There's tea in the pot. It's pretty past it, and probably not very hot, but there's water in the tap. There is also a letter from your father, clearly the one you were waiting for.'

Her voice was like ice, her gaze too as she watched Leah dive for the letter, and hold it up, screeching, 'You've opened it?'

Claire pounded the dough. 'Yes, since it was addressed to me it seemed the sensible thing to do.' Leah yanked the letter from the envelope and scanned it once, then a second time. For a long moment she did nothing, then she screwed it up, tossed it on to the breakfast bar, turned away to stare out across the garden, her hands dug into her pockets, humming as though she didn't care. As she watched, Claire felt her own anger evaporate and she came to her daughter's side and held her unyielding body to her, whispering into her hair, 'I've something to tell you, Leah. Something I should have talked to you about ages ago. Come and sit down.'

Leah broke free of her, moving closer to the window, turning to face her mother, her voice shaking. 'It's all your fault. All you want to do is potter around being Lady Bountiful, being the CO's wife, having people think you're perfect. Anna would have ruined it for you, wouldn't she? Well, you've cocked everything up anyway.' She pushed past Claire and headed for the door into the hall. Claire caught up with her before she

396

reached it, grabbing hold of her arm, but Leah shook her off. There was flour on her black sweater. Leah stared at it. 'Well, thanks, but I suppose that's what you do—leave a mess wherever you've been.'

It was one of the few times Claire had ever slapped her daughter and now she caught her across her upper arm. It shocked them both. Claire said, 'You don't understand, and that's what I want to talk to you about.'

At that moment the phone rang, and Leah ran into the hall. 'Come back, Leah,' Claire shouted, rushing after her. Leah had stopped by the phone, her hand reaching for the receiver. Claire said, 'Let it ring, for heaven's sake. I need to talk to you.'

But Leah had lifted the receiver. She listened, and said 'Yes, she'll come right round.' She turned with a grim smile on her face and said without bothering to put her hand over the mouthpiece. 'You're needed, Lady Bountiful. Better go and keep your image intact.' Claire lunged for the phone but Leah was too quick. She replaced it, then ran for the stairs, taking them two at a time with Claire in her wake. Leah reached her bedroom, dived in and locked the door, leaving Claire to pound on it, shouting 'Let me in, Leah, we need to talk.'

'Oh go away, I've got a headache. I just want to lie down.'

The phone rang again. Claire swore, and rushed down the stairs, snatching up the receiver. It was Sally, the RSM's wife. 'Claire, are you all right? I've just had a strange conversation with Leah.'

Claire struggled for composure, but her breath was still heaving in her chest when she panted, 'Bit

397

of a do, you know, Sally. Look, Rob's doing the calls today, I'm trying to sort a few things out.'

She could hear voices in the background at Sally's end, and Sally said quickly, 'Just a minute, Claire.'

Claire hung on to the receiver, tapping her foot. Come on, come on. She craned to see up the stairs, to listen. Not a sound from Leah. She was about to put the receiver down when Sally came back on the line. 'Sorry, Claire. It's a bit hectic here, Angie's had an unexpected visitor.'

Claire pressed her hand to her forehead. For God's sake, what had Turbogob's visitor got to do with her. She blurted, 'I can't do this now, Sally.'

Again there was a kerfuffle at Sally's end and now Angie came on to the phone, and she was crying. Claire closed her eyes in resignation. 'Calm down, Angie. Whatever's the matter?'

Angie told her that a woman had turned up at the front door with a kid in a pushchair, a kid she said was Angie's husband's. Claire felt very, very weary as she listened to Angie crying again but with another glance up the stairs she said firmly, 'I can't come just now, Angie. Please let Sally help you. I've got a problem here I've got to sort out. When I have, I'll come, try and understand. Now put Sally back on the line.'

Angie stammered, 'I don't know how I can cope. How are we going to cope, Mrs Baird? How do you stay so calm? Perhaps you don't care what he does, but I do. I care. I still love my husband. Why do they have to have these slags?'

Claire struggled to keep up with Angie, to sort through what she was saying and when she did, she grew very still, feeling as though a fist had been plunged into her gut. 'What are you saying, Angie?'

But by now Sally had taken the phone. 'It's OK Claire, I can cope. She's just got overexcited, you know what she's like.' She whispered into the phone: 'Turbogob, remember.'

Claire shouted, 'Shut up, Sally, put her back on, or you tell me.'

'Claire this isn't the time or the place.'

Claire was shouting louder. 'It never is the right time, or right place. What does she know about my husband? What do you know?'

Sally told her hesitantly the gossip that some of the husbands had repeated about an interpreter called Gordana Sevo, who accompanied Mark on patrols and had sometimes stayed at his house. She had been overheard discussing a trip they were making to an island in the Adriatic. Sally insisted, when she'd finished, 'The Colonel's not like that though. I asked my old man when he was back on R & R, and he said it was a load of nonsense. Anyway, how could he go anywhere with her when he's coming back here for his leave, or our last night, anyway?'

Claire nodded into the phone, looking into the mirror, nodding to herself, nodding like some stupid toy dog on the back shelf of a car and now the chattering groups which had been falling silent at her approach made sense. 'Take care of Angie,' she instructed then replaced the phone, turning to Leah who stood at the foot of the stairs, Leah whom she had also seen in the mirror.

Leah was gripping the newel post, her face contorted. 'I heard about it at the Youth Club. I heard he'd got this woman. I heard about it, and I didn't believe it, and then there was that letter, and

399

it's all your fault, it's all your fault. If you hadn't . . .' She stopped and just cried, and looked about three.

Claire walked to her and held her, close, dragging her down to sit on the bottom of the stairs with her, letting her cry, letting her rage, letting her accuse her of driving her father into the arms of this other woman.

All the time Claire felt quite detached as she held her daughter, quite devoid of anger towards Mark because there'd been too much over the past twenty-four hours, just too damned much for the whole of her life, and she merely examined the situation as though it were a specimen under a microscope, as though they were all swimming in some sort of solution, coming together, breaking away, colourless, soundless, getting nowhere, trapped between two sheets of glass.

At length she said, 'You're probably right, it is my fault. Perhaps he felt threatened by Anna, disappointed in me. Perhaps he needed someone, some reassurance?'

Leah sat upright, wiping her eyes with the sleeves of her sweater. 'Why did it all have to happen? Perhaps it's because I wrote? I shouldn't have, but you shouldn't have sent her away. Oh, for God's sake, Mum, why did you have to have her in the first place?'

It was now, as they sat together on the stairs, that Claire told her of the rape, explaining at the end that she'd managed to put it away in her mind, pretending it had never happened, but that the photo had brought it all back and that she knew that she could never tell a child of hers that she was born of such an act and she marvelled that she

400

could tell Leah all this, and sound calm and matter-of-fact, in spite of the sounds of the surf.

Leah looked at her mother's hands that were gripped tightly together in her lap, and listened and almost heard the sea, and felt the fear, and recognized it as the feeling she had had at the hotel swimming pool with Steve at Christmas. There didn't seem to be anything she could say as her mother finished.

There didn't seem anything that would be big enough, anything that could take all that away and make it better. She did the only thing she could, and that was to place her own hand over her mother's. 'I'm so sorry, Mum. I really am so sorry for you.'

For a moment they were quiet together, and Leah played that beach over and over in her mind, and wanted to kill the boy, wanted to stand between him and her mother, wanted to take back all the things she had ever done and said to hurt her mother, wanted to be the perfect daughter. She said, 'You should have told me, I'd have understood.'

Claire moved slightly and her voice was so tired when she spoke that Leah put her arm around her, rubbing her back, her shoulder, her arm. 'Then you're a bigger person than most. My mother did not understand. I started to tell her about the rape when my pregnancy was recognized. It was as we walked to the bus that took us home from school, though I didn't tell her who the father was because of my father's job, I even changed it from a beach to a field. I just said I'd been walking with a young man, that I'd let him kiss me because I was too shy, too eager not to be rude, then I told her that he wanted more, that he'd been too strong, that he'd got me down on the ground. I said I was frightened, but I fought. She stopped me there. She said that to be there in the first place was asking for it, that I must have led the boy on. She said what he said, you see, Leah. She also said I must spend the rest of my life atoning for the deed and for the lie. That I must be good, that I had no right to anything other than shame. I got angry, at her and the boy. It was all tangled up, all muddled, and then she hit me, and said I would never from that day on have a right to be angry with anyone, because I was a total disgrace and didn't deserve a mother's love.'

Leah held her now, stroking her hair, just as Liz had done. 'She was an old witch. She's got no idea. She had no right to say that, no right at all. It's changed now, Mum, everything's changed, people don't think like that any more, not the people who matter, anyway. What did Dad say when you told him—or doesn't he know?'

Claire let herself be held, let her child be the mother for a moment longer, because at the mention of Mark the detachment was fading, the specimens were escaping from the glass, they were becoming colourful, real, wounding. She said, 'No. I tried to tell him before we were married but he didn't want to hear any more about it and when Anna came back into our lives I was still denying it to myself. Perhaps, because I still wondered why I hadn't said that one word, no. I still wonder.'

Liz's voice reached them from the kitchen and grew louder as she walked towards them. 'You did, in everything you said and did, you old slapper.' She approached like a breath of fresh air, and stood before them, resplendent in bright red

402

lipstick, and her dangling earrings which matched the scarlet of her cardigan. 'I got a call from Sally which excused me nicely from playgroup, so I'm back, to dispel gloom and despondency and tell you both that it's probably a load of gossip. Mark and an interpreter? Good grief, he'd be scared to death. He's a one woman man, and he adores your mother, Leah, and besides, Ben would have said something. That man is a hopeless gossip, can't keep a secret to save his life. Now I'm going to make us all a cup of tea and we can either squeeze on to the same step or behave like civilized people and huddle round the kitchen table to scheme our way to some sensible outcome.'

She swept back to the kitchen, her heels clicking on the tiles. Leah looked incredulously at her mother. 'Liz was at playgroup?'

Claire was on her feet, pulling her daughter up with her, holding her close for a moment longer, then kissing her still damp cheek, smiling even though the image of Mark with another woman had not gone; instead it was becoming clearer and clearer. She said, 'Indeed she was, and in earrings to die for, apparently.'

Liz called from the kitchen: 'Do you think I have no sense? I took them off and stuck them way up high. Some things I will do for you, Claire Baird, but letting your little horrors swing on my ears is where I draw the line. This bread, by the way, is expanding alarmingly and taking over the kitchen. It should be dealt with.'

They could hear the clatter of mugs and spoons and the soft slap of the fridge door closing. 'How about fetching your glass down from your room, Leah?' Claire said quietly, acknowledging Leah's questioning look, smiling when she asked: 'Big girl talk?'

'Just for a moment.'

Leah made for the stairs, turning back to look at her mother, and Claire saw that the tears were close again, and started towards her. Leah shook her head. 'I'm OK, go and talk to Liz.' Claire waited until she was on the landing before moving into the kitchen which smelt of yeast and flour. The dough had risen and flopped out of control all over the breakfast bar. She washed her hands while Liz flipped open the lid of the tea caddy and spooned tea into the pot. As Claire began to knock the dough into shape she asked, 'Are you sure Ben didn't say anything? I need to know if this other woman is flesh and blood or just a mythical titbit.'

Liz murmured as she poured boiling water on to the tea. 'Ben doesn't know. Yes, there's a friendship that worried him, and quite why she'd stay in his house . . . but who knows?' She put the teapot on the tray and carried it to the table, sitting down wearily.

Claire finished kneading. Rubbing her hands free of the dough, she reached for Mark's letter. She smoothed it, then joined Liz, saying, 'Angie says he's going to an island in the Adriatic with the girl, but how can he, on a purely practical level? After all, he *has* to leave the deployment area. But if he is . . . How can he use me and the photo as an excuse? You say he adores me, but . . .'

They could hear Leah moving around in the bathroom. Liz said as she began to pour the tea, 'He thinks you've let him down, ignoring the fact that he's let you down for the last eighteen months. I don't know, I sometimes wonder if these men

404

have any balls.'

Claire said, 'Presumably in this case, yes.'

Liz stopped, and roared with laughter, putting the teapot down, flapping her hand at Claire. 'You've been watching too many pantomimes.'

The two women looked at one another. Claire said, 'I need to go and see Anna this afternoon, and then I will phone Mark.'

Liz finished pouring the three teas. 'In that case I'll have Leah at my house, and she and the girls can catch up on project work and hopefully make a good fist of it before they return to school tomorrow.'

'It sounds so normal.' The tea was good and strong. Claire hadn't realized how parched she was.

'When actually it's a damned nightmare?' Liz said. 'Isn't that what you're thinking? Well, I have to say I rather agree with you.'

CHAPTER TWENTY-EIGHT

Mark was in his office briefing Gordana in preparation for the journey to Zenica tomorrow. He was weary from the seminar he'd just attended along with all the other UN commanding officers in Bosnia, a seminar designed to reinforce a unified approach. It had been comforting to be with others who held the reins, who looked as stressed as he did. It had been less comforting to arrive back at base and receive a message that Claire had rung and that she would ring back at 6.30.

Ben knocked and entered, his face noncommittal, though his voice was steely as he laid another message slip carefully on Mark's desk, and stood just to the right of Gordana's chair. 'I wasn't sure if you had received the message referring to Mrs Baird's call, Colonel. I have made sure that you will have no other call upon your time. It is now 6.20.' He inclined his head pointedly towards Gordana.

She rose immediately, tucking her notebook in her backpack, brushing back her short hair which Irvana had turned into something resembling a haircut. Ben indicated that she should precede him from the room and dogged her down the corridor. Mark listened to their footsteps. Ben wasn't sure, my Aunt Fanny. Damn it, he'd given him the first ruddy message. Outside the hills were shrouded in mist. Were the skiers bunkered down? Were they wrapping their mittens round flasks of slivovitz, talking of military matters, stamping their boots, trying to keep warm? That seemed so simple.

He rubbed his eyes. He had hoped Claire wouldn't ring. He had hoped that somehow she would fade into silence, accept his letter, allow him this time. She'd always been so reasonable, so patient, so good . . . He silenced his mind. No, he didn't want to think of the past, all the good things about her. All that had changed. She had changed. It was she who had brought this about, who had somehow manoeuvred him into this.

Damn it to hell. He slammed his hands down on the desk. The lamp jolted, the ballpoint she had given him shuddered. He fingered it, feeling sick. What the bloody hell had he done?

'Cocked up good and proper,' Ben had said when Mark had blurted out his R & R plans just before the seminar. Mark had nodded as they

406

stood together in the bitter cold by the Land Rover. He had bitten his thumbnail, before ramming his hand into his glove. 'I can't change it now. I'm in too deep, it's happened and there's no turning back. I mean, it's only a week, and Claire won't know.'

Ben had just looked at him as though he'd appeared from another planet, and shaken his head, coming up close, murmuring, 'It's a bloody lifetime you're in danger of throwing away.'

Mark had looked around quickly. 'What else can I do?'

'Just say no, like the good boys do—and you can forget any idea of keeping your little away-week a secret. There's gossip. It will already have reached the patch with the men going home on leave.'

Mark had felt the keenness of the wind, the wet flurry of snow. His eyes were stinging with the cold. Had he managed to keep the panic from his voice when he'd asked, 'Has Liz mentioned it?'

'Yes, it's in circulation but more than that, she won't be drawn, which is strange. She says it's between the two of you, and nothing to do with her or me. Have a good seminar.' His voice had been almost as cold as the weather.

At dead on 6.30 the phone rang. He just looked at it. On the third ring he reached out his hand to pick up the receiver just as someone knocked on the door and entered. It was Gordana. She stood uncertainly in the doorway, pointing towards her chair, whispering, 'Forgive me, I dropped my pen.'

He could hear Claire's voice. 'Mark, are you there, Mark?'

Gordana was approaching. He didn't want her here, not now, not at the island, not ever, but she

407

was thin, pale, desperate and he'd promised. He shook his head at her, his hand over the mouthpiece. 'Not now.'

She stopped, her eyes on the receiver, her eyes so tired, her shoulders thin beneath her jacket, her hands trembling slightly as she adjusted the small backpack, easing its weight, just as she did at checkpoints and roadblocks, as she did at line crossings, holding steady, always sound, always supportive in spite of the fact that her life had fallen down round her ears. He found himself picking up Claire's pen, holding it out to her. 'Take this for now.'

Claire said again, her voice becoming angry, 'Mark, are you there?'

Gordana took it, held it, knowing it was Claire's, and then she smiled, and it was a smile of gratitude, a smile that assumed the gesture indicated much more. Again Claire spoke. Mark fingered the blotter, his eyes on that, not on Gordana as she left and he was sweating, and he could hardly see, let alone speak because he didn't know what the hell he was up to.

'Claire, it's me. Sorry to hold you up, just had a bit of unfinished business.'

The line was pretty bad. She said, 'Yes, but it isn't just unfinished, is it? From the sounds of it, it's just getting under way. Are you both packed and ready for your escape from reality?'

He sat back, and sighed. So, she definitely did know and he felt despair at the hurt in her voice, but then through this sprang the anger and it was typical of the seesaw he had been for days now. He tried to sound distant but firm as he reasoned: 'Look Claire, is it any wonder I don't want to rush home with all the drama back there. I need some peace, damn it, why can't you accept that? There is no both.' All the time he was talking he was looking at the blotter which was covered with his doodles, calculations, reminders, written with her pen and he felt the sweat break out again, and the anger died and all he wanted was for her to make it all go away, for her to tell him a way out of this because there was no one who knew him so well, or cared, or was so kind. Into this the harsh rage of Claire's voice was like a thunderbolt.

'Don't lie to me. Don't you *dare* lie to me, you total and utter shit.'

He sat upright with shock, then yelled back: 'Nothing's happening here, I just want a bit of bloody peace! Is that so very surprising when you scream down the phone at me, when you cock up my home life? It's enough of a hotbed out here, without having one at home—'

She cut across, 'So instead you're going to fall into a hotbed on some idyllic island, are you?'

'There you are, you see, I don't know where I am with you any more. If you're not lying you're being hysterical, imagining God knows what, so I suggest you take a hold of yourself. I'm just not listening to this fabrication, Claire.' He was panting, his collar was wet from sweat.

'Then listen to this, then. You have a pantomime waiting for you here, a panto I've been slogging out my guts on at your instigation to keep up morale, a pantomime on top of everything else, I might add. What will it do to morale if you're not here? Think very carefully Mark, all those endless open days, all the extra effort by the men will count for nothing, all the leadership they need right now will go down

409

the drain. You are *expected* back, Mark.'

Mark heard the desperation in her voice as she tried to disguise it behind concern for the patch, the men, for his career, and he didn't want to hear it because it stirred up too much in him and he knew even less why he was doing what he was doing.

He said quietly, 'I'm tired, Claire. I'm just knackered.'

Her voice softened. 'Then come home.'

He rubbed and rubbed at the blotting paper, destroying his writing, smearing it. 'I can't. I can't. You don't understand. You don't know what it's like out here. I owe . . . Oh, you just wouldn't understand.'

For a moment Claire didn't speak, but he could picture her there, in the hall, by the mirror, his mirror. God, he wanted to be there, to be with her. The line was breaking up. She said, 'Your daughter needs you, I need you. I'm not going to make this easy for you.'

The door was opening, and Gordana stood in the doorway, holding out Claire's pen. She walked towards him, saying very quietly, 'Thank you, I have finished with it.' Her fingers were trembling as she laid it on the blotter, her deep sun lines seemed more marked in the dim light, her tiredness more obvious. She smiled and it was as though for a moment all the pain of her life dropped away. She turned and walked towards the door.

He said to Claire: 'But it's all different now, isn't it. It's all changed. You've changed. I don't know who you are.' The anger was coming back and he welcomed it. 'God almighty you reject your daughter twice, three times, it causes all sorts of fallout just when I don't need it, and I can't understand why. I mean, would it be surprising if I were to try to find comfort where I can? I mean, who's going to come popping out of the woodwork next? The first Mr Right, the one with Anna's eyes? Who else am I going to have to share my home with, my life with? I mean, look at it, everything has changed, Claire, and you most of all.'

The door was slowly closing behind Gordana when Claire said, 'There is no first Mr Right, Mark. You've never let me talk about it before but I should have made you. I was raped and I was frightened all over again when Anna sent the photo, then came from the bush. I was shocked, because I'd made myself pretend it had never happened. That's why I sent her away, and also because I knew that if she came back into my life I'd have to tell her about her father. It's something I've just had to do, and I didn't enjoy it, and neither did she.'

Mark could hardly breathe. 'Rape?' Before him were tumbling images of the women and girls in the hostels who had been raped; their eyes, their dead eyes. He felt as though he were choking. He had pins and needles in his hands, his feet. He saw Claire in the darkness of a street, a man leaping, grabbing.

'Oh God, Claire. Oh my God. Who was it? I'll bloody kill him. How did it happen? Oh Claire.' His eyes flickered around the room, seeing the shadows where the desk lamp didn't reach, the half-identifiable shapes, hearing the noise of the wind outside, and he imagined her fear as a shape moved in the darkness, pouncing as Claire walked

411

home.

Her voice was shaking now. 'Listen to me Mark, it's difficult. It's not straightforward. You see, I was walking home from a party with this boy. We went along the shore, then took a short cut through the dunes.'

Mark shook his head, trying to picture it, not wanting to hear what came next, because how many boys would it take to attack a young couple, how many for God's sake? As many as attacked these poor girls in their Bosnian villages.

He interrupted, feeling sick, ashamed of his sex, heartbroken. 'How many, Claire?'

'How many?'

His voice was gentle. 'Yes, how many attacked you?'

'Just one, it was more than enough.' Her tone was defensive.

Mark was confused. 'But why didn't your boyfriend fight him off?' The door was opening again, slowly, but he didn't notice. His head was bent down as he tried to understand.

'Mark, he wasn't my boyfriend, he was the boss's son. It was *he* who raped me, as he was walking me home from the party. He stopped in the dunes and he kissed me again.'

Outside the sky lit up as a mortar landed in the distance. He heard the crump but ignored it. 'Again?'

'Yes, he'd kissed me by the sea, then we ran through the dunes and he kissed me again and I didn't want him to, but it seemed rude to say no. I was scared, young, stupid. It was difficult.' Mark was staring at the blotter, seeing the hole he had rubbed, feeling the paper in his nail, trying to

412

understand, to visualize, to sort out the sense of it.

'Difficult? You didn't like to say no? Hang on a minute.' Visions of the raped women in the hostel jumbled up with a girl and a boy on a beach. 'Hang on, I don't understand. He kissed you, you didn't like it, but you went to the dunes with him anyway?'

She rushed in. 'No, I didn't mind the kiss on the shore, but it got too much in the dunes. I wanted to stop him after the first one but I didn't want to be rude, then when—'

'What the hell *is* all this? I mean, you went with him to the dunes then didn't like to say no because it was rude. Oh, come on, Claire. If you went to the dunes with the guy, what the hell was he supposed to think?'

There was silence.

Claire said, 'I'll make your apologies for the last night. Phone me, by all means, if you need any duty performed. Goodbye, Mark.'

There was a click. The line went dead.

CHAPTER TWENTY-NINE

'I thought the dress rehearsal was ace.' Leah pushed herself forward against the rear seat belt. 'This belt is creasing my top.'

'The Dames came up trumps.' Anna sat next to Claire tracing their route on the road map. 'You have to hand it to Mollie, the costumes are very good.'

Claire laughed, checking her mirror, indicating right and overtaking a struggling Morris Minor.

'Sickening, isn't it.'

Leah groaned. 'I'll have to live with it morning, noon and night now from her girls. Thank heavens I don't share their dorm.'

Claire kept to a steady sixty, too fraught beneath the banter to really push the car. Besides, their appointment wasn't until eleven. She glanced at the clock. Anna murmured, 'We're fine for time. Another hour and we've only got thirty miles to go.'

Leah said, her voice serious, 'We've got to find it once we get there, though, and then somewhere to park, or do you remember where his office is, Mum?'

As Claire changed down for a roundabout, easing into the traffic without having to stop, her mind clanged open and she saw the office of Turnbull, Turnbull and Watkins, but only the inside. It had been so dark where she and her mother had waited, long ago, in reception, perching nervously on the long bench-type seat, hardly daring to speak as they waited for her father to finish work early. It had been her seventh birthday and they were taking the Greenline to London for the theatre. What was the show? She'd forgotten.

She said, 'I've been once, but as a child and I've absolutely no recollection of where it is, or the façade even.'

Anna shut the map and leaned back, closing her eyes. Claire asked, 'Are you all right?'

Anna opened her eyes and smiled at her mother. 'Yes, are you?'

'I think so.'

Leah strained forward against the belt again.

414

'That was Dad on the phone, wasn't it, while I was in the bathroom?'

'Yes.'

'Did you speak to him?'

Claire braked slightly for a long bend that was signalled by signs, changing down, keeping the car as steady as she could, ever mindful of Leah's propensity to upchuck when she sat in the back. 'The answer machine was on. Look, are you sure you don't want to change places with Anna?'

Leah groaned. 'Oh Mum.' Their eyes met in the mirror and Leah grinned. 'It's OK, I've come prepared.' She waved a couple of carrier bags in the air.

Anna shrieked with laughter. 'Are you expecting an avalanche—did you have a three-course breakfast?'

Again all three of them laughed, but Claire wondered if there was a similar hollowness inside everyone else. She felt almost as though she was at a funeral tea where everyone launched into the cold ham, and talked of the price of things, and the kids of today, then suddenly remembered the dear departed with a desperate shaft of emotion. Though it wasn't the dear departed who kept breaking in. It was Alex Turnbull, Anna's father.

After a moment, Leah asked, 'Will you phone Dad back?'

Again their eyes met in the mirror. 'Yes, when I've been to see Anna's father. You told him that last night when he phoned, didn't you?'

The anxiety was reflected in Leah's voice as she said, 'Yes, I just wanted to make sure. He's going to Chianciamo for his leave, he said. *All* his leave except for the last night of the panto.'

'I know, you told me.' Claire's eyes were back on the road, assessing the distance from the car in front carefully, too carefully.

'He's not seeing the interpreter. He said to say he was sorry. He was a fool. He just couldn't take it in. It's not that he didn't believe you, not really, not deep down. He says he's been all kinds of a pillock. He says he's so sorry, for everything. For the last eighteen months, for Gordana, for everything.'

Claire repeated. 'I know, Leah, you've told me, he's told me.'

'So what are you going to say?'

'I don't know, I really don't know. I'll apologize about messing my side up, but beyond that I don't know.' Claire felt Leah's hand on her shoulder, felt her squeeze, heard her say, 'OK, Mum.'

After a moment Claire heard Anna say, 'Are you sure you want to do this? It's not just for me?'

'I've never been so sure of anything. I don't know why I didn't do it before. It was so obvious it was the thing to do, so obvious that he'd be in the phone book.'

Leah piped up again: 'It isn't obvious when you're in denial. As far as you were concerned it hadn't happened.'

Out of the mouths of babes and sucklings, Claire thought, hearing Liz's words here.

Anna called back to Leah, 'And you Leah, you don't have to come. You really don't.'

Leah's reply was swift. 'I know, but it gives me the day off school.' Again there was laughter but almost immediately Leah's voice rose above it. 'I want to be there. I want to make sure you're both all right.'

Anna and Claire smiled but Anna felt her

416

stomach fluttering as it had done when she first went to meet Claire and so she searched for road signs, checking again on the map, knowing the route by heart but needing to do something. All the while the houses, shops and offices flicked by.

'What time is the appointment again?' Leah asked, needing to hear someone speak.

Claire said gently, 'It's not so long ago that you used to ask ten million times on a journey "How much longer?" I suppose you'll be driving within three years and that'll be an end of that. I wonder if we'll be able to run to a Mini?'

Leah thought. We, she said we. She sat on her hands, and stared out of the window. Her father had been beside himself, so sorry, so distraught, but her mother had refused to discuss anything until all this was over. Would she go to Chianciamo? Leah got a grip and just stared ahead.

Anna had heard the strain in Leah's voice and berated herself as she'd done so often since Claire's disclosure. She'd been wrong to come back, to start opening doors, letting genies out of bottles. She felt Claire's hand on her knee. 'I'm so glad you returned.'

Anna smiled, comforted by the rapport between the two of them, and the accommodation that had been achieved between the two families. How many natural and adopted mothers would have worked in unison as Claire and Lynne Weaver had done on the day Claire had driven over to the flat to tell her of the truth of her origins?

It was Claire who had phoned Lynne Weaver, put her in the picture, asked her to come over, where all three had talked until midnight, when Claire had dashed back to be with Leah, leaving

417

Anna free to talk of things that might hurt Claire. To talk of her sense of self-disgust and fear that she might contain that man's genes, of her guilt that she was the issue of such a union, of her sadness that love had not existed, of her anger, her colossal anger against that man. But ultimately to realize that the love she was being allowed to display and feel for both sets of parents was a rare and generous gift.

She had phoned Claire during the course of the next morning, feeling strong, knowing that there would be good and bad moments but free enough to let the guilt, self-disgust and fear slide from her, and the anger soar. 'Don't get mad, get even, isn't that what they say,' she'd said to Claire on the phone. Claire had by then found that Alex Turnbull was still at Turnbull, Turnbull and Watkins. Together they had decided that they would visit.

Soon they were entering Woking. Anna switched to the town map Liz had found for them, but only after she had sat all three of them down and talked them through their feelings.

Leah released her belt and peered at the map over Anna's shoulder. 'Right at the next lights, Mum.'

'Get back in your belt, Leah,' Claire ordered as she slid into the right-hand lane and waited for the green filter arrow. The outskirts of Woking had spread and it was difficult to get her bearings but suddenly she began to recognize and remember. Wasn't that the road to the open air swimming pool she and Liz had sometimes cycled to? Wasn't that the park? Nostalgia for that time of innocence cut her to the quick.

418

On she drove, and now they were in the town proper, and it had been modernised, though parts were the same and it was these that were beginning to guide her. She turned right, and right again, at which point Leah banged on the back of her seat. 'This is the road.'

It was indeed and now Claire saw that it ran parallel to the station. How could she forget that? It seemed so much smaller. Back then Turnbull, Turnbull and Watkins and its environs had seemed so prestigious, so overpowering.

Leah banged on the back of her seat again. 'There it is.' She was pointing ahead. About twenty yards away a sign hung from an ornamental wrought iron post. It waved in the wind. Claire flexed her hand on the steering wheel. 'Get in your seat belt, Leah. I've told you once and won't tell you again.' Leah took no notice and neither did she expect her to, but it was something to say while her heart pounded out of her body.

Leah said, 'Clients' car park, there, you see?' Claire had slowed almost to a crawl. A car behind tooted, and she speeded up and sailed past. 'Mum,' Leah wailed. Anna said nothing, just looked. Claire indicated left at the next street. 'Might need a quick getaway. We'll park on the road, rather than get boxed in the car park.'

Instead they found a pay and display. Claire manoeuvred into a slot and sent Leah to the machine, saying, 'Young legs.'

'I hate it when you say that. I keep telling you that your cellulite would improve with exercise.' Leah's familiar grumbles grew fainter as she walked away.

Anna put out her hand. 'I'm frightened.' Claire

419

gripped it. 'Join the club.'

They got out of the car as Leah returned complete with ticket but she didn't hand it to Claire. Instead she said, shielding her eyes against the low midwinter sun, 'I don't think I want to come after all. I'll wait here if that's all right. I just don't want to see you being upset.'

Claire smiled and opened the driver's door. 'Good, I don't think you should.'

As Leah slipped into the driver's seat her hand was already reaching for the radio, and as Claire and Anna walked away they could hear the blaring music of Radio 1. 'Lucky old Woking,' Claire murmured. Suddenly they heard Leah's shout. 'Good luck both of you.' They turned and she was hanging out of the window waving with crossed fingers.

*   *   *

At Turnbull, Turnbull and Watkins the reception area was smarter and lighter than Claire remembered. It had white walls, not the dark green of the past. The long bench was gone. Now spindly chrome chairs were carefully placed against the walls. At a glass table where there had once been a big old oak desk, a receptionist sat. She looked up, a formula smile on her face. There had once been a very old woman with grey hair and bifocals. Claire half shook her head. Poor old soul, she'd probably only been forty.

It was hard to imagine the time when she had sat here with her mother, to imagine her father working here, to be here, now, to see Alex Turnbull whom she had met for just one evening, and at the thought it seemed to become dark, as dark as it had been when she had waited on the bench, or been pushed to the sand. She stared at the receptionist, confused, leaving Anna to give their names. The receptionist announced their presence into the intercom. There was a tinny response. 'Splendid, ask them to come in.'

She did so, wafting a limp hand towards a door at the end of the short corridor leading off the reception area. Together Claire and Anna headed towards it and as they did so, the door opened and a man who was recognizably Alex Turnbull, though older, plumper, stood full square at the entrance to his office. Claire grasped her handbag firmly and would not allow herself to hesitate, would not allow the confusion to remain for a second longer. He greeted them with a handshake, a pleasant smile reaching his eyes, his dark eyes. 'So pleased to meet you, do take a seat.'

His voice was pleasant too, mellifluous, wasn't that the word? His handshake was firm, restrained, just right. Was she mistaken? How could this man have done what he did? Perhaps her mother was right, perhaps he was right, perhaps she had given the wrong message, perhaps she was misremembering?

Alex Turnbull gestured to the two seats at the desk in front of the window and escorted them across the tasteful grey carpet. There was a glass coffee table to their right with three low leather armchairs. The room was lined with books. Alex Turnbull bustled behind his desk to sit in a swivel chair which swung just a bit as he sat down. It was an expensive modern desk on which sat a similar intercom to the receptionist's, a framed

421

photograph, and a tall thin glass containing two lilies. It was a neat desk, belonging to a neat man. This man was neat. This man who was the father of her child was neat. This man she didn't know was neat.

Claire's breathing seemed so slow, every movement seemed slow. She crossed her legs, those legs he'd . . . She tried to slam her memory shut, to slap the fear of him away, making herself face him, trying to push aside the remembered horror, the wind in the marram grass, the sound of the surf, of her scream. Why hadn't she said no?

Alex Turnbull pulled forward a clean sheet of paper, unscrewing his fountain pen. Claire made herself study those fingers, examine the pen: it was mottled green, the nib was gold. She liked black ink, and a fine nib. Was Alex Turnbull's fine, medium or thick? Was the ink blue or black? Suddenly she needed to know, needed to shake him, scream at him, force him to tell her because he was the father of her child and she knew nothing of him. She closed her eyes. Get a grip, take a deep breath and get a grip.

She opened her eyes, staring at his hands which were not the same as they had been that night. The skin was coarser, the pores larger. Then they had been soft as he had lifted her hand to his lips. She studied his face. He was lined. He had bags under his eyes, those eyes. His hair was grey. There was a photo frame on his desk, its back to her. She needed to know this man.

She reached forward, slowly, so slowly. He watched her turn the frame round, watched her examine the black and white studio photograph of a middle-aged woman and two daughters. The two

422

daughters had dark eyes, Anna's eyes. She showed Anna.

Anna nodded, but did not speak. She didn't know what to say, what to think because this man was her father, her father was a rapist. He was a rapist with children and a wife and he meant nothing to her, and she wouldn't allow herself to think that she was half of him, that perhaps his brutality was in her, because it wasn't. Or was it? because the anger and hatred she was feeling was so intense. She drew a shuddering breath, and wanted to smash the photo down on the desk. Instead she smiled at her mother.

Claire met her eyes, saw the rage. Good; rage was good. For a long moment they drew strength from one another, then she turned back to Alex Turnbull. Everything seemed so slow but then he reached forward, his arm brushing the sheet of paper as he took the photograph from her. For a moment his fingers were so close. For a wild moment Claire thought of wrenching it from him, denying him his own property, making him beg for its return. She released it into his care. He placed it in precisely the same position. His expression was still pleasant, his tone still charming. He addressed her, straightening the pristine sheet of paper, poising his pen above it in readiness. 'My family, taken last year, and now, it's Mrs Baird, that's correct, is it?'

He smiled at her with no recognition, one eyebrow raised. His lips were a little wet and she wanted to recoil. Claire said, 'You don't recognize me?'

He cocked his head and blinked, and Claire could almost see his mind flicking through his social calendar. Had they met at a dinner, at a cocktail party, a point-to-point maybe? Ah yes, she'd forgotten the talk of that at the party. She shivered as the sound of the sea grew loud again.

She heard, as though from a distance, 'I'm so sorry, you have me at a disadvantage.' He was looking at her as though in query, and now there was impatience in his voice.

She sat straight. 'Your father had a clerk, a Mr Riddick.'

He relaxed in his swivel chair, thinking, then said, 'Good heavens, I'd forgotten all about him. Yes, he retired soon after I returned from America, shadowy short of chap, always here, but hard to remember. Mark you, after Harvard and various places it's amazing how things fade.' He laughed. 'Best few years of my life, it's been downhill all the way since then. I mean, how can Woking compare?'

'Perhaps West Wittering would be better?'

He looked confused, then marginally irritated, flicking an obvious glance at his office clock which hung, chrome clean on the wall. I read your message, she felt like saying, but I'm taking no notice.

She repeated, 'West Wittering.'

'Oh, you know that too? That's where we met, is it?'

Lowering his pen, giving her this moment because she was a client after all. 'We used to have a house there, oh for about three summers before we bought the place in Portugal.'

Claire persisted. 'I am the daughter of your father's clerk.'

He checked his watch again, relieved she'd revealed the connection though visibly

424

disappointed that she was the equivalent of below-stairs. After a moment he gave himself permission to increase his impatience. He said, 'Oh well, what a pleasant surprise, and look, I'm sure the connection can be reflected in the costs. Don't worry, we like to offer preferential terms to our employees. So, to business: in what way can I help?'

By dying, she thought. Dying painfully, grotesquely here at my feet. How dare you forget my father, how dare you forget his daughter, the one you raped. She felt she must look as though she was drowning, as though she was gasping, clawing for air, because this man did not remember, even now he did not remember when it was something she'd always had to fight to forget. Claire said, 'I am the former Claire Riddick.'

He hesitated, ducked his head, and smiled in confirmation. 'Quite, I think I've grasped that, so shall we proceed? I repeat that you will be charged at a favourable rate.'

She wanted to tear at the collar of her high-necked blouse. She needed air. She blurted out. 'My younger daughter, Leah, is fourteen. This is my elder daughter, Anna. She is twenty-five. She was born on 10 April.'

The only response was ill-concealed exasperation. Alex Turnbull pulled at the sleeve of his dark suit, revealing a gold Rolex watch. He examined it, not looking at her as he asked, 'But, my dear Mrs Baird, how can I help you?'

At the sight of the Rolex and at the tone of his voice something snapped in Claire: some tight band that had coiled tighter with the years suddenly, sharply with a great gush, snapped and

425

immediately air flooded into her lungs, great gulps of it and it fed the rage that had been building and now it was flaring, blazing so that she was surprised it didn't roar out of her eyes and mouth.

Alex Turnbull was shaking his suit sleeve down over his watch. How could he do that when he must have felt the change? How could he do that in the presence of such violent hatred? He couldn't, not if she tore his office down around him, if she ripped his bloody Rolex from his wrist, stamped on it, and then on him.

Claire took another shuddering breath. 'You were . . .' She hesitated as though seeking the right word, but in fact trying not to leap to her feet, not to scream like a madwoman. 'You were kind enough to walk me home twenty-six years ago in West Wittering. But we didn't go straight home.' She saw Anna tense.

He stared at her, still with no recognition, no fear, no anything, and part of her anger was directed against herself now for allowing every second, every minute of that night to control her subsequent life while he looked at her and could not remember. He said, 'I'm sorry?'

She wanted to shout but she didn't, she fought for calm saying in a detached voice, 'Dear God, I do hope you are. We left your father and mother's party before midnight and walked along the beach.' She examined him for a response but there was none beyond the same confusion. 'The sea splashed my boots, those long white boots. You stopped and kissed my hand.'

Alex Turnbull coughed slightly, raising his hand to his mouth, his eyes darting to Anna then back to Claire. 'Um, this hardly seems appropriate, Mrs

426

Baird, especially with your daughter present. I'm—'

'You said there was a short cut through the dunes.' He was checking his watch, fiddling with his pen, and his only reaction was embarrassment at her lack of taste. 'Look,' he began, 'this is all very interesting, but I do have a tight schedule so perhaps we should come straight to the matter on which you need advice.'

Claire watched his nicotine-stained fingers, which had endlessly turned the pen, now move to his mouth, tapping against his lips and suddenly memory stirred, the final layer that she didn't know existed peeled back and she could taste the nicotine and feel that hand on her mouth, pressing. She remembered the split lip, the taste, his other hand pinioning her arms above her head. She felt the abrasive sand. She remembered her mouth moving on that hand, forming the silent words. No. No. No. At last she recalled that she had screamed again and again that word no against the hand that gagged her.

She sat back, staring at him, staring back at that moment and now she remained calm no longer, because at long last she was totally free of personal blame, utterly and totally free for the first time since the age of seventeen. She shouted. 'You kissed my hand, my mouth and said "I know a path through the dunes to Hope Cottage." We ran. You held my hand. We stopped. You kissed me again, too much and too hard and it felt wrong. It was too dark. You were too pressing. But you were the son of my father's boss, perhaps one day you would be his boss too. I didn't want to be rude to you but then I became frightened.'

She was on her feet, leaning on the desk, close

427

enough to strike, close enough to hurt him as he'd hurt her. For a moment he flinched, leaning sharply away from her but as he did so she saw that suddenly he had remembered. For a moment he stared, his mouth half open, but then he ducked his head, reaching swiftly into his drawer, taking out a packet of cigarettes. His fingers trembled as he placed a cigarette between his lips, those lips. She said, her head thrust forward, her voice quiet, full of intent to do damage, 'I said, please, please.'

He flashed his lighter, inhaled, swinging his chair round to the right, staring out of the window. She watched him fight for calm, watched him rearrange his features into a display of boredom. But still his hand trembled. She could wait. Oh, yes she could wait. He inhaled deeply, then stared down at the gold lighter in his hand. He exhaled, then swung back to her, placing the lighter neatly beside his pen, smiling up at her, and though his fingers were still unsteady his voice was composed, even superior. 'Please, please?' He arched his eyebrows. 'Exactly, and at this point this young woman should leave the room. It isn't correct that any daughter should listen to her mother's past exploits.'

Claire addressed Anna without turning. 'Would you like to leave?'

Anna said, 'I'd like to stay. I'd very much like to stay.' Her voice was as angry as Claire's and yes, she did want to stay. She must for as long as she could because this was something she had to face, this was something that she had told Claire she was owed. This was her salvation.

Claire continued to stare at Alex Turnbull. 'You remember now, then?'

His voice was contemptuous. 'Yes, as a matter of

428

fact I do remember. I remember you saying please. I remember the fuss afterwards. The ridiculous accusations. Good God, why else were you there if you didn't want it?' He nodded an apology to Anna. 'You shouldn't have to listen to this, so sorry. Quite unforgivable.' Jabbing a finger at Claire he said, 'You've just said you ran to the dunes and here you are, back out of the blue complete with your poor wretched posse, all steamed up over an insignificant event. Well, you've had your say and I'll bill you for it, and no employees' preferential rates, let me assure you.'

He stubbed out his cigarette in a green Venetian glass ashtray. Claire stood up straight. She turned to Anna. 'I think you should leave now.'

'No, Mum.'

Claire shook her head, a new authority in her voice. 'You really must leave.' She waited as Anna rose, but before she left, her daughter kissed her, whispering, 'I'll just be outside the door. I love you.'

As Anna walked away she knew her mother was right. She had heard enough, seen enough. The other details were private and would not affect how she felt about herself, or him. For him she had only contempt and disgust. For herself she had neither of these. Yes, she was the child of this man, but her rage wasn't his violence. Her rage was moral indignation. It was clean, it was hers. She was Claire's child, and Lynne's and Harry's, that was all.

Claire watched Alex rise and gesture to the door. 'Now might be an appropriate time to bring this meeting to a close.'

'Sit down,' Claire shouted, turning to him. She

429

heard the door open, then close. Alex Turnbull sat down, the sweat breaking out on his forehead, and somehow he seemed diminished. She wondered if he was hearing the wind in the marram grass, feeling the young girl beneath him, remembering what it felt like to commit rape. In case the details were hazy she explained in a clear, constrained, businesslike voice, her eyes never leaving his face, so that she could see the acknowledgement in them, see his eyes search for and find the photograph of his family.

As she paused to draw breath he started to stand. 'I haven't finished,' she snapped. He sat again, but even before he was settled she was saying, 'Finally you tore into me, damaged me, bruised me, then told me no one would believe me in a court of law, no one would employ my father again. You made me believe I had asked for it. You took away my truth, you took away my knowledge of who I was. For the whole of my life since, I have been without self-esteem, without the justification to feel angry, and never separated from fear and guilt. That insignificant event that you speak of changed my life. I will not allow that change to persist.'

He had reached for his pen. He was screwing the top back on, putting the clean sheet of paper back in his drawer. She said nothing more. He leaned back, clasped his hands on the desk and met her eyes. He said quite clearly, and in a voice as businesslike as hers, 'This is a diabolical accusation. You are hysterical, you obviously need help and to allow your daughter to witness any of this meeting is beyond imagination. It's quite sick.'

Claire leaned on his desk again, thrusting her

head forward, shouting, jabbing at him now. 'Anna is *our* daughter, the product of that rape. She found me a few months ago. She wanted to see you, to meet you, now that she knows the truth.'

His mouth became slack, his hands limp, and he sat speechless for a moment. Trucks were passing. A train, then another. Finally, with a visible effort he pulled himself together, swallowing, firming up his mouth. He reached towards the drawer. 'It's money you want, is it? That's the bottom line? Well, I deny everything, especially that your daughter is mine. But if it means I can get on with my afternoon, well, so be it.'

'Sit still,' she said and her whisper was far more formidable than any of his bluster. She picked up the photo of his family, held it out to him. He didn't move to take it so she let it drop to the desk. The glass broke. Alex Turnbull instinctively reached forward, snatching it to him and now she recognized his fear. He shouted, pressing back in his chair, 'You're bloody mad.'

'I am full of rage, full of hate and I'm glad you're feeling scared, but you should really be feeling terrified, just as I was.' Her voice was still a whisper. She pointed to the photograph he clutched to him. 'It's the eyes, all your children have your eyes.'

He sat back in his chair, all pretence gone. He spluttered, 'It was by mutual consent. You know you agreed.'

She shook her head. 'Don't be any more pathetic than you already are. I know I didn't. You know I didn't.'

He rubbed his face, swinging round to look out of the window then back at her, and there was a

431

difference in him, a nakedness, a cowed acceptance. 'What do you want?'

She stayed quite immobile, her voice still that strange whisper. 'I want an admission of guilt, an apology to your daughter and to me.'

He laughed, he actually laughed, then in a flurry stood up, towering over her, but there was no way in which anyone could intimidate her any more, fear had gone for ever. She had lost it when the coils had snapped. She faced him unflinching as he ranted: 'Why should I admit to something I didn't do? Just turn off any tape recorders right now, Mrs Baird, or Claire, or whatever you call yourself.' She laughed.

For the moment neither said anything and in the end it was he who backed down, he who moved across to the window, staring out as though she was not there. She followed him. He edged away. She stood on the other side of the window. Together they watched the stream of traffic, the high wall which edged the railway line, the cold blue sky. As a white Escort braked sharply behind a slow lorry she said, 'I want to call in my daughter. I want an admission of guilt, and an apology or you will have to live with the repercussions.'

He tapped the window, scaring off a sparrow on the windowsill, and it was as though his courage had returned, as though by the simple action of seeing off a sparrow he had reminded himself he was Alex Turnbull of Turnbull, Turnbull and Watkins and she was a Riddick. 'Forget it.' His breath misted the pane. 'And understand this. You'd be laughed out of court if you try to take it that far. It'd be my word against yours. Yes, I'll admit to my daughter, but what man could say,

432

hand on heart, that there weren't any by-blows of his scattered about the place? Take your threats and leave.' He crossed his arms in victory.

Claire shrugged. It was no more than she had expected. 'I have no intention of taking it to court. The justice I wanted was an admission and an apology, for me, and for Anna. It would have given her a little something to be proud of.'

She began to walk towards the door. He was incredulous. 'So that's it? All this bloody rigmarole and that's it?'

She stopped within touching distance of the door and slowly faced him, smiling, but there was no smile in her voice. That was icy and implacable. 'Oh no, that's not "it". In the absence of justice one seeks revenge, and you will have to wait and see whether I take it into my head one fine day to phone your wife, your daughters, and explain about that night.'

He started across the grey carpet towards her. She stopped him with a gesture of her hand. He muttered defiantly. 'Do it. My family wouldn't believe you.'

Claire's hand was on the door knob. 'I've medical records and Anna's DNA would be interesting. It would be enough to sow doubts in your wife's mind, in your daughters' minds. Every time the phone goes now you'll wonder if it could be me, every time the postman comes your heart will stop for just a moment. Being vulnerable, being destroyed is a learning experience, Alex.'

'You fucking bitch.' He rushed at her. She opened the door and stood in the doorway. 'One learns to be,' she said. He was looming over her and she didn't care. Anna came to stand by her as

433

he grabbed Claire's arm, insisting, 'I was drunk.'

She replied, 'Obviously not that drunk.'

He dropped his hand. He was flushed, and wiped his mouth. 'Do I hear an apology?' Claire queried.

'I have done nothing. I was drunk. You consented.' His whisper was hoarse, his eyes flicking to the receptionist at her desk.

Claire walked with Anna to the main door. She heard him call, 'Please, please.'

Anna and she stopped and looked, seeing the pleading in his eyes. Anna was as unmoved as Claire because she didn't need the apology that would never come, and neither did Claire, not really. Revenge would be enough for them. It would cauterize, it would finish it. She held open the glass door. 'Come on, Mum.' They left.

*   *   *

On their return to the patch there was yet another message from Mark on the answer machine saying that she need not phone him. 'You will have more than enough on your hands with the pantomime, you will need time to think, I understand that now. Claire, I want to know how today went, I long for it to have given you what you needed. I wish I could have been there with you. I love you, I will be there for the last night. I don't ask for anything else—that's up to you.'

The pantomime was to run from Wednesday to Saturday. At the end of the first night Jo grinned as she hugged Claire. 'The best I've ever put on, and the audience will grow, don't you worry.'

They had played to an only partially full house,

434

which was disappointing, but the audience had stood up, sat down and generally made fools of themselves as Buttons exhorted. They oooed and aaahed over the transformation scene, laughing when the Warrior tank descended instead of the coach, laughing even more when it crashed fairly definitely as one of the pulley ropes broke.

The journalist from the local paper who Claire had seen arrive through the spyhole joined them for the impromptu party after the first night. Anna and Angie were sent out for Claire's cases of Belle's wine. At the same time, the newly promoted Lt. Samuel Williams, who had arrived home on leave bearing Mark's message of goodwill for the cast, nipped to his parents' home a few doors from Muriel. He returned with Mum and Dad and crisps and Lord knows what.

Word must have spread—or perhaps Muriel had taken it upon herself to whip up ticket sales— because it was a full house for Thursday's performance and that went some way to curing the hangovers which most of the cast were suffering.

On that night as the transformation scene approached, Claire ducked behind the stage and checked with the deputy warden that all was well. Stan said: 'It'd better bloody well be, I've changed all the ropes, checked the knots, and if I have either you or Jo round here once more we can forget the Warrior because I'll make a noose and it'll be one of you coming down looking a funny colour, so clear off.'

Mollie, who had overheard, thought it was an appalling way for a Christian to behave, which made Liz dive for the lavatory so she could have a cigarette.

Friday's performance was another full house, thanks partly to a rollicking review in the local press, in which the journalist made no mention of plummeting Warriors. Again the performance went well, and again that night Claire slept, and again, as she had told herself every night so far, she wouldn't think further than the end of the panto.

On Saturday she and Jo arrived at six as usual to prepare the hall with a small team, whilst Liz collected the dancers who attended Leah's boarding school. By 6 p.m. the cast had arrived. By 6.30 Mollie was in her usual tizz and Claire sent her to place 'Reserved' notices on five front-row seats. Claire said, 'The mayor and mayoress can talk to one another, and Muriel can field the Brigadier's wife. I think that's suitable punishment for inflicting this damn production on us.'

Mollie trotted off tutting, and rolling her shoulders as Claire had known she would, but it broke the tension of the dressing room, as she had also known it would. As the laughter grew she winked at Jo. 'Some things never change.'

All around was bedlam, but organized bedlam, she assured Liz when she arrived with the girls. Liz lit a cigarette. 'Don't be so bloody daft, darling, there's nothing organized about this.'

Jo passed on her way to the Uglies' dressing room, and snatched the cigarette from Liz's hand, taking a puff, looking at Claire who pleaded, 'Me too, me too.'

It made her cough but took her mind off curtain-up, and she went in search of Turbogob whose makeup was being applied by Anna. In the makeup room, which was really the kitchen, Angie was sitting on a stool toying with her black wig as Anna stood putting the finishing touches to her white makeup. Claire hadn't managed to chat to her since Wednesday night, and then it had only been for a moment. Now she touched Angie's knee. 'How's it going?'

Angie kept her face quite still as Anna drew red warts on her cheek. 'My nerves or my life?'

'Both,' Claire said, smiling.

Anna stepped back, holding a mirror up for Angie. Staring at herself, Angie said, 'Well, it could be worse. I could look like this all the time.'

Anna laughed. Claire squatted down beside her, waiting. Angie confided, as Anna took the wig from her, 'The old bugger's home on leave soon so we'll sort it out then, either that or I'll bite his bloody head off. I mean, we're going to have to help keep that other baby, even if he stays with me. I mean, where do they keep their brains, Claire?'

Claire squeezed her hand, groaning as she stood up. 'We both know that. Call me if you need me, and not just to straighten your wig. Call me any time, remember that. The small hours of the morning are worse.'

This time it was Angie who held her arm. 'You remember you can do the same to me. It's not over for you two, either.'

Claire hurried up on to the stage, making sure that the curtains were fully drawn while Jo checked that the props were in place. 'How's the audience, Claire?'

Claire was already heading for the spyhole on the left of the stage. She peered through. 'Trickling in. Mollie's still out there, directing traffic.'

Jo called: 'I suggested to the WI that they celebrate the last night by giving her something

437

important to do and getting her out from under their feet. She's fine on measuring and making, but lousy on soothing frayed nerves.'

Claire was still at the spyhole. 'Tell me something I don't know.'

Jo came up behind her. 'Can't do that, but I'll ask you something. Is Mark going to come, do you think?'

Claire let the spyhole trap fall shut and closed her eyes. 'He said he was, but I've heard nothing all day. Perhaps he's coming straight here. It feels odd not to know. I'm half glad, half not.'

Jo took her place at the spyhole. 'Well, I've told everyone that we're expecting him, but if he's not here, it'll be because there's an emergency meeting in London. I'll task Mollie, and make sure she puts him next to Muriel.' She bustled off, and Claire ignored the Uglies who were prancing across the stage doing 'Knees up Mother Brown', a ritual Rob insisted upon. It put him in the right frame of mind, he'd said the first night, hitching up one of his boobs.

She returned to the spyhole and saw Lt. Samuel Williams, sitting in the last row, again. She shook her head and smiled. He'd met Anna on the first night as she'd slaved over the Uglies in their underwear, and he'd even offered to be chief dresser for the chicken until Muriel had chased him out of the way.

There had been no keeping him away from the party afterwards, however, and he had seldom left Anna's side since then. He'd taken her out for lunch yesterday and today, skidding down Claire's drive in his MG to collect her, grinning a welcome at Claire as she'd driven in at a more sedate pace

438

behind him—Anna had been staying with her while the panto was on and had been concerned that Claire would mind her spending so much time with Samuel. Claire had said, 'We're in no hurry, you and I. We've our lives ahead of us, but that young man is going back soon. Have some fun, the pair of you.'

Claire scanned the audience again, turning away only when Sparks called her. He was in the prompt corner, waving his lighting script at her, bawling, 'Claire, I need to talk to you.' She pressed her finger to her mouth, pointing towards the audience behind the curtain as she walked calmly across to him. What was the great adage, something about keeping your head whilst all around are panicking?

Sparks thrust his script in her face. 'Last night the blinds let in light, it buggered up the ultraviolet scene. We can't have that, Mrs Baird, we just can't.'

Claire grinned and dealt with the first of the evening's problems.

*   *   *

The first half romped along on time and with gusto. The Uglies flounced about, the chicken was almost good enough to eat; but he'd have to be plucked first, Claire told him. He threatened to peck her to death if she laid one hand on him.

Each time she was near the spyhole she looked, and always Mark's place was empty. During the interval the Brigadier's wife swept through the dressing rooms in Muriel's wake, dispensing congratulations but looking as though this was the last place on earth she wished to be. As soon as decently possible she fled back into the hall leaving

439

Muriel sipping a mug of tea, and striding after Claire and Jo who needed to supervise the ball scene set change.

Linking arms with Claire, Muriel peered up at the Warrior tank which was hanging good and high, well out of sight from the audience. 'Smashing idea, girls. What fun. Heard all about the leak of light from Sparks last night. What a palaver. I'm sure he suspected fifth column activity. As for my gardener—well, he's never going to look quite the same in my eyes. It'll go to his head, you mark my words. My dears, he was preening when he downed the 'Orrible Oracle in scene iii. The problem is that he's caught the bug, so you'll have to find something for him in next year's production.'

Jo and Claire screeched, 'Next year's production?'

Muriel raised her eyebrows, then hastily checked her watch. 'Good Lord, is that the time. Curtain up any minute, girls. Don't want to get in your way.' She escaped across the stage and down the stairs into Cinderella's dressing room, or dressing space would be more like it. Claire laughed but then Muriel's bellow reached them: 'Claire, a quiet word, dear.'

She grimaced and handed her script to Jo. 'Can you manage for a moment?'

Jo pushed her. 'Go on, answer the summons but don't let her back on stage, and just make sure the dancers are ready, and Cinders mustn't forget her necklace tonight.'

In the dressing room Muriel was gazing fascinated at Liz's snowman earrings which she had borrowed from Angie for the last night, and Claire was in time to hear her bark, 'You really must make

440

sure you plonk yourself on top of the mess Christmas tree next year, Liz. It will make you realize that medicine is just a by-blow, your true vocation is sitting with a pine tree up your—'

Jo interrupted valiantly, 'Quiet, backstage. One minute to curtain-up. Claire, check the dancers and Cinders.'

'I'll do that,' Liz said and flew off.

Claire steered Muriel towards the door to the auditorium. 'You need to hop back to your seat, Muriel.'

Muriel shoved the empty tea mug into her hand. 'But I did just want to know if Mark will be coming?'

Claire opened the door and waited. Muriel looked at her keenly. Claire just shook her head. 'He's supposed to be, but I have no more idea than you.'

Muriel's glance was shrewd and sad. 'And you care even less?'

Claire studied the cold dregs of Muriel's tea. 'I don't know. I haven't decided, and before you ask, I don't know what is going to happen after that. We've both made mistakes and now we need some time.' Her voice was firm.

Muriel started to enter the auditorium, then turned back to Claire. 'I love you, Claire Baird; so does that daft pillock you married all those years ago, but you must do what is best for you. Really best for you.'

'I know.' Claire's voice was still firm. 'It's just the business of deciding what that is.'

Just before the finale, as everyone was rushing and tearing to take up their positions, Claire peered through the spyhole. Mark's seat was still

441

empty. She checked for Samuel Williams. Yes, he was still at the back. She smiled and her eyes travelled over the audience just before the curtain rose again. The door into the auditorium hall opened and in slipped Anna. Claire watched as Sam turned, rose and joined her, propping himself against the back wall alongside the other members of the drama group.

The curtain rose. Behind Claire the last of the dance troupe pushed past and squeezed on to the stage, taking their place as the music struck up. Jo joined her and they grinned at one another as the audience joined in. Across, by the right-hand flats, Liz and Mollie stood. Liz lifted her hand and waved, then gave a thumbs-up as the cast began the last dance routine and all got off on the right foot for once.

Claire and Jo danced in the wings with them, sang with them, clapping them silently as they began the final chorus and now the audience were clapping, and the cast were taking their bows and Jo and Claire looked at one another, shaking their heads. It was over and tears were close for both of them. They turned and clapped their cast as they prepared to take their individual bows, and the audience whooped and whistled and cheered.

The Youth Club came first, and bowed, then danced down the centre steps to line up in front of the stage, then the Sunflower troop, the supporting cast, the 'Orrible Oracle and her witchlets. The cheer that greeted their bow was huge, and Claire wished that Angie's husband could have been here to see her moment of triumph, and so too Cinderella's. The Uglies and the stepmother performed 'Knees up Mother Brown', whilst the chicken clucked so hard that Claire was amazed he didn't lay an egg. Finally it was Buttons, arm in arm with Cinderella's dad.

Still the applause went on, until finally the calls went up from the audience for 'The boss, the boss.'

Jo pushed Claire forward, but she pulled Jo on to centre stage with her, and beckoned Liz from the other side. She came on, flashing, to another round of applause.

As the house lights went up, Claire thanked Muriel, the cast, the music, the back-up crew, everyone. She looked at Mark's empty seat and finally felt a certain emptiness. She clapped the audience, the cast, the backstage crew, turning to the wings to do so—and there stood Mark. He carried a huge cellophane wrapped bouquet. She faltered, her hands fell to her sides.

Mark walked on to the stage. He handed her the flowers. He turned to the audience, who had fallen silent.

He said, 'My plane was delayed, but I'm assured there is a video.' He grinned at Claire, who nodded, seeing how thin he was, how tired, and beneath the smile, the calm voice, she recognized the desperation. She stared down at the flowers. They were white, her favourite.

Mark said, 'How can we thank our wives, and their friends who have struggled on in spite of everything, as they always do? It's impossible to single anyone out, but on this occasion I must because I want to thank my wife. This pantomime was in addition to her already heavy load of responsibilities. As always, she has performed wonderfully. But I also want to thank her two daughters, Anna and Leah. I look forward to getting to know Anna, and to catching up with Leah.'

He was looking at Claire now, and there was a question in his eyes. She smiled, and held out her hand, and together they faced the audience, joined by Jo and Liz, but Mark knew when the smile did not reach her eyes that there would be no easy path to a decision, and as Claire bowed she still did not know whether she wanted this man to remain in her life.

EPILOGUE

Eighteen months later at the villa in Chianciamo, as the midday sun bore down on the vineyard and the cypress shimmered darkly on distant hills, Claire and Liz sipped iced mineral water at the long table beneath the vine-shaded loggia. Just beyond them was the swimming pool, approached via the stone steps Mark's father had originally created and which Mark had tarted up, just this winter. Geraniums stood in pots on each step, whilst bougainvillaea and cypress led the eye to the boundary of the pool area, and from there to the sweeping hills beyond, some of which were harvested of their corn, whilst others were furrowed with vines, or dotted with olive trees.

It was at the pool, however, that they were looking. The water was inviting and blue from the tiles Claire and Mark had laboriously laid during the spring, and barely a ripple disturbed the surface as Anna and Leah floated on lilos while Sarah and Louise half sat, half flopped in huge inner tubes. Liz said, smoking one of her five cigarettes of the day, 'They maintain that if their bums are in water it stops them overheating.'

Claire grinned. 'That's the line they fed me, but as you can see they've had to bow to hat parade.'

The girls all wore rather dreadful heavy cotton hats which would survive any amount of water. 'Ah,' Liz mused. 'So the new Claire is still a neurotic, a worrier, a darned pain in the ass?' She deflected the olive that Claire had picked from the bowl on the table, and thrown. She managed to

445

catch the second and ate it. 'Very nice too. Your own, of course.' Liz's expansive gesture took in the olive groves, pale grey-green and stoic.

'Absolutely. Not bad, eh?' Claire fanned herself with the copy of *The Times* that Liz, Ben and the girls had brought with them from the UK last night. Already it was yellowed from the sun, already the cicadas were in full cry, already the scents of the earth were all around, and the bird song sounded sweet as it always did. Claire stirred herself to modest action and called down to the girls: 'Careful, we don't want peeling skin for the wedding.'

Liz stretched out her legs. Her toenails were the same rich red as her fingernails and dangling earrings. The red was picked up in her wrap-around skirt and matching top, though her sandals were gold, and too fragile to cope with even a short tour of the vineyard. A fact she had announced the moment she appeared for an al-fresco breakfast of strong coffee and bread rolls. Now she asked, 'When are Harry and Lynne Weaver coming out?'

'The day after tomorrow. Belle's in Florence with Muriel even as we speak, rushing around because she's decided the Weavers must have new curtains for their room. She's in her element, nothing has made her happier than organizing the wedding and all the brouhaha that goes with it. The Weavers will be her most favourite people until the day she dies, for letting her take control.'

Liz roared with laughter, shading her eyes as she looked towards the vineyard, but Claire had already seen Mark and Ben strolling between the vines towards the house. Ben's shorts were new and looked it, especially against Mark's faded denim.

446

Claire felt she and Mark must look like the country cousins, her own shorts were cut-down jeans. It wasn't that they didn't have the money, it was just that it didn't matter how they looked to other people any more and she gloried in the fact. The wedding, though, would mean dress parade— and how.

Mark was leading Ben towards the cellars which lay between the upper vineyard and the villa. 'Oops, the tasting's about to begin,' Claire said.

She and Liz returned the waves of the men, though Liz groaned. 'When is it our turn?'

'Everything comes to those who wait, so calm . . .' At a shriek from the pool they looked round in time to see Anna tipped from the lilo into the water by Liz's girls, her hat floating free, laughter bursting from all the girls. Claire said quietly, touching her friend's arm, gaining her full attention, 'It's ironic that as I move out of that world my new daughter moves in. Is there some great plan somewhere or is it all just as chaotic as it always feels?'

Liz smiled gently. 'Your guess is as good as mine.' Claire kept hold of Liz's arm, her voice urgent. 'You'll look after her?'

Liz shook her head firmly. 'Oh no, I'll ignore her from the moment she arrives on the patch. Come on Claire, you know that young Samuel Williams is protective enough as it is; a veritable warrior where she's concerned. He also knows his CO Ben Gibbons and his lady are just as concerned. Don't fret, that young couple will do just fine and don't forget that both Ben and Mark say Sam proved himself nicely in Bosnia, but then the perception all round is that the British have been the most

447

consistently effective of all the troops out there.'

Claire examined her friend closely. She looked relaxed, confident, happy. 'Any regrets Ben stayed in, Liz?'

Immediately Liz responded. 'Absolutely not, except for the panto precedent you set. God almighty, I just wish that first one had failed dismally.'

'And Mollie?'

'She seems to have got over the divorce, or so Jean tells us all. It's made her humbler, if that's not too trite a word, though I dare say she rules her local WI drama group with an iron fist. Must be a bit of a facer when your old man finds himself and in so doing tells you to shut up and ship out. Nigel's gone from strength to strength though after Bosnia. Just been made up to Lieutenant-Colonel, you know.'

To Claire it all seemed a world away and she laid *The Times* on the table, sitting back, closing her eyes, soaking in the sounds and scents of her life, coming to only when she heard Mark calling, 'You simply must try this.'

Rousing herself she grinned across at Liz who said, 'I hope that he means he comes bearing a particularly good wine, because if it's an olive he can find a home for it in someone's Martini.'

'It's wine, you old soak.' Claire watched as Mark hurried towards them, his face alight, his stride as lithe and young as it had been before his promotion. He clutched two glasses and almost cuddled a bottle of the 1986. He placed the glasses on the table, pouring only a little each.

Liz instructed him to stop being a tease and fill them to the brim. 'I trust your judgement.' He raised his eyebrows at Claire, and filled her glass to the brim also, making a great to-do of placing the bottle midway between the two of them, saying, 'It's up for grabs, no favours to either of you.' Before he left he kissed Claire's hand. 'Tell your sainted friend that were Bacchus here with us he'd recognize a kindred spirit.'

He dodged the olives that pelted him on his way back to the cellar and they could hear his laugh all the way. Licking her fingers Liz raised her glass to Claire. 'Is it as good as it looks?'

'The wine, or us?'

'You.'

Claire ran her finger round the rim of her glass, then drank. 'Oh yes, it's as good. It's very good. But it's taken time.'

Liz flicked the ash from her cigarette into the brass ashtray. 'I thought I could stop worrying when Mark came for the last night of the panto. Good grief, girl, there wasn't a dry eye in the house when he gave you that bouquet and thanked you, and Anna and Leah for all you'd done. Then, you old ratbag, you sent him to Chianciamo alone. I nearly died.'

'Nonsense, you were too bloody vocal about it to be near death. Anyway I had a lot of guff to sort out in my head and so had he.' Claire stared into the distance. 'Apparently it was the very best present a husband could have when Leah and I turned up here on Christmas Eve last year, though I'm still not sure whether it was us, or the bottle of malt whisky we threw in first.' Her laugh was contented.

The girls were clambering out of the pool and retreating into the shade, throwing off their hats, dragging their sunbeds into close order before lying back, talking and laughing. What about? No prize for guessing it was Anna's wedding, and as she watched, Leah stood up, using her hands to explain her bridesmaid's dress.

Liz was sipping the wine appreciatively. 'This really is excellent. By the way, when are you going to let your victim off the hook, or aren't you?'

The mention of Alex Turnbull did nothing to disturb the calm of the day. Claire merely smiled and shrugged. 'With Anna's permission I faxed him in February and told him he could relax, he'd hear no more from us. I hope he suffered though. I hope he forgot what a good night's sleep was.'

'Any response from him?'

'You must be joking.'

Liz nodded. 'I thought I probably was, but how about Anna? She went through a bad patch when the anger wore off, didn't she?'

They looked across at the girls who were all now lying flat out on the sunbeds with their personal stereos rigged for action. Claire took a photograph with the camera that would be near her for the next two weeks as their friends and relations arrived in stages to attend the wedding. She said thoughtfully, 'Yes, she did, but only for a very short while. You know, Liz, the new generation are tougher than us, they've more of a sense of their own worth, they're more inclined to tell someone, or something— including the past—to take a running jump. Quite right too. Then, of course, young Samuel was ever attentive and what with one thing and another, including a great deal of "sucking face", we were on to entirely different things.'

The two women were laughing as they let the

soft sun lull them.

*   *   *

In the muted light of the cellar Mark and Ben sat on old half-barrels, tasting, spitting, appreciating. As Mark held up his glass and swirled the wine around, pointing out the depth of colour, Ben said, 'You're really into this, aren't you?'

Mark sipped, rolled the wine around his mouth and this time swallowed. 'Now, Mother would never swallow, so don't tell her, but it's just too good. Here, try some.' While he poured a half-glass he continued: 'Yes, I think I'm getting better. I find it easy. It's in the bones, Mother says. Claire of course disagrees, and mentions the liver quite frequently. Mother wants us to take the reins completely by next year, but my guess is the old trout'll never bow out completely, and neither do we want her to.'

'She's happy in the top flat?' Ben was looking around the cellar at the casks and bottles.

'For now. She says the stairs keep her young, but I think she should turn that one into the holiday flat, and take the ground floor. She will do exactly as she sees fit, however. That's what I mean about her never letting go.' His laugh was rich and long.

Ben grinned, brushing at his pale legs, feeling the sting from the sun already. 'She's just like her son, stubborn as hell. I really miss you, Mark.'

For a moment they fell silent. Mark stared into his glass. It seemed so long ago, just a nightmare, a bloody nightmare. 'I miss you, but not "it". Taking redundancy was the best decision of my life. I'd reached the level of my incompetence as you well

451

know, Ben. I wasn't enjoying it, it was all too much responsibility and I was giving everyone else a hard time. Not to mention going off at half cock, getting into a tangle and making a bloody fool of myself. It was really nothing to do with Claire, or Anna. None of it. It was all down to me.'

Ben went over to the bottles which were stacked on their sides, walking the length of them, only speaking when he reached the end. 'You did a good job, you saved the regiment, albeit in a fairly obnoxious way.' He grinned and raised his hand in apology, but Mark was nodding. Ben continued: 'You also took the mandate to the limit, everyone knew that, including the locals.' He hesitated. 'Do you ever hear from Gordana?'

Mark tensed. They had not discussed it since he had told Gordana that he must go home, explaining the rape, explaining that he would have gone home without the rape, because he loved Claire. For a moment he had thought she would cry, but instead she had just said sadly, 'I knew, all along I knew, but for a moment I wanted to believe in escape. I wanted to live outside my life.'

She had then walked to her flat, and each day she had worked with him, though never again had they referred to anything other than the job, never again had she agreed to eat at his house, and there had been no way she would allow him to show the extent of his gratitude and admiration and his sense of shame. No way at all, though he and Claire had wanted to help her family resettle, wanted to do something.

Ben repeated his question. 'Have you heard from her?'

'No, not from her, but of her. Charlie tells me

she's based in Zagreb working with refugees in some capacity or other. He's sworn he'll let us know if we can ever do anything. God, I behaved so badly. I took advantage of a kid already in a mess. That's what really got to Claire; it was too reminiscent of her own experience. I just lost the plot, Ben, completely lost the bloody plot. I don't even like thinking of it. It was unforgivable.' He reached for the bottle. 'Come on, have a top-up, forget the tasting. Let's just hope I go ever onwards without being more of a pillock than strictly necessary.'

Ben peered at an interesting rack of wine. 'You and Gordana both needed someone, something, don't forget that. It happened; you made it unhappen as kindly as anyone could, even Charlie and Arthur saw that. Why else wasn't it splashed all over the tabloids?'

*   *   *

That night Claire stood at the bedroom window looking out at the pool and the vineyard, and the distant rolling hills where corn had been grown and already harvested. 'Busy day tomorrow with the caterers coming for a final meeting, and the rep from the wine warehouse here too. When's your guy arriving?' She could feel the heat from the shutters and the outside walls, hear the cicadas, see the cypress dark in the moonlight.

Mark was standing behind her, his arms around her. Now he pulled her to him. 'Ten hundred hours.' He stopped, then started again. 'Ten o'clock. Keep your fingers crossed, darling, it could be the big order we're waiting for. How about your essay? Is it finished?' His kisses were soft on her neck.

She turned to him, kissing his mouth, saying against it, 'Indeed it is.'

His arms tightened. 'I'm so glad you're back. I can't bear it when you go away.'

Together they watched over their land. 'It was only a week.'

'But all those Open University students.' He groaned. 'They're probably young virile, sensitive new men.'

Her laugh rang out. 'Chance would be a fine thing.'

He kissed her throat and she could sense his amusement. Below them now, they could hear the girls drive in from the town. The car doors slammed, the sound ringing across the valley. Somewhere a dog barked. The giggling and chatter grew louder as they came to sit beneath the loggia. Together they listened to the young excited voices and then Mark whispered, 'I feel as though we've been flung up on a safe shore, or am I in danger of waxing poetic, as Leah would say?'

Claire reached up, and stroked his face. 'The only danger you're in is of being kissed to death.'

He held her tight and neither moved, they just listened to their world.

*   *   *

Gordana's flat in Zagreb, was stifling, even though night had fallen and across the table from Gordana in the kitchen cum living room cum sleeping room Charlie attempted to fan himself with his handkerchief. Gordana laughed slightly and

454

handed him one of her notebooks. 'Use this, or perhaps you should bring a fan with you next time, my dear Charlie.'

Against one wall was her bed-settee; against another was Stevo's. In the next room, a converted box room with paper-thin walls, her mother slept. Charlie gratefully fanned himself and used the handkerchief to wipe his forehead, saying softly so as not to disturb her mother, 'Frankly, old dear, I'd rather have the geisha who should be wielding it, but I dare say I could make do with a fan. Anyway, how have you been keeping?'

They sat in the light from the moon, without the lamp which would only have attracted moths and mosquitoes. With the lowering of the sun she'd thrown back the shutters, longing for a breeze, any breeze, and in had walked Charlie and that was almost as good.

She felt the waft of air as Charlie fanned frantically. 'I'm keeping very well, my dear Charlie.'

Outside in the city the sounds of the evening continued. Zagreb was a city where poverty vied with wealth, a wealth that was held firmly in the hands of those hand-picked by the Tudjman regime, a wealth that eluded her, and her mother, her cousin and her friends, just as their Bosnian homes still eluded them, just as peace between factions, and a deep internal peace eluded them.

She stared out towards Bosnia where the tragedy continued. Just how did those who had experienced *etnicko cis cenje*—ethnic cleansing—obtain that peace? How did they obtain justice? How did they ever regain their homes, their history?

They forgot, they put them behind them, they started again, her mother said.

455

'We face them. We bring them to court,' she and Stevo insisted.

Charlie said, still fanning, his voice uncharacteristically careful, 'I'm off to the Baird wedding next week, or the Weaver/Williams wedding, perhaps I should say.'

Gordana pushed a can of the lager he had brought nearer to him. It was warm and poor Charlie hated warm lager. She took one herself, and fingered the tins of corned beef and artichoke hearts he had plonked on the table. She drank directly from the can. 'So, they are happy?'

Charlie had placed the notebook on top of the other five and was drinking his lager, and checking his watch. 'Yes, they seem to be pulling it together and making a good life for themselves.'

'I'm glad.' She drained the can. Yes, she supposed she was but it all seemed so long ago.

Charlie squeezed the empty can and tossed it into the bucket by the sink. 'Goal,' he crowed. 'There you are, you see, I should have joined the netball team but it was those damned little skirts I'd have had to wear that put me off. I haven't got the legs, old flower.'

She laughed as she always did at Charlie, but all the while she was trying to make out the image of her father in the photograph frame on the plain wood shelf, but it was too dark. Yes, it was all so long ago. She drained her own can, and squeezed it as Charlie had done, squeezed it until her fingers hurt. Mark had been a good man, and suddenly she saw his face more clearly than she had done since he'd left. Yes, he'd been a good man and her heart jolted. Did he walk those hills they'd spoken of?

Charlie was tapping the table with his fingers as

456

though he was playing jazz and she knew signalled his going. Sure enough he stood, leaned down and kissed her. 'Flying visit, sorry. But you should leave, my dear old turnip. You really should leave. There's a world out there, waiting for you, and in it is Arthur with his face down to his knees for want of you. Mind you, he'll wait until the seas freeze over, or his kangaroo tail gets so long even Rumpelstiltskin would offer him a fiver for it.' He kissed her, gripped her shoulders. 'You're young, your life is ahead of you, you've done enough here. Escape for good.' He kissed her again, and hugged her. She leaned into him, wanting to cry, wanting to leave with him. She shook her head and said against his shirt, 'Take care, my Charlie.'

She saw him to the door, opening it on to the fetid corridor, then watched until he disappeared down the stairs. All around was the muted sound of poverty-stricken refugee lives eked out in overcrowded rooms. She came back to the window and peered out, knowing Charlie would turn as he set off up the road, and wave, and blow a kiss. The moon was high and large, the heat was still in the stone walls. This weather was ideal for vines.

She looked down and waved as Charlie waved, but it was Mark she saw.

She returned to the table, returned to her notebooks, to the letter that had arrived this morning, and now she smiled. Tomorrow Arthur would be here. Arthur Pierce whose ponytail Charlie was always so very rude about. Arthur who came when he could, who held her and asked her to leave with him, offered to turn her Cinderella's pumpkin into a coach, offered to take her and her mother and Stevo riding off towards the sunset.

457

It was Arthur who had travelled with her to ᴌorcula, who had held her for more than just a moment, and she was glad it was. Quite suddenly she knew how glad she was that it was he who had taken her, for their happiness had not been clouded by the guilt of a wife in the background, by a sense of wrongdoing amongst so much wrongdoing.

'But how can I leave?' she said aloud. 'It means they will have finally beaten me.' It was what she said to Arthur every time, and to her father's image, and to herself, especially to herself because she so wanted to go, to feel young again, for life to be as it had once been.

She reached out and touched the notebooks. Yes, she should go, for her mother's sake . . . but just a little longer, that is all. It would be just a little longer until peace was brokered, until the wheels of justice turned, until those men who had taken so much from so many, including their dignity and self-esteem, were brought to justice, until the international communities dragged them before their judges. Just a little longer before their victims received a measure of satisfaction.

She took the notebooks, held them, staring out at the night sky above Zagreb, the same sky that hung over Bosnia and the rest of the world, like a conscience.

Just a little longer, she assured herself.

ACKNOWLEDGEMENTS

This book could not have been written without the help of numerous people who have been more than generous in revealing their moving experiences of adoption. I hope I've done them justice and they certainly have my sincere gratitude. I also want to thank Sherie Williams Ellen of The Army Families Federation (previously the Federation of Army Wives), and other service wives I've spoken to, and my own few short years as a service wife. Since that time, quite some years ago now, I've wanted to write about the stoicism and day to day endurance I observed which enables our servicemen's wives to carve a life for themselves and their families. I am filled with awed admiration at the good fist they make of it and the support they give their husbands in what is becoming an increasingly difficult and stressful job.

I must also thank Yeovil and Martock Libraries, Sylvia Fortnum, and Shelagh Smith, not forgetting Barry Pegrum for his introduction to an invaluable and appreciated contact.

It is clear that our troops in Bosnia did, and are doing, a magnificent job under enormously difficult circumstances and I'm grateful to those servicemen who have talked to me but reiterate that the Severn Regiment and its personnel and experiences are not based on any actual regiment.

I am indebted to the award-winning Tintinhull Drama Group for allowing me to follow their production of *Cinderella*. (I can assure you that Mollie and Turbogob are not based on any members of the group!) What rollicking good fun it was, and they even let me participate—behind the scenes. Oh yes they did!